The Lamp in the Desert

Ethel M. Dell

Copyright © 2017 Okitoks Press

All rights reserved.

ISBN: 1981945156

ISBN-13: 978-1981945153

Table of Contents

PART I 5
   CHAPTER I 5
   BEGGAR'S CHOICE 5
   CHAPTER II 7
   THE PRISONER AT THE BAR 7
   CHAPTER III 12
   THE TRIUMPH 12
CHAPTER IV 14
   THE BRIDE 14
CHAPTER V 16
   THE DREAM 16
CHAPTER VI 20
   THE GARDEN 20
CHAPTER VII 23
   THE SERPENT IN THE GARDEN 23
CHAPTER VIII 28
   THE FORBIDDEN PARADISE 28
   PART II 31
   CHAPTER I 31
   THE MINISTERING ANGEL 31
   CHAPTER II 33
   THE RETURN 33
   CHAPTER III 36
   THE BARREN SOIL 36
   CHAPTER IV 38
   THE SUMMONS 38
   CHAPTER V 43
   THE MORNING 43
   CHAPTER VI 45
   THE NIGHT-WATCH 45
   CHAPTER VII 49
   SERVICE RENDERED 49
   CHAPTER VIII 53
   THE TRUCE 53
   CHAPTER IX 55
   THE OASIS 56
   CHAPTER X 57
   THE SURRENDER 57
PART III 62
   CHAPTER I 62
   BLUEBEARD'S CHAMBER 62
   CHAPTER II 64
   EVIL TIDINGS 64

- CHAPTER III ... 68
  - THE BEAST OF PREY ... 68
- CHAPTER IV ... 73
  - THE FLAMING SWORD ... 73
- CHAPTER V ... 77
  - TESSA ... 77
- CHAPTER VI ... 82
  - THE ARRIVAL ... 82
- CHAPTER VII ... 84
  - FALSE PRETENCES ... 84
- CHAPTER VIII ... 87
  - THE WRATH OF THE GODS ... 87

PART IV ... 90
- CHAPTER I ... 90
  - DEVILS' DICE ... 90
- CHAPTER II ... 92
  - OUT OF THE DARKNESS ... 92
- CHAPTER III ... 95
  - PRINCESS BLUEBELL ... 96
- CHAPTER IV ... 99
  - THE SERPENT IN THE DESERT ... 99
- CHAPTER V ... 102
  - THE WOMAN'S WAY ... 102
- CHAPTER VI ... 105
  - THE SURPRISE PARTY ... 105
- CHAPTER VII ... 109
  - RUSTAM KARIN ... 109
- CHAPTER VIII ... 112
  - PETER ... 112
- CHAPTER IX ... 113
  - THE CONSUMING FIRE ... 113
- CHAPTER X ... 115
  - THE DESERT PLACE ... 115

PART V ... 118
- CHAPTER I ... 118
  - GREATER THAN DEATH ... 118
- CHAPTER II ... 122
  - THE LAMP ... 122
- CHAPTER III ... 125
  - TESSA'S MOTHER ... 125
- CHAPTER IV ... 128
  - THE BROAD ROAD ... 128
- CHAPTER V ... 131
  - THE DARK NIGHT ... 131
- CHAPTER VI ... 135
  - THE FIRST GLIMMER ... 135
- CHAPTER VII ... 137
  - THE FIRST VICTIM ... 137
- CHAPTER VIII ... 140
  - THE FIERY VORTEX ... 140

CHAPTER IX	142
THE DESERT OF ASHES	142
CHAPTER X	146
THE ANGEL	146
CHAPTER XI	149
THE DAWN	149
CHAPTER XII	152
THE BLUE JAY	152
THE END	154

PART I

CHAPTER I

BEGGAR'S CHOICE

A great roar of British voices pierced the jewelled curtain of the Indian night. A toast with musical honours was being drunk in the sweltering dining-room of the officers' mess. The enthusiastic hubbub spread far, for every door and window was flung wide. Though the season was yet in its infancy, the heat was intense. Markestan had the reputation in the Indian Army for being one of the hottest corners in the Empire in more senses than one, and Kurrumpore, the military centre, had not been chosen for any especial advantages of climate. So few indeed did it possess in the eyes of Europeans that none ever went there save those whom an inexorable fate compelled. The rickety, wooden bungalows scattered about the cantonment were temporary lodgings, not abiding-places. The women of the community, like migratory birds, dwelt in them for barely four months in the year, flitting with the coming of the pitiless heat to Bhulwana, their little paradise in the Hills. But that was a twenty-four hours' journey away, and the men had to be content with an occasional week's leave from the depths of their inferno, unless, as Tommy Denvers put it, they were lucky enough to go sick, in which case their sojourn in paradise was prolonged, much to the delight of the angels.

But on that hot night the annual flitting of the angels had not yet come to pass, and notwithstanding the heat the last dance of the season was to take place at the Club House. The occasion was an exceptional one, as the jovial sounds that issued from the officers' mess-house testified. Round after round of cheers followed the noisy toast, filling the night with the merry uproar that echoed far and wide. A confusion of voices succeeded these; and then by degrees the babel died down, and a single voice made itself heard. It spoke with easy fluency to the evident appreciation of its listeners, and when it ceased there came another hearty cheer. Then with jokes and careless laughter the little company of British officers began to disperse. They came forth in lounging groups on to the steps of the mess-house, the foremost of them—Tommy Denvers—holding the arm of his captain, who suffered the familiarity as he suffered most things, with the utmost indifference. None but Tommy ever attempted to get on familiar terms with Everard Monck. He was essentially a man who stood alone. But the slim, fair-haired young subaltern worshipped him openly and with reason. For Monck it was who, grimly resolute, had pulled him through the worst illness he had ever known, accomplishing by sheer force of will what Ralston, the doctor, had failed to accomplish by any other means. And in consequence and for all time the youngest subaltern in the mess had become Monck's devoted adherent.

They stood together for a moment at the top of the steps while Monck, his dark, lean face wholly unresponsive and inscrutable, took out a cigar. The night was a wonderland of deep spaces and glittering stars. Somewhere far away a native *tom-tom* throbbed like the beating of a fevered pulse, quickening spasmodically at intervals and then dying away again into mere monotony. The air was scentless, still, and heavy.

"It's going to be deuced warm," said Tommy.

"Have a smoke?" said Monck, proffering his case.

The boy smiled with swift gratification. "Oh, thanks awfully! But it's a shame to hurry over a good cigar, and I promised Stella to go straight back."

"A promise is a promise," said Monck. "Have it later!" He added rather curtly, "I'm going your way myself."

"Good!" said Tommy heartily. "But aren't you going to show at the Club House? Aren't you going to dance?"

Monck tossed down his lighted match and set his heel on it. "I'm keeping my dancing for to-morrow," he said. "The best man always has more than enough of that."

Tommy made a gloomy sound that was like a groan and began to descend the steps by his side. They walked several paces along the dim road in silence; then quite suddenly he burst into impulsive speech.

"I'll tell you what it is, Monck!"

"I shouldn't," said Monck.

Tommy checked abruptly, looking at him oddly, uncertainly. "How do you know what I was going to say?" he demanded.

"I don't," said Monck.

"I believe you do," said Tommy, unconvinced.

Monck blew forth a cloud of smoke and laughed in his brief, rather grudging way. "You're getting quite clever for a child of your age," he observed. "But don't overdo it, my son! Don't get precocious!"

Tommy's hand grasped his arm confidentially. "Monck, if I don't speak out to someone, I shall bust! Surely you don't mind my speaking out to you!"

"Not if there's anything to be gained by it," said Monck.

He ignored the friendly, persuasive hand on his arm, but yet in some fashion Tommy knew that it was not unwelcome. He kept it there as he made reply.

"There isn't. Only, you know, old chap, it does a fellow good to unburden himself. And I'm bothered to death about this business."

"A bit late in the day, isn't it?" suggested Monck.

"Oh yes, I know; too late to do anything. But," Tommy spoke with force, "the nearer it gets, the worse I feel. I'm downright sick about it, and that's the truth. How would you feel, I wonder, if you knew your one and only sister was going to marry a rotter? Would you be satisfied to let things drift?"

Monck was silent for a space. They walked on over the dusty road with the free swing of the conquering race. One or two 'rickshaws met them as they went, and a woman's voice called a greeting; but though they both responded, it scarcely served as a diversion. The silence between them remained.

Monck spoke at last, briefly, with grim restraint. "That's rather a sweeping assertion of yours. I shouldn't repeat it if I were you."

"It's true all the same," maintained Tommy. "You know it's true."

"I know nothing," said Monck. "I've nothing whatever against Dacre."

"You've nothing in favour of him anyway," growled Tommy.

"Nothing particular; but I presume your sister has." There was just a hint of irony in the quiet rejoinder.

Tommy winced. "Stella! Great Scott, no! She doesn't care the toss of a halfpenny for him. I know that now. She only accepted him because she found herself in such a beastly anomalous position, with all the spiteful cats of the regiment arrayed against her, treating her like a pariah."

"Did she tell you so?" There was no irony in Monck's tone this time. It fell short and stern.

Again Tommy glanced at him as one uncertain. "Not likely," he said.

"Then why do you make the assertion? What grounds have you for making the assertion?" Monck spoke with insistence as one who meant to have an answer.

And the boy answered him, albeit shamefacedly. "I really can't say, Monck. I'm the sort of fool that sees things without being able to explain how. But that Stella has the faintest spark of real love for that fellow Dacre,—well, I'd take my dying oath that she hasn't."

"Some women don't go in for that sort of thing," commented Monck dryly.

"Stella isn't that sort of woman." Hotly came Tommy's defence. "You don't know her. She's a lot deeper than I am."

Monck laughed a little. "Oh, you're deep enough, Tommy. But you're transparent as well. Now your sister on the other hand is quite inscrutable. But it is not for us to interfere. She probably knows what she is doing—very well indeed."

"That's just it. Does she know? Isn't she taking a most awful leap in the dark?" Keen anxiety sounded in Tommy's voice. "It's been such horribly quick work, you know. Why, she hasn't been out here six weeks. It's a shame for any girl to marry on such short notice as that. I said so to her, and she—she laughed and said, 'Oh, that's beggar's choice! Do you think I could enjoy life with your angels in paradise in unmarried bliss? I'd sooner stay down in hell with you.' And she'd have done it too, Monck. And it would probably have killed her. That's partly how I came to know."

"Haven't the women been decent to her?" Monck's question fell curtly, as if the subject were one which he was reluctant to discuss.

Tommy looked at him through the starlight. "You know what they are," he said bluntly. "They'd hunt anybody if once Lady Harriet gave tongue. She chose to eye Stella askance from the very outset, and of course all the rest followed suit. Mrs. Ralston is the only one in the whole crowd who has ever treated her decently, but of course she's nobody. Everyone sits on her. As if," he spoke with heat, "Stella weren't as good as the best of 'em—and better! What right have they to treat her like a social outcast just because she came out here to me on her own? It's hateful! It's iniquitous! What else could she have done?"

"It seems reasonable—from a man's point of view," said Monck.

"It was reasonable. It was the only thing possible. And just for that they chose to turn the cold shoulder on her,—to ostracize her practically. What had she done to them? What right had they to treat her like that?" Fierce resentment sounded in Tommy's voice.

"I'll tell you if you want to know," said Monck abruptly. "It's the law of the pack to rend an outsider. And your sister will always be that—married or otherwise. They may fawn upon her later, Dacre being one to hold his own with women. But they will always hate her in their hearts. You see, she is beautiful."

"Is she?" said Tommy in surprise. "Do you know, I never thought of that!"

Monck laughed—a cold, sardonic laugh. "Quite so! You wouldn't! But Dacre has—and a few more of us."

"Oh, confound Dacre!" Tommy's irritation returned with a rush. "I detest the man! He behaves as if he were conferring a favour. When he was making that speech to-night, I wanted to fling my glass at him."

"Ah, but you mustn't do those things." Monck spoke reprovingly. "You may be young, but you're past the schoolboy stage. Dacre is more of a woman's favourite than a man's, you must remember. If your sister is not in love with him, she is about the only woman in the station who isn't."

"That's the disgusting part of it," fumed Tommy. "He makes love to every woman he meets."

They had reached a shadowy compound that bordered the dusty road for a few yards. A little eddying wind made a mysterious whisper among its thirsty shrubs. The bungalow it surrounded showed dimly in the starlight, a wooden structure with a raised verandah and a flight of steps leading up to it. A light thrown by a red-shaded lamp shone out from one of the rooms, casting a shaft of ruddy brilliance into the night as though it defied the splendour without. It shone upon Tommy's face as he paused, showing it troubled and anxious.

"You may as well come in," he said. "She is sure to be ready. Come in and have a drink!"

Monck stood still. His dark face was in shadow. He seemed to be debating some point with himself.

Finally, "All right. Just for a minute," he said. "But, look here, Tommy! Don't you let your sister suspect that you've been making a confidant of me! I don't fancy it would please her. Put on a grin, man! Don't look bowed down with family cares! She is probably quite capable of looking after herself—like the rest of 'em."

He clapped a careless hand on the lad's shoulder as they turned up the path together towards the streaming red light.

"You're a bit of a woman-hater, aren't you?" said Tommy.

And Monck laughed again his short, rather bitter laugh; but he said no word in answer.

CHAPTER II

THE PRISONER AT THE BAR

In the room with the crimson-shaded lamp Stella Denvers sat waiting. The red glow compassed her warmly, striking wonderful copper gleams in the burnished coils of her hair. Her face was bent over the long white gloves that she was pulling over her wrists, a pale face that yet was extraordinarily vivid, with features that were delicate and proud, and lips that had the exquisite softness and purity of a flower.

She raised her eyes from her task at sound of the steps below the window, and their starry brightness under her straight black brows gave her an infinite allurement. Certainly a beautiful woman, as Monck had said, and possessing the brilliance and the wonder of youth to an almost dazzling degree! Perhaps it was not altogether surprising that the ladies of the regiment had not been too enthusiastic in their welcome of this sister of Tommy's who had come so suddenly into their midst, defying convention. Her advent had been utterly unexpected—a total surprise even to Tommy, who, returning one day from the polo-ground, had found her awaiting him in the bachelor quarters which he had shared with three other subalterns. And her arrival had set the whole station buzzing.

Led by the Colonel's wife, Lady Harriet Mansfield, the women of the regiment had—with the single exception of Mrs. Ralston whose opinion was of no account—risen and condemned the splendid stranger who had come amongst them with such supreme audacity and eclipsed the fairest of them. Stella's own simple explanation that she had, upon attaining her majority and fifty pounds a year, decided to quit the home of some distant relatives who did not want her and join Tommy who was the only near relation she had, had satisfied no one. She was an interloper, and as such they united to treat her. As Lady Harriet said, no nice girl would have dreamed of taking such an extraordinary step, and she had not the smallest intention of offering her the chaperonage that she so conspicuously lacked. If Mrs. Ralston chose to do so, that was her own affair. Such action on the part of the surgeon's very ordinary wife would make no difference to any one. She was glad to think that all the other ladies were too well-bred to accept without reservation so unconventional a type.

The fact that she was Tommy's sister was the only consideration in her favour. Tommy was quite a nice boy, and they could not for his sake entirely exclude her from the regimental society, but to no intimate gathering was she ever invited, nor from the female portion of the community was there any welcome for her at the Club.

The attitude of the officers of the regiment was of a totally different nature. They had accepted her with enthusiasm, possibly all the more marked on account of the aloofness of their women folk, and in a very short time they were paying her homage as one man. The subalterns who had shared their quarters with Tommy turned out to make room for her, treating her like a queen suddenly come into her own, and like a queen she entered into possession, accepting all courtesy just as she ignored all slights with a delicate self-possession that yet knew how to be gracious when occasion demanded.

Mrs. Ralston would have offered her harbourage had she desired it, but there was pride in Stella—a pride that surged and rebelled very far below her serenity. She received favours from none.

And so, unshackled and unchaperoned, she had gone her way among her critics, and no one—not even Tommy—suspected how deep was the wound that their barely-veiled hostility had inflicted. In bitterness of soul she hid it from all the world, and only her brother and her brother's grim and somewhat unapproachable captain were even vaguely aware of its existence.

Everard Monck was one of the very few men who had not laid themselves down before her dainty feet, and she had gradually come to believe that this man shared the silent, side-long disapproval manifested by the women. Very strangely that belief hurt her even more deeply, in a subtle, incomprehensible fashion, than any slights inflicted by her own sex. Possibly Tommy's warm enthusiasm for the man had made her more sensitive regarding his good opinion. And possibly she was over ready to read condemnation in his grave eyes. But—whatever the reason—she would have given much to have had him on her side. Somehow it mattered to her, and mattered vitally.

But Monck had never joined her retinue of courtiers. He was never other than courteous to her, but he did not seek her out. Perhaps he had better things to do. Aloof, impenetrable, cold, he passed her by, and she would have been even more amazed than Tommy had she heard him describe her as beautiful, so convinced was she that he saw in her no charm.

It had been a disheartening struggle, this hewing for herself a way along the rocky paths of prejudice, and many had been the thorns under her feet. Though she kept a brave heart and never faltered, she had tired inevitably of the perpetual effort it entailed. Three weeks after her arrival, when the annual exodus of the ladies of the regiment to the Hills was drawing near, she became engaged to Ralph Dacre, the handsomest and most irresponsible man in the mess.

With him at least her power to attract was paramount. He was blindly, almost fulsomely, in love. Her beauty went to his head from the outset; it fired his blood. He worshipped her hotly, and pursued her untiringly, caring little whether she returned his devotion so long as he ultimately took possession. And when finally, half-disdainfully, she yielded to his insistence, his one all-mastering thought became to clinch the bargain before she could repent of it. It was a mad and headlong passion that drove him—not for the first time in his life; and the subtle pride of her and the soft reserve made her all the more desirable in his eyes.

He had won her; he did not stop to ask himself how. The women said that the luck was all on her side. The men forebore to express an opinion. Dacre had attained his captaincy, but he was not regarded with great respect by any one. His fellow-officers shrugged their shoulders over him, and the commanding officer, Colonel Mansfield, had been heard to call him "the craziest madman it had ever been his fate to meet." No one, except Tommy, actively disliked him, and he had no grounds for so doing, as Monck had pointed out. Monck, who till then had occupied the same bungalow, declared he had nothing against him, and he was surely in a position to form a very shrewd opinion. For Monck was neither fool nor madman, and there was very little that escaped his silent observation.

He was acting as best man at the morrow's ceremony, the function having been almost thrust upon him by Dacre who, oddly enough, shared something of Tommy's veneration for his very reticent brother-officer. There was scant friendship between them. Each had been accustomed to go his own way wholly independent of the other. They were no more than casual acquaintances, and they were content to remain such. But undoubtedly Dacre entertained a certain respect for Monck and observed a wariness of behaviour in his presence that he never troubled to assume for any other man. He was careful in his dealings with him, being at all times not wholly certain of his ground.

Other men felt the same uncertainty in connection with Monck. None—save Tommy—was sure what manner of man he was. Tommy alone took him for granted with whole-hearted admiration, and at his earnest wish it had been arranged between them that Monck should take up his abode with him when the forthcoming marriage had deprived each of a companion. Tommy was delighted with the idea, and he had a gratifying suspicion that Monck himself was inclined to be pleased with it also.

The Green Bungalow had become considerably more homelike since Stella's arrival, and Tommy meant to keep it so. He was sure that Monck and he would have the same tastes.

And so on that eve of his sister's wedding, the thought of their coming companionship was the sole redeeming feature of the whole affair, and he turned in his impulsive fashion to say so just as they reached the verandah steps.

But the words did not leave his lips, for the red glow flung from the lamp had found Monck's upturned face, and something—something about it—checked all speech for the moment. He was looking straight up at the lighted window and the face of a beautiful woman who gazed forth into the night. And his eyes were no longer cold and unresponsive, but burning, ardent, intensely alive. Tommy forgot what he was going to say and only stared.

The moment passed; it was scarcely so much as a moment. And Monck moved on in his calm, unfaltering way.

"Your sister is ready and waiting," he said.

They ascended the steps together, and the girl who sat by the open window rose with a stately movement and stepped forward to meet them.

"Hullo, Stella!" was Tommy's greeting. "Hope I'm not awfully late. They wasted such a confounded time over toasts at mess to-night. Yours was one of 'em, and I had to reply. I hadn't a notion what to say. Captain Monck thinks I made an awful hash of it though he is too considerate to say so."

"On the contrary I said 'Hear, hear!' to every stutter," said Monck, bowing slightly as he took the hand she offered.

She was wearing a black lace dress with a glittering spangled scarf of Indian gauze floating about her. Her neck and shoulders gleamed in the soft red glow. She was superb that night.

She smiled at Monck, and her smile was as a shining cloak hiding her soul. "So you have started upon your official duties already!" she said. "It is the best man's business to encourage and console everyone concerned, isn't it?"

The faint cynicism of her speech was like her smile. It held back all intrusive curiosity. And the man's answering smile had something of the same quality. Reserve met reserve.

"I hope I shall not find it very arduous in that respect," he said. "I did not come here in that capacity."

"I am glad of that," she said. "Won't you come in and sit down?"

She motioned him within with a queenly gesture, but her invitation was wholly lacking in warmth. It was Tommy who pressed forward with eager hospitality.

"Yes, and have a drink! It's a thirsty right. It's getting infernally hot. Stella, you're lucky to be going out of it."

"Oh, I am very lucky," Stella said.

They entered the lighted room, and Tommy went in search of refreshment.

"Won't you sit down?" said Stella.

Her voice was deep and pure, and the music in it made him wonder if she sang. He sat facing her while she returned with apparent absorption to the fastening of her gloves. She spoke again after a moment without raising her eyes. "Are you proposing to take up your abode here to-morrow?"

"That's the idea," said Monck.

"I hope you and Tommy will be quite comfortable," she said. "No doubt he will be a good deal happier with you than he has been for the past few weeks with me."

"I don't know why he should be," said Monck.

"No?" She was frowning slightly over her glove. "You see, my sojourn here has not been—a great success. I think poor Tommy has felt it rather badly. He likes a genial atmosphere."

"He won't get much of that in my company," observed Monck.

She smiled momentarily. "Perhaps not. But I think he will not be sorry to be relieved of family cares. They have weighed rather heavily upon him."

"He will be sorry to lose you," said Monck.

"Oh, of course, in a way. But he will soon get over that." She looked up at him suddenly. "You will all be rather thankful when I am safely married, Captain Monck," she said.

There was a second or two of silence. Monck's eyes looked straight back into hers while it lasted, but they held no warmth, scarcely even interest.

"I really don't know why you should say that, Miss Denvers," he said stiffly at length.

Stella's gloved hands clasped each other. She was breathing somewhat hard, yet her bearing was wholly regal, even disdainful.

"Only because I realize that I have been a great anxiety to all the respectable portion of the community," she made careless reply. "I think I am right in classing you under that heading, am I not?"

He heard the challenge in her tone, delicately though she presented it, and something in him that was fierce and unrestrained sprang up to meet it. But he forced it back. His expression remained wholly inscrutable.

"I don't think I can claim to be anything else," he said. "But that fact scarcely makes me in any sense one of a community. I think I prefer to stand alone."

Her blue eyes sparkled a little. "Strangely, I have the same preference," she said. "It has never appealed to me to be one of a crowd. I like independence—whatever the crowd may say. But I am quite aware that in a woman that is considered a dangerous taste. A woman should always conform to rule."

"I have never studied the subject," said Monck.

He spoke briefly. Tommy's confidences had stirred within him that which could not be expressed. The whole soul of him shrank with an almost angry repugnance from discussing the matter with her. No discussion could make any difference at this stage.

Again for a second he saw her slight frown. Then she leaned back in her chair, stretching up her arms as if weary of the matter. "In fact you avoid all things feminine," she said. "How discreet of you!"

A large white moth floated suddenly in and began to beat itself against the lamp-shade. Monck's eyes watched it with a grim concentration. Stella's were half-closed. She seemed to have dismissed him from her mind as an unimportant detail. The silence widened between them.

Suddenly there was a movement. The fluttering creature had found the flame and fallen dazed upon the table. Almost in the same second Monck stooped forward swiftly and silently, and crushed the thing with his closed fist.

Stella drew a quick breath. Her eyes were wide open again. She sat up.

"Why did you do that?"

He looked at her again, a smouldering gleam in his eyes. "It was on its way to destruction," he said.

"And so you helped it!"

He nodded. "Yes. Long-drawn-out agonies don't attract me."

Stella laughed softly, yet with a touch of mockery. "Oh, it was an act of mercy, was it? You didn't look particularly merciful. In fact, that is about the last quality I should have attributed to you."

"I don't think," Monck said very quietly, "that you are in a position to judge me." She leaned forward. He saw that her bosom was heaving. "That is your prerogative, isn't it?" she said. "I—I am just the prisoner at the bar, and—like the moth—I have been condemned—without mercy."

He raised his brows sharply. For a second he had the look of a man who has been stabbed in the back. Then with a swift effort he pulled himself together.

In the same moment Stella rose. She was smiling, and there was a red flush in her cheeks. She took her fan from the table.

"And now," she said, "I am going to dance—all night long. Every officer in the mess—save one—has asked me for a dance."

He was on his feet in an instant. He had checked one impulse, but even to his endurance there were limits. He spoke as one goaded.

"Will you give me one?"

She looked him squarely in the eyes. "No, Captain Monck."

His dark face looked suddenly stubborn. "I don't often dance," he said. "I wasn't going to dance to-night. But—I will have one—I must have one—with you."

"Why?" Her question fell with a crystal clearness. There was something of crystal hardness in her eyes.

But the man was undaunted. "Because you have wronged me, and you owe me reparation."

"I—have wronged—you!" She spoke the words slowly, still looking him in the eyes.

He made an abrupt gesture as of holding back some inner force that strongly urged him. "I am not one of your persecutors," he said. "I have never in my life presumed to judge you—far less condemn you."

His voice vibrated as though some emotion fought fiercely for the mastery. They stood facing each other in what might have been open antagonism but for that deep quiver in the man's voice.

Stella spoke after the lapse of seconds. She had begun to tremble.

"Then why—why did you let me think so? Why did you always stand aloof?"

There was a tremor in her voice also, but her eyes were shining with the light half-eager, half-anxious, of one who seeks for buried treasure.

Monck's answer was pitched very low. It was as if the soul of him gave utterance to the words. "It is my nature to stand aloof. I was waiting."

"Waiting?" Her two hands gripped suddenly hard upon her fan, but still her shining eyes did not flinch from his. Still with a quivering heart she searched.

Almost in a whisper came his reply. "I was waiting—till my turn should come."

"Ah!" The fan snapped between her hands; she cast it from her with a movement that was almost violent.

Monck drew back sharply. With a smile that was grimly cynical he veiled his soul. "I was a fool, of course, and I am quite aware that my foolishness is nothing to you. But at least you know now how little cause you have to hate me."

She had turned from him and gone to the open window. She stood there bending slightly forward, as one who strains for a last glimpse of something that has passed from sight.

Monck remained motionless, watching her. From another room near by there came the sound of Tommy's humming and the cheery pop of a withdrawn cork.

Stella spoke at last, in a whisper, and as she spoke the strain went out of her attitude and she drooped against the wood-work of the window as if spent. "Yes; but I know—too late."

The words reached him though he scarcely felt that they were intended to do so. He suffered them to go into silence; the time for speech was past.

The seconds throbbed away between them. Stella did not move or speak again, and at last Monck turned from her. He picked up the broken fan, and with a curious reverence he laid it out of sight among some books on the table.

Then he stood immovable as granite and waited.

There came the sound of Tommy's footsteps, and in a moment the door was flung open. Tommy advanced with all a host's solicitude.

"Oh, I say, I'm awfully sorry to have kept you waiting so long. That silly ass of a *khit* had cleared off and left us nothing to drink. Stella, we shall miss all the fun if we don't hurry up. Come on, Monck, old chap, say when!"

He stopped at the table, and Stella turned from the window and moved forward. Her face was pale, but she was smiling.

"Captain Monck is coming with us, Tommy," she said.

"What?" Tommy looked up sharply. "Really? I say, Monck, I'm pleased. It'll do you good."

Monck was smiling also, faintly, grimly. "Don't mix any strong waters for me, Tommy!" he said. "And you had better not be too generous to yourself! Remember, you will have to dance with Lady Harriet!"

Tommy grimaced above the glasses. "All right. Have some lime-juice! You will have to dance with her too. That's some consolation!"

"I?" said Monck. He took the glass and handed it to Stella, then as she shook her head he put it to his own lips and drank as a man drinks to a memory. "No," he said then. "I am dancing only one dance to-night, and that will not be with Lady Harriet Mansfield."

"Who then?" questioned Tommy.

It was Stella who answered him, in her voice a note that sounded half-reckless, half-defiant. "It isn't given to every woman to dance at her own funeral," she said: "Captain Monck has kindly consented to assist at the orgy of mine."

"Stella!" protested Tommy, flushing. "I hate to hear you talking like that!"

Stella laughed a little, softly, as though at the vagaries of a child. "Poor Tommy!" she said. "What it is to be so young!"

"I'd sooner be a babe in arms than a cynic," said Tommy bluntly.

CHAPTER III

THE TRIUMPH

Lady Harriet's lorgnettes were brought piercingly to bear upon the bride-elect that night, and her thin, refined features never relaxed during the operation. She was looking upon such youth and loveliness as seldom came her way; but the sight gave her no pleasure. She deemed it extremely unsuitable that Stella should dance at all on the eve of her wedding, and when she realized that nearly every man in the room was having his turn, her disapproval by no means diminished. She wondered audibly to one after another of her followers what Captain Dacre was about to permit such a thing. And when Monck—Everard Monck of all people who usually avoided all gatherings at the Club and had never been known to dance if he could find any legitimate means of excusing himself—waltzed Stella through the throng, her indignation amounted almost to anger. The mess had yielded to the last man.

"I call it almost brazen," she said to Mrs. Burton, the Major's wife. "She flaunts her unconventionality in our faces."

"A grave mistake," agreed Mrs. Burton. "It will not make us think any the more highly of her when she is married."

"I am in two minds about calling on her," declared Lady Harriet. "I am very doubtful as to the advisability of inviting any one so obviously unsuitable into our inner circle. Of course Mrs. Ralston," she raised her long pointed chin upon the name, "will please herself in the matter. She will probably be the first to try and draw her in, but what Mrs. Ralston does and what I do are two very different things. She is not particular as to the society she keeps, and the result is that her opinion is very justly regarded as worthless."

"Oh, quite," agreed Mrs. Burton, sending an obviously false smile in the direction of the lady last named who was approaching them in the company of Mrs. Ermsted, the Adjutant's wife, a little smart woman whom Tommy had long since surnamed "The Lizard."

Mrs. Ralston, the surgeon's wife, had once been a pretty girl, and there were occasions still on which her prettiness lingered like the gleams of a fading sunset. She had a diffident manner in society, but yet she was the only woman in the station who refused to follow Lady Harriet's lead. As Tommy had said, she was a nobody. Her influence was of no account, but yet with unobtrusive insistence she took her own way, and none could turn her therefrom.

Mrs. Ermsted held her up to ridicule openly, and yet very strangely she did not seem to dislike the Adjutant's sharp-tongued little wife. She had been very good to her on more than one occasion, and the most appreciative remark that Mrs. Ermsted had ever found to make regarding her was that the poor thing was so fond of drudging for somebody that it was a real kindness to let her. Mrs. Ermsted was quite willing to be kind to any one in that respect.

They approached now, and Lady Harriet gave to each her distinctive smile of royal condescension.

"I expected to see you dancing, Mrs. Ermsted," she said.

"Oh, it's too hot," declared Mrs. Ermsted. "You want the temperament of a salamander to dance on a night like this."

She cast a barbed glance towards Stella as she spoke as Monck guided her to the least crowded corner of the ball-room. Stella's delicate face was flushed, but it was the exquisite flush of a blush-rose. Her eyes were of a starry brightness; she had the radiant look of one who has achieved her heart's desire.

"What a vision of triumph!" commented Mrs. Ermsted. "It's soothing anyway to know that that wild-rose complexion won't survive the summer. Captain Monck looks curiously out of his element. No doubt he prefers the bazaars."

"But Stella Denvers is enchanting to-night," murmured Mrs. Ralston.

Lady Harriet overheard the murmur, and her aquiline nose was instantly elevated a little higher. "So many people never see beyond the outer husk," she said.

Mrs. Burton smiled out of her slitty eyes. "I should scarcely imagine Captain Monck to be one of them," she said. "He is obviously here as a matter of form to-night. The best man must be civil to the bride—whatever his feelings."

Lady Harriet's face cleared a little, although her estimate of Mrs. Burton's opinion was not a very high one. "That may account for Captain Dacre's extremely complacent attitude," she said. "He regards the attentions paid to his *fiancée* as a tribute to himself."

"He may change his point of view when he is married," laughed Mrs. Ermsted. "It will be interesting to watch developments. We all know what Captain Dacre is. I have never yet seen him satisfied to take a back seat."

Mrs. Burton laughed with her. "Nor content to occupy even a front one at the same show for long," she observed. "I marvel to see him caught in the noose so easily."

"None but an adventuress could have done it," declared Mrs. Ermsted. "She has practised the art of slinging the lasso before now."

"My dear," said Mrs. Ralston, "forgive me, but that is unworthy of you."

Mrs. Ermsted flicked an eyelid in Mrs. Burton's direction with an *insouciance* that somehow robbed the act of any serious sting. "Poor Mrs. Ralston holds such a high opinion of everybody," she said, "that she must meet with a hundred disappointments in a day."

Lady Harriet's down-turned lips said nothing, but they were none the less eloquent on that account.

Mrs. Ralston's eyes of faded blue watched Stella with a distressed look. She was not hurt on her own account, but she hated to hear the girl criticized in so unfriendly a spirit. Stella was more brilliantly beautiful that night than she had ever before seen her, and she longed to hear a word of appreciation from that hostile group of women. But she knew very well that the longing was vain, and it was with relief that she saw Captain Dacre himself saunter up to claim Mrs. Ermsted for a partner.

Smiling, debonair, complacent, the morrow's bridegroom had a careless quip for all and sundry on that last night. It was evident that his *fiancée's* defection was a matter of no moment to him. Stella was to have her fling, and he, it seemed, meant to have his. He and Mrs. Ermsted had had many a flirtation in the days that were past and it was well known that Captain Ermsted heartily detested him in consequence. Some even hinted that matters had at one time approached very near to a climax, but Ralph Dacre knew how to handle difficult situations, and with considerable tact had managed to avoid it. Little Mrs. Ermsted, though still willing to flirt, treated him with just a tinge of disdain, now-a-days; no one knew wherefore. Perhaps it was more for Stella's edification than her own that she condescended to dance with him on that sweltering evening of Indian spring.

But Stella was evidently too engrossed with her own affairs to pay much attention to the doings of her *fiancé*. His love-making was not of a nature to be carried on in public. That would come later when they walked home through the glittering night and parted in the shadowy verandah while Tommy tramped restlessly about within the bungalow. He would claim that as a right she knew, and once or twice remembering the methods of his courtship a little shudder went through her as she danced. Very willingly would she have left early and foregone all intercourse with her lover that night. But there was no escape for her. She was pledged to the last dance, and for the sake of the pride that she carried so high she would not shrink under the malicious eyes that watched her so unsparingly. Her dance with Monck was quickly over, and he left her with the briefest word of thanks. Afterwards she saw him no more.

The rest of the evening passed in a whirl of gaiety that meant very little to her. Perhaps, on the whole, it was easier to bear than an evening spent in solitude would have been. She knew that she would be too utterly weary to lie awake when bedtime came at last. And the night would be so short—ah, so short! And so she danced and laughed with the gayest of the merrymakers, and when it was over at last even the severest of her critics had to admit that her triumph was complete. She had borne herself like a queen at a banquet of rejoicing, and like a queen she finally quitted the festive scene in a 'rickshaw drawn by a team of giddy subalterns, scattering her careless favours upon all who cared to compete for them.

As she had foreseen, Dacre accompanied the procession. He had no mind to be cheated of his rights, and it was he who finally dispersed the irresponsible throng at the steps of the verandah, handing her up them with a royal air and drawing her away from the laughter and cheering that followed her.

With her hand pressed lightly against his side, he led her away to the darkest corner, and there he pushed back the soft wrap from her shoulders and gathered her into his arms.

She stood almost stiffly in his embrace, neither yielding nor attempting to avoid. But at the touch of his lips upon her neck she shivered. There was something sensual in that touch that revolted her—in spite of herself.

"Ralph," she said, and her voice quivered a little, "I think you must say good-bye to me. I am tired to-night. If I don't rest, I shall never be ready for to-morrow."

He made an inarticulate sound that in some fashion expressed what the drawing of his lips had made her feel. "Sweetheart—to-morrow!" he said, and kissed her again with a lingering persistence that to her overwrought nerves had in it something that was almost unendurable. It made her think of an epicurean tasting some favourite dish and smacking his lips over it.

A hint of irritation sounded in her voice as she said, drawing slightly away from him, "Yes, I want to rest for the few hours that are left. Please say good night now, Ralph! Really I am tired."

He laughed softly, his cheek laid to hers. "Ah, Stella!" he said. "What a queen you have been to-night! I have been watching you with the rest of the world, and I shouldn't mind laying pretty heavy odds that there isn't a single man among 'em that doesn't envy me."

Stella drew a deep breath as if she laboured against some oppression. "It's nice to be envied, isn't it?" she said.

He kissed her again. "Ah! You're a prize!" he said. "It was just a question of first in, and I never was one to let the grass grow. I plucked the fruit while all the rest were just looking at it. Stella—mine! Stella—mine!"

His lips pressed hers between the words closely, possessively, and again involuntarily she shivered. She could not return his caresses that night.

His hold relaxed at last. "How cold you are, my Star of the North!" he said. "What is it? Surely you are not nervous at the thought of to-morrow after your triumph to-night! You will carry all before you, never fear!"

She answered him in a voice so flat and emotionless that it sounded foreign even to herself. "Oh, no, I am not nervous. I'm too tired to feel anything to-night."

He took her face between his hands. "Ah, well, you will be all mine this time to-morrow. One kiss and I will let you go. You witch—you enchantress! I never thought you would draw old Monck too into your toils."

Again she drew that deep breath as of one borne down by some heavy weight. "Nor I," she said, and gave him wearily the kiss for which he bargained.

He did not stay much longer, possibly realizing his inability to awake any genuine response in her that night. Her remoteness must have chilled any man less ardent. But he went from her too encompassed with blissful anticipation to attach any importance to the obvious lack of corresponding delight on her part. She was already in his estimation his own property, and the thought of her happiness was one which scarcely entered into his consideration. She had accepted him, and no doubt she realized that she was doing very well for herself. He had no misgivings on that point. Stella was a young woman who knew her own mind very thoroughly. She had secured the finest catch within reach, and she was not likely to repent of her bargain at this stage.

So, unconcernedly, he went his way, throwing a couple of *annas* with careless generosity to a beggar who followed him along the road whining for alms, well-satisfied with himself and with all the world on that wonderful night that had witnessed the final triumph of the woman whom he had chosen for his bride, asking nought of the gods save that which they had deigned to bestow—Fortune's favourite whom every man must envy.

CHAPTER IV

THE BRIDE

It was remarked by Tommy's brother-officers on the following day that it was he rather than the bride who displayed all the shyness that befitted the occasion.

As he walked up the aisle with his sister's hand on his arm, his face was crimson and reluctant, and he stared straight before him as if unwilling to meet all the watching eyes that followed their progress. But the bride walked proudly and firmly, her head held high with even the suspicion of an upward, disdainful curve to her beautiful mouth, the ghost of a defiant smile. To all who saw her she was a splendid spectacle of bridal content.

"Unparalleled effrontery!" whispered Lady Harriet, surveying the proud young face through her lorgnettes.

"Ah, but she is exquisite," murmured Mrs. Ralston with a wistful mist in her faded eyes.

"'Faultily faultless, icily regular, splendidly null,'" scoffed little Mrs. Ermsted upon whose cheeks there bloomed a faint fixed glow.

Yes, she was splendid. Even the most hostile had to admit it. On that, the day of her final victory, she surpassed herself. She shone as a queen with majestic self-assurance, wholly at her ease, sublimely indifferent to all criticism.

At the chancel-steps she bestowed a brief smile of greeting upon her waiting bridegroom, and for a single moment her steady eyes rested, though without any gleam of recognition, upon the dark face of the best man.

Then the service began, and with the utmost calmness of demeanour she took her part.

When the service was over, Tommy extended his hesitating invitation to Lady Harriet and his commanding officer to follow the newly wedded pair to the vestry. They went. Colonel Mansfield with a species of jocose pomposity specially assumed for the occasion, his wife, upright, thin-lipped, forbidding, instinct with wordless disapproval.

The bride,—the veil thrown back from her beautiful face,—stood laughing with her husband. There was no fixity in the soft flush of those delicately rounded cheeks. Even Lady Harriet realized that, though she had never seen so much colour in the girl's face before. She advanced stiffly, and Ralph Dacre with smiling grace took his wife's arm and drew her forward.

"This is good of you, Lady Harriet," he declared. "I was hoping for your support. Allow me to introduce—my wife!"

His words had a pride of possession that rang clarion-like in every syllable, and in response Lady Harriet was moved to offer a cold cheek in salutation to the bride. Stella bent instantly and kissed it with a quick graciousness that would have melted any one less austere, but in Lady Harriet's opinion the act was marred by its very impulsiveness. She did not like impulsive people. So, with chill repression, she accepted the only overture from Stella that she was ever to receive.

But if she were proof against the girl's ready charm, with her husband it was quite otherwise. Stella broke through his pomposity without effort, giving him both her hands with a simplicity that went straight to his heart. He held them in a tight, paternal grasp.

"God bless you, my dear!" he said. "I wish you both every happiness from the bottom of my soul."

She turned from him a few seconds later with a faintly tremulous laugh to give her hand to the best man, but it did not linger in his, and to his curtly proffered felicitations she made no verbal response whatever.

Ten minutes later, as she left the vestry with her husband, Mrs. Ralston pressed forward unexpectedly, and openly checked her progress in full view of the whole assembly.

"My dear," she murmured humbly, "my dear, you'll allow me I know. I wanted just to tell you how beautiful you look, and how earnestly I pray for your happiness."

It was a daring move, and it had not been accomplished without courage. Lady Harriet in the background stiffened with displeasure, nearer to actual anger than she had ever before permitted herself to be with any one so contemptible as the surgeon's wife. Even Major Ralston himself, most phlegmatic of men, looked momentarily disconcerted by his wife's action.

But Stella—Stella stopped dead with a new light in her eyes, and in a moment dropped her husband's arm to fling both her own about the gentle, faded woman who had dared thus openly to range herself on her side.

"Dear Mrs. Ralston," she said, not very steadily, "how more than kind of you to tell me that!"

The tears were actually in her eyes as she kissed the surgeon's wife. That spontaneous act of sympathy had pierced straight through her armour of reserve and found its way to her heart. Her face, as she passed on down the aisle by her husband's side, was wonderfully softened, and even Mrs. Ermsted found no gibe to fling after her. The smile that quivered on Stella's lips was full of an unconscious pathos that disarmed all criticism.

The sunshine outside the church was blinding. It smote through the awning with pitiless intensity. Around the carriage a curious crowd had gathered to see the bridal procession. To Stella's dazzled eyes it seemed a surging sea of unfamiliar faces. But one face stood out from the rest—the calm countenance of Ralph Dacre's magnificent Sikh servant clad in snowy linen, who stood at the carriage door and gravely bowed himself before her, stretching an arm to protect her dress from the wheel.

"This is Peter the Great," said Dacre's careless voice, "a highly honourable person, Stella, and a most efficient bodyguard."

"How do you do?" said Stella, and held out her hand.

She acted with the utmost simplicity. During her four weeks' sojourn in India she had not learned to treat the native servant with contempt, and the majestic presence of this man made her feel almost as if she were dealing with a prince.

He straightened himself swiftly at her action, and she saw a sudden, gleaming smile flash across his grave face. Then he took the proffered hand, bending low over it till his turbaned forehead for a moment touched her fingers.

"May the sun always shine on you, my *mem-sahib!*" he said.

Stella realized afterwards that in action and in words there lay a tacit acceptance of her as mistress which was to become the allegiance of a lifelong service.

She stepped into the carriage with a feeling of warmth at her heart which was very different from the icy constriction that had bound it when she had arrived at the church a brief half-hour before with Tommy.

Her husband's arm was about her as they drove away. He pressed her to his side. "Oh, Star of my heart, how superb you are!" he said. "I feel as if I had married a queen. And you weren't even nervous."

She bent her head, not looking at him. "Poor Tommy was," she said.

He smiled tolerantly. "Tommy's such a youngster."

She smiled also. "Exactly one year younger than I am."

He drew her nearer, his eyes devouring her. "You, Stella!" he said. "You are as ageless as the stars."

She laughed faintly, not yielding herself to the closer pressure though not actually resisting it. "That is merely a form of telling me that I am much older than I seem," she said. "And you are quite right. I am."

His arm compelled her. "You are you," he said. "And you are so divinely young and beautiful that there is no measuring you by ordinary standards. They all know it. That is why you weren't received into the community with open arms. You are utterly above and beyond them all."

She flinched slightly at the allusion. "I hope I am not so extraordinary as all that," she said.

His arm became insistent. "You are unique," he said. "You are superb."

There was passion barely suppressed in his hold and a sudden swift shiver went through her. "Oh, Ralph," she said, "don't—- don't worship me too much!"

Her voice quivered in its appeal, but somehow its pathos passed him by. He saw only her beauty, and it thrilled every pulse in his body. Fiercely almost, he strained her to him. And he did not so much as notice that her lips trembled too piteously to return his kiss, or that her submission to his embrace was eloquent of mute endurance rather than glad surrender. He stood as a conqueror on the threshold of a newly acquired kingdom and exulted over the splendour of its treasures because it was all his own.

It did not even occur to him to doubt that her happiness fully equalled his. Stella was a woman and reserved; but she was happy enough, oh, she was happy enough. With complacence he reflected that if every man in the mess envied him, probably every woman in the station would have gladly changed places with her. Was he not Fortune's favourite? What happier fate could any woman desire than to be his bride?

CHAPTER V

THE DREAM

It was a fortnight after the wedding, on an evening of intense heat, that Everard Monck, now established with Tommy at The Green Bungalow, came in from polo to find the mail awaiting him. He sauntered in through the verandah in search of a drink which he expected to find in the room which Stella during her brief sojourn had made more dainty and artistic than the rest, albeit it had never been dignified by the name of drawing-room. There was light green matting on the floor and there were also light green cushions in each of the long wicker chairs. Curtains of green gauze hung before the windows, and the fierce sunlight filtering through gave the room a strangely translucent effect. It was like a chamber under the sea.

It had been Monck's intention to have his drink and pass straight on to his own quarters for a bath, but the letters on the table caught his eye and he stopped. Standing in the green dimness with a tumbler in one hand, he sorted them out. There were two for himself and two for Tommy, the latter obviously bills, and under these one more, also for Tommy in a woman's clear round writing. It came from Srinagar, and Monck stood for a second or two holding it in his hand and staring straight out before him with eyes that saw not. Just for those seconds a mocking vision danced gnomelike through his brain. Just at this moment probably most of the other men were opening letters from their wives in the Hills. And he saw the chance he had not taken like a flash of far, elusive sunlight on the sky-line of a troubled sea.

The vision passed. He laid down the letter and took up his own correspondence. One of the letters was from England. He poured out his drink and flung himself down to read it.

It came from the only relation he possessed in the world—his brother. Bernard Monck was the elder by fifteen years—a man of brilliant capabilities, who had long since relinquished all idea of worldly advancement in the all-absorbing interest of a prison chaplaincy. They had not met for over five years, but they maintained a regular correspondence, and every month brought to Everard Monck the thin envelope directed in the square, purposeful handwriting of the man who had been during the whole of his life his nearest and best friend. Lying back in the wicker-chair, relaxed and weary, he opened the letter and began to read.

Ten minutes later, Tommy Denvers, racing in, also in polo-kit, stopped short upon the threshold and stared in shocked amazement as if some sudden horror had caught him by the throat.

"Great heavens above, Monck! What's the matter?" he ejaculated.

Perhaps it was in part due to the green twilight of the room, but it seemed to him in that first startled moment that Monck's face had the look of a man who had received a deadly wound. The impression passed almost immediately, but the memory of it was registered in his brain for all time.

Monck raised the tumbler to his lips and drank before replying, and as he did so his customary grave composure became apparent, making Tommy wonder if his senses had tricked him. He looked at the lad with sombre eyes as he set down the glass. His brother's letter was still gripped in his hand.

"Hullo, Tommy!" he said, a shadowy smile about his mouth. "What are you in such a deuce of a hurry about?"

Tommy glanced down at the letters on the table and pounced upon the one that lay uppermost. "A letter from Stella! And about time, too! She isn't much of a correspondent now-a-days. Where are they now? Oh, Srinagar. Lucky beggar—Dacre! Wish he'd taken me along as well as Stella! What am I in such a hurry about? Well, my dear chap, look at the time! You'll be late for mess yourself if you don't buck up."

Tommy's treatment of his captain was ever of the airiest when they were alone. He had never stood in awe of Monck since the days of his illness; but even in his most familiar moments his manner was not without a certain deference. His respect for him was unbounded, and his pride in their intimacy was boyishly whole-hearted. There was no sacrifice great or small that he would not willingly have offered at Monck's behest.

And Monck knew it, realized the lad's devotion as pure gold, and valued it accordingly. But, that fact notwithstanding, his faith in Tommy's discretion did not move him to bestow his unreserved confidence upon him. Probably to no man in the world could he have opened his secret soul. He was not of an expansive nature. But Tommy occupied an inner place in his regard, and there were some things that he veiled from all beside which he no longer attempted to hide from this faithful follower of his. Thus far was Tommy privileged.

He got to his feet in response to the boy's last remark. "Yes, you're right. We ought to be going. I shall be interested to hear what your sister thinks of Kashmir. I went up there on a shooting expedition two years after I came out. It's a fine country."

"Is there anywhere that you haven't been?" said Tommy. "I believe you'll write a book one of these days."

Monck looked ironical. "Not till I'm on the shelf, Tommy," he said, "where there's nothing better to do."

"You'll never be on the shelf," said Tommy quickly. "You'll be much too valuable."

Monck shrugged his shoulders slightly and turned to go. "I doubt if that consideration would occur to any one but you, my boy," he said.

They walked to the mess-house together a little later through the airless dark, and there was nothing in Monck's manner either then or during the evening to confirm the doubt in Tommy's mind. Spirits were not very high at the mess just then. Nearly all the women had left for the Hills, and the increasing heat was beginning to make life a burden. The younger officers did their best to be cheerful, and one of them, Bertie Oakes, a merry, brainless youngster, even proposed an impromptu dance to enliven the proceedings. But he did not find many supporters. Men were tired after the polo. Colonel Mansfield and Major Burton were deeply engrossed with some news that had been brought by Barnes of the Police, and no one mustered energy for more than talk.

Tommy soon decided to leave early and return to his letters. Before departing, he looked round for Monck as was his custom, but finding that he and Captain Ermsted had also been drawn into the discussion with the Colonel, he left the mess alone.

Back in The Green Bungalow he flung off his coat and threw himself down in his shirt-sleeves on the verandah to read his sister's letter. The light from the red-shaded lamp streamed across the pages. Stella had written very fully of their wanderings, but her companion she scarcely mentioned.

It was like a gorgeous dream, she said. Each day seemed to bring greater beauties. They had spent the first two at Agra to see the wonderful Taj which of course was wholly beyond description. Thence they had made their way to Rawal Pindi where Ralph had several military friends to be introduced to his bride. It was evident that he was anxious to display his new possession, and Tommy frowned a little over that episode, realizing fully why Stella touched so lightly upon it. For some reason his dislike of Dacre was increasing rapidly, and he read the letter very critically. It was the first with any detail that she had written. From Rawal Pindi they had journeyed on to exquisite Murree set in the midst of the pines where only to breathe was the keenest pleasure. Stella spoke almost wistfully of this place; she would have loved to linger there.

"I could be happy there in perfect solitude," she wrote, "with just Peter the Great to take care of me." She mentioned the Sikh bearer more than once and each time with growing affection. "He is like an immense and kindly watch-dog," she said in one place. "Every material comfort that I could possibly wish for he manages somehow to procure, and he is always on guard, always there when wanted, yet never in the way."

Their time being limited and Ralph anxious to use it to the utmost, they had left Murree after a very brief stay and pressed on into Kashmir, travelling in a *tonga* through the most glorious scenery that Stella had ever beheld.

"I only wished you could have been there to enjoy it with me," she wrote, and passed on to a glowing description of the Hills amidst which they had travelled, all grandly beautiful and many capped with the eternal snows. She told of the River Jhelum, swift and splendid, that flowed beside the way, of the flowers that bloomed in dazzling profusion on every side—wild roses such as she had never dreamed of, purple acacias, jessamine yellow and white, maiden-hair ferns that hung in sprays of living green over the rushing waterfalls, and the vivid, scarlet pomegranate blossom that grew like a spreading fire.

And the air that blew through the mountains was as the very breath of life. Physically, she declared, she had never felt so well; but she did not speak of happiness, and again Tommy's brow contracted as he read.

For all its enthusiasm, there was to him something wanting in that letter—a lack that hurt him subtly. Why did she say so little of her companion in the wilderness? No casual reader would have dreamed that the narrative had been written by a bride upon her honeymoon.

He read on, read of their journey up the river to Srinagar, punted by native boatmen, and again, as she spoke of their sad, droning chant, she compared it all to a dream. "I wonder if I am really asleep, Tommy," she wrote, "if I shall wake up in the middle of a dark night and find that I have never left England after all. That is what I feel like sometimes—almost as if life had been suspended for awhile. This strange existence cannot be real. I am sure that at the heart of me I must be asleep."

At Srinagar, a native *fête* had been in progress, and the howling of men and din of *tom-toms* had somewhat marred the harmony of their arrival. But it was all interesting, like an absorbing fairy-tale, she said, but quite unreal. She felt sure it couldn't be true. Ralph had been disgusted with the hubbub and confusion. He compared the place to an asylum of filthy lunatics, and they had left it without delay. And so at last they had come to their present abiding-place in the heart of the wilderness with coolies, pack-horses, and tents, and were camped beside a rushing stream that filled the air with its crystal music day and night. "And this is Heaven," wrote Stella; "but it is the Heaven of the Orient, and I am not sure that I have any part or lot in it. I believe I shall feel myself an interloper for all time. I dread to turn each corner lest I should meet the Angel with the Flaming Sword and be driven forth into the desert. If only you were here, Tommy, it would be more real to me. But Ralph is just a part of the dream. He is almost like an Eastern potentate himself with his endless cigarettes and his wonderful capacity for doing nothing all day long without being bored. Of course, I am not bored, but then no one ever feels bored in a dream. The lazy well-being of it all has the effect of a narcotic so far as I am concerned. I cannot imagine ever feeling active in this lulling atmosphere. Perhaps there is too much champagne in the air and I am never wholly sober. Perhaps it is only in the desert that any one ever lives to the utmost. The endless singing of the stream is hushing me into a sweet drowsiness even as I write. By the way, I wonder if I have written sense. If not, forgive me! But I am much too lazy to read it through. I think I must have eaten of the lotus. Good-bye, Tommy dear! Write when you can and tell me that all is well with you, as I think it must be—though I cannot tell—with your always loving, though for the moment strangely bewitched, sister, Stella."

Tommy put down the letter and lay still, peering forth under frowning brows. He could hear Monck's footsteps coming through the gate of the compound, but he was not paying any attention to Monck for once. His troubled mind scarcely even registered the coming of his friend.

Only when the latter mounted the steps on to the verandah and began to move along it, did he turn his head and realize his presence. Monck came to a stand beside him.

"Well, Tommy," he said, "isn't it time to turn in?"

Tommy sat up. "Oh, I suppose so. Infernally hot, isn't it? I've been reading Stella's letter."

Monck lodged his shoulder against the window-frame. "I hope she is all right," he said formally.

His voice sounded pre-occupied. It did not convey to Tommy the idea that he was greatly interested in his reply.

He answered with something of an effort. "I believe she is. She doesn't really say. I wish they had been content to stay at Bhulwana. I could have got leave to go over and see her there."

"Where exactly are they now?" asked Monck.

Tommy explained to the best of his ability. "Srinagar seems their nearest point of civilization. They are camping in the wilderness, but they will have to move before long. Dacre's leave will be up, and they must allow time to get back. Stella talks as if they are fixed there for ever and ever."

"She is enjoying it then?" Monck's voice still sounded as if he were thinking of something else.

Tommy made grudging reply. "I suppose she is, after a fashion. I'm pretty sure of one thing." He spoke with abrupt force. "She'd enjoy it a deal more if I were with her instead of Dacre."

Monck laughed, a curt, dry laugh. "Jealous, eh?"

"No, I'm not such a fool." The boy spoke recklessly. "But I know—I can't help knowing—that she doesn't care twopence about the man. What woman with any brains could?"

"There's no accounting for women's tastes or actions at any time," said Monck. "She liked him well enough to marry him."

Tommy made an indignant sound. "She was in a mood to marry any one. She'd probably have married you if you'd asked her."

Monck made an abrupt movement as if he had lost his balance, but he returned to his former position immediately. "Think so?" he said in a voice that sounded very ironical. "Then possibly she has had a lucky escape. I might have been moved to ask her if she had remained free much longer."

"I wish to Heaven you had!" said Tommy bluntly.

And again Monck uttered his short, sardonic laugh. "Thank you, Tommy," he said.

There fell a silence between them, and a hot draught eddied up through the parched compound and rattled the scorched twigs of the creeping rose on the verandah with a desolate sound, as if skeleton hands were feeling along the trellis-work. Tommy suppressed a shudder and got to his feet.

In the same moment Monck spoke again, deliberately, emotionlessly, with a hint of grimness. "By the way, Tommy, I've a piece of news for you. That letter I had from my brother this, evening contained news of an urgent business matter which only I can deal with. It has come at a rather unfortunate moment as Barnes, the policeman, brought some disturbing information this evening from Khanmulla and the Chief wanted to make use of me in that quarter. They are sending a Mission to make investigations and they wanted me to go in charge of it."

"Oh, man!" Tommy's eyes suddenly shone with enthusiasm. "What a chance!"

"A chance I'm not taking to take," rejoined Monck dryly. "I applied for leave instead. In any case it is due to me, but Dacre had his turn first. The Chief didn't want to grant it, but he gave way in the end. You boys will have to work a little harder than usual, that's all."

Tommy was staring at him in amazement. "But, I say, Monck!" he protested. "That Mission business! It's the very thing you'd most enjoy. Surely you can't be going to let such an opportunity slip!"

"My own business is more pressing," Monck returned briefly.

Then Tommy remembered the stricken look that he had surprised on his friend's face that evening, and swift concern swallowed his astonishment. "You had bad news from Home! I say, I'm awfully sorry. Is your brother ill, or what?"

"No. It's not that. I can't discuss it with you, Tommy. But I've got to go. The Chief has granted me eight weeks and I am off at dawn." Monck made as if he would turn inwards with the words.

"You're going Home?" ejaculated Tommy. "By Jove, old fellow, it'll be quick work." Then, his sympathy coming uppermost again, "I say, I'm confoundedly sorry. You'll take care of yourself?"

"Oh, every care." Monck paused to lay an unexpected hand upon the lad's shoulder. "And you must take care of yourself, Tommy," he said. "Don't get up to any tomfoolery while I am away! And if you get thirsty, stick to lime-juice!"

"I'll be as good as gold," Tommy promised, touched alike by action and admonition. "But it will be pretty beastly without you. I hate a lonely life, and Stella will be stuck at Bhulwana for the rest of the hot weather when they get back."

"Well, I shan't stay away for ever," Monck patted his shoulder and turned away. "I'm not going for a pleasure trip, and the sooner it's over, the better I shall be pleased."

He passed into the room with the words, that room in which Stella had sat on her wedding-eve, gazing forth into the night. And there came to Tommy, all-unbidden, a curious, wandering memory of his friend's face on that same night, with eyes alight and ardent, looking upwards as though they saw a vision. Perplexed and vaguely troubled, he thrust her letter away into his pocket and went to his own room.

CHAPTER VI

THE GARDEN

The Heaven of the Orient! It was a week since Stella had penned those words, and still the charm held her, the wonder grew. Never in her life had she dreamed of a land so perfect, so subtly alluring, so overwhelmingly full of enchantment. Day after day slipped by in what seemed an endless succession. Night followed magic night, and the spell wound closer and ever closer about her. She sometimes felt as if her very individuality were being absorbed into the marvellous beauty about her, as if she had been crystallized by it and must soon cease to be in any sense a being apart from it.

The siren-music of the torrent that dashed below their camping-ground filled her brain day and night. It seemed to make active thought impossible, to dull all her senses save the one luxurious sense of enjoyment. That was always present, slumbrous, almost cloying in its unfailing sweetness, the fruit of the lotus which assuredly she was eating day by day. All her nerves seemed dormant, all her energies lulled. Sometimes she wondered if the sound of running water had this stultifying effect upon her, for wherever they went it followed them. The snow-fed streams ran everywhere, and since leaving Srinagar she could not remember a single occasion on which they had been out of earshot of their perpetual music. It haunted her like a ceaseless refrain, but yet she never wearied of it. There was no thought of weariness in this mazed, dream-world of hers.

At the beginning of her married life, so far behind her now that she scarcely remembered it, she had gone through pangs of suffering and fierce regret. Her whole nature had revolted, and it had taken all her strength to quell it. But that was long, long past. She had ceased to feel anything now, but a dumb and even placid acquiescence in this lethargic existence, and Ralph Dacre was amply satisfied therewith. He had always been abundantly confident of his power to secure her happiness, and he was blissfully unconscious of the wild impulse to rebellion which she had barely stifled. He had no desire to sound the deeps of her. He was quite content with life as he found it, content to share with her the dreamy pleasures that lay in this fruitful wilderness, and to look not beyond.

He troubled himself but little about the future, though when he thought of it that was with pleasure too. He liked, now and then, to look forward to the days that were coming when Stella would shine as a queen—his queen—among an envious crowd. Her position assured as his wife, even Lady Harriet herself would have to lower her flag. And how little Netta Ermsted would grit her teeth! He laughed to himself whenever he thought of that. Netta had become too uppish of late. It would be amusing to see how she took her lesson.

And as for his brother-officers, even the taciturn Monck had already shown that he was not proof against Stella's charms. He wondered what Stella thought of the man, well knowing that few women liked him, and one evening, as they sat together in the scented darkness with the roar of their mountain-stream filling the silences, he turned their fitful conversation in Monck's direction to satisfy his lazy curiosity in this respect.

"I suppose I ought to write to the fellow," he said, "but if you've written to Tommy it's almost the same thing. Besides, I don't suppose he would be in the smallest degree interested. He would only be bored."

There was a pause before Stella answered; but she was often slow of speech in those days. "I thought you were friends," she said.

"What? Oh, so we are." Ralph Dacre laughed, his easy, complacent laugh. "But he's a dark horse, you know. I never know quite how to take him. Your brother Tommy is a deal more intimate with him than I am, though I have stabled with him for over four years. He's a very clever fellow, there's no doubt of that—altogether too brainy for my taste. Clever fellows always bore me. Now I wonder how he strikes you."

Again there was that slight pause before Stella spoke, but there was nothing very vital about it. She seemed to be slow in bringing her mind to bear upon the subject. "I agree with you," she said then. "He is clever. And he is kind too. He has been very good to Tommy."

"Tommy would lie down and let him walk over him," remarked Dacre. "Perhaps that is what he likes. But he's a cold-blooded sort of cuss. I don't believe he has a spark of real affection for anybody. He is too ambitious."

"Is he ambitious?" Stella's voice sounded rather weary, wholly void of interest.

Dacre inhaled a deep breath of cigar-smoke and puffed it slowly forth. His curiosity was warming. "Oh yes, ambitious as they're made. Those strong, silent chaps always are. And there's no doubt he will make his mark some day. He is a positive marvel at languages. And he dabbles in Secret Service matters too, disguises himself and goes among the natives in the bazaars as one of themselves. A fellow like that, you know, is simply priceless to the Government. And he is as tough as leather. The climate never touches him. He could sit on a grille and be happy. No doubt he will be a very big pot some day." He tipped the ash from his cigar. "You and I will be comfortably growing old in a villa at Cheltenham by that time," he ended.

A little shiver went through Stella. She said nothing and silence fell between them again. The moon was rising behind a rugged line of snow-hills across the valley, touching them here and there with a silvery radiance, casting mysterious shadows all about them, sending a magic twilight over the whole world so that they saw it dimly, as through a luminous veil. The scent of Dacre's cigar hung in the air, fragrant, aromatic, Eastern. He was sleepily watching his wife's pure profile as she gazed into her world of dreams. It was evident that she took small interest in Monck and his probable career. It was not surprising. Monck was not the sort of man to attract women; he cared so little about them—this silent watcher whose eyes were ever searching below the surface of Eastern life, who studied and read and knew so much more than any one else and yet who guarded knowledge and methods so closely that only those in contact with his daily life suspected what he hid.

"He will surprise us all some day," Dacre placidly reflected. "Those quiet, ambitious chaps always soar high. But I wouldn't change places. with him even if he wins to the top of the tree. People who make a specialty of hard work never get any fun out of anything. By the time the fun comes along, they are too old to enjoy it."

And so he lay at ease in his chair, feasting his eyes upon his young wife's grave face, savouring life with the zest of the epicurean, placidly at peace with all the world on that night of dreams.

It was growing late, and the moon had topped the distant peaks sending a flood of light across the sleeping valley before he finally threw away the stump of his cigar and stretched forth a lazy arm to draw her to him.

"Why so silent, Star of my heart? Where are those wandering thoughts of yours?"

She submitted as usual to his touch, passively, without enthusiasm. "My thoughts are not worth expressing, Ralph," she said.

"Let us hear them all the same!" he said, laying his head against her shoulder.

She sat very still in his hold. "I was only watching the moonlight," she said. "Somehow it made me think—of a flaming sword."

"Turning all ways?" he suggested, indolently humorous. "Not driving us forth out of the garden of Eden, I hope? That would be a little hard on two such inoffensive mortals as we are, eh, sweetheart?"

"I don't know," she said seriously. "I doubt if the plea of inoffensiveness would open the gates of Heaven to any one."

He laughed. "I can't talk ethics at this time of night, Star of my heart. It's time we went to our lair. I believe you would sit here till sunrise if I would let you, you most ethereal of women. Do you ever think of your body at all, I wonder?"

He kissed her neck with the careless words, and a quick shiver went through her. She made a slight, scarcely perceptible movement to free herself.

But the next moment sharply, almost convulsively, she grasped his arm. "Ralph! What is that?"

She was gazing towards the shadow cast by a patch of flowering azalea in the moonlight about ten yards from where they sat. Dacre raised himself with leisurely self-assurance and peered in the same direction. It was not his nature to be easily disturbed.

But Stella's hand still clung to his arm, and there was agitation in her hold. "What is it?" she whispered. "What can it be? I have seen it move—twice. Ah, look! Is it—is it—a panther?"

"Good gracious, child, no!" Carelessly he made response, and with the words disengaged himself from her hand and stood up. "It's more probably some filthy old beggar who fondly thinks he is going to get *backsheesh* for disturbing us. You stay here while I go and investigate!"

But some nervous impulse goaded Stella. She also started up, holding him back. "Oh, don't go, Ralph! Don't go! Call one of the men! Call Peter!"

He laughed at her agitation. "My dear girl, don't be absurd! I don't want Peter to help me kick a beastly native. In fact he probably wouldn't lower himself to do such a thing."

But still she clung to him. "Ralph, don't go! Please don't go! I have a feeling—I am afraid—I—" She broke off panting, her fingers tightly clutching his sleeve. "Don't go!" she reiterated.

He put his arm round her. "My dear, what do you think a tatterdemalion gipsy is going to do to me? He may be a snake-charmer, and if so the sooner he is got rid of the better. There! What did I tell you? He is coming out of his corner. Now, don't be frightened! It doesn't do to show funk to these people."

He held her closely to him and waited. Beside the flowering azalea something was undoubtedly moving, and as they stood and watched, a strange figure slowly detached itself from the shadows and crept towards them. It was clad in native garments and shuffled along in a bent attitude as if deformed. Stella stiffened as she stood. There was something unspeakably repellent to her in its toadlike advance.

"Make one of the men send him away!" she whispered urgently. "Please do! It may be a snake-charmer as you say. He moves like a reptile himself. And I—abhor snakes."

But Dacre stood his ground. He felt none of her shrinking horror of the bowed, misshapen creature approaching them. In fact he was only curious to see how far a Kashmiri beggar's audacity would carry him.

Within half a dozen paces of them, in the full moonlight, the shambling figure halted and salaamed with clawlike hands extended. His deformity bent him almost double, but he was so muffled in rags that it was difficult to discern any tangible human shape at all. A tangled black beard hung wisplike from the dirty *chuddah* that draped his head, and above it two eyes, fevered and furtive, peered strangely forth.

The salaam completed, the intruder straightened himself as far as his infirmity would permit, and in a moment spoke in the weak accents of an old, old man. "Will his most gracious excellency be pleased to permit one who is as the dust beneath his feet to speak in his presence words which only he may hear?"

It was the whine of the Hindu beggar, halting, supplicatory, almost revoltingly servile. Stella shuddered with disgust. The whole episode was so utterly out of place in that moonlit paradise. But Dacre's curiosity was evidently aroused. To her urgent whisper to send the man away he paid no heed. Some spirit of perversity—or was it the hand of Fate upon him?—made him bestow his supercilious attention upon the cringing visitor.

"Speak away, you son of a centipede!" he made kindly rejoinder. "I am all ears—the *mem-sahib* also."

The man waved a skinny, protesting arm. "Only his most gracious excellency!" he insisted, seeming to utter the words through parched lips. "Will not his excellency deign to give his unworthy servant one precious moment that he may speak in the august one's ear alone?"

"This is highly mysterious," commented Dacre. "I think I shall have to find out what he wants, eh, Stella? His information may be valuable."

"Oh, do send him away!" Stella entreated. "I am not used to these natives. They frighten me."

"My dear child, what nonsense!" laughed Dacre. "What harm do you imagine a doddering old fool like this could do to any one? If I were Monck, I should invite him to join the party. Not being Monck, I propose to hear what he has to say and then kick him out. You run along to bed, dear! I'll soon settle him and follow you. Don't be uneasy! There is really no need."

He kissed her lightly with the words, flattered by her evident anxiety on his behalf though fully determined to ignore it.

Stella turned beside him in silence, aware that he could be immovably obstinate when once his mind was made up. But the feeling of dread remained upon her. In some fantastic fashion the beauty of the night had become marred, as though evil spirits were abroad. For the first time she wanted to keep her husband at her side.

But it was useless to protest. She was moreover half-ashamed herself at her uneasiness, and his treatment of it stung her into the determination to dismiss it. She parted with him before their tent with no further sign of reluctance.

He on his part kissed her in his usual voluptuous fashion. "Good-night, darling!" he said lightly. "Don't lie awake for me! When I have got rid of this old Arabian Nights sinner, I may have another smoke. But don't get impatient! I shan't be late."

She withdrew herself from him almost with coldness. Had she ever been impatient for his coming? She entered the tent proudly, her head high. But the moment she was alone, reaction came. She stood with her hands gripped together, fighting the old intolerable misgiving that even the lulling magic all around her had never succeeded in stilling. What was she doing in this garden of delights with a man she did not love? Had she not entered as it were by stealth? How long would it be before her presence was discovered and she thrust forth into the outermost darkness in shame and bitterness of soul?

Another thought was struggling at the back of her mind, but she held it firmly there. Never once had she suffered it to take full possession of her. It belonged to that other life which she had found too hard to endure. Vain regrets and futile longings—she would have none of them. She had chosen her lot, she would abide by the choice. Yes, and she would do her duty also, whatever it might entail. Ralph should never know, never dimly suspect. And that other—he would never know either. His had been but a passing fancy. He trod the way of ambition, and there was no room in his life for anything besides. If she had shown him her heart, it had been but a momentary glimpse; and he had forgotten already. She was sure he had forgotten. And she had desired that he should forget. He had penetrated her stronghold indeed, but it was only as it were the outer defences that had fallen. He had not reached the inner fort. No man would ever reach that now—certainly, most certainly, not the man to whom she had given herself. And to none other would the chance be offered.

No, she was secure; she was secure. She guarded her heart from all. And she could not suffer deeply—so she told herself—so long as she kept it close. Yet, as the wonder-music of the torrent lulled her to sleep, a face she knew, dark, strong, full of silent purpose, rose before her inner vision and would not be driven forth. What was he doing to-night? Was he wandering about the bazaars in some disguise, learning the secrets of that strange native India that had drawn him into her toils? She tried to picture that hidden life of his, but could not. The keen, steady eyes, set in that calm, emotionless face, held her persistently, defeating imagination. Of one thing only was she certain. He might baffle others, but by no amount of ingenuity could he ever deceive her. She would recognize him in a moment whatever his disguise. She was sure that she would know him. Those grave, unflinching eyes would surely give him away to any who really knew him. So ran her thoughts on that night of magic till at last sleep came, and the vision faded. The last thing she knew was a memory that awoke and mocked her—the sound of a low voice that in spite of herself she had to hear.

"I was waiting," said the voice, "till my turn should come."

With a sharp pang she cast the memory from her—and slept.

CHAPTER VII

THE SERPENT IN THE GARDEN

"Now, you old sinner! Let's hear your valuable piece of information!" Carelessly Ralph Dacre sauntered forth again into the moonlight and confronted the tatterdemalion figure of his visitor.

The contrast between them was almost fantastic so strongly did the arrogance of the one emphasize the deep abasement of the other. Dacre was of large build and inclined to stoutness. He had the ruddy complexion of the English country squire. He moved with the swagger of the conquering race.

The man who cringed before him, palsied, misshapen, a mere wreck of humanity, might have been a being from another sphere—some underworld of bizarre creatures that crawled purblind among shadows.

He salaamed again profoundly in response to Dacre's contemptuous words, nearly rubbing his forehead upon the ground. "His most noble excellency is pleased to be gracious," he murmured. "If he will deign to follow his miserably unworthy servant up the goat-path where none may overhear, he will speak his message and depart."

"Oh, it's a message, is it?" With a species of scornful tolerance Dacre turned towards the path indicated. "Well, lead on! I'm not coming far—no, not for untold wealth. Nor am I going to waste much time over you. I have better things to do."

The old man turned also with a cringing movement. "Only a little way, most noble!" he said in his thin, cracked voice. "Only a little way!"

Hobbling painfully, he began the ascent in front of the strolling Englishman. The path ran steeply up between close-growing shrubs, following the winding of the torrent far below. In places the hillside was precipitous and the roar of the stream rose louder as it dashed among its rocks. The heavy scent of the azalea flowers hung like incense everywhere, mingling aromatically with the smoke from Dacre's newly lighted cigar.

With his hands in his pockets he followed his guide with long, easy strides. The ascent was nothing to him, and the other's halting progress brought a smile of contemptuous pity to his lips. What did the old rascal expect to gain from the interview he wondered?

Up and up the narrow path they went, till at length a small natural platform in the shoulder of the hill was reached, and here the ragged creature in front of Dacre paused and turned.

The moonlight smote full upon him, revealing him in every repulsive detail. His eyes burned in their red-rimmed sockets as he lifted them. But he did not speak even after the careless saunter of the Englishman had ceased at his side. The dash of the stream far below rose up like the muffled roar of a train in a tunnel. The bed of it was very narrow at that point and the current swift.

For a moment or two Dacre stood waiting, the cigar still between his lips, his eyes upon the gleaming caps of the snow-hills far away. But very soon the spell of them fell from him. It was not his nature to remain silent for long.

With his easy, superior laugh he turned and looked his motionless companion up and down. "Well?" he said. "Have you brought me here to admire the view? Very fine no doubt; but I could have done it without your guidance."

There was no immediate reply to his carelessly flung query, and faint curiosity arose within him mingling with his strong contempt. He pulled a hand out of his pocket and displayed a few *annas* in his palm.

"Well?" he said again. "What may this valuable piece of information be worth?"

The other made an abrupt movement; it was almost as if he curbed some savage impulse to violence. He moved back a pace, and there in the moonlight before Dacre's insolent gaze—he changed.

With a deep breath he straightened himself to the height of a tall man. The bent contorted limbs became lithe and strong. The cringing humility slipped from him like a garment. He stood upright and faced Ralph Dacre—a man in the prime of life.

"That," he said, "is a matter of opinion. So far as I am concerned, it has cost a damned uncomfortable journey. But—it will probably cost you more than that."

"Great—Jupiter!" said Dacre.

He stood and stared and stared. The curt speech, the almost fiercely contemptuous bearing, the absolute, unwavering assurance of this man whom but a moment before he had so arrogantly trampled underfoot sent through him such a shock of amazement as nearly deprived him of the power to think. Perhaps for the first time in his life he was utterly and completely at a loss. Only as he gazed at the man before him, there came upon him, sudden as a blow, the memory of a certain hot day more than a year before when he and Everard Monck had wrestled together in the Club gymnasium for the benefit of a little crowd of subalterns who had eagerly betted upon the result. It had been sinew *versus* weight, and after a tough struggle sinew had prevailed. He remembered the unpleasant sensation of defeat even now though he had had the grit to take it like a man and get up laughing. It was one of the very few occasions he could remember upon which he had been worsted.

But now—to-night—he was face to face with something of an infinitely more serious nature. This man with the stern, accusing eyes and wholly merciless attitude—what had he come to say? An odd sensation stirred at Dacre's heart like an unsteady hand knocking for admittance. There was something wrong here—something wrong.

"You—madman!" he said at length, and with the words pulled himself together with a giant effort. "What in the name of wonder are you doing here?" He had bitten his cigar through in his astonishment, and he tossed it away as he spoke with a gesture of returning confidence. He silenced the uneasy foreboding within and met the hard eyes that confronted him without discomfiture. "What's your game?" he said. "You have come to tell me something, I suppose. But why on earth couldn't you write it?"

"The written word is not always effectual," the other man said.

He put up a hand abruptly and stripped the ragged hair from his face, pushing back the heavy folds of the *chuddah* that enveloped his head as he did so. His features gleamed in the moonlight, lean and brown, unmistakably British.

"Monck!" said Dacre, in the tone of one verifying a suspicion.

"Yes—Monck." Grimly the other repeated the name. "I've had considerable trouble in following you here. I shouldn't have taken it if I hadn't had a very urgent reason."

"Well, what the devil is it?" Dacre spoke with the exasperation of a man who knows himself to be at a disadvantage. "If you want to know my opinion, I regard such conduct as damned intrusive at such a time. But if you've any decent excuse let's hear it!"

He had never adopted that tone to Monck before, but he had been rudely jolted out of his usually complacent attitude, and he resented Monck's presence. Moreover, an unpleasant sense of inferiority had begun to make itself felt. There was something judicial about Monck—something inexorable and condemnatory—something that aroused in him every instinct of self-defence.

But Monck met his blustering demand with the utmost calm. It was as if he held him in a grip of iron intention from which no struggles, however desperate, could set him free.

He took an envelope from the folds of his ragged raiment. "I believe you have heard me speak of my brother Bernard," he said, "chaplain of Charthurst Prison."

Dacre nodded. "The fellow who writes to you every month. Well? What of him?"

Monck's steady fingers detached and unfolded a letter. "You had better read for yourself," he said, and held it out.

But curiously Dacre hung back as if unwilling to touch it.

"Can't you tell me what all the fuss is about?" he said irritably.

Monck's hand remained inflexibly extended. He spoke, a jarring note in his voice. "Oh yes, I can tell you. But you had better see for yourself too. It concerns you very nearly. It was written in Charthurst Prison nearly six weeks ago, where a woman who calls herself your wife is undergoing a term of imprisonment for forgery."

"Damnation!" Ralph Dacre actually staggered as if he had received a blow between the eyes. But almost in the next moment he recovered himself, and uttered a quivering laugh. "Man alive! You are not fool enough to believe such a cock-and-bull story as that!" he said. "And you have come all this way in this fancy get-up to tell me! You must be mad!"

Monck was still holding out the letter. "You had better see for yourself," he reiterated. "It is damnably circumstantial."

"I tell you it's an infernal lie!" flung back Dacre furiously. "There is no woman on this earth who has any claim on me—except Stella. Why should I read it? I tell you it's nothing but damned fabrication—a tissue of abominable falsehood!"

"You mean to deny that you have ever been through any form of marriage before?" said Monck slowly.

"Of course I do!" Dacre uttered another angry laugh. "You must be a positive fool to imagine such a thing. It's preposterous, unheard of! Of course I have never been married before. What are you thinking of?"

Monck remained unmoved. "She has been a music-hall actress," he said. "Her name is—or was—Madelina Belleville. Do you tell me that you have never had any dealings whatever with her?"

Dacre laughed again fiercely, scoffingly. "You don't imagine that I would marry a woman of that sort, do you?" he said.

"That is no answer to my question," Monck said firmly.

"Confound you!" Dacre blazed into open wrath. "Who the devil are you to enquire into my private affairs? Do you think I am going to put up with your damned impertinence? What?"

"I think you will have to." Monck spoke quietly, but there was deadly determination in his words. "It's a choice of evils, and if you are wise you will choose the least. Are you going to read the letter?"

Dacre stared at him for a moment or two with eyes of glowering resentment; but in the end he put forth a hand not wholly steady and took the sheet held out to him. Monck stood beside him in utter immobility, gazing out over the valley with a changeless vigilance that had about it something fateful.

Minutes passed. Dacre seemed unable to lift his eyes from the page. But it fluttered in his hold, though the night was still, as if a strong wind were blowing.

Suddenly he moved, as one who violently breaks free from some fettering spell. He uttered a bitter oath and tore the sheet of paper passionately to fragments. He flung them to the ground and trampled them underfoot.

"Ten million curses on her!" he raved. "She has been the bane of my life!"

Monck's eyes came out of the distance and surveyed him, coldly curious. "I thought so," he said, and in his voice was an odd inflection as of one who checks a laugh at an ill-timed jest.

Dacre stamped again like an infuriated bull. "If I had her here—I'd strangle her!" he swore. "That brother of yours is an artist. He has sketched her to the life—the she-devil!" His voice cracked and broke. He was breathing like a man in torture. He swayed as he stood.

And still Monck remained passive, grim and cold and unyielding. "How long is it since you married her?" he questioned at last.

"I tell you I never married her!" Desperately Dacre sought to recover lost ground, but he had slipped too far.

"You told me that lie before," Monck observed in his even judicial tones. "Is it—worth while?"

Dacre glared at him, but his glare was that of the hunted animal trapped and helpless. He was conquered, and he knew it.

Calmly Monck continued. "There is not much doubt that she holds proof of the marriage, and she will probably try to establish it as soon as she is free."

"She will never get anything more out of me," said Dacre. His voice was low and sullen. There was that in the other man's attitude that stilled his fury, rendering it futile, even in a fashion ridiculous.

"I am not thinking of you." Monck's coldness had in it something brutal. "You are not the only person concerned. But the fact remains—this woman is your wife. You may as well tell the truth about it as not—since I know."

Dacre jerked his head like an angry bull, but he submitted. "Oh well, if you must have it, I suppose she was—once," he said. "She caught me when I was a kid of twenty-one. She was a bad 'un even then, and it didn't take me long to find it out. I could have divorced her several times over, only the marriage was a secret and I didn't want my people to know. The last I heard of her was that her name was among the drowned on a wrecked liner going to America. That was six years ago or more; and I was thankful to be rid of her. I regarded her death as one of the biggest slices of luck I'd ever had. And now—curse her!"—he ended savagely—"she has come to life again!"

He glanced at Monck with the words, almost as if seeking sympathy; but Monck's face was masklike in its unresponsiveness. He said nothing whatever.

In a moment Dacre took up the tale. "I've considered myself free ever since we separated, after only six weeks together. Any man would. It was nothing but a passing fancy. Heaven knows why I was fool enough to marry her, except that I had high-flown ideas of honour in those days, and I got drawn in. She never regarded it as binding, so why in thunder should I?" He spoke indignantly, as one who had the right of complaint.

"Your ideas of honour having altered somewhat," observed Monck, with bitter cynicism.

Dacre winced a little. "I don't profess to be anything extraordinary," he said. "But I maintain that marriage gives no woman the right to wreck a man's life. She has no more claim upon me now than the man in the moon. If she tries to assert it, she will soon find her mistake." He was beginning to recover his balance, and there was even a hint of his customary complacence audible in his voice as he made the declaration. "But there is no reason to believe she will," he added. "She knows very well that she has nothing whatever to gain by it. Your brother seems to have gathered but a vague idea of the affair. You had better write and tell him that the Dacre he means is dead. Your brother-officer belongs to another branch of the family. That ought to satisfy everybody and no great harm done, what?"

He uttered the last word with a tentative, disarming smile. He was not quite sure of his man, but it seemed to him that even Monck must see the utter futility of making a disturbance about the affair at this stage. Matters had gone so far that silence was the only course—silence on his part, a judicious lie or two on the part of Monck. He did not see how the latter could refuse to render him so small a service. As he himself had remarked but a few moments before, he, Dacre, was not the only person concerned.

But the absolute and uncompromising silence with which his easy suggestion was received was disquieting. He hastened to break it, divining that the longer it lasted the less was it likely to end in his favour.

"Come, I say!" he urged on a friendly note. "You can't refuse to do this much for a comrade in a tight corner! I'd do the same for you and more. And remember, it isn't my happiness alone that hangs in the balance! We've got to think of—Stella!"

Monck moved at that, moved sharply, almost with violence. Yet, when he spoke, his voice was still deliberate, cuttingly distinct. "Yes," he said. "And her honour is worth about as much to you, apparently, as your own! I am thinking of her—and of her only. And, so far as I can see, there is only one thing to be done."

"Oh, indeed!" Dacre's air of half-humorous persuasion dissolved into insolence. "And I am to do it, am I? Your humble servant to command!"

Monck stretched forth a sinewy arm and slowly closed his fist under the other man's eyes. "You will do it—yes," he said. "I hold you—like that."

Dacre flinched slightly in spite of himself. "What do you mean? You would never be such a—such a cur—as to give me away?"

Monck made a sound that was too full of bitterness to be termed a laugh. "You're such an infernal blackguard," he said, "that I don't care a damn whether you go to the devil or not. The only thing that concerns me is how to protect a woman's honour that you have dared to jeopardize, how to save her from open shame. It won't be an easy matter, but it can be done, and it shall be done. Now listen!" His voice rang suddenly hard, almost metallic. "If this thing is to be kept from her—as it must be—as it shall be—you must drop out—vanish. So far as she is concerned you must die to-night."

"I?" Dacre stared at him in startled incredulity. "Man, are you mad?"

"I am not." Keen as bared steel came the answer. Monck's impassivity was gone. His face was darkly passionate, his whole bearing that of a man relentlessly set upon obtaining the mastery. "But if you imagine her safety can be secured without a sacrifice, you are wrong. Do you think I am going to stand tamely by and see an innocent woman dragged down to your beastly level? What do you suppose her point of view would be? How would she treat the situation if she ever came to know? I believe she would kill herself."

"But she never need know! She never shall know!" There was a note of desperation in Dacre's rejoinder. "You have only got to hush it up, and it will die a natural death. That she-devil will never take the trouble to follow me out here. Why should she? She knows very well that she has no claim whatever upon me. Stella is the only woman who has any claim upon me now."

"You are right." Grimly Monck took him up. "And her claim is the claim of an honourable woman to honourable treatment. And so far as lies in your power and mine, she shall have it. That is why you will do this thing—disappear to-night, go out of her life for good, and let her think you dead. I will undertake then that the truth shall never reach her. She will be safe. But there can be no middle course. She shall not be exposed to the damnable risk of finding herself stranded."

He ceased to speak, and in the moonlight their eyes met as the eyes of men who grip together in a death-struggle.

The silence between them was more terrible than words. It held unutterable things.

Dacre spoke at last, his voice low and hoarse. "I can't do it. There is too much involved. Besides, it wouldn't really help. She would come to know inevitably."

"She will never know." Inexorably came the answer, spoken with pitiless insistence. "As to ways and means, I have provided for them. It won't be difficult in this wilderness to cover your tracks. When the news has gone forth that you are dead, no one will look for you."

A hard shiver went through Dacre. His hands clenched. He was as a man in the presence of his executioner. The paralysing spell was upon him again, constricting as a rope about his neck. But sacrifice was no part of his nature. With despair at his heart, he yet made a desperate bid for freedom.

"The whole business is outrageous!" he said. "It is out of the question. I refuse to do it. Matters have gone too far. To all intents and purposes, Stella is my wife, and I'm damned if any one shall come between us. You may do your worst! I refuse."

Defiance was his only weapon, and he hurled it with all his strength; but the moment he had done so, he realized the hopelessness of the venture. Monck made a single, swift movement, and in a moment the moonlight glinted upon the polished muzzle of a Service revolver. He spoke, briefly, with iron coldness.

"The choice is yours. Only—if you refuse to give her—the sanctuary of widowhood—I will! After all it would be the safest way for all concerned."

Dacre went back a pace. "Going to murder me, what?" he said.

Monck's teeth gleamed in a terrible smile. "You need not—refuse," he said.

"True!" Dacre was looking him full in the eyes with more of curiosity than apprehension. "And—as you have foreseen—I shall not refuse under those circumstances. It would have saved time if you had put it in that light before."

"It would. But I hoped you might have the decency to act without—persuasion." Monck was speaking between his teeth, but the revolver was concealed again in the folds of his garment. "You will leave to-night—at once—without seeing her again. That is understood."

It was the end of the conflict. Dacre attempted no further resistance. He was not the man to waste himself upon a cause that he realized to be hopeless. Moreover, there was about Monck at that moment a force that restrained him, compelled instinctive respect. Though he hated the man for his mastery, he could not despise him. For he knew that what he had done had been done through a rigid sense of honour and that chivalry which goes hand in hand with honour—the chivalry with which no woman would have credited him.

That Monck had nought but the most disinterested regard for any woman, he firmly believed, and probably that conviction gave added strength to his position. That he should fight thus for a mere principle, though incomprehensible in Dacre's opinion, was a circumstance that carried infinitely more weight than more personal championship. Monck was the one man of his acquaintance who had never displayed the smallest desire to compete for any woman's favour, who had never indeed shown himself to be drawn by any feminine attractions, and his sudden assumption of authority was therefore unassailable. In yielding to the greater power, Dacre yielded to a moral force rather than to human compulsion. And though driven sorely against his will, he respected the power that drove. His dumb gesture of acquiescence conveyed as much as he turned away relinquishing the struggle.

He had fought hard, and he had been defeated. It was bitter enough, but after all he had had his turn. The first hot rapture was already passing. Love in the wilderness could not last for ever. It had been fierce enough—too fierce to endure. And characteristically he reflected that Stella's cold beauty would not have held him for long. He preferred something more ardent, more living. Moreover, his nature demanded a certain meed of homage from the object of his desire, and undeniably this had been conspicuously lacking. Stella was evidently one to accept rather than to give, and there had been moments when this had slightly galled him. She seemed to him fundamentally incapable of any deep feeling, and though this had not begun to affect their relations at present, he had realized in a vague fashion that because of it she would not hold him for ever. So, after the first, he knew that he would find consolation. Certainly he would not break his heart for her or for any woman, nor did he flatter himself that she would break hers for him.

Meantime—he prepared to shrug his shoulders over the inevitable. Things might have been much worse. And perhaps on the whole it was safer to obey Monck's command and go. An open scandal would really be a good deal worse for him than for Stella, who had little to lose, and there was no knowing what might happen if he took the risk and remained. Emphatically he had no desire to face a personal reckoning at some future date with the she-devil who had been the bane of his existence. It was an unlikely contingency but undoubtedly it existed, and he hated unpleasantness of all kinds. So, philosophically, he resolved to adjust himself to this burden. There was something of the adventurer in his blood and he had a vast belief in his own ultimate good luck. Fortune might frown for awhile, but he knew that he was Fortune's favourite notwithstanding. And very soon she would smile again.

But for Monck he had only the bitter hate of the conquered. He cast a malevolent look upon him with eyes that were oddly narrowed—a measuring, speculative look that comprehended his strength and registered the infallibility thereof with loathing. "I wonder what happened to the serpent," he said, "when the man and woman were thrust out of the garden."

Monck had readjusted his disguise. He looked back with baffling, inscrutable eyes, his dark face masklike in its impenetrability. But he spoke no word in answer. He had said his say. Like a mantle he gathered his reserve about him again, as a man resuming a solitary journey through the desert which all his life he had travelled alone.

CHAPTER VIII

THE FORBIDDEN PARADISE

Looking back later upon that fateful night, it seemed to Stella that she must indeed have slept the sleep of the lotus-eater, for no misgivings pierced the numb unconsciousness that held her through the still hours. She lay as one in a trance, wholly insensible of the fact that she was alone, aware only of the perpetual rush and fall of the torrent below, which seemed to act like a narcotic upon her brain.

When she awoke at length broad daylight was all about her, and above the roar of the stream there was rising a hubbub of voices like the buzzing of a swarm of bees. She lay for awhile listening to it, lazily wondering why the coolies should bring their breakfast so much nearer to the tent than usually, and then, suddenly and terribly, there came a cry that seemed to transfix her, stabbing her heavy senses to full consciousness.

For a second or two she lay as if petrified, every limb struck powerless, every nerve strained to listen. Who had uttered that dreadful wail? What did it portend? Then, her strength returning, she started up, and knew that she was alone. The camp-bed by her side was empty. It had not been touched. Fear, nameless and chill, swept through her. She felt her very heart turn cold.

Shivering, she seized a wrap, and crept to the tent-entrance. The flap was unfastened, just as it had been left by her husband the night before. With shaking fingers she drew it aside and looked forth.

The hubbub of voices had died down to awed whisperings. A group of coolies huddled in the open space before her like an assembly of monkeys holding an important discussion.

Further away, with distorted limbs and grim, impassive countenance, crouched the black-bearded beggar whose importunity had lured Ralph from her side the previous evening. His red-rimmed, sunken eyes gazed like the eyes of a dead man straight into the sunrise. So motionless were they, so utterly void of expression, that she thought they must be blind. There was something fateful, something terrible in the aloofness of him. It was as if an invisible circle surrounded him within which none might intrude.

And close at hand—so close that she could have touched his turbaned head as she stood—the great Sikh bearer, Peter, sat huddled in a heap on the soft green earth and rocked himself to and fro like a child in trouble. She knew at the first glance that it was he who had uttered that anguished wail.

To him she turned, as to the only being she could trust in that strange scene.

"Peter," she said, "what has happened? What is wrong? Where—where is the captain *sahib*?"

He gave a great start at the sound of her voice above him, and instantly, with a rapid noiseless movement, arose and bent himself before her.

"The *mem-sahib* will pardon her servant," he said, and she saw that his dark face was twisted with emotion. "But there is bad news for her to-day. The captain *sahib* has gone."

"Gone!" Stella echoed the word uncomprehendingly, as one who speaks an unknown language.

Peter's look fell before the wide questioning of hers. He replied almost under his breath: "*Mem-sahib*, it was in the still hour of the night. The captain *sahib* slept on the mountain, and in his sleep he fell—and was taken away by the stream."

"Taken away!" Again, numbly, Stella repeated his words. She felt suddenly very weak and sick.

Peter stretched a hand towards the inscrutable stranger. "This man, *mem-sahib*," he said with reverence, "he is a holy man, and while praying upon the mountain top, he saw the *sahib*, sunk in a deep sleep, fall forward over the rock as if a hand had touched him. He came down and searched for him, *mem-sahib*; but he was gone. The snows are melting, and the water runs swift and deep."

"Ah!" It was a gasp rather than an exclamation. Stella was blindly tottering against the tent-rope, clutching vaguely for support.

The great Sikh caught her ere she fell, his own distress subdued in a flash before the urgency of her need. "Lean on me, *mem-sahib!*" he said, deference and devotion mingling in his voice.

She accepted his help instinctively, scarcely knowing what she did, and very gently, with a woman's tenderness, he led her back into the tent.

"My *mem-sahib* must rest," he said. "And I will find a woman to serve her."

She opened her eyes with a dizzy sense of wonder. Peter had never failed before to procure anything that she wanted, but even in her extremity she had a curiously irrelevant moment of conjecture as to where he would turn in the wilderness for the commodity he so confidently mentioned.

Then, the anguish returning, she checked his motion to depart. "No, no, Peter," she said, commanding her voice with difficulty. "There is no need for that. I am quite all right. But—but—tell me more! How did this happen? Why did he sleep on the mountain?"

"How should the *mem-sahib's* servant know?" questioned Peter, gently and deferentially, as one who reasoned with a child. "It may be that the opium of his cigar was stronger than usual. But how can I tell?"

"Opium! He never smoked opium!" Stella gazed upon him in fresh bewilderment. "Surely—surely not!" she said, as though seeking to convince herself.

"*Mem-sahib*, how should I know?" the Indian murmured soothingly.

She became suddenly aware that further inaction was unendurable. She must see for herself. She must know the whole, dreadful truth. Though trembling from head to foot, she spoke with decision. "Peter, go outside and wait for me! Keep that old beggar too! Don't let him go! As soon as I am dressed, we will go to—the place—and—look for him."

She stumbled over the last words, but she spoke them bravely. Peter straightened himself, recognizing the voice of authority. With a deep salaam, he turned and passed out, drawing the tent-flap decorously into place behind him.

And then with fevered energy, Stella dressed. Her hands moved with lightning speed though her body felt curiously weighted and unnatural. The fantastic thought crossed her brain that it was as though she prepared herself for her own funeral.

No sound reached her from without, save only the monotonous and endless dashing of the torrent among its boulders. She was beginning to feel that the sound in some fashion expressed a curse.

When she was ready at length, she stood for a second or two to gather her strength. She still felt ill and dizzy, as though the world she knew had suddenly fallen away from her and left her struggling in unimaginable space, like a swimmer in deep waters. But she conquered her weakness, and, drawing aside the tent-flap once more, she stepped forth.

The morning sun struck full upon her. It was as if the whole earth rushed to meet her in a riot of rejoicing; but she was in some fashion outside and beyond it all. The glow could not reach her.

With a sharp sense of revulsion, she saw the deformed man squatting close to her, his *chuddah*-draped head lodged upon his knees. He did not stir at her coming though she felt convinced that he was aware of her, aware probably of everything that passed within a considerable radius of his disreputable person. His dark face, lined and dirty, half-covered with ragged black hair that ended in a long thin wisp like a goat's beard on his shrunken chest, was still turned to the east as though challenging the sun that was smiting a swift course through the heavens as if with a flaming sword. The simile rushed through her mind unbidden. Where would she be—what would have happened to her—by the time that sword was sheathed?

She conquered her repulsion and approached the man. As she did so, Peter glided silently up like a faithful watch-dog and took his place at her right hand. It was typical of the position he was to occupy in the days that were coming.

Within a pace or two of the huddled figure, Stella stopped. He had not moved. It was evident that he was so rapt in meditation that her presence at that moment was no more to him than that of an insect crawling across his path. His eyes, red-rimmed, startlingly bright, still challenged the coming day. His whole expression was so grimly aloof, so sternly unsympathetic, that she hesitated to disturb him.

Humbly Peter came to her assistance. "May I be allowed to speak to him, *mem-sahib?*" he asked.

She turned to him thankfully. "Yes, tell him what I want!"

Peter placed himself in front of the stranger. "The noble lady desires your service," he said. "Her gracious excellency is waiting."

A quiver went through the crouching form. He seemed to awake, his mind returning as it were from a far distance. He turned his head, and Stella saw that he was not blind. For his eyes took her in, for the moment appraised her. Then with ungainly, tortoiselike movements, he arose.

"I am her excellency's servant," he said, in hollow, quavering accents. "I live or die at her most gracious command."

It was abjectly spoken, yet she shuddered at the sound of his voice. Her whole being revolted against holding any converse with the man. But she forced herself to persist. Only this monstrous, half-bestial creature could give her any detail of the awful thing that had happened in the night. If Ralph were indeed dead, this man was the last who had seen him in life.

With a strong effort she subdued her repugnance and addressed him. "I want," she said, "to be guided to the place from which you say he fell. I must see for myself."

He bent himself almost to the earth before her. "Let the gracious lady follow her servant!" he said, and forthwith straightened himself and hobbled away.

She followed him in utter silence, Peter walking at her right hand. Up the steep goat-path which Dacre had so arrogantly ascended in the wake of his halting guide they made their slow progress in dumb procession. Stella moved as one rapt in some terrible dream. Again that drugged feeling was upon her, that sense of being bound by a spell, and now she knew that the spell was evil. Once or twice her brain stirred a little when Peter offered his silent help, and she thanked him and accepted it while scarcely realizing what she did. But for the most part she remained in that state of awful quiescence, the inertia of one about whom the toils of a pitiless Fate were closely woven. There was no escape for her. She knew that there could be no escape. She had been caught trespassing in a forbidden paradise, and she was about to be thrust forth without mercy.

High up on a shelf of naked rock their guide stood and waited—a ragged, incongruous figure against the purity of the new day. The early sun had barely topped the highest mountains, but a great gap between two mighty peaks revealed it. As Stella pressed forward, she came suddenly into the splendour of the morning.

It affected her strangely. She felt as Moses must have felt when the Glory of God was revealed to him. The brightness was intolerable. It seemed to pierce her through and through. She was not able to look upon it.

"Excellency," the stranger said, "it was here."

She moved forward and stood beside him. Quiveringly, in a voice she hardly recognized as her own, she spoke. "You were with him. You brought him here."

He made a gesture as of one who repudiates responsibility. "I, excellency, I am the servant of the Holy Ones," he said. "I had a message for him. I knew that the Holy Ones were angry. It was written that the white *sahib* should not tread the sacred ground. I warned him, excellency, and then I left him. And now the Holy Ones have worked their will upon him, and lo, he is gone."

Stella gazed at the man with fascinated eyes. The confidence with which he spoke somehow left no room for question.

"He is mad," she murmured, half to herself and half to Peter. "Of course he is mad."

And then, as if a hand had touched her also, she moved forward to the edge of the precipice and looked down.

The rush of the torrent rose up like the tumult of many voices calling to her, calling to her. The depth beneath her feet widened to an abyss that yawned to engulf her. With a sick sense of horror she realized that ghastly, headlong fall—from warm, throbbing life on the enchanted height to instant and terrible destruction upon the green, slimy boulders over which the water dashed and roared continuously far below. Here he had sat, that arrogant lover of hers, and slipped from somnolent enjoyment into that dreadful gulf. At her feet—proof indisputable of the truth of the story she had been told—lay a charred fragment of the cigar that had doubtless been between his lips when he had sunk into that fatal sleep. The memory of Peter's words flashed through her brain. He had smoked opium. She wondered if Peter really knew. But of what avail now to conjecture? He was gone, and only this mad native vagabond had witnessed his going.

And at that, another thought pierced her keen as a dagger, rending its way through living tissues. The manner of the man's appearing, the horror with which he had inspired her, the mystery of him, all combined to drive it home to her heart. What if a hand had indeed touched him? What if a treacherous blow had hurled him over that terrible edge?

She turned to look again upon the stranger, but he had withdrawn himself. She saw only the Indian servant, standing close beside her, his dark eyes following her every action with wistful vigilance.

Meeting her desperate gaze, he pressed a little nearer, like a faithful dog, protective and devoted. "Come away, my *mem-sahib!*" he entreated very earnestly. "It is the Gate of Death."

That pierced her anew. Her desolation came upon her in an overwhelming wave. She turned with a great cry, and threw her arms wide to the risen sun, tottering blindly towards the emptiness that stretched beneath her feet. And as she went, she heard the roar of the torrent dashing down over its grim boulders to the great river up which they two had glided in their dream of enchantment aeons and aeons before....

She knew nothing of the sinewy arms that held her back from death though she fought them fiercely, desperately. She did not hear the piteous entreaties of poor harassed Peter as he forced her back, back, back, from those awful depths. She only knew a great turmoil that seemed to her unending—a fearful striving against ever-increasing odds—and at the last a swirling, unfathomable darkness descending like a wind-blown blanket upon her—enveloping her, annihilating her....

And British eyes, keen and grey and stern, looked on from afar, watching silently, as the Indian bore his senseless *mem-sahib* away.

PART II

CHAPTER I

THE MINISTERING ANGEL

"And what am I going to do?" demanded Mrs. Ermsted fretfully. She was lounging in the easiest chair in Mrs. Ralston's drawing-room with a cigarette between her fingers. A very decided frown was drawing her delicate brows. "I had no idea you could be so fickle," she said.

"My dear, I shall welcome you here just as heartily as I ever have," Mrs. Ralston assured her, without lifting her eyes from the muslin frock at which she was busily stitching.

Mrs. Ermsted pouted. "That may be. But I shan't come very often when she is here. I don't like widows. They are either so melancholy that they give you the hump or so self-important that you want to slap them. I never did fancy this girl, as you know. Much too haughty and superior."

"You never knew her, dear," said Mrs. Ralston.

Mrs. Ermsted's laugh had a touch of venom. "As I have tried more than once to make you realize," she said, "there are at least two points of view to everybody. You, dear Mrs. Ralston, always wear rose-coloured spectacles, with the unfortunate result that your opinion is so unvaryingly favourable that nobody values it."

Mrs. Ralston's faded face flushed faintly. She worked on in silence.

For a space Netta Ermsted smoked her cigarette with her eyes fixed upon space; then very suddenly she spoke again. "I wonder if Ralph Dacre committed suicide."

Mrs. Ralston started at the abrupt surmise. She looked up for the first time. "Really, my dear! What an extraordinary thing to say!"

Little Mrs. Ermsted jerked up her chin aggressively. "Why extraordinary, I wonder? Nothing could be more extraordinary than his death. Either he jumped over the precipice or she pushed him over when he wasn't looking. I wonder which."

But at that Mrs. Ralston gravely arose and rebuked her. She never suffered any nervous qualms when dealing with this volatile friend of hers. "It is more than foolish," she said with decision; "it is wicked, to talk like that. I will not sit and listen to you. You have a very mischievous brain, Netta. You ought to keep it under better control."

Mrs. Ermsted stretched out her dainty feet in front of her and made a grimace. "When you call me Netta, I always know it is getting serious," she remarked. "I withdraw it all, my dear angel, with the utmost liberality. You shall see how generous I can be to my supplanter. But do like a good soul finish those tiresome tucks before you begin to be really cross with me! Poor little Tessa really needs that frock, and *ayah* is such a shocking worker. I shan't be able to turn to you for anything when the estimable Mrs. Dacre is here. In fact I shall be driven to Mrs. Burton for companionship and counsel, and shall become more catty than ever."

"My dear, please"—Mrs. Ralston spoke very earnestly—"do not imagine for an instant that having that poor girl to care for will make the smallest difference to my friendship for you! I hope to see as much of you and little Tessa as I have ever seen. I feel that Stella would be fond of children. Your little one would be a comfort to any sore heart."

"She can be a positive little devil," observed Tessa's mother dispassionately. "But it's better than being a saint, isn't it? Look at that hateful child, Cedric Burton—detestable little ape! That Burton complacency gets on my nerves, especially in a child. But then look at the Burtons! How could they help having horrible little self-opinionated apes for children?"

"My dear, your tongue—your tongue!" protested Mrs. Ralston.

Mrs. Ermsted shot it out and in again with an impudent smile. "Well, what's the matter with it? It's quite a candid one—like your own. A little more pointed perhaps and something venomous upon occasion. But it has its good qualities also. At least it is never insincere."

"Of that I am sure." Mrs. Ralston spoke with ready kindliness. "But, oh, my dear, if it were only a little more charitable!"

Netta Ermsted smiled at her like a wayward child. "I like saying nasty things about people," she said. "It amuses me. Besides, they're nearly always true. Do tell me what you think of that latest hat erection of Lady Harriet's! I never saw her look more aristocratically hideous in my life than she looked at the Rajah's garden-party yesterday. I felt quite sorry for the Rajah, for he's a nice boy notwithstanding his forty wives, and he likes pretty things." She gave a little laugh, and stretched her white arms up, clasping her hands behind her head. "I have promised to ride with him in the early mornings now and then. Won't darling Dick be jealous when he knows?"

Mrs. Ralston uttered a sigh. There were times when all her attempts to reform this giddy little butterfly seemed unavailing. Nevertheless, being sound of principle and unfailingly conscientious, she made a gallant effort. "Do you think you ought to do that, dear? I always think that we ought to live more circumspectly here at Bhulwana than down at Kurrumpore. And—if I may be allowed to say so—your husband is such a good, kind man, so indulgent, it seems unfair to take advantage of it."

"Oh, is he?" laughed Netta. "How ill you know my doughty Richard! Why, it's half the fun in life to make him mad. He nearly turned me over his knee and spanked me the last time."

"My dear, I wish he had!" said Mrs. Ralston, with downright fervour. "It would do you good."

"Think so?" Netta flicked the ash from her cigarette with a disdainful gesture. "It all depends. I should either worship him or loath him afterwards. I wonder which. Poor old Richard! It's silly of him to stay in love with the same person always, isn't it? I couldn't be so monotonous if I tried."

"In fact if he cared less about you, you would think more of him," remarked Mrs. Ralston, with a quite unusual touch of severity.

Netta Ermsted laughed again, her light, heartless laugh. "How crushingly absolute! But it is the literal truth. I certainly should. He's cheap now, poor old boy. That's why I lead him such a dog's life. A man should never be cheap to his wife. Now look at your husband! Indifference personified! And you have never given him an hour's anxiety in his life."

Mrs. Ralston's pale blue eyes suddenly shone. She looked almost young again. "We understand each other," she said simply.

A mocking smile played about Mrs. Ermsted's lips, but she said nothing for the moment. In her own fashion she was fond of the surgeon's wife, and she would not openly deride her, dear good soul.

"When you've quite finished that," she remarked presently, "there's a tussore frock of my own I want to consult you about. There's one thing about Stella; she won't be wanting many clothes, so I shall be able to retain your undivided attention in that respect. I really don't know what Tessa and I would do without you. The tiresome little thing is always tearing her clothes to picces."

Mrs. Ralston smiled, a soft mother-smile. "You're a lucky, lucky girl," she said, "though you don't realize it, and probably never will. When are you going to bring the little monkey to see me again?"

"She will probably come herself when the mood takes her," carelessly Mrs. Ermsted made reply. "I assure you, you stand very high on her visiting list. But I hardly ever take her anywhere. She is always so naughty with me." She chose another cigarette with the words. "She is sure to be a pretty frequent visitor while Tommy Denvers is here. She worships him."

"He is a nice boy," observed Mrs. Ralston. "I wish he could have got longer leave. It would have comforted Stella to have him."

"I suppose she can go down to him at Kurrumpore if she doesn't mind sacrificing that rose-leaf complexion," rejoined Mrs. Ermsted, shutting her matchbox with a spiteful click. "You stayed down last hot weather."

"Gerald was not well and couldn't leave his post," said Mrs. Ralston. "That was different. I felt he needed me."

"And so you nearly killed yourself to satisfy the need," commented Mrs. Ermsted. "I sometimes think you are rather a fine woman, notwithstanding appearances." She glanced at the watch on her wrist. "By Jove, how late it is! Your latest *protégée* will be here immediately. You must have been aching to tell me to go for the last half-hour. You silly saint! Why didn't you?"

"I have no wish for you to go, dear," responded Mrs. Ralston tranquilly. "All my visitors are an honour to my house."

Mrs. Ermsted sprang to her feet with a swift, elastic movement. "Mary, I love you!" she said. "You are a ministering angel, faithful friend, and priceless counsellor, all combined. I laugh at you for a frump behind your back, but when I am with you, I am spellbound with admiration. You are really superb."

"Thank you, dear," said Mrs. Ralston.

She returned the impulsive kiss bestowed upon her with a funny look in her blue eyes that might almost have been compassionate if it had not been so unmistakably humorous. She did not attempt to make the embrace a lingering one, however, and Netta Ermsted took her impetuous departure with a piqued sense of uncertainty.

"I wonder if she really has got any brains after all," she said aloud, as she sped away in her "rickshaw." "She is a quaint creature anyhow. I rather wonder that I bother myself with her."

At which juncture she met the Rajah, resplendent in green *puggarree* and riding his favourite bay Arab, and forthwith dismissed Mrs. Ralston and all discreet counsels to the limbo of forgotten things. She had dubbed the Rajah her Arabian Knight. His name for her was of too intimate an order to be pronounced in public. She was the Lemon-scented Lily of his dreams.

CHAPTER II

THE RETURN

Stella's first impression of Bhulwana was the extremely European atmosphere that pervaded it. Bungalows and pine-woods seemed to be its main characteristics, and there was about it none of the languorous Eastern charm that had so haunted the forbidden paradise. Bhulwana was a cheerful place, and though perched fairly high among the hills of Markestan it was possible to get very hot there. For this reason perhaps all the energies of its visitors were directed towards the organizing of gaieties, and in the height of the summer it was very gay indeed.

The Rajah's summer palace, white and magnificent, occupied the brow of the hill, and the bungalows that clustered among the pines below it looked as if there had been some competition among them as to which could get the nearest.

The Ralstons' bungalow was considerably lower down the hill. It stood upon more open ground than most, and overlooked the race-course some distance below. It was an ugly little place, and the small compound surrounding it was a veritable wilderness. It had been named "The Grand Stand" owing to its position, but no one less racy than its present occupant could well have been found. Mrs. Ralston's wistful blue eyes seldom rested upon the race-course. They looked beyond to the mist-veiled plains.

The room she had prepared for Stella's reception looked in an easterly direction towards the winding, wooded road that led up to the Rajah's residence. Great care had been expended upon it. Her heart had yearned to the girl ever since she had heard of her sudden bereavement, and her delight at the thought of receiving her was only second to her sorrow upon Stella's account.

Higher up the hill stood the dainty bungalow which Ralph Dacre had taken for his bride. The thought of it tore Mrs. Ralston's tender heart. She had written an urgent epistle to Tommy imploring him not to let his sister go there in her desolation. And, swayed by Tommy's influence, and, it might be, touched by Mrs. Ralston's own earnest solicitude, Stella, not caring greatly whither she went, had agreed to take up her abode for a time at least with the surgeon's wife. There was no necessity to make any sudden decision. The whole of her life lay before her, a dreary waste of desert. It did not seem to matter at that stage where she spent those first forlorn months. She was tired to the soul of her, and only wanted to rest.

She hoped vaguely that Mrs. Ralston would have the tact to respect this wish of hers. Her impression of this the only woman who had shown her any kindness since her arrival in India was not of a very definite order. Mrs. Ralston with her faded prettiness and gentle, retiring ways did not possess a very arresting personality. No one seeing her two or three times could have given any very accurate description of her. Lady Harriet had more than once described her as a negligible quantity. But Lady Harriet systematically neglected everyone who had no pretensions to smartness. She detested all dowdy women.

But Stella still remembered with gratitude the warmth of affectionate admiration and sympathy that had melted her coldness on her wedding-day, and something within her, notwithstanding her utter weariness, longed to feel that warmth again. Though she scarcely realized it, she wanted the clasp of motherly arms, shielding her from the tempest of life.

Tommy, who had met her at Rawal Pindi on the dreadful return journey, had watched over her and cared for her comfort with the utmost tenderness; but Tommy, like Peter, was somehow outside her confidence. He was just a blundering male with the best intentions. She could not have opened her heart to him had she tried. She was unspeakably glad to have him with her, and later on she hoped to join him again at The Green Bungalow down at Kurrumpore where they had dwelt together during the weeks preceding her marriage. For Tommy was the only relative she had in the world who cared for her. And she was very fond of Tommy, but she was not really intimate with him. They were just good comrades.

As a married woman, she no longer feared the veiled shafts of malice that had pierced her before. Her position was assured. Not that she would have cared greatly in any case. Such trivial things belonged to the past, and she marvelled now at the thought that they had ever seriously affected her. She was changed, greatly changed. In one short month she had left her girlhood behind her. Her proud shyness had utterly departed. She had returned a grave, reserved woman, indifferent, almost apathetic, wholly self-contained. Her natural stateliness still clung about her, but she did not cloak herself therewith. She walked rather as one rapt in reverie, looking neither to the right nor to the left.

Mrs. Ralston nearly wept when she saw her, so shocked was she by the havoc that strange month had wrought. All the soft glow of youth had utterly passed away. White and cold as alabaster, a woman empty and alone, she returned from the forbidden paradise, and it seemed to Mrs. Ralston at first that the very heart of her had been shattered like a beautiful flower by the closing of the gates.

But later, when Stella had been with her for a few hours, she realized that life still throbbed deep down below the surface, though, perhaps in self-defence, it was buried deep, very far from the reach of all casual investigation. She could not speak of her tragedy, but she responded to the mute sympathy Mrs. Ralston poured out to her with a gratitude that was wholly unfeigned, and the latter understood clearly that she would not refuse her admittance though she barred out all the world beside.

She was deeply touched by the discovery, reflecting in her humility that Stella's need must indeed have been great to have drawn her to herself for comfort. It was true that nearly all her friends had been made in trouble which she had sought to alleviate, but Mary Ralston was too lowly to ascribe to herself any virtue on that account. She only thanked God for her opportunities.

On the night of their arrival, when Stella had gone to her room, Tommy spoke very seriously of his sister's state and begged Mrs. Ralston to do her utmost to combat the apathy which he had found himself wholly unable to pierce.

"I haven't seen her shed a single tear," he said. "People who didn't know would think her heartless. I can't bear to see that deadly coldness. It isn't Stella."

"We must be patient," Mrs. Ralston said.

There were tears in the boy's own eyes for which she liked him, but she did not encourage him to further confidence. It was not her way to discuss any friend with a third person, however intimate.

Tommy left the subject without realizing that she had turned him from it.

"I don't know in the least how she is left," he said restlessly. "Haven't an idea what sort of state Dacre's affairs were in. I ought to have asked him, but I never had the chance; and everything was done in such a mighty hurry.

I don't suppose he had much to leave if anything. It was a fool marriage," he ended bitterly. "I always hated it. Monck knew that."

"Doesn't Captain Monck know anything?" asked Mrs. Ralston.

"Oh, goodness knows. Monck's away on urgent business, been away for ever so long now. I haven't seen him since Dacre's death. I daresay he doesn't even know of that yet. He had to go Home. I suppose he is on his way back again now; I hope so anyway. It's pretty beastly without him."

"Poor Tommy!" Mrs. Ralston's sympathy was uppermost again. "It's been a tragic business altogether. But let us be thankful we have dear Stella safely back! I am going to say good night to her now. Help yourself to anything you want!"

She went, and Tommy stretched himself out on a long chair with a sigh of discontent over things in general. He had had no word from Monck throughout his absence, and this was almost the greatest grievance of all.

Treading softly the passage that led to Stella's door, Mrs. Ralston nearly stumbled over a crouching, white-clad figure that rose up swiftly and noiselessly on the instant and resolved itself into the salaaming person of Peter the Sikh. He had slept across Stella's threshold ever since her bereavement.

"My *mem-sahib* is still awake," he told her with a touch of wistfulness. "She sleeps only when the night is nearly spent."

"And you sleep at her door?" queried Mrs. Ralston, slightly disconcerted.

The tall form bent again with dignified courtesy. "That is my privilege, *mem-sahib*," said Peter the Great.

He smiled mournfully, and made way for her to pass.

Mrs. Ralston knocked, and heard a low voice speak in answer. "What is it, Peter?"

Softly she opened the door. "It is I, my dear. Are you in bed? May I come and bid you good night?"

"Of course," Stella made instant reply. "How good you are! How kind!"

A shaded night-lamp was burning by her side. Her face upon the pillow was in deep shadow. Her hair spread all around her, wrapping her as it were in mystery.

As Mrs. Ralston drew near, she stretched out a welcoming hand. "I hope my watch-dog didn't startle you," she said. "The dear fellow is so upset that I don't want an *ayah*, he is doing his best to turn himself into one. I couldn't bear to send him away. You don't mind?"

"My dear, I mind nothing." Mrs. Ralston stooped in her warm way and kissed the pale, still face. "Are you comfortable? Have you everything you want?"

"Everything, thank you," Stella answered, drawing her hostess gently down to sit on the side of the bed. "I feel rested already. Somehow your presence is restful."

"Oh, my dear!" Mrs. Ralston flushed with pleasure. Not many were the compliments that came her way. "And you feel as if you will be able to sleep?"

Stella's eyes looked unutterably weary; yet she shook her head. "No. I never sleep much before morning. I think I slept too much when I was in Kashmir. The days and nights all seemed part of one long dream." A slight shudder assailed her; she repressed it with a shadowy smile. "Life here will be very different," she said. "Perhaps I shall be able to wake up now. I am not in the least a dreamy person as a rule."

The quick tears sprang to Mrs. Ralston's eyes; she stroked Stella's hand without speaking.

"I wanted to go back to Kurrumpore with Tommy," Stella went on, "but he won't hear of it, though he tells me that you stayed there through last summer. If you could stand it, so could I. I feel sure that physically I am much stronger."

"Oh no, dear, no. You couldn't do it." Mrs. Ralston looked down upon the beautiful face very tenderly. "I am tough, you know, dried up and wiry. And I had a very strong motive. But you are different. You would never stand a hot season at Kurrumpore. I can't tell you what it is like there. At its worst it is unspeakable. I am very glad that Tommy realizes the impossibility of it. No, no! Stay here with me till I go down! I am always the first. And it will give me so much pleasure to take care of you."

Stella relinquished the discussion with a short sigh. "It doesn't seem to matter much what I do," she said. "Tommy certainly doesn't need me. No one does. And I expect you will soon get very tired of me."

"Never, dear, never." Mrs. Ralston's hand clasped hers reassuringly. "Never think that for a moment! From the very first day I saw you I have wanted to have you to love and care for."

A gleam of surprise crossed Stella's face. "How very kind of you!" she said.

"Oh no, dear. It was your own doing. You are so beautiful," murmured the surgeon's wife. "And I knew that you were the same all through—beautiful to the very soul."

"Oh, don't say that!" Sharply Stella broke in upon her. "Don't think it! You don't know me in the least. You—you have far more beauty of soul than I have, or can ever hope to have now."

Mrs. Ralston shook her head.

"But it is so," Stella insisted. "I—What am I?" A tremor of passion crept unawares into her low voice. "I am a woman who has been denied everything. I have been cast out like Eve, but without Eve's compensations. If I had been given a child to love, I might have had hope. But now I have none—I have none. I am hard and bitter,—old before my time, and I shall never now be anything else."

"Oh, darling, no!" Very swiftly Mrs. Ralston checked her. "Indeed you are wrong. We can make of our lives what we will. Believe me, the barren woman can be a joyful mother of children if she will. There is always someone to love."

Stella's lips were quivering. She turned her face aside. "Life is very difficult," she said.

"It gets simpler as one goes on, dear," Mrs. Ralston assured her gently. "Not easy, oh no, not easy. We were never meant to make an easy-chair of circumstance however favourable. But if we only press on, it does get simpler, and the way opens out before us as we go. I have learnt that at least from life." She paused a moment, then bent suddenly down and spoke into Stella's ear. "May I tell you something about myself—something I have never before breathed to any one—except to God?"

Stella turned instantly. "Yes, tell me!" she murmured back, clasping closely the thin hand that had so tenderly stroked her own.

Mrs. Ralston hesitated a second as one who pauses before making a supreme effort. Then under her breath she spoke again. "Perhaps it will not interest you much. I don't know. It is only this. Like you, I wanted—I hoped for—a child. And—I married without loving—just for that. Stella, my sin was punished. The baby came—and went—and there can never be another. I thought my heart was broken at the time. Oh, it was bitter—bitter. Even now—sometimes—" She stopped herself. "But no, I needn't trouble you with that. I only want to tell you that very beautiful flowers bloom sometimes out of ashes. And it has been so with me. My rose of love was slow in growing, but it blossoms now, and I am training it over all the blank spaces. And it grew out of a barren soil, dear, out of a barren soil."

Stella's arms were close about her as she finished. "Oh, thank you," she whispered tremulously, "thank you for telling me that."

But though she was deeply stirred, no further confidence could she bring herself to utter. She had found a friend—a close, staunch friend who would never fail her; but not even to her could she show the blackness of the gulf into which she had been hurled. Even now there were times when she seemed to be still falling, falling, and always, waking or sleeping, the nightmare horror of it clung cold about her soul.

CHAPTER III

THE BARREN SOIL

No one could look askance at poor Ralph Dacre's young widow. Lady Harriet Mansfield graciously hinted as much when she paid her state call within a week of her arrival. Also, she desired to ascertain Stella's plans for the future, and when she heard that she intended to return to Kurrumpore with Mrs. Ralston she received the news with a species of condescending approval that seemed to indicate that Stella's days of probation were past. With the exercise of great care and circumspection she might even ultimately be admitted to the fortunate circle which sunned itself in the light of Lady Harriet's patronage.

Tommy elevated his nose irreverently when the august presence was withdrawn and hoped that Stella would not have her head turned by the royal favour. He prophesied that Mrs. Burton would be the next to come simpering round, and in this he was not mistaken; but Stella did not receive this visitor, for on the following day she was in bed with an attack of fever that prostrated her during the rest of his leave.

It was not a dangerous illness, and Mrs. Ralston nursed her through it with a devotion that went far towards cementing the friendship already begun between them. Tommy, though regretful, consoled himself by the ready means of the station's gaieties, played tennis with zest, inaugurated a gymkhana, and danced practically every night into the early morning. He was a delightful companion for little Tessa Ermsted who followed him everywhere and was never snubbed, an inquiring mind notwithstanding. Truly a nice boy was Tommy, as everyone agreed, and the regret was general when his leave began to draw to a close.

On the afternoon of his last day he made his appearance on the verandah of The Grand Stand for tea, with his faithful attendant at his heels, to find his sister reclining there for the first time on a *charpoy* well lined with cushions, while Mrs. Ralston presided at the tea-table beside her.

She looked the ghost of her former self, and for a moment though he had visited her in bed only that morning, Tommy was rudely startled.

"Great Jupiter!" he ejaculated. "How ill you look!"

She smiled at his exclamation, while his small, sharp-faced companion pricked up attentive ears. "Do people look like that when they're going to die?" she asked.

"Not in the least, dear," said Mrs. Ralston tranquilly. "Come and speak to Mrs. Dacre and tell us what you have been doing!"

But Tessa would only stand on one leg and stare, till Stella put forth a friendly hand and beckoned her to a corner of her *charpoy*.

She went then, still staring with wide round eyes of intensest blue that gazed out of a somewhat pinched little face of monkey-like intelligence.

"What have you and Tommy been doing?" Stella asked.

"Oh, just hobnobbing," said Tessa. "Same as Mother and the Rajah."

"Have some cake!" said Tommy. "And tell us all about the mongoose!"

"Oh, Scooter! He's such a darling! Shall I bring him to see you?" asked Tessa, lifting those wonderful unchildlike eyes of hers to Stella's. "You'd love him! I know you would. He talks—almost. Captain Monck gave him to me. I never liked him before, but I do now. I wish he'd come back, and so does Tommy. Don't you think he's a nice man?"

"I don't know him very well," said Stella.

"Oh, don't you? That's because he's so quiet. I used to think he was surly. But he isn't really. He's only shy. Is he, Aunt Mary?" The blue eyes whisked round to Mrs. Ralston and were met by a slightly reproving shake of the head. "No, but really," Tessa protested, "he is a nice man. Tommy says so. Mother doesn't like him, but that's nothing to go by. The people she likes are hardly ever nice. Daddy says so."

"Tessa," said Mrs. Ralston gently, "we don't want to hear about that. Tell us some more about Captain Monck's mongoose instead!"

Tessa frowned momentarily. Such nursery discipline was something of an insult to her eight years' dignity, but in a second she sent a dazzling smile to her hostess, accepting the rebuff. "All right, Aunt Mary, I'll bring him to see you to-morrow, shall I?" she said brightly. "Mrs. Dacre will like that too. It'll be something to amuse us when Tommy's gone."

Tommy looked across with a grin. "Yes, keep your spirits up!" he said. "It's dull work with the boys away, isn't it, Aunt Mary? And Scooter is a most sagacious animal—almost as intelligent as Peter the Great who coils himself on Stella's threshold every night as if he thought the bogeyman was coming to spirit her away. He's developing into a habit, isn't he Stella? You'd better be careful."

Stella smiled her faint, tired smile. "I like to have him there," she said. "I am not nervous, of course, but he is a friend."

"You'll never shake him off," predicted Tommy. "He comes of a romantic stock. Hullo! Here is his high mightiness with the mail! Look at the sparkle in Aunt Mary's eyes! Did you ever see the like? She expects to draw a prize evidently."

He stretched a leisurely arm and took the letter from the salver that the Indian extended. It was for Mrs. Ralston, and she received it blushing like an eager girl.

"Why does Aunt Mary look like that?" piped Tessa, ever observant. "It's only from the Major. Mother never looks like that when Daddy writes to her."

"Perhaps Daddy's letters are not so interesting," suggested Tommy.

Tessa chuckled. "Shall I tell you what? She'd ever so much rather have a letter from the Rajah. I know she would. She keeps his locked up, but she never bothers about Daddy's. I can't think what the Rajah finds to write about when they are always meeting. I think it's silly, don't you?"

"Very silly," said Tommy. "I hate writing letters myself. Beastly dull work."

"Perhaps you will excuse me while I read mine," said Mrs. Ralston.

Stella smiled at her. "Oh do! Perhaps there will be some interesting news of Kurrumpore in it."

"News of Monck perhaps," suggested Tommy. "There's a fellow who never writes a letter. I haven't the faintest idea where he is or what he is doing, except that he went to his brother somewhere in England. He is due back in about a fortnight, but I probably shan't hear a word of him until he's there."

"You have not written to him either?" questioned Stella.

"I couldn't. I didn't know where to write." Tommy's eyes met hers with slight hesitation. "I haven't been able to tell him anything of our affairs. It's quite possible though that he will have heard before he gets back to The Green Bungalow. He generally gets hold of things."

"It need not make any difference." Stella spoke slowly, her eyes fixed upon the green race-course that gleamed in the sun below them. "So far as I am concerned, he is quite welcome to remain at The Green Bungalow. I daresay we should not get in each other's way. That is," she looked at her brother, "if you prefer that arrangement."

"I say, that's jolly decent of you!" Tommy's face was flushed with pleasure. "Sure you mean it?"

"Quite sure." Stella spoke rather wearily. "It really doesn't matter to me—except that I don't want to come between you and your friend. Now that I have been married—" a tinge of bitterness sounded in her voice—"I suppose no one will take exception. But of course Captain Monck may see the matter in a different light. If so, pray let him do as he thinks fit!"

"You bet he will!" said Tommy. "He's about the most determined cuss that ever lived."

"He's a very nice man," put in Tessa jealously.

Tommy laughed. "He's one of the best," he agreed heartily. "And he's the sort that always comes out on top sooner or later. Just you remember that, Tessa! He's a winner, and he's straight—straight as a die." "Which is all that matters," said Mrs. Ralston, without lifting her eyes from her letter.

"Hear, hear!" said Tommy. "Why do you look like that, Stella? Mean to say he isn't straight?"

"I didn't say anything." Stella still spoke wearily, albeit she was faintly smiling. "I was only wondering."

"Wondering what?" Tommy's voice had a hint of sharpness; he looked momentarily aggressive.

"Just wondering how much you knew of him, that's all," she made answer.

"I know as much as any one," asserted Tommy quickly. "He's a man to be honoured. I'd stake my life on that. He is incapable of anything mean or underhand."

Stella was silent. The boy's faith was genuine, she knew, but, remembering what Ralph Dacre had told her on their last night together, she could not stifle the wonder as to whether Tommy had ever grasped the actual quality of his friend's character. It seemed to her that Tommy's worship was of too humble a species to afford him a very comprehensive view of the object thereof. She was sure that unlike herself—he would never presume to criticize, would never so much as question any action of Monck's. Her own conception of the man, she was aware, had altered somewhat since that night. She regarded him now with a wholly dispassionate interest. She had attracted him, but she much doubted if the attraction had survived her marriage. For herself, that chapter in her life was closed and could never, she now believed, be reopened. Monck had gone his way, she hers, and they had drifted apart. Only by the accident of circumstance would they meet again, and she was determined that when this meeting took place their relations should be of so impersonal a character that he should find it well-nigh impossible to recall the fact that any hint of romance had ever hovered even for a fleeting moment between them. He had his career before him. He followed the way of ambition, and he should continue to follow it, unhindered by any thought of her. She was dependent upon no man. She would pick up the threads of her own life and weave of it something that should be worth while. With the return of health this resolution was forming within her. Mrs. Ralston's influence was making itself felt. She believed that the way would open out before her as she went. She had made one great mistake. She would never make such another. She would be patient. It might be in time that to her, even as to her friend, a blossoming might come out of the barren soil in which her life was cast.

CHAPTER IV

THE SUMMONS

During those months spent at Bhulwana with the surgeon's wife a measure of peace did gradually return to Stella. She took no part in the gaieties of the station, but her widow's mourning made it easy for her to hold aloof. Undoubtedly she earned Lady Harriet's approval by so doing, but Mrs. Ermsted continued to look at her askance, notwithstanding the fact that her small daughter had developed a warm liking for the sister of her beloved Tommy.

"Wait till she gets back to Kurrumpore," said Mrs. Ermsted. "We shall see her in her true colours then."

She did not say this to Mrs. Ralston. She visited The Grand Stand less and less frequently. She was always full of engagements and seldom had a moment to spare for the society of this steady friend of hers. And Mrs. Ralston never sought her out. It was not her way. She was ready for all, but she intruded upon none.

Mrs. Ralston's affection for Stella had become very deep. There was between them a sympathy that was beyond words. They understood each other.

As the wet season drew on, their companionship became more and more intimate though their spoken confidences were few. Mrs. Ralston never asked for confidences though she probably received more than any other woman in the station.

It was on a day in September of drifting clouds and unbroken rain that Stella spoke at length of a resolution that had been gradually forming in her mind. She found no difficulty in speaking; in fact it seemed the natural thing to do. And she felt even as she gave utterance to the words that Mrs. Ralston already knew their import.

"Mary," she said, "after Christmas I am going back to England."

Mrs. Ralston betrayed no surprise. She was in the midst of an elaborate darn in the heel of a silk sock. She looked across at Stella gravely.

"And when you get there, my dear?" she said.

"I shall find some work to do." Stella spoke with the decision of one who gives utterance to the result of careful thought. "I think I shall go in for hospital training. It is hard work, I know; but I am strong. I think hard work is what I need."

Mrs. Ralston was silent.

Stella went on. "I see now that I made a mistake in ever coming out here. It wasn't as if Tommy really wanted me. He doesn't, you know. His friend Captain Monck is all-sufficing—and probably better for him. In any case—he doesn't need me."

"You may be right, dear," Mrs. Ralston said, "though I doubt if Tommy would view it in the same light. I am glad anyhow that you will spend Christmas out here. I shall not lose you so soon."

Stella smiled a little. "I don't want to hurt Tommy's feelings, and I know they would be hurt if I went sooner. Besides I would like to have one cold weather out here."

"And why not?" said Mrs. Ralston. She added after a moment, "What will you do with Peter?"

Stella hesitated. "That is one reason why I have not come to a decision sooner. I don't like leaving poor Peter. It occurred to me possibly that down at Kurrumpore he might find another master. Anyway, I shall tell him my plans when I get there, and he will have the opportunity"—she smiled rather sadly—"to transfer his devotion to someone else."

"He won't take it," said Mrs. Ralston with conviction. "The fidelity of these men is amazing. It puts us to shame."

"I hate the thought of parting with him," Stella said. "But what can I do?"

She broke off short as the subject of their discussion came softly into the room, salver in hand. He gave her a telegram and stood back decorously behind her chair while she opened it.

Mrs. Ralston's grave eyes watched her, and in a moment Stella looked up and met them. "From Kurrumpore," she said.

Her face was pale, but her hands and voice were steady.

"From Tommy?" questioned Mrs. Ralston.

"No. From Captain Monck. Tommy is ill—very ill. Malaria again. He thinks I had better go to him."

"Oh, my dear!" Mrs. Ralston's exclamation held dismay.

Stella met it by holding out to her the message. "Tommy down with malaria," it said. "Condition serious. Come if you are able. Monck."

Mrs. Ralston rose. She seemed to be more agitated than Stella. "I shall go too," she said.

"No, dear, no!" Stella stopped her. "There is no need for that. I shall be all right. I am perfectly strong now, stronger than you are. And they say malaria never attacks newcomers so badly. No. I will go alone. I won't be answerable to your husband for you. Really, dear, really, I am in earnest."

Her insistence prevailed, albeit Mrs. Ralston yielded very unwillingly. She was not very strong, and she knew well that her husband would be greatly averse to her taking such a step. But the thought of Stella going alone was even harder to face till her look suddenly fell upon Peter the Great standing motionless behind her chair.

"Ah well, you will have Peter," she said with relief.

And Stella, who was bending already over her reply telegram, replied instantly with one of her rare smiles. "Of course I shall have Peter!"

Peter's responding smile was good to see. "I will take care of my *mem-sahib*," he said.

Stella's reply was absolutely simple. "Starting at once," she wrote; and within half an hour her preparations were complete.

She knew Monck well enough to be certain that he would not have telegraphed that urgent message had not the need been great. He had nursed Tommy once before, and she knew that in Tommy's estimation at least he had been the means of saving his life. He was a man of steady nerve and level judgment. He would not have sent for her if his faith in his own powers had not begun to weaken. It meant that Tommy was very ill, that he might be dying. All that was great in Stella rose up impulsively at the call. Tommy had never really wanted her before.

To Mrs. Ralston who at the last stood over her with a glass of wine she was as a different woman. There was nothing headlong about her, but the quiet energy of her made her realize that she had been fashioned for better things than the social gaieties with which so many were content. Stella would go to the deep heart of life.

She yearned to accompany her upon her journey to the plains, but Stella's solemn promise to send for her if she were taken ill herself consoled her in a measure. Very regretfully did she take leave of her, and when the rattle of the wheels that bore Stella and the faithful Peter away had died at last in the distance she turned back into her empty bungalow with tears in her eyes. Stella had become dear to her as a sister.

It was an all-night journey, and only a part of it could be accomplished by train, the line ending at Khanmulla which was reached in the early hours of the morning. But for Peter's ministrations Stella would probably have fared ill, but he was an experienced traveller and surrounded her with every comfort that he could devise. The night was close and dank. They travelled through pitch darkness. Stella lay back and tried to sleep; but sleep would not come to her. She was tired, but repose eluded her. The beating of the unceasing rain upon the tin roof, and the perpetual rattle of the train made an endless tattoo in her brain from which there was no escape. She was haunted by the memory of the last journey that she had made along that line when leaving Kurrumpore in the spring, of Ralph and the ever-growing passion in his eyes, of the first wild revolt within her which she had so barely quelled. How far away seemed those days of an almost unbelievable torture! She could regard them now dispassionately, albeit with wonder. She marvelled now that she had ever given herself to such a man. By the light of experience she realized how tragic had been her blunder, and now that the awful sense of shock and desolation had passed she could be thankful that no heavier penalty had been exacted. The man had been taken swiftly, mercifully, as she believed. He had been spared much, and she—she had been delivered from a fate far worse. For she could never have come to love him. She was certain of that. Lifelong misery would have been her portion, school herself to submission though she might. She believed that the awakening from that dream of lethargy could not have been long deferred for either of them, and with it would have come a bitterness immeasurable. She did not think he had ever honestly believed that she loved him. But at least he had never guessed at the actual repulsion with which at times she had been filled. She was thankful to think that he could never know that now, thankful that now she had come into her womanhood it was all her own. She valued her freedom almost extravagantly since it had been given back to her. And she also valued the fact that in no worldly sense was she the richer for having been Ralph Dacre's wife. He had had no private means, and she was thankful that this was so. She could not have endured to reap any benefit from what she now regarded as a sin. She had borne her punishment, she had garnered her experience. And now she walked once more with unshackled feet; and though all her life she would carry the marks of the chain that had galled her she had travelled far enough to realize and be thankful for her liberty.

The train rattled on through the night. Anxiety came, wraith-like at first, drifting into her busy brain. She had hardly had time to be anxious in the rush of preparation and departure. But restlessness paved the way. She began to ask herself with growing uneasiness what could be awaiting her at the end of the journey. The summons had been so clear and imperative. Her first thought, her instinct, had been to obey. Till the enforced inaction of this train journey she had not had time to feel the gnawing torture of suspense. But now it came and racked her. The thought of Tommy and his need became paramount. Did he know that she was hastening to him, she wondered? Or had he—had he already passed beyond her reach? Men passed so quickly in this tropical wilderness. The solemn music of an anthem she had known and loved in the old far-off days of her girlhood rose and surged through her. She found herself repeating the words:

"Our life is but a shadow; So soon passeth it away, And we are gone,— So soon,—so soon."

The repetition of those last words rang like a knell. But Tommy! She could not think of Tommy's eager young life passing so. Those words were written for the old and weary. But for such as Tommy—a thousand times No! He was surely too ardent, too full of life, to pass so. She felt as if he were years younger than herself.

And then another thought came to her, a curious haunting thought. Was the Nemesis that had overtaken her in the forbidden paradise yet pursuing her with relentless persistence? Was the measure of her punishment not yet complete? Did some further vengeance still follow her in the wilderness of her desolation? She tried to fling the thought from her, but it clung like an evil dream. She could not wholly shake off the impression that it had made upon her.

Slowly the night wore away. The heat was intense. She felt as if she were sitting in a tank of steaming vapour. The oppression of the atmosphere was like a physical weight. And ever the rain beat down, rattling, incessant, upon the tin roof above her head. She thought of Nemesis again, Nemesis wielding an iron flail that never missed its mark. There was something terrible to her in this perpetual beating of rain. She had never imagined anything like it.

It was in the dark of the early morning that she began at last to near her destination. A ten-mile drive through the jungle awaited her, she knew. She wondered if Monck had made provision for this or if all arrangements would be left in Peter's capable hands. She had never felt more thankful for this trusty servant of hers than now with the loneliness and darkness of this unfamiliar world hedging her round. She felt almost as one in a hostile country, and even the thought of Tommy and his need could not dispel the impression.

The train rattled into the little iron-built station of Khanmulla. The rainfall seemed to increase as they stopped. It was like the beating of rods upon the station-roof. There came the usual hubbub of discordant cries, but in foreign voices and in a foreign tongue.

Stella gathered her property together in readiness for Peter. Then she turned, somewhat stiff after her long journey, and found the door already swinging open and a man's broad shoulders blocking the opening.

"How do you do?" said Monck.

She started at the sound of his voice. His face was in the shadow, but in a moment his features, dark and dominant, flashed to her memory. She bent to him swiftly, with outstretched hand.

"How good of you to meet me! How is Tommy?"

He held her hand for an instant, and she was aware of a sharp tingling throughout her being, as though by means of that strong grasp he had imparted strength. "He is about as bad as a man can be," he said. "Ralston has been with him all night. I've borrowed his two-seater to fetch you. Don't waste any time!"

Her heart gave a throb of dismay. The brief words were as flail-like as the rain. They demanded no answer, and she made none; only instant submission, and that she gave.

She had a glimpse of Peter's tall form standing behind Monck, and to him for a moment she turned as she descended.

"You will see to everything?" she said. "You will follow."

"Leave all to me, my *mem-sahib*!" he said, deeply bowing; and she took him at his word.

Monck had a military overcoat on his arm in which he wrapped her before they left the station-shelter. Ralston's little two-seater car shed dazzling beams of light through the dripping dark. She floundered blindly into a pool of water before she reached it, and was doubly startled by Monck lifting her bodily, without apology, out of the mire, and placing her on the seat. The beat of the rain upon the hood made her wonder if they could make any headway under it. And then, while she was still wondering, the engine began to throb like a living thing, and she was aware of Monck squeezing past her to his seat at the wheel.

He did not speak, but he wrapped the rug firmly about her, and almost before she had time to thank him, they were in motion.

That night-ride was one of the wildest experiences that she had ever known. Monck went like the wind. The road wound through the jungle, and in many places was little more than a rough track. The car bumped and jolted, and seemed to cry aloud for mercy. But Monck did not spare, and Stella crouched beside him, too full of wonder to be afraid.

They emerged from the jungle at length and ran along an open road between wide fields of rice or cotton. Their course became easier, and Stella realized that they were nearing the end of their journey. They were approaching the native portion of Kurrumpore.

She turned to the silent man beside her. "Is Tommy expecting me?" she asked.

He did not answer her immediately; then, "He was practically unconscious when I left," he said.

He put on speed with the words. They shot forward through the pelting rain at a terrific pace. She divined that his anxiety was such that he did not wish to talk.

They passed through the native quarter as if on wings. The rain fell in a deluge here. It was like some power of darkness striving to beat them back. She pictured Monck's face, grim, ruthless, forcing his way through the opposing element. The man himself she could barely see.

And then, almost before she realized it, they were in the European cantonment, and she heard the grinding of the brakes as they reached the gate of The Green Bungalow. Monck turned the little car into the compound, and a light shone down upon them from the verandah.

The car came to a standstill. "Do you mind getting out first?" said Monck.

She got out with a dazed sense of unreality. He followed her immediately; his hand, hard and muscular, grasped her arm. He led her up the wooden steps all shining and slippery in the rain.

In the shelter of the verandah he stopped. "Wait here a moment!" he said.

But Stella turned swiftly, detaining him. "No, no!" she said. "I am coming with you. I would rather know at once."

He shrugged his shoulders without remonstrance, and stood back for her to precede him. Later it seemed to her that it was the most merciful thing he could have done. At the time she did not pause to thank him, but went swiftly past, taking her way straight along the verandah to Tommy's room.

The window was open, and a bar of light stretched therefrom like a fiery sword into the streaming rain. Just for a second that gleaming shaft daunted her. Something within her shrank affrighted. Then, aware of Monck immediately behind her, she conquered her dread and entered. She saw that the bar of light came from a hooded lamp which was turned towards the window, leaving the bed in shadow. Over the latter a man was bending. He straightened himself sharply at her approach, and she recognized Major Ralston.

And then she had reached the bed, and all the love in her heart pulsed forth in yearning tenderness as she stooped. "Tommy!" she said. "My darling!"

He did not stir in answer. He lay like a figure carved in marble. Suddenly the rays of the lamp were turned upon him, and she saw that his face was livid. The eyes were closed and sunken. A terrible misgiving stabbed her. Almost involuntarily she drew back.

In the same moment she felt Monck's hands upon her. He was unbuttoning the overcoat in which she was wrapped. She stood motionless, feeling cold, powerless, strangely dependent upon him.

As he stripped the coat back from her shoulders, he spoke, his voice very measured and quiet, but kind also, even soothing.

"Don't give up!" he said. "We'll pull him through between us."

A queer little thrill went through her. Again she felt as if he had imparted strength. She turned back to the bed.

Major Ralston was on the other side. Across that silent form he spoke to her.

"See if you can get him to take this! I am afraid he's past it. But try!"

She saw that he was holding a spoon, and she commanded herself and took it from him. She wondered at the steadiness of her own hand as she put it to the white, unconscious lips. They were rigidly closed, and for a few moments she thought her task was hopeless. Then very slowly they parted. She slipped the spoon between.

The silence in the room was deathly, the heat intense, heavy, pall-like. Outside, the rain fell monotonously, and, mingling with its beating, she heard the croaking of innumerable frogs. Neither Ralston nor Monck stirred a finger. They were watching closely with bated breath.

Tommy's breathing was wholly imperceptible, but in that long, long pause she fancied she saw a slight tremor at his throat. Then the liquid that had been in the spoon began to trickle out at the corner of his mouth.

She stood up, turning instinctively to the man beside her. "Oh, it's no use," she said hopelessly.

He bent swiftly forward. "Let me try! Quick, Ralston! Have it ready! That's it. Now then, Tommy! Now, lad!"

He had taken her place almost before she knew it. She saw him stoop with absolute assurance and slip his arm under the boy's shoulders. Tommy's inert head fell back against him, but she saw his strong right hand come out and take the spoon that Ralston held out. His dark face was bent to his task, and it held no dismay, only unswerving determination.

"Tommy!" he said again, and in his voice was a certain grim tenderness that moved her oddly, sending the tears to her eyes before she could check them. "Tommy, wake up, man! If you think you're going out now, you're damn well mistaken. Wake up, do you hear? Wake up and swallow this stuff! There! You've got it. Now swallow—do you hear?—swallow!"

He held the spoon between Tommy's lips till it was emptied of every drop; then thrust it back at Ralston.

"Here take it! Pour out some more! Now, Tommy lad, it's up to you! Swallow it like a dear fellow! Yes, you can if you try. Give your mind to it! Pull up, boy, pull up! play the damn game! Don't go back on me! Ah, you didn't know I was here, did you? Thought you'd slope while my back was turned. You weren't quick enough, my lad. You've got to come back."

There was a strange note of passion in his voice. It was obvious to Stella that he had utterly forgotten himself in the gigantic task before him. Body and soul were bent to its fulfillment. She could see the perspiration running down his face. She stood and watched, thrilled through and through with the wonder of what she saw.

For at the call of that curt, insistent voice Tommy moved and made response. It was like the return of a departing spirit. He came out of that deathly inertia. He opened his eyes upon Monck's face, staring up at him with an expression half-questioning and half-expectant.

"You haven't swallowed that stuff yet," Monck reminded him. "Get rid of that first! What a child you are, Tommy! Why can't you behave yourself?"

Tommy's throat worked spasmodically, he made a mighty effort and succeeded in swallowing. Then, through lips that twitched as if he were going to cry, weakly he spoke.

"Hullo—hullo—you old bounder!"

"Hullo!" said Monck in stern rejoinder. "A nice game this! Aren't you ashamed of yourself? You ought to be. I'm furious with you. Do you know that?"

"Don't care—a damn," said Tommy, and forced his quivering lips to a smile.

"You will presently, you—puppy!" said Monck witheringly. "You're more bother than you're worth. Come on, Ralston! Give him another dose! Tommy, you hang on, or I'll know the reason why! There, you little ass! What's the matter with you?"

For Tommy's smile had crumpled into an expression of woe in spite of him. He turned his face into Monck's shoulder, piteously striving to hide his weakness.

"Feel—so beastly—bad," he whispered.

"All right, old fellow, all right! I know." Monck's hand was on his head, soothing, caressing, comforting. "Stick to it like a Briton! We'll pull you round. Think I don't understand? What? But you've got to do your bit, you know. You've got to be game. And here's your sister waiting to lend a hand, come all the way to this filthy hole on purpose. You are not going to let her see you go under. Come, Tommy lad!"

The tears overflowed down Stella's cheeks. She dared not show herself. But, fortunately for her, Tommy did not desire it. Monck's words took effect upon him, and he made a trembling effort to pull himself together.

"Don't let her see me—like this!" he murmured. "I'll be better presently. You tell her, old chap, and—I say—look after her, won't you?"

"All right, you cuckoo," said Monck.

CHAPTER V

THE MORNING

Day broke upon a world of streaming rain. Stella sat before a meal spread in the dining-room and wanly watched it. Peter hovered near her; she had a suspicion that the meal was somehow of his contriving. But how he had arrived she had not the least idea and was too weary to ask.

Tommy had fallen into natural sleep, and Ralston had persuaded her to leave him in his care for a while, promising to send for her at once if occasion arose. She had left Monck there also, but she fancied Ralston did not mean to let him stay. Her thoughts dwelt oddly upon Monck. He had surprised her; more, in some fashion he had pierced straight through her armour of indifference. Wholly without intention he had imposed his personality upon her. He had made her recognize him as a force that counted. Though Major Ralston had been engaged upon the same task, she realized that it was his effort alone that had brought Tommy back. And—she saw it clearly—it was sheer love and nought else that had obtained the mastery. This man whom she had always regarded as a being apart, grimly self-contained, too ambitious to be capable of more than a passing fancy, had shown her something in his soul which she knew to be Divine. He was not, it seemed, so aloof as she had imagined him to be. The friendship between himself and Tommy was not the one-sided affair that she and a good many others had always believed it. He cared for Tommy, cared very deeply. Somehow that fact made a vast difference to her, such a difference as seemed to reach to the very centre of her being. She felt as if she had underrated something great.

The rush of the rain on the roof of the verandah seemed to make coherent thought impossible. She gazed at the meal before her and wondered if she could bring herself to partake of it. Peter had put everything ready to her hand, and in justice to him she felt as if she ought to make the attempt. But a leaden weariness was upon her. She felt more inclined to sink back in her chair and sleep.

There came a sound behind her, and she was aware of someone entering. She fancied it was Peter returned to mark her progress, and stretched her hand to the coffee-urn. But ere she touched it she knew that she was mistaken. She turned and saw Monck.

By the grey light of the morning his face startled her. She had never seen it look so haggard. But out of it the dark eyes shone, alert and indomitable, albeit she suspected that they had not slept for many hours.

He made her a brief bow. "May I join you?" he said.

His manner was formal, but she could not stand on her dignity with him at that moment. Impulsively, almost involuntarily it seemed to her later, she rose, offering him both her hands. "Captain Monck," she said, "you are—splendid!"

Words and action were alike wholly spontaneous. They were also wholly unexpected. She saw a strange look flash across his face. Just for a second he hesitated. Then he took her hands and held them fast.

"Ah—Stella!" he said.

With the name his eyes kindled. His weariness vanished as darkness vanishes before the glare of electricity. He drew her suddenly and swiftly to him.

For a few throbbing seconds Stella was so utterly amazed that she made no resistance. He astounded her at every turn, this man. And yet in some strange and vital fashion her moods responded to his. He was not beyond comprehension or even sympathy. But as she found his dark face close to hers and felt his eyes scorch her like a flame, expediency rather than dismay urged her to action. There was something so sublimely natural about him at that moment that she could not feel afraid.

She drew back from him gasping. "Oh please—please!" she said. "Captain Monck, let me go!"

He held her still, though he drew her no closer. "Must I?" he said. And in a lower voice, "Have you forgotten how once in this very room you told me—that I had come to you—too late? And—now!"

The last words seemed to vibrate through and through her. She quivered from head to foot. She could not meet the passion in his eyes, but desperately she strove to cope with it ere it mounted beyond her control.

"Ah no, I haven't forgotten," she said. "But I was a good deal younger then. I didn't know much of life. I have changed—I have changed enormously."

"You have changed—in that respect?" he asked her, and she heard in his voice that note of stubbornness which she had heard on that night that seemed so long ago—the night before her marriage.

She freed one hand from his hold and set it pleadingly against his breast. "That is a difficult question to answer," she said. "But do you think a slave would willingly go back into servitude when once he has felt the joy of freedom?"

"Is that what marriage means to you?" he said.

She bent her head. "Yes."

But still he did not let her go. "Stella," he said, "I haven't changed since that night."

She trembled again, but she spoke no word, nor did she raise her eyes.

He went on slowly, quietly, almost on a note of fatalism. "It is beyond the bounds of possibility that I should change. I loved you then, I love you now. I shall go on loving you as long as I live. I never thought it possible that you could care for me—until you told me so. But I shall not ask you to marry me so long as the thought of marriage means slavery to you. All I ask is that you will not hold yourself back from loving me—that you will not be afraid to be true to your own heart. Is that too much?"

His voice was steady again. She raised her eyes and met his look. The passion had gone out of it, but the dominance remained. She thrilled again to the mastery that had held Tommy back from death.

For a moment she could not speak. Then, as he waited, she gathered her strength to answer. "I mean to be true," she said rather breathlessly. "But I—I value my freedom too much ever to marry again. Please, I want you to understand that. You mustn't think of me in that way. You mustn't encourage hopes that can never be fulfilled."

A faint gleam crossed his face. "That is my affair," he said.

"Oh, but I mean it." Quickly she broke in upon him. "I am in earnest. I am in earnest. It wouldn't be right of me to let you imagine—to let you think—" she faltered suddenly, for something obstructed her utterance. The next moment swiftly she covered her face. "My dear!" he said.

He led her back to the table and made her sit down. He knelt beside her, his arms comfortingly around her.

"I've made you cry," he said. "You're worn out. Forgive me! I'm a brute to worry you like this. You've had a rotten time of it, I know, I know. No, don't be afraid of me! I won't say another word. Just lean on me, that's all. I won't let you down, I swear."

She took him at his word for a space and leaned upon him; for she had no alternative. She was weary to the soul of her; her strength was gone.

But gradually his strength helped her to recover. She looked up at length with a quivering smile. "There! I am going to be sensible. You must be worn out too. I can see you are. Sit down, won't you, and let us forget this?"

He met her look steadily. "No, I can't forget," he said. "But I shan't pester you. I don't believe in pestering any one. I shouldn't have done it now, only—" he broke off faintly smiling—"it's all Tommy's fault, confound him!" he said, and rose, giving her shoulder a pat that was somehow more reassuring to her than any words.

She laughed rather tremulously. "Poor Tommy! Now please sit down and have a rational meal! You are looking positively gaunt. It will be Tommy's and my turn to nurse you next if you are not careful."

He pulled up a chair and seated himself. "What a pleasing suggestion! But I doubt if Tommy's assistance will be very valuable to any one for some little time to come. No milk in that coffee, please. I will have some brandy."

Looking back upon that early breakfast, Stella smiled to herself though not without misgiving. For somehow, in spite of what had preceded it, it was a very light-hearted affair. She had never seen Monck in so genial a mood. She had not believed him capable of it. For though he looked wretchedly ill, his spirits were those of a conqueror.

Doubtless he regarded the turn in Tommy's illness as a distinct and personal victory. But was that his only cause for triumph? She wished she knew.

CHAPTER VI

THE NIGHT-WATCH

When Stella saw Tommy again, he greeted her with a smile of welcome that told her that for him the worst was over. He had returned. But his weakness was great, greater than he himself realized, and she very quickly comprehended the reason for Major Ralston's evident anxiety. Sickness was rife everywhere, and now that the most imminent danger was past he was able to spare but little time for Tommy's needs. He placed him in Stella's care with many repeated injunctions that she did her utmost to fulfil.

For the first two days Monck helped her. His management of Tommy was supremely arbitrary, and Tommy submitted himself with a meekness that sometimes struck Stella as excessive. But it was so evident that the boy loved to have his friend near him, whatever his mood, that she made no comments since Monck was not arbitrary with her. She saw but little of him after their early morning meal together, for when he could spare the time to be with Tommy, she took his advice and went to her room for the rest she so sorely needed.

She hoped that Monck rested too during the hours that she was on duty in the sick-room. She concluded that he did so, though his appearance gave small testimony to the truth of her supposition. Once or twice coming upon him suddenly she was positively startled by the haggardness of his look. But upon this also she made no comment. It seemed advisable to avoid all personal matters in her dealings with him. She was aware that he suffered no interference from Major Ralston whose time was in fact so fully occupied at the hospital and elsewhere that he was little likely to wish to add him to his sick list.

Tommy's recovery, however, was fairly rapid, and on the third night after her arrival she was able to lie down in his room and rest between her ministrations. Ralston professed himself well satisfied with his progress in the morning, and she looked forward to imparting this favourable report to Monck. But Monck did not make an appearance. She watched for him almost unconsciously all through the day, but he did not come. Tommy also watched for him, and finally concluded somewhat discontentedly that he had gone on some mission regarding which he had not deemed it advisable to inform them.

"He is like that," he told Stella, and for the first time he spoke almost disparagingly of his hero. "So beastly discreet. He never thinks any one can keep a secret besides himself."

"Ah well, never mind," Stella said. "We can do without him."

But Tommy had reached the stage when the smallest disappointment was a serious matter. He fretted and grew feverish over his friend's absence.

When Major Ralston saw him that evening he rated him soundly, and even, Stella thought, seemed inclined to blame her also for the set-back in his patient's condition.

"He must be kept quiet," he insisted. "It is absolutely essential, or we shall have the whole trouble over again. I shall have to give him a sedative and leave him to you. I can't possibly look in again to-night, so it will be useless to send for me. You will have to manage as best you can."

He departed, and Stella arranged to divide the night-watches with Peter the Great. She did not privately believe that there was much ground for alarm, but in view of the doctor's very emphatic words she decided to spend the first hours by Tommy's side. Peter would relieve her an hour after midnight, when at his earnest request she promised to go to her room and rest.

The sedative very speedily took effect upon Tommy and he slept calmly while she sat beside him with the light from the lamp turned upon her book. But though her eyes were upon the open page her attention was far from it. Her thoughts had wandered to Monck and dwelt persistently upon him. The memory of that last conversation she had had with Ralph Dacre would not be excluded from her brain. What was the meaning of this mysterious absence? What was he doing? She felt uneasy, even troubled. There was something about this Secret Service employment which made her shrink, though she felt that had their mutual relations been of the totally indifferent and casual order she would not have cared. It seemed to her well-nigh impossible to place any real confidence in a man who deliberately concealed so great a part of his existence. Her instinct was to trust him, but her reason forbade. She was beginning to ask herself if it would not be advisable to leave India just as soon as Tommy could spare her. It seemed madness to remain on if she desired to avoid any increase of intimacy with this man who had already so far overstepped the bounds of convention in his dealing with her.

And yet—in common honesty she had to admit it—she did not want to go. The attraction that held her was as yet too intangible to be definitely analyzed, but she could not deny its existence. She did not love the man—oh, surely she did not love him—for she did not want to marry him. She brought her feelings to that touchstone and it seemed that they were able to withstand the test. But neither did she want to cut herself finally adrift from all chance of contact with him. It would hurt her to go. Probably—almost certainly—she would wish herself back again. But, the question remained unanswered, ought she to stay? For the first time her treasured independence arose and mocked her. She had it in her heart to wish that the decision did not rest with herself.

It was at this point, while she was yet deep in her meditations, that a slight sound at the window made her look up. It was almost an instinctive movement on her part. She could not have said that she actually heard anything besides the falling rain which had died down to a soft patter among the trees in the compound. But something induced her took up, and so doing, she caught a glimpse of a figure on the verandah without that sent all the blood in her body racing to her heart. It was but a momentary glimpse. The next instant it was gone, gone like a shadow, so that she found herself asking breathlessly if it had ever been, or if by any means her imagination had tricked her. For in that fleeting second it seemed to her that the past had opened its gates to reveal to her a figure which of late had drifted into the back alleys of memory—the figure of the dreadful old native who, in some vague fashion, she had come to regard as the cause of her husband's death.

She had never seen him again since that awful morning when oblivion had caught her as it were on the very edge of the world, but for long after he had haunted her dreams so that the very thought of sleep had been abhorrent to her. But now—like the grim ghost of that strange life that she had so resolutely thrust behind her—the whole revolting personality of the man rushed vividly back upon her.

She sat as one petrified. Surely—surely—she had seen him in the flesh! It could not have been a dream. She was certain that she had not slept. And yet—how had that horrible old Kashmiri beggar come all these hundreds of miles from his native haunts? It was not likely. It was barely possible. And yet she had always been convinced that in some way he had known her husband beforehand. Had he come then of set intention to seek her out, perhaps to attempt to extract money from her?

She could not answer the question, and her whole being shrank from the thought of going out into the darkness to investigate. She could not bring herself to it. Actually she dared not.

Minutes passed. She sat still gazing and gazing at the blank darkness of the window. Nothing moved there. The wild beating of her heart died gradually down. Surely it had been a mistake after all! Surely she had fallen into a doze in the midst of her reverie and dreamed this hateful apparition with the gleaming eyes and famished face!

She exerted her self-command and turned at last to look at Tommy. He was sleeping peacefully with his head on his arm. He would sleep all night if undisturbed. She laid aside her book and softly rose.

Her first intention was to go to the door and see if Peter were in the passage. But the very fact of moving seemed to give her courage. The man's rest would be short enough; it seemed unkind to disturb him.

Resolutely she turned to the window, stifling all qualms. She would not be a wretched coward. She would see for herself.

The night was steaming hot, and there was a smell of mildew in the air. A swarm of mosquitoes buzzed in the glare thrown by the lamp with a shrill, attenuated sound like the skirl of far-away bagpipes. A creature with bat-like wings flapped with a monstrous ungainliness between the outer posts of the verandah. From across the compound an owl called on a weird note of defiance. And in the dim waste of distance beyond she heard the piercing cry of a jackal. But close at hand, so far as the rays of the lamp penetrated, she could discern nothing.

Stay! What was that? A bar of light from another lamp lay across the verandah, stretching out into the darkness. It came from the room next to the one in which she stood. Her heart gave a sudden hard throb. It came from Monck's room.

That meant—that meant—what did it mean? That Monck had returned at that unusual hour? Or that there really was a native intruder who had found the window unfastened and entered?

Again the impulse to retreat and call Peter to deal with the situation came upon her, but almost angrily she shook it off. She would see for herself first. If it were only Monck, then her fancy had indeed played her false and no one should know it. If it were any one else, it would be time enough then to return and raise the alarm.

So, reasoning with herself, seeking to reassure herself, crying shame on her fear, she stepped noiselessly forth into the verandah and slipped, silent as that shadow had been, through the intervening space of darkness to the open window of Monck's room.

She reached it, was blinded for a moment by the light that poured through it, then, recovering, peered in.

A man, dressed in pyjamas, stood facing her, so close to her that he seemed to be in the act of stepping forth. She recognized him in a second. It was Monck,—but Monck as she never before had seen him, Monck with eyes alight with fever and lips drawn back like the lips of a snarling animal. In his right hand he gripped a revolver.

He saw her as suddenly as she saw him, and a rapid change crossed his face. He reached out and caught her by the shoulder.

"Come in! Come in!" he said, his words rushing over each other in a confused jumble utterly unlike his usual incisive speech. "You're safe in here. I'll shoot the brute if he dares to come near you again."

She saw that he was not himself. The awful fire in his eyes alone would have told her that. But words and action so bewildered her that she yielded to the compelling grip. In a moment she was in the room, and he was closing and shuttering the window with fevered haste.

She stood and watched him, a cold sensation beginning to creep about her heart. When he turned round to her, she saw that he was smiling, a fierce, triumphant smile.

He threw down the revolver, and as he did so, she found her voice. "Captain Monck, what does that man want? What—what is he doing?"

He stood looking at her with that dreadful smile about his lips and the red fire leaping, leaping in his eyes. "Can't you guess what he wants?" he said. "He wants—you."

"Me?" She gazed back at him astounded. "But why—why? Does he want to get money out of me? Where has he gone?"

Monck laughed, a low, terrible laugh. "Never mind where he has gone! I've frightened him off, and I'll shoot him—I'll shoot him—if he comes back! You're mine now—not his. You were right to come to me, quite right. I was just coming to you. But this is better. No one can come between us now. I know how to protect my wife."

He reached out his hands to her as he ended. His eyes shocked her inexpressibly. They held a glare that was inhuman, almost devilish.

She drew back from him in open horror. "Captain Monck! I am not your wife! What can you be thinking of? You—you are not yourself."

She turned with the words, seeking the door that led into the passage. He made no attempt to check her. Instinct told her, even before she laid her hand upon it, that it was locked.

She turned back, facing him with all her courage. "Captain Monck, I command you to let me go!"

Clear and imperious her voice fell, but it had no more visible effect upon him than the drip of the rain outside. He came towards her swiftly, with the step of a conqueror, ignoring her words as though they had never been uttered.

"I know how to protect my wife," he reiterated. "I will shoot any man who tries to take you from me."

He reached her with the words, and for the first time she flinched, so terrible was his look. She shrank away from him till she stood against the closed door. Through lips that felt stiff and cold she forced her protest.

"Indeed—indeed—you don't know what you are doing. Open the door and—let me—go!"

Her voice sounded futile even to herself. Before she ceased to speak, his arms were holding her, his lips, fiercely passionate, were seeking hers.

She struggled to avoid them, but her strength was as a child's. He quelled her resistance with merciless force. He choked the cry she tried to utter with the fiery insistence of his kisses. He held her crushed against his heart, so overwhelming her with the volcanic fires of his passion that in the end she lay in his hold helpless and gasping, too shattered to oppose him further.

She scarcely knew when the fearful tempest began to abate. All sense of time and almost of place had left her. She was dizzy, quivering, on fire, wholly incapable of coherent thought, when at last it came to her that the storm was arrested.

She heard a voice above her, a strangely broken voice. "My God!" it said. "What—have I done?"

It sounded like the question of a man suddenly awaking from a wild dream. She felt the arms that held her relax their grip. She knew that he was looking at her with eyes that held once more the light of reason. And, oddly, that fact affected her rather with dismay than relief. Burning from head to foot, she turned her own away.

She felt his hand pass over her shamed and quivering face as though to assure himself that she was actually there in the flesh. And then abruptly—so abruptly that she tottered and almost fell—he set her free.

He turned from her. "God help me! I am mad!" he said.

She stood with throbbing pulses, gasping for breath, feeling as one who had passed through raging fires into a desert of smouldering ashes. She seemed to be seared from head to foot. The fiery torment of his kisses had left her tingling in every nerve.

He moved away to the table on which he had flung his revolver, and stood there with his back to her. He was swaying a little on his feet.

Without looking at her, he spoke, his voice shaky, wholly unfamiliar. "You had better go. I—am not safe. This damned fever has got into my brain."

She leaned against the door in silence. Her physical strength was coming back to her, but yet she could not move, and she had no words to speak. He seemed to have reft from her every faculty of thought and feeling save a burning sense of shame. By his violence he had broken down all her defences. She seemed to have lost both the power and the will to resist. She remained speechless while the dreadful seconds crept away.

He turned round upon her at length suddenly, almost with a movement of exasperation. And then something that he saw checked him. He stood silent, as if not knowing how to proceed.

Across the room their eyes met and held for the passage of many throbbing seconds. Then slowly a change came over Monck. He turned back to the table and deliberately picked up the revolver that lay there.

She watched him fascinated. Over his shoulder he spoke. "You will think me mad. Perhaps it is the most charitable conclusion you could come to. But I fully realize that when a thing is beyond an apology, it is an insult to offer one. The key of the door is under the pillow on the bed. Perhaps you will not mind finding it for yourself."

He sat down with the words in a heavy, dogged fashion, holding the revolver dangling between his knees. There was grim despair in his attitude; his look was that of a man utterly spent. It came to Stella at that moment that the command of the situation had devolved upon her, and with it a heavier responsibility than she had ever before been called upon to bear.

She put her own weakness from her with a resolution born of expediency, for the need for strength was great. She crossed the room to the bed, felt for and found the key, returned to the door and inserted it in the lock. Then she paused.

He had not moved. He was not watching her. He sat as one sunk deep in dejection, bowed beneath a burden that crushed him to the earth. But there was even in his abasement a certain terrible patience that sent an icy misgiving to her heart. She did not dare to leave him so.

It needed all the strength she could muster to approach him, but she compelled herself at last. She came to him. She stood before him.

"Captain Monck!" she said.

Her voice sounded small and frightened even in her own ears. She clenched her hands with the effort to be strong.

He scarcely stirred. His eyes remained downcast. He spoke no word.

She bent a little. "Captain Monck, if you have fever, you had better go to bed."

He moved slightly, influenced possibly by the increasing steadiness of her voice. But still he did not look at her or speak.

She saw that his hold upon the revolver had tightened to a grip, and, prompted by an inner warning that she could not pause to question, she bent lower and laid her hand upon his arm. "Please give that to me!" she said.

He started at her touch; he almost recoiled. "Why?" he said.

His voice was harsh and strained, even savage. But the needed strength had come to Stella, and she did not flinch.

"You have no use for it just now," she said. "Please be sensible and let me have it!"

"Sensible!" he said.

His eyes sought hers suddenly, involuntarily, and she had a sense of shock which she was quick to control; for they held in their depths the torment of hell.

"You are wrong," he said, and the deadly intention of his voice made her quiver afresh. "I have a use for it. At least I shall have—presently. There are one or two things to be attended to first."

It was then that a strange and new authority came upon Stella, as if an unknown force had suddenly inspired her. She read his meaning beyond all doubting, and without an instant's hesitation she acted.

"Captain Monck," she said, "you have made a mistake. You have done nothing that is past forgiveness. You must take my word for that, for just now you are ill and not in a fit state to judge for yourself. Now please give me that thing, and let me do what I can to help you!"

Practical and matter-of-fact were her words. She marvelled at herself even as she stooped and laid a steady hand upon the weapon he held. Her action was purposeful, and he relinquished it. The misery in his eyes gave place to a dumb curiosity.

"Now," Stella said, "get to bed, and I will bring you some of Tommy's quinine."

She turned from him, revolver in hand, but paused and in a moment turned back.

"Captain Monck, you heard what I said, didn't you? You will go straight to bed?"

Her voice held a hint of pleading, despite its insistence. He straightened himself in his chair. He was still looking at her with an odd wonder in his eyes—wonder that was mixed with a very unusual touch of reverence.

"I will do—whatever you wish," he said.

"Thank you," said Stella. "Then please let me find you in bed when I come back!"

She turned once more to go, went to the door and opened it. From the threshold she glanced back.

He was on his feet, gazing after her with the eyes of a man in a trance.

She lifted her hand. "Now remember!" she said, and with that passed quietly out, closing the door behind her.

Her brain was in a seething turmoil and her heart was leaping within her like a wild thing suddenly caged. But, very strangely, all fear had departed from her.

Only a brief interval before, she had found herself wishing that the decision of her life's destiny had not rested entirely with herself. It seemed to her that a great revelation had been vouchsafed between the amazing present and those past moments of troubled meditation. And she knew now that it did not.

CHAPTER VII

SERVICE RENDERED

The news that Monck was down with the fever brought both the Colonel and Major Ralston early to the bungalow on the following morning.

They found Stella and the ever-faithful Peter in charge of both patients. Tommy was better though weak. Monck was in a high fever and delirious.

Stella was in the latter's room, for he would not suffer her out of his sight. She alone seemed to have any power to control him, and Ralston noted the fact with astonishment.

"There's some magic about you," he observed in his blunt fashion. "Are you going to take on this job? It's no light one but you'll probably do it better than any one else."

It was a tacit invitation, and Stella knowing how widespread was the sickness that infected the station, accepted it without demur.

"It rather looks as if it were my job, doesn't it?" she said. "I am willing, anyway to do my best."

Ralston looked at her with a gleam of approval, but the Colonel drew her aside to remonstrate.

"It's not fit for you. You'll be ill yourself. If Ralston weren't nearly at his wit's end he'd never dream of allowing it."

But Stella heard the protest with a smile. "Believe me, I am only too glad to be able to do something useful for a change," she assured him. "As to being ill myself, I will promise not to behave so badly as that."

"You're a brick, my dear," said Colonel Mansfield. "I wish there were more like you. Mind you take plenty of quinine!" With which piece of fatherly advice he left her with the determination to keep an eye on her and see that Ralston did not work her too hard.

Stella, however, had no fears on her own account. She went to her task resolute and undismayed, feeling herself actually indispensable for almost the first time in her life. Her influence upon Monck was beyond dispute. She alone possessed the power to calm him in his wildest moments, and he never failed to recognize her or to control himself to a certain extent in her presence.

The attack was a sharp one, and for a while Ralston was more uneasy than he cared to admit. But Monck's constitution was a good one, and after three days of acute illness the fever began to subside. Tommy was by that time making good progress, and Stella, who till then had snatched her rest when and how she could, gave her charge into Peter's keeping and went to bed for the first time since her arrival at Kurrumpore.

Till she actually lay down she did not realize how utterly worn out she was, or how little the odd hours of sleep that she had been able to secure had sufficed her. But as she laid her head upon the pillow, slumber swept upon her on soundless wings. She slept almost before she had time to appreciate the exquisite comfort of complete repose.

That slumber of hers lasted for many hours. She had given Peter express injunctions to awake her in good time in the morning, and she rested secure in the confidence that he would obey her orders. But it was the light of advancing evening that filled the room when at last she opened her eyes.

There had come a break in the rain, and a bar of misty sunshine had penetrated a chink in the green blinds and lay golden across the Indian matting on the floor. She lay and gazed at it with a bewildered sense of uncertainty as to her whereabouts. She felt as if she had returned from a long journey, and for a time her mind dwelt hazily upon the Himalayan paradise from which she had been so summarily cast forth. Vague figures flitted to and fro through her brain till finally one in particular occupied the forefront of her thoughts. She found herself recalling every unpleasant detail of the old Kashmiri beggar who had lured Ralph Dacre from her side on that last fateful night. The old question arose within her and would not be stifled. Had the man murdered and robbed him ere flinging him down to the torrent that had swept his body away? The wonder tormented her as of old, but with renewed intensity. She had awaked with the conviction strong upon her that the man was not far away, that she had seen him recently, and that Everard Monck had seen him also.

That brought her thoughts very swiftly to the present, to Monck's illness and dependence upon her, and in a flash to the realization that she had spent nearly the whole day as well as the night in sleep. In keen dismay she started from her bed and began a rapid toilet.

A quarter of an hour later she heard Peter's low, discreet knock at the door, and bade him enter. He came in with a tea-tray, smiling upon her with such tender solicitude that she had it not in her heart to express any active annoyance with him.

"Oh, Peter, you should have called me hours ago!" was all she found to say.

He set down the tray with a deep salaam. "But the captain *sahib* would not permit me," he said.

"He is better?" Stella asked quickly.

"He is much better, my *mem-sahib*. The doctor *sahib* smiled upon him only this afternoon and told him he was a damn' fraud. So my *mem-sahib* may set her mind at rest."

Obviously the term constituted a high compliment in Peter's estimation and the evident satisfaction that it afforded to Stella seemed to confirm the impression. He retired looking as well pleased as Stella had ever seen him.

She finished dressing as speedily as possible, ate a hasty meal, and hastened to Tommy's room. To her surprise she found it empty, but as she turned on the threshold the sound of her brother's laugh came to her through the passage. Evidently Tommy was visiting his fellow sufferer.

With a touch of anxiety as to Monck's fitness to receive a visitor, she turned in the direction of the laugh. But at Monck's door she paused, constrained by something that checked her almost like a hand laid upon her. The blood ran up to her temples and beat through her brain. She found she could not enter.

As she stood there hesitating, Monck's voice came to her, quiet and rational. She could not hear what he said, but Tommy's more impetuous tones cutting in were clearly audible.

"Oh, rats, my dear fellow! Don't be so damn' modest! You're worth a score of Dacres and you bet she knows it."

Stella tingled from head to foot. In another moment she would have passed swiftly on, but even as the impulse came to her it was frustrated. The door in front of her suddenly opened, and she was face to face with Monck himself.

He stood leaning slightly on the handle of the door. He was draped in a long dressing-gown of Oriental silk that hung upon him dejectedly as if it yearned for a stouter tenant. In it he looked leaner and taller than he had ever seemed to her before. He had a cigarette between his lips, but this he removed with a flicker of humour as he observed her glance.

"Caught in the act," he remarked. "Please come in!"

Something that was very far from humour impelled Stella to say quickly, "I hope you don't imagine I was eavesdropping."

He looked sardonic for an instant. "No, I do not so far flatter myself," he said. "I was referring to my cigarette."

She entered, striving for dignity. Then as his attitude caught her attention she forgot herself and turned upon him in genuine dismay. "What are you doing out of bed? You know you are not fit for it. Oh, how wrong of you! Take my arm!"

He transferred his hand from the door to her shoulder, and she felt it tremble though his hold was strong.

"May I not sit up to tea with you, nurse *sahib*?" he suggested, as she piloted him firmly to the bedside.

"Of course not," she made answer. The consciousness of his weakness had fully restored her confidence and her authority. "Besides, I have had mine. Tommy, you too! It is too bad, I shall never dare to close my eyes again."

At this point Monck laughed so suddenly and boyishly that she found it utterly impossible to continue her reproaches. He humbly apologized as he subsided upon the bed, and turning to Tommy who, fully dressed, was reclining at his ease in a deck-chair by its side said with a smile, "You get back to your own compartment, my son. It isn't good for me to have two people in the room with me at the same time. And your sister wants to take my pulse undisturbed."

"Or listen to your heart?" suggested Tommy irreverently as he rose.

"Turn him out!" said Monck, leaning luxuriously upon the pillows that Stella arranged for him.

Tommy laughed as he sauntered away, pulling the door carelessly after him but recalled by Monck to shut it.

A sudden silence followed his departure. Stella was at the window, looping back the curtains. The vague sunlight still smote across the dripping compound; the whole plain was smoking like a mighty cauldron. Stella finished her task and stood still.

Across the silence came Monck's voice. "Aren't you going to give me my medicine?"

She turned slowly round. "I think you are nearly equal to doctoring yourself now," she said.

He was lying raised on his elbow, his eyes, intent and searching, fixed upon her. Abruptly, in a different tone, he spoke. "In other words, quit fooling and play the game!" he said. "All right, I will—to the best of my ability. First of all, may I tell you something that Ralston said to me this morning?"

"Certainly." Stella's voice sounded constrained and formal. She remained with her back to the window; for some reason she did not want him to see her face too clearly.

"It was only this," said Monck. "He said that I had you to thank for pulling me through this business, that but for you I should probably have gone under. Ralston isn't given to saying that sort of thing. So—if you will allow me—I should like to thank you for the trouble you have taken and for the service rendered."

"Please don't!" Stella said. "After all, it was no more than you did for Tommy, nor so much." She spoke nervously, avoiding his look.

The shadow of a smile crossed Monck's face. "I chance to be rather fond of Tommy," he said, "so my motive was more or less a selfish one. But you had not that incentive, so I should be all the more grateful. I am afraid I have given you a lot of trouble. Have you found me very difficult to manage?"

He put the question suddenly, almost imperiously. Stella was conscious of a momentary surprise. There was something in the tone rather than the words that puzzled her. She hesitated over her reply.

"You have?" said Monck. "That means I have been very unruly. Do you mind telling me what happened on the night I was taken ill?"

She felt a burning blush rush up to her face and neck before she could check it. It was impossible to attempt to hide her distress from him. She forced herself to speak before it overwhelmed her. "I would rather not discuss it or think of it. You were not yourself, and I—and I—"

"And you?" said Monck, his voice suddenly sunk very low.

She commanded herself with a supreme effort. "I wish to forget it," she said with firmness.

He was silent for a moment or two. She began to wonder if it would be possible to make her escape before he could pursue the subject further. And then he spoke, and she knew that she must remain.

"You are very generous," he said, "more generous than I deserve. Will it help matters at all if I tell you that I would give all I have to be able to forget it too, or to believe that the thing I remember was just one of the wild delusions of my brain?"

His voice was deep and sincere. In spite of herself she was moved by it. She came forward to his side. "The past is past," she said, and gave him her hand.

He took it and held it, looking at her in his straight, inscrutable way. "True, most gracious!" he said. "But I haven't quite done with it yet. Will you hear me a moment longer? You have of your goodness pardoned my outrageous behaviour, so I make no further allusion to that, except to tell you that I had been tempted to try a native drug which in its effects was worse than the fever pure and simple. But there is one point which only you can make clear. How was it you came to seek me out that night?"

His grasp upon her hand was reassuring though she felt the quiver of physical weakness in its hold. It was the grasp of a friend, and her embarrassment began to fall away from her.

"I came," she said, "because I had been startled. I had no idea you were anywhere near. I was really investigating the verandah because of—of something I had seen, when the light from this window attracted me. I thought possibly someone had broken in."

"Will you tell me what startled you?" Monck said.

She looked at him. "It was a man—an old native beggar. I only saw him for a moment. I was in Tommy's room, and he came and looked in at me. You—you must have seen him too. You were talking very excitedly about him. You threatened to shoot him."

"Was that how you came to deprive me of my revolver?" questioned Monck.

She coloured again vividly. "No, I thought you were going to shoot yourself. I will give it back to you presently."

"When you consider that I can be safely trusted with it?" he suggested, with his brief smile. "But tell me some more about this mysterious old beggar of yours! What was he like?"

She hesitated momentarily. "I only had a very fleeting glimpse of him. I can't tell you what he was really like. But—he reminded me of someone I never want to think of or suffer myself to think of again if I can help it."

"Who?" said Monck.

His voice was quiet, but it held insistence. She felt as if his eyes pierced her, compelling her reply.

"A horrible old native—a positive nightmare of a man—whom I shall always regard as in some way the cause of my husband's death."

In the pause that followed her words, Monck's hand left hers. He lay still looking at her, but with that steely intentness that told her nothing. She could not have said whether he were vitally interested in the matter or not when he spoke again.

"You think that he was murdered then?"

A sharp shudder went through her. "I am very nearly convinced of it," she said. "But I shall never know for certain now."

"And you imagine that the murderer can have followed you here?" he pursued.

"No! Oh no!" Hastily she made answer. "It is ridiculous of course. He would never be such a fool as to do that. It was only my imagination. I saw the figure at the window and was reminded of him."

"Are you sure the figure at the window was not imagination too?" said Monck. "Forgive my asking! Such things have happened."

"Oh, I know," Stella said. "It is a question I have been asking myself ever since. But, you know—" she smiled faintly—"I had no fever that night. Besides, I fancy you saw him too."

His smile met hers. "I saw many things that night as they were not. And you also were overwrought and very tired. Perhaps you had had an exciting supper!"

She saw that he meant to turn the subject away from her husband's death, and a little thrill of gratitude went through her. He had seen how reluctant she was to speak of it. She followed his lead with relief.

"Perhaps—perhaps," she said. "We will say so anyhow. And now, do you know, I think you had better have your tea and rest. You have done a lot of talking, and you will be getting feverish again if I let you go on. I will send Peter in with it."

He raised one eyebrow with a wry expression. "Must it be Peter?" he said.

She relented. "I will bring it myself if you will promise not to talk."

"Ah!" he said. "And if I promise that—will you promise me one thing too?"

She paused. "What is that?"

His eyes met hers, direct but baffling. "Not. to run away from me," he said.

The quick blood mounted again in her face. She stood silent.

He lifted an urgent hand. "Stella, in heaven's name, don't be afraid of me!"

She laid her hand again in his. She could not do otherwise. She wanted to beg him to say nothing further, to let her go in peace. But no words would come. She stood before him mute.

And—perhaps he knew what was in her mind—Monck was silent also after that single earnest appeal of his. He held her hand for a few seconds, and then very quietly let it go. She knew by his action that he would respect her wish for the time at least and say no more.

CHAPTER VIII

THE TRUCE

Tommy was in a bad temper with everyone—a most unusual state of affairs. The weather was improving every day; the rains were nearly over. He was practically well again, too well to be sent to Bhulwana on sick leave, as Ralston brutally told him; but it was not this fact that had upset his internal equilibrium. He did not want sick leave, and bluntly said so.

"Then what the devil do you want?" said Ralston, equally blunt and ready to resent irritation from one who in his opinion was too highly favoured of the gods to have any reasonable grounds for complaint.

Tommy growled an inarticulate reply. It was not his intention to confide in Ralston whatever his grievance. But Ralston, not to be frustrated, carried the matter to Monck, then on the high road to recovery.

"What in thunder is the matter with the young ass?" he demanded. "He gets more lantern-jawed and obstreperous every day."

"Leave him to me!" said Monck. "Discharge him as cured! I'll manage him."

"But that's just what he isn't," grumbled Ralston. "He ought to be well. So far as I can make out, he is well. But he goes about looking like a sick fly and stinging before you touch him."

"Leave him to me!" Monck said again.

That afternoon as he and Tommy lounged together on the verandah after the lazy fashion of convalescents, he turned to the boy in his abrupt fashion.

"Look here, Tommy!" he said. "What are you making yourself so conspicuously unpleasant for? It's time you pulled up."

Tommy turned crimson. "I?" he stammered. "Who says so? Stella?"

There was the suspicion of a smile about Monck's grim mouth as he made reply. "No; not Stella, though she well might. I've heard you being beastly rude to her more than once. What's the matter with you? Want a kicking, eh?"

Tommy hunched himself in his wicker chair with his chin on his chest. "No, want to kick," he said in a savage undertone.

Monck laughed briefly. He was standing against a pillar of the verandah. He turned and sat down unexpectedly on the arm of Tommy's chair. "Who do you want to kick?" he said.

Tommy glanced at him and was silent.

"Significant!" commented Monck. He put his hand with very unwonted kindness upon the lad's shoulder. "What do you want to kick me for, Tommy?" he asked.

Tommy shrugged the shoulder under his hand. "If you don't know, I can't tell you," he said gruffly.

Monck's fingers closed with quiet persistence. "Yes, you can. Out with it!" he said.

But Tommy remained doggedly silent.

Several seconds passed. Then very suddenly Monck raised his hand and smote him hard on the back.

"Damn!" said Tommy, straightening involuntarily.

"That's better," said Monck. "That'll do you good. Don't curl up again! You're getting disgracefully round-shouldered. Like to have a bout with the gloves?"

There was not a shade of ill-feeling in his voice. Tommy turned round upon him with a smile as involuntary as his exclamation had been.

"What a brute you are, Monck! You have such a beastly trick of putting a fellow in the wrong."

"You are in the wrong," asserted Monck. "I want to get you out of it if I can. What's the grievance? What have I done?"

Tommy hesitated for a moment, then finally reached up and gripped the hand upon his shoulder. "Monck! I say, Monck!" he said boyishly. "I feel such a cur to say it. But—but—" he broke off abruptly. "I'm damned if I can say it!" he decided dejectedly.

Monck's fingers suddenly twisted and closed upon his. "What a funny little ass you are, Tommy!" he said.

Tommy brightened a little. "It's infernally difficult—taking you to task," he explained blushing a still fiercer red. "You'll never speak to me again after this."

Monck laughed. "Yes, I shall. I shall respect you for it. Get on with it, man! What's the trouble?"

With immense effort Tommy made reply. "Well, it's pretty beastly to have to ask any fellow what his intentions are with regard to his sister, but you pretty nearly told me yours."

"Then what more do you want?" questioned Monck.

Tommy made a gesture of helplessness. "Damn it, man! Don't you know she is making plans to go Home?"

"Well?" said Monck.

Tommy faced round. "I say, like a good chap,—you've practically forced this, you know—you're not going to—to let her go?"

Monck's eyes looked back straight and hard. He did not speak for a moment; then, "You want to know my intentions, Tommy," he said. "You shall. Your sister and I are observing a truce for the present, but it won't last for ever. I am making plans for a move myself. I am going to live at the Club."

"Is that going to help?" demanded Tommy bluntly.

Monck looked sardonic. "We mustn't offend the angels, you know, Tommy," he said.

Tommy made a sound expressive of gross irreverence. "Oh, that's it, is it? Now we know where we are. I've been feeling pretty rotten about it, I can tell you."

"You always were an ass, weren't you?" said Monck, getting up.

Tommy got up too, giving himself an impatient shake. He pushed an apologetic hand through Monck's arm. "I can't expect ever to get even with a swell like you," he said humbly,

Monck looked at him. Something in the boy's devotion seemed to move him, for his eyes were very kindly though his laugh was ironic. "You'll have an almighty awakening one of these days, my son," he said. "By the way, if we are going to be brothers, you had better call me by my Christian name."

"By Jove, I will," said Tommy eagerly. "And if there is anything I can do, old chap—anything under the sun—"

"I'll let you know," said Monck.

So, like the lifting of a thunder cloud, Tommy's very unwonted fit of temper merged into a mood of great benignity and Ralston complained no more.

Monck took up his abode at the Club before the brief winter season brought the angels flitting back from Bhulwana to combine pleasure with duty at Kurrumpore.

Stella accepted his departure without comment, missing him when gone after a fashion which she would have admitted to none. She did not wholly understand his attitude, but Tommy's serenity of demeanour made her somewhat suspicious; for Tommy was transparent as the day.

Mrs. Ralston's return made her life considerably easier. They took up their friendship exactly where they had left it and found it wholly satisfactory. When Lady Harriet Mansfield made her stately appearance, Stella's position was assured. No one looked askance at her any longer. Even Mrs. Burton's criticism was limited to a strictly secret smile.

Netta Ermsted was the last to leave Bhulwana. She returned nervous and fretful, accompanied by Tessa whose joy over rejoining her friends was as patent as her mother's discontent. Tessa had a great deal to say in disparagement of the Rajah of Markestan, and said it so often and with such emphasis that at last Captain Ermsted's patience gave way and he forbade all mention of the man under penalty of a severe slapping. When Tessa had ignored the threat for the third time he carried it out with such thoroughness that even Netta was startled into remonstrance.

"You are quite right to keep the child in order," she said. "But you needn't treat her like that. I call it brutal."

"You can call it what you like," said Ermsted. "I did it quite as much for your benefit as for hers."

Netta tossed her head. "I'm not a sentimental mother," she observed. "You won't punish me in that way. I object to a commotion, that's all."

He took her by the shoulder. "Do you?" he said. "Then I advise you to be mighty careful, for, I warn you, my blood is up."

She made a face at him, albeit there was a quality of menace in his hold. "Are you going to treat me as you have just treated Tessa?"

His teeth were clenched upon his lower lip. "Don't be a little devil, Netta!" he said.

She snapped her fingers. "Then don't you be a big fool, most noble Richard! It doesn't pay to bully a woman. She can always get her own back one way or another. Remember that!"

He gripped her suddenly by both arms. "By Heaven!" he said passionately. "I'll do worse than beat you if you dare to trifle with me!"

She tried to laugh, but his look frightened her. She turned as white as the muslin wrap she wore. "Richard—Dick—don't," she gasped helplessly.

He held her locked to him. "You've gone too far," he said.

"I haven't, Dick! I haven't!" she protested. "Dick, I swear to you—I have never—I have never—"

He stopped the words upon her lips with his own, but his kiss was terrible. She shrank from it trembling, appalled.

In a moment he let her go, and she sank upon her couch, hiding her quivering face with convulsive weeping.

"You are cruel! You are cruel!" she sobbed.

He remained beside her, looking down at her till some of the sternness passed from his face.

He bent at last and touched her. "I'm not cruel," he said. "I'm just in earnest, that's all. You be careful for the future! There's a bit of the devil in me too when I'm goaded."

She drew herself away from him, half-frightened still and half petulant. "You used to be—ever so much nicer than you are now," she said, keeping her face averted.

He answered her sombrely as he turned away, "I used to have a wife that I honoured before all creation."

She sprang to her feet. "Dick! How can you be so horrid?"

He shrugged his shoulders as he walked to the door. "I was—a big fool," he said very bitterly.

The door closed upon him. Netta stood staring at it, tragic and tear-stained.

Suddenly she stamped her foot and whirled round in a rage. "I won't be treated like a naughty child! I won't—I won't! I'll write to my Arabian Knight—I'll write now—and tell him how wretched I am! If Dick objects to our friendship I'll just leave him, that's all. I was a donkey ever to marry him. I always knew we shouldn't get on."

She paused, listening, half-fearing, half-hoping, that she had heard him returning. Then she heard his voice in the next room. He was talking to Tessa.

She set her lips and went to her writing-table. "Oh yes, he can make it up with his child when he knows he has been brutal; but never a single kind word to his wife—not one word!"

She took up a pen with fingers that trembled with indignation, and began to write.

CHAPTER IX

THE OASIS

For two months Tommy possessed his impulsive soul in patience. For two months he watched Monck go his impassive and inscrutable way, asking no further question. The gaieties of the station were in full swing. Christmas was close at hand.

Stella was making definite plans for departure in the New Year. She could not satisfy herself with an idle life, though Tommy vehemently opposed the idea of her going. Monck never opposed it. He listened silently when she spoke of it, sometimes faintly smiling. She often saw him. He came to the Green Bungalow in Tommy's company at all hours of the day. She met him constantly at the Club, and he never failed to come to her side there and by some means known only to himself to banish the crowd of subalterns who were wont to gather round her. He asserted no claim, but the claim existed and was mutely recognized. He never spoke to her intimately. He never attempted to pass the bounds of ordinary friendship. Only very rarely did he make her aware that her company was a pleasure to him. But the fact remained that she was the only woman that he ever sought, and the tongues of all the rest were busy in consequence.

As for Stella, she still told herself that she would escape with her freedom. He would speak, she was convinced, before she left. She even sometimes told herself that after what had passed between them, it was almost incumbent upon him to speak. But she believed that he would accept her refusal philosophically, possibly even with relief. She restrained herself forcibly from dwelling upon the thought of him. Again and again she reminded herself that he trod the way of ambition. His heart was given to his work, and a man may not serve two masters. He cared for her, probably, but in a calm, judicial fashion that could never satisfy her. If she married him she would come second—and a very poor second—to his profession. And so she did not mean to marry him. And so she checked the fevered memory of passionate kisses that had burned her to the soul, of arms that had clasped and held her by a force colossal. That had been only the primitive man in him, escaped for the moment beyond his control—the primitive man which he had well-nigh succeeded in stifling with the bonds of his servitude. Had he not told her that he would have given all he had to forget that single wild lapse into savagery? She was sure that he despised himself for it. He would never for an instant suffer such an impulse again. He did not really love her. It was not in him to love any woman. He would make her a formal offer of marriage, and when she had refused him he would dismiss the matter from his mind and return to his work undisturbed.

So she schooled herself to make her plans, leaving him out of the reckoning, telling herself ever that her newly restored freedom was too dear ever to be sacrificed again. In Mrs. Ralston's company she attended some of the social gatherings of the station, but she took no keen pleasure in them. She disliked Lady Harriet, she distrusted Mrs. Burton, and more often than not she remained away. The coming Christmas festivities did not attract her. She held aloof till Tommy who was in the thick of everything suddenly and vehemently demanded her presence.

"It's ridiculous to be so stand-offish," he maintained. "Don't let 'em think you're afraid of 'em! Come anyway to the moonlight picnic at Khanmulla on Christmas Eve! It's going to be no end of a game."

Stella smiled a little. "Do you know, Tommy, I think I'd rather go to bed?"

"Absurd!" declared Tommy. "You used to be much more sporting."

"I wasn't a widow in those days," Stella said.

"What rot! What damn' rot!" cried Tommy wrathfully.

"There is no altering the fact," said Stella.

He left her, fuming.

That evening as she sat on the Club verandah with Mrs. Ralston, watching some tennis, Monck came up behind her and stood against the wall smoking a cigarette.

He did not speak for some time and after a word of greeting Stella turned back to the play. But presently Mrs. Ralston got up and went away, and after an interval Monck came silently forward and took the vacant seat.

Tommy was among the players. His play was always either surprisingly brilliant or amazingly bad, and on this particular evening he was winning all the honours.

Stella was joining in the general applause after a particularly fine stroke when suddenly Monck's voice spoke at her side.

"Why don't you take a hand sometimes instead of always looking on?"

The question surprised her. She glanced at him in momentary embarrassment, met his straight look, and smiled.

"Perhaps I am lazy."

"That isn't the reason," he said. "Why do you lead a hermit's life? Do you follow your own inclination in so doing? Or are you merely proving yourself a slave to an unwritten law?"

His voice was curt; it held mastery. But yet she could not resent it, for behind it was a masked kindness which deprived it of offence.

She decided to treat the question lightly. "Perhaps a little of both," she said. "Besides, it seems scarcely worth while to try to get into the swim now when I am leaving so soon."

He made an abrupt movement which seemed to denote suppressed impatience. "You are too young to say that," he said.

She laughed a little. "I don't feel young. I think life moves faster in tropical countries. I have lived years since I have been here, and I am glad of a rest."

He was silent for a space; then again abruptly he returned to the charge. "You're not going to waste all the best of your life over a memory, are you? The finest man in the world isn't worth that."

She felt the colour rise in her face as she made reply. "I hope I am not going to waste my life at all. Is it a waste not to spend it in a feverish round of social pleasures? If so, I do not think you are in a position to condemn me."

She saw his brief smile for an instant. "My life is occupied with other things," he said. "But I don't lead a hermit's existence. I am going to the officers' picnic at Khanmulla on the twenty-fourth for instance."

"Being a case of 'Needs must'," suggested Stella.

"By no means." Monck leaned forward to light another cigarette. "I am going for a particular purpose. If that purpose is not fulfilled—" he paused a moment and she felt his eyes upon her again—"I shall come straight back," he ended with a certain doggedness of determination that did not escape her.

Stella's gaze was fixed upon the court below her and she kept it there, but she saw nothing of the game. Her heart was beating oddly in leaps and jerks. She felt curiously as if she were under the influence of an electric battery; every nerve and every vein seemed to be tingling.

He had not asked a question, yet she felt that in some fashion he had made it incumbent upon her to speak in answer. In the silence that followed his words she was aware of an insistence that would not be denied. She tried to put it from her, but could not. In the end, more than half against her will, she yielded.

"I suppose I shall have to go," she said, "if only to pacify Tommy."

"A very good and sufficient reason," commented Monck enigmatically.

He lingered on beside her for a while, but nothing further of an intimate nature passed between them. She felt that he had gained his objective and would say no more. The truce between them was to be observed until the psychological moment arrived to break it, and that moment would occur some time on Christmas Eve in the moonlit solitudes of Khanmulla.

Later she reflected that perhaps it was as well to go and get it over. She could not deny him his opportunity, and it would not take long—she was sure it would not take long to convince him that they were better as they were.

Had he been younger, less wedded to his work, less the slave of his ambition, things might have been different. Had she never been married to Ralph Dacre, never known the bondage of those few strange weeks, she might have been more ready to join her life to his.

But Fate had intervened between them, and their paths now lay apart. He realized it as well as she did. He would not press her. Their eyes were open, and if the oasis in the desert had seemed desirable to either for a space, yet each knew that it was no abiding-place.

Their appointed ways lay in the waste beyond, diverging ever more and more, till presently even the greenness of that oasis in which they had met together would be no more to either than a half-forgotten dream.

CHAPTER X

THE SURRENDER

The moon was full on Christmas Eve. It shone in such splendour that the whole world was transformed into a fairyland of black and silver. Stella stood on the verandah of the Green Bungalow looking forth into the dazzling night with a tremor at her heart. The glory of it was in a sense overwhelming. It made her feel oddly impotent, almost afraid, as if some great power menaced her. She had never felt the ruthlessness of the East more strongly than she felt it that night. But the drugged feeling that had so possessed her in the mountains was wholly absent from her now. She felt vividly alive, almost painfully conscious of the quick blood pulsing through her veins. She was aware of an intense longing to escape even while the magic of the night yet drew her irresistibly. Deep in her heart there lurked an uncertainty which she could not face. Up to that moment she had been barely aware of its existence, but now she felt it stirring, and strangely she was afraid. Was it the call of the East, the wonder of the moonlight? Or was it some greater thing yet, such as had never before entered into her life? She could not say; but her face was still firmly set towards the goal of liberty. Whatever was in store for her, she meant to extricate herself. She meant to cling to her freedom at all costs. When next she stood upon that verandah, the ordeal she had begun to dread so needlessly, so unreasonably, would be over, and she would have emerged triumphant.

So she told herself, even while the shiver of apprehension which she could not control went through her, causing her to draw her wrap more closely about her though there was nought but a pleasant coolness in the soft air that blew across the plain.

She and Tommy were to drive with the Ralstons to the ruined palace in the jungle of Khanmulla where the picnic was to take place. She had never seen it, but had heard it described as the most romantic spot in Markestan. It had been the site of a fierce battle in some bye-gone age, and its glories had departed. For centuries it had lain deserted and crumbling. Yet some of its ancient beauty remained. Its marble floors and walls of carved stone were not utterly obliterated though only owls and flying-foxes made it their dwelling-place. Natives regarded it with superstitious awe and seldom approached it. But Europeans all looked upon it as the most beautiful corner within reach, and had it been nearer to Kurrumpore, it would have been a far more frequented playground than it was.

The hoot of a motor-horn broke suddenly upon the silence, and Stella started. It was the horn of Major Ralston's little two-seater; she knew it well. But they had not proposed using it that night. She and Tommy were to accompany them in a waggonette. The crunching of wheels and throb of the engine at the gate told her it was stopping. Then the Ralstons had altered their plans, unless—Something suddenly leapt up within her. She was conscious of a curious constriction at the throat, a sense of suffocation. The fuss and worry of the engine died down into silence, and in a moment there came the sound of a man's feet entering the compound. Standing motionless, with hands clenched against her sides, she gazed forth. A tall, straight figure was coming towards her between the whispering tamarisks. It was not Major Ralston. He walked with a slouch, and this man's gait was firm and purposeful. He came up to the verandah-steps with unfaltering determination. He was looking full at her, and she knew that she stood revealed in the marvellous Indian moonlight. He mounted the steps with the same absolute self-assurance that yet held nought of arrogance. His face remained in shadow, but she did not need to see it. The reason of his coming was proclaimed in every line, in every calm, unwavering movement.

He came to her, and she waited there in the merciless moonlight; for she had no choice.

"I have come for you," he said.

The words were brief, but they thrilled her strangely. Her eyes fluttered and refused to meet his look.

"The Ralstons are taking us," she said.

Her tone was cold, her bearing aloof. She was striving for self-control. He could not have known of the tumult within her. Yet he smiled. "They are taking Tommy," he said.

She heard the stubborn note in his voice and suddenly and completely the power to resist went from her.

She held out her hand to him with a curious gesture of appeal, "Captain Monck, if I come with you—"

His fingers closed about her own. "If?" he said.

She made a rather piteous attempt to laugh. "Really I don't want to," she said.

"Really?" said Monck. He drew a little nearer to her, still holding her hand. His grasp was firm and strong. "Really?" he said again.

She stood in silence, for she could not give him any answer.

He waited for a moment or two; then, "Stella," he said, "are you afraid of me?"

She shook her head. Her lips had begun to tremble inexplicably. "No—no," she said.

"What then?" He spoke with a gentleness that she had never heard from him before. "Of yourself?"

She turned her face away from him. "I am afraid—of life," she told him brokenly. "It is like a great Wheel—a vast machinery. I have been caught in it once—caught and crushed. Oh can't you understand?"

"Yes," he said.

Again for a space he was silent, his hand yet holding hers. There was subtle comfort in his grasp. It held protection.

"And so you want to run away from it?" he said at length. "Do you think that's going to help you?"

She choked back a sob. "I don't know. I have no judgment. I don't trust myself."

"You believe in sincerity?" he said. "In being true to yourself?" Then, as she winced, "No, I don't want to go over old ground. We are talking of present things. I'm not going to pester you, not going to ask you to marry me even—" again she was aware of his smile though his speech sounded grim—"until you have honestly answered the question that you are trying to shirk. Perhaps you won't thank me for reminding you a second time of a conversation that you and I once had on this very spot, but I must. I told you that I had been waiting for my turn. And you told me that I had come—too late."

He paused, but she did not speak. She was trembling from head to foot.

He leaned towards her. "Stella, I'm not such a fool as to make the same mistake twice over. I'm not going to miss my turn a second time. I loved you then—though I had never flattered myself that I had a chance. And my love isn't the kind that burns and goes out." His voice suddenly quivered. "I don't know whether you have any use for it. You have been too discreet and cautious to betray yourself. Your heart has been a closed book to me. But to-night—I am going to open that book. I have the right, and you can't deny it to me. If you were queen of the whole earth I should still have the right, because I love you, to ask you—as I ask you now—have you any love for me? There! I have done it. If you can tell me honestly that I am nothing to you, that is the end. But if not—if not—" again she heard a deep vibration in his voice—"then don't be afraid—in the name of Heaven! Marriage with me would not mean slavery."

He stopped abruptly and turned from her. From the room behind them there came a cheery hail. Tommy came tramping through.

"Hullo, old chap! You, is it? Has Stella been attending to your comfort? Have you had a drink?"

Monck's answer had a sardonic note, "Your sister has been kindness itself—as she always is. No drinks for me, thanks. I am just off in Ralston's car to Khanmulla." He turned deliberately back again to Stella. "Will you come with me? Or will you go with Tommy—and the Ralstons?"

There was neither anxiety nor persuasion in his voice. Tommy frowned over its utter lack of emotion. He did not think his friend was playing his cards well.

But to Stella that coolness had a different meaning. It stirred her to an impulse more headlong than at the moment she realized.

"I will come with you," she said.

"Good!" said Monck simply, and stood back for her to pass.

She went by him without a glance. She felt as if the wild throbbing of her heart would choke her. He had spoken in such a fashion as she had dreamed that he could ever speak. He had spoken and she had not sent him away. That was the thought that most disturbed her. Till that moment it had seemed a comparatively easy thing to do. Her course had been clear. But he had appealed to that within her which could not be ignored. He had appealed to the inner truth of her nature, and she could not close her ears to that. He had asked her only to be true to herself. He had taken his stand on higher ground than that on which she stood. He had not urged any plea on his own behalf. He had only urged her to be honest. And in so doing he had laid bare that ancient mistake of hers that had devastated her life. He did not desire her upon the same terms as those upon which she had bestowed herself upon Ralph Dacre. He made that abundantly clear. He did not ask her to subordinate her happiness to his. He only asked for straight dealing from her, and she knew that he asked it as much for her sake as for his own. He would not seek to hold her if she did not love him. That was the great touchstone to which he had brought her, and she knew that she must face the test. The mastery of his love compelled her. As he had freely asserted, he had the right—just because he was an honourable man and he loved her honourably.

But how far would that love of his carry him? She longed to know. It was not the growth of a brief hour's passion. That at least she knew. It would not burn and go out. It would endure; somehow she realized that now past disputing. But was it first and greatest with him? Were his cherished career, his ambition, of small account beside it? Was he willing to do sacrifice to it? And if so, how great a sacrifice was he prepared to offer?

She yearned to ask him as he sped her in silence through the chequered moonlight of the Khanmulla jungle. But some inner force restrained her. She feared to break the spell.

The road was deserted, just as it had been on that dripping night when she had answered his summons to Tommy's sick bed. She recalled that wild rush through the darkness, his grim strength, his determination. The iron of his will had seemed to compass her then. Was it the same to-night? Had her freedom already been wrested from her? Was there to be no means of escape?

Through the jungle solitudes there came the call of an owl, weird and desolate and lonely. Something in it pierced her with a curious pain. Was freedom then everything? Did she truly love the silence above all?

She drew her cloak closer about her. Was there something of a chill in the atmosphere? Or was it the chill of the desert beyond the oasis that awaited her?

They emerged from the thickest part of the jungle into a space of tangled shrubs that seemed fighting with each other for possession of the way. The road was rough, and Monck slackened speed.

"We shall have to leave the car," he said. "There is a track here that leads to the ruined palace. It is only a hundred yards or so. We shall have to do it on foot."

They descended. The moonlight poured in a flood all about them. They were alone.

Stella turned up the narrow path he indicated, but in a moment he overtook her. "Let me go first!" he said.

He passed her with the words and walked ahead, holding the creepers back from her as she followed.

She suffered him silently, with a strange sense of awe, almost as though she trod holy ground. But the old feeling of trespass was wholly absent. She had no fear of being cast forth from this place that she was about to enter.

The path began to widen somewhat and to ascend. In a few moments they came upon a crumbling stonewall crossing it at right angles.

Monck paused. "One way leads to the palace, the other to the temple," he said. "Which shall we take?"

Stella faced him in the moonlight. She thought he looked stern. "Is not the picnic to be at the palace?" she said.

"Yes." He answered her without hesitation. "You will find Lady Harriet and Co. there. The temple on the other hand is probably deserted."

"Ah!" His meaning flashed upon her. She stood a second in indecision. Then "Is it far?" she said.

She saw his faint smile for an instant. "A very long way—for you," he said.

"I can come back?" she said.

"I shall not prevent you." She heard the smile in his voice, and something within her thrilled in answer.

"Let us go then!" she said.

He turned without further words and led the way.

They entered the shadow of the jungle once more. For a space the path ran beside the crumbling wall, then it diverged from it, winding darkly into the very heart of the jungle. Monck walked without hesitation. He evidently knew the place well.

They came at length upon a second clearing, smaller than the first, and here in the centre of a moonlit space there stood the ruined walls of a little native temple or mausoleum.

A flight of worn, marble steps led to the dark arch of the doorway. Monck stretched a hand to his companion, and they ascended side by side. A bubbling murmur of water came from within. It seemed to fill the place with gurgling, gnomelike laughter. They entered and Monck stood still.

For a space of many seconds he neither moved nor spoke. It was almost as if he were waiting for some signal. They looked forth into the moonlight they had left through the cave-like opening. The air around them was chill and dank. Somewhere in the darkness behind them a frog croaked, and tiny feet scuttled and scrambled for a few moments and then were still.

Again Stella shivered, drawing her cloak more closely round her. "Why did you bring me to this eerie place?" she said, speaking under her breath involuntarily.

He stirred as if her words aroused him from a reverie. "Are you afraid?" he said.

"I should be—— by myself," she made answer. "I don't think I like India at too close quarters. She is so mysterious and so horribly ruthless."

He passed over the last two sentences as though they had not been uttered. "But you are not afraid with me?" he said.

She quivered at something in his question. "I am not sure," she said. "I sometimes think that you are rather ruthless too."

"Do you know me well enough to say that?" he said.

She tried to answer him lightly. "I ought to by this time. I have had ample opportunity."

"Yes," he said rather bitterly. "But you are prejudiced. You cling to a preconceived idea. If you love me—it is in spite of yourself."

Something in his voice hurt her like the cry of a wounded thing. She made a quick, impulsive movement towards him. "Oh, but that is not so!" she said. "You don't understand. Please don't think anything so—so hard of me!"

"Are you sure it is not so?" he said. "Stella! Stella! Are you sure?"

The words pierced her afresh. She suddenly felt that she could bear no more. "Oh, please!" she said. "Oh, please!" and laid a quivering hand upon his arm. "You are making it very difficult for me. Don't you realize how much better it would be for your own sake not to press me any further?"

"No!" he said; just the one word, spoken doggedly, almost harshly. His hands were clenched and rigid at his sides.

Almost instinctively she began to plead with him as one who pleads for freedom. "Ah, but listen a moment! You have your life to live. Your career means very much to you. Marriage means hindrance to a man like you. Marriage means loitering by the way. And there is no time to loiter. You have taken up a big thing, and you must carry it through. You must put every ounce of yourself into it. You must work like a galley slave. If you don't you will be—a failure."

"Who told you that?" he demanded.

She met the fierceness of his eyes unflinchingly. "I know it. Everyone knows it. You have given yourself heart and soul to India, to the Empire. Nothing else counts—or ever can count now—in the same way. It is quite right that it should be so. You are a builder, and you must follow your profession. You will follow it to the end. And you will do great things,—immortal things." Her voice shook a little. "But you must keep free from all hampering burdens, all private cares. Above all, you must not think of marriage with a woman whose chief desire is to escape from India and all that India means, whose sympathies are utterly alien from her, and whose youth has died a violent death at her hands. Oh, don't you see the madness of it? Surely you must see!"

A quiver of deep feeling ran through her words. She had not meant to go so far, but she was driven, driven by a force that would not be denied. She wanted him to see the matter with her eyes. Somehow that seemed essential now. Things had gone so far between them. It was intolerable now that he should misunderstand.

But as she ceased to speak, she abruptly realized that the effect of her words was other than she intended. He had listened to her with a rigid patience, but as her words went into silence it seemed as if the iron will by which till then he had held himself in check had suddenly snapped.

He stood for a second or two longer with an odd smile on his face and that in his eyes which startled her into a momentary feeling that was almost panic; then with a single, swift movement he bent and caught her to him.

"And you think that counts!" he said. "You think that anything on earth counts—but this!"

His lips were upon hers as he ended, stopping all protest, all utterance. He kissed her hotly, fiercely, holding her so pressed that above the wild throbbing of her own heart she felt the deep, strong beat of his. His action was passionate and overwhelming. She would have withstood him, but she could not; and there was that within her that rejoiced, that exulted, because she could not. Yet as at last his lips left hers, she turned her face aside, hiding it from him that he might not see how completely he had triumphed.

He laughed a little above her bent head; he did not need to see. "Stella, you and I have got to sink or swim together. If you won't have success with me, then I will share your failure."

She quivered at his words; she was clinging to him almost without knowing it. "Oh, no! Oh, no!" she said.

His hand came gently upwards and lay upon her head. "My dear, that rests with you. I have sworn that marriage to me shall not mean bondage. If India is any obstacle between us, India will go."

"Oh, no!" she said again. "No, Everard! No!"

He bent his face to hers. His lips were on her hair. "You love me, Stella," he said.

She was silent, her breathing short, spasmodic, difficult.

His cheek pressed her forehead. "Why not own it?" he said softly. "Is it—so hard?"

She lifted her face swiftly; her arms clasped his neck. "And if—if I do,—will you let me go?" she asked him tremulously.

The smile still hovered about his lips. "No," he said.

"It is madness," she pleaded desperately.

"It is—Kismet," he made answer, and took her face between his hands looking deeply, steadily, into her eyes. "Your life is bound up with mine. You know it. Stella, you know it."

She uttered a sob that yet was half laughter. "I have done my best," she said. "Why are you so—so merciless?"

"You surrender?" he said.

She gave herself to the drawing of his hands. "Have I any choice?"

"Not if you are honest," he said.

"Ah!" She coloured rather painfully. "I have at least been honest in trying to keep you from this—this big mistake. I know you will repent it. When this—fever is past, you will regret—oh, so bitterly."

He set his jaw and all the grim strength of the man was suddenly apparent. "Shall I tell you the secret of success?" he said abruptly. "It is just never to look back. It is the secret of happiness also, if people only realized it. If you want to make the best of life, you've got to look ahead. I'm going to make you do that, Stella. You've been sitting mourning by the wayside long enough."

She smiled almost in spite of herself, for the note of mastery in his voice was inexplicably sweet. "I've thought that myself," she said. "But I'm not going to let you patch up my life with yours. If this must be—and you are sure—you are sure that it must?"

"I have spoken," he said.

She faced him resolutely. "Then India shall have us both. Now I have spoken too."

His face changed. The grimness became eagerness. "Stella, do you mean that?" he said. "It's a big sacrifice—too big for you."

Her eyes were shining as stars shine through a mist. She was drawing his head downwards that her lips might reach his. "Oh, my darling," she said, and the thrill of love triumphant was in her words, "nothing would be—too big. It simply ceases to be a sacrifice—if it is done—for your dear sake."

Her lips met his upon the words, and in that kiss she gave him all she had. It was the rich bestowal of a woman's full treasury, than which it may be there is nought greater on earth.

PART III

CHAPTER I

BLUEBEARD'S CHAMBER

Bhulwana in early spring! Bhulwana of the singing birds and darting squirrels! Bhulwana of the pines!

Stella stood in the green compound of the bungalow known as The Grand Stand, gazing down upon the green racecourse with eyes that dreamed.

The evening was drawing near. They had arrived but a few minutes before in Major Ralston's car, and the journey had taken the whole day. Her mind went back to that early hour almost in the dawning when she and Everard Monck had knelt together before the altar of the little English Church at Kurrumpore and been pronounced man and wife. Mrs. Ralston and Tommy alone had attended the wedding. The hour had been kept a strict secret from all besides. And they had gone straight forth into the early sunlight of the new day and sped away into the morning, rejoicing. A blue jay had laughed after them at starting, and a blue jay was laughing now in the budding acacia by the gate. There seemed a mocking note in its laughter, but it held gaiety as well. Listening to it, she forgot all the weary miles of desert through which they had travelled. The world was fair, very fair, here at Bhulwana. And they were alone.

There fell a step on the grass behind her; she thrilled and turned. He came and put his arm around her.

"Do you think you can stand seven days of it?" he said.

She leaned her head against him. "I want to catch every moment of them and hold it fast. How shall we make the time pass slowly?"

He smiled at the question. "Do you know, I was afraid this place wouldn't appeal to you?"

Her hand sought and closed upon his. "Ah, why not?" she said.

He did not answer her. Only, with his face bent down to hers, he said, "The past is past then?"

"For ever," she made swift reply. "But I have always loved Bhulwana—even in my sad times. Ah, listen! That is a *koïl*!"

They listened to the bird's flutelike piping, standing closely linked in the shadow of a little group of pines. In the bungalow behind them Peter the Great was decking the table for their wedding-feast. The scent of white roses was in the air, languorous, exquisite.

The blue jay laughed again in the acacia by the gate, laughed and flew away. "Good riddance!" said Monck.

"Don't you like him?" said Stella.

"I'm not particularly keen on being jeered at," he answered.

She laughed at him in her turn. "I never thought you cared a single *anna* what any one thought of you."

He smiled. "Perhaps I have got more sensitive since I knew you."

She lifted her lips to his with a sudden movement. "I am like that too, Everard. I care—terribly now."

He kissed her, and his kiss was passionate. "No one shall ever think anything but good of you, my Stella," he said.

She clung to him. "Ah, but the outside world doesn't matter," she said. "It is only we ourselves, and our secret, innermost hearts that count. Everard, let us be more than true to each other! Let us be quite, quite open—always!"

He held her fast, but he made no answer to her appeal.

Her eyes sought his. "That is possible, isn't it?" she pleaded. "My heart is open to you. There is not a single corner of it that you may not enter."

His arms clasped her closer. "I know," he said. "I know. But you mustn't be hurt or sorry if I cannot say the same. My life is a more complex affair than yours, remember."

"Ah! That is India!" she said. "But let me share that part too! Let me be a partner in all! I can be as secret as the wiliest Oriental of them all. I would so love to be trusted. It would make me so proud!"

He kissed her again. "You might be very much the reverse sometimes," he said, "if you knew some of the secrets I had to keep. India is India, and she can be very lurid upon occasion. There is only one way of treating her then; but I am not going to let you into any unpleasant secrets. That is Bluebeard's Chamber, and you have got to stay outside."

She made a small but vehement gesture in his arms. "I hate India!" she said. "She dominates you like—like—"

"Like what?" he said.

She hid her face from him. "Like a horrible mistress," she whispered.

"Stella!" he said.

She throbbed in his hold. "I had to say it. Are you angry with me?"

"No," he said.

"But you don't like me for it all the same." Her voice came muffled from his shoulder. "You don't realize—very likely you never will—how near the truth it is."

He was silent, but in the silence his hold tightened upon her till it was almost a grip.

She turned her face up again at last. "I told you it was madness to marry me," she said tremulously. "I told you you would repent."

He looked at her with a strange smile. "And I told you it was—Kismet," he said. "You did it because it was written that you should. For better for worse—" his voice vibrated—"you and I are bound by the same Fate. It was inevitable, and there can be no repentance, just as there can be no turning back. But you needn't hate India on that account. I have told you that I will give her up for your sake, and that stands. But I will not give you up for India—or for any other power on earth. Now are you satisfied?"

Her face quivered at the question. "It is—more than I deserve," she said. "You shall give up nothing for me."

He put his hand upon her forehead. "Stella, will you give her a trial? Give her a year! Possibly by that time I may tell you more than I am able to tell you now. I don't know if you would welcome it, but there are always a chosen few to whom success comes. I may be one of the few. I have a strong belief in my own particular star. Again I may fail. If I fail, I swear I will give her up. I will start again at some new job. But will you be patient for a year? Will you, my darling, let me prove myself? I only ask—one year."

Her eyes were full of tears. "Everard! You make me feel—ashamed," she said. "I won't—won't—be a drag on you, spoil your career! You must forgive me for being jealous. It is because I love you so. But I know it is a selfish form of love, and I won't give way to it. I will never separate you from the career you have chosen. I only wish I could be a help to you."

"You can only help me by being patient—just at present," he said.

"And not asking tiresome questions!" She smiled at him though her tears had overflowed. "But oh, you won't take risks, will you? Not unnecessary risks? It is so terrible to think of you in danger—to think—to think of that horrible deformed creature who sent—Ralph—" She broke off shuddering and clinging to him. It was the first time she had ever spoken of her first husband by name to him.

He dried the tears upon her cheeks. "My own girl, you needn't be afraid," he said, and though his words were kind she wondered at the grimness of his voice. "I am not the sort of person to be disposed of in that way. Shall we talk of something less agitating? I can't have you crying on our wedding-night."

His tone was repressive. She was conscious of a chill. Yet it was a relief to turn from the subject, for she recognized that there was small satisfaction to be derived therefrom. The sun was setting moreover, and it was growing cold. She let him lead her back into the bungalow, and they presently sat down at the table that Peter had prepared with so much solicitude.

Later they lingered for awhile on the verandah, watching the blazing stars, till it came to Monck that his bride was nearly dropping with weariness and then he would not suffer her to remain any longer.

When she had gone within, he lit a pipe and wandered out alone into the starlight, following the deserted road that led to the Rajah's summer palace.

He paced along slowly with bent head, deep in thought. At the great marble gateway that led into the palace-garden he paused and stood for a space in frowning contemplation. A small wind had sprung up and moaned among the cypress-trees that overlooked the high wall. He seemed to be listening to it. Or was it to the hoot of an owl that came up from the valley?

Finally he drew near and deliberately tapped the ashes from his half-smoked pipe upon the shining marble. The embers smouldered and went out. A black stain remained upon the dazzling white surface of the stone column. He looked at it for a moment or two, then turned and retraced his steps with grim precision.

When he reached the bungalow, he turned into the room in which they had dined; and sat down to write.

Time passed, but he took no note of it. It was past midnight ere he thrust his papers together at length and rose to go.

The main passage of the bungalow was bright with moonlight as he traversed it. A crouching figure rose up from a shadowed doorway at his approach. Peter the Great looked at him with reproach in his eyes.

Monck stopped short. He accosted the man in his own language, but Peter made answer in the careful English that was his pride.

"Even so, *sahib*, I watch over my *mem-sahib* until you come to her. I keep her safe by night as well as by day. I am her servant."

He stood back with dignity that Monck might pass, but Monck stood still. He looked at Peter with a level scrutiny for a few moments. Then: "It is enough," he said, with brief decision. "When I am not with your *mem-sahib*, I look to you to guard her."

Peter made his stately *salaam*. Without further words, he conveyed the fact that without his permission no man might enter the room behind him and live.

Very softly Monck turned the handle of the door and passed within, leaving him alone in the moonlight.

CHAPTER II

EVIL TIDINGS

They walked on the following morning over the pine-clad hill and down into the valley beyond, a place of running streams and fresh spring verdure. Stella revelled in its sweetness. It made her think of Home.

"You haven't told me anything about your brother," she said, as they sat together on a grey boulder and basked in the sunshine.

"Haven't I?" Monck spoke meditatively. "I've got a photograph of him somewhere. You must see it. You'll like my brother," he added, with a smile. "He isn't a bit like me."

She laughed. "That's a recommendation certainly. But tell me what he is like! I want to know."

Monck considered. "He is a short, thick-set chap, stout and red, rather like a comedian in face. I think he appreciates a joke more than any one I know."

"He sounds a dear!" said Stella; and added with a gay side-glance, "and certainly not in the least like you. Have you written yet to break the news of your very rash marriage?"

"Yes, I wrote two days ago. He will probably cable his blessing. That is the sort of chap he is."

"It will be rather a shock for him," Stella observed. "You had no idea of changing your state when you saw him last summer."

There fell a somewhat abrupt silence. Monck was filling his pipe and the process seemed to engross all his thoughts. Finally, rather suddenly, he spoke. "As a matter of fact, I didn't see him last summer."

"You didn't see him!" Stella opened her eyes wide. "Not when you went Home?"

"I didn't go Home." Monck's eyes were still fixed upon his pipe. "No one knows that but you," he said, "and one other. That is the first secret out of Bluebeard's chamber that I have confided in you. Keep it close!"

Stella sat and gazed; but he would not meet her eyes. "Tell me," she said at last, "who is the other? The Colonel?"

He shook his head. "No, not the Colonel, You mustn't ask questions, Stella, if I ever expand at all. If you do, I shall shut up like a clam, and you may get pinched in the process."

She slipped her hand through his arm. "I will remember," she said. "Thank you—ever so much—for telling me. I will bury it very deep. No one shall ever suspect it through me."

"Thanks," he said. He pressed her hand, but he kept his eyes lowered. "I know I can trust you. You won't try to find out the things I keep back."

"Oh, never!" she said. "Never! I shall never try to pry into affairs of State."

He smiled rather cynically. "That is a very wise resolution," he said. "I shall tell Bernard that I have married the most discreet woman in the Empire—as well as the most beautiful."

"Did you marry her for her beauty or for her discretion?" asked Stella.

"Neither," he said.

"Are you sure?" She leaned her cheek against his shoulder. "It's no good pretending with me you know, I can see through anything, detect any disguise, so far as you are concerned."

"Think so?" said Monck.

"Answer my question!" she said.

"I didn't know you asked one." His voice was brusque; he pushed his pipe into his mouth without looking at her.

She reached up and daringly removed it. "I asked what you married me for," she said. "And you suck your horrid pipe and won't even look at me."

His arm went round her. He looked down into her eyes and she saw the fiery worship in his own. For a moment its intensity almost frightened her. It was like the red fire of a volcano rushing forth upon her—a fierce, unshackled force. For a space he held her so, gazing at her; then suddenly he crushed her to him, he kissed her burningly till she felt as if caught and consumed by the flame.

"My God!" he said passionately. "Can I put—that—into words?"

She clung to him, but she was trembling. There was that about him at the moment that startled her. She was in the presence of something terrible, something she could not fathom. There was more than rapture in his passion. It was poignant with a fierce defiance that challenged all the world.

She lay against his breast in silence while the storm that she had so unwittingly raised spent itself. Then at last as his hold began to slacken she took courage.

She laid her cheek against his hand. "Ah, don't love me too much at first, darling," she said. "Give me the love that lasts!"

"And you think my love will not last?" he said, his voice low and very deep.

She softly kissed the hand she held. "No, I didn't say—or mean—that. I believe it is the greatest thing that I shall ever possess. But—shall I tell you a secret? There is something in it that frightens me—even though I glory in it."

"My dear!" he said.

She raised her lips again to his. "Yes, I know. That is foolish. But I don't know you yet, remember. I have never yet seen you angry with me."

"You never will," he said.

"Yes, I shall." Her eyes were gazing into his, but they saw beyond. "There will come a day when something will come between us. It may be only a small thing, but it will not seem small to you. And you will be angry because I do not see with your eyes. And I think the very greatness of your love will make it harder for us both. You mustn't worship me, Everard. I am only human. And you will be so bitterly disappointed afterwards when you discover my limitations."

"I will risk that," he said.

"No. I don't want you to take any risks. If you set up an idol, and it falls, you may be—I think you are—the kind of man to be ruined by it."

She spoke very earnestly, but his faint smile told her that her words had failed to convince.

"Are you really afraid of all that?" he asked curiously.

She caught her breath. "Yes, I am afraid. I don't think you know yourself, your strength, or your weakness. You haven't the least idea what you would say or do—or even feel—if you thought me unkind or unjust to you."

"I should probably sulk," he said.

She shook her head. "Oh, no! You would explode—sooner or later. And it would be a very violent explosion. I wonder if you have ever been really furious with any one you cared about—with Tommy for instance."

"I have," said Monck. "But I don't fancy you will get him to relate his experiences. He survived it anyway."

"You tell me!" she said.

He hesitated. "It's rather a shame to give the boy away. But there is nothing very extraordinary in it. When Tommy first came out, he felt the heat—like lots of others. He was thirsty, and he drank. He doesn't do it now. I don't mind wagering that he never will again. I stopped him."

"Everard, how?" Stella was looking at him with the keenest interest.

"Do you really want to know how?" he still spoke with slight hesitation.

"Of course I do. I suppose you were very angry with him?"

"I was—very angry. I had reason to be. He fell foul of me one night at the Club. It doesn't matter how he did it. He wasn't responsible in any case. But I had to act to keep him out of hot water. I took him back to my quarters. Dacre was away that night and I had him to myself. I kept my temper with him at first—till he showed fight and tried to kick me. Then I let him have it. I gave him a licking—such a licking as he never got at school. It sobered him quite effectually, poor little beggar." An odd note of tenderness crept through the grimness of Monck's speech. "But I didn't stop then. He had to have his lesson and he had it. When I had done with him, there was no kick left in him. He was as limp as a wet rag. But he was quite sober. And to the best of my belief he has never been anything else from that day to this. Of course it was all highly irregular, but it saved a worse row in the end." Monck's faint smile appeared. "He realized that. In fact he was game enough to thank me for it in the morning, and apologized like a gentleman for giving so much trouble."

"Oh, I'm glad he did that!" Stella said, with shining eyes. "And that was the beginning of your friendship?"

"Well, I had always liked him," Monck admitted. "But he didn't like me for a long time after. That thrashing stuck in his mind. It was a pretty stiff one certainly. He was always very polite to me, but he avoided me like the plague. I think he was ashamed. I left him alone till one day he got ill, and then I went round to see if I could do anything. He was pretty bad, and I stayed with him. We got friendly afterwards."

"After you had saved his life," Stella said.

Monck laughed. "That sort of thing doesn't count in India. If it comes to that, you saved mine. No, we came to an understanding, and we've managed to hit it ever since."

Stella got to her feet. "Were you very brutal to him, Everard?"

He reached a brown hand to her as she stood. "Of course I was. He deserved it too. If a man makes a beast of himself he need never look for mercy from me."

She looked at him dubiously. "And if a woman makes you angry—" she said.

He got to his feet and put his arm about her shoulders. "But I don't treat women like that," he said, "not even—my wife. I have quite another sort of treatment for her. It's curious that you should credit me with such a vindictive temperament. I don't know what I have done to deserve it."

She leaned her head against him. "My darling, forgive me! It is just my horrid, suspicious nature."

He pressed her to him. "You certainly don't know me very well yet," he said.

They went back to the bungalow in the late afternoon, walking hand in hand as children, supremely content.

The blue jay laughed at the gate as they entered, and Monck looked up, "Jeer away, you son of a satyr!" he said. "I was going to shoot you, but I've changed my mind. We're all friends in this compartment."

Stella squeezed his hand hard. "Everard, I love you for that!" she said simply. "Do you think we could make friends with the monkeys too?"

"And the jackals and the scorpions and the dear little *karaits*," said Monck. "No doubt we could if we lived long enough."

"Don't laugh at me!" she protested. "I am quite in earnest. There are plenty of things to love in India."

"There's India herself," said Monck.

She looked at him with resolution shining in her eyes. "You must teach me," she said.

He shook his head. "No, my dear. If you don't feel the lure of her, then you are not one of her chosen and I can never make you so. She is either a goddess in her own right or the most treacherous old she-devil who ever sat in a heathen temple. She can be both. To love her, you must be prepared to take her either way."

They went up into the bungalow. Peter the Great glided forward like a magnificent genie and presented a scrap of paper on a salver to Monck.

He took it, opened it, frowned over it.

"The messenger arrived three hours ago, *sahib*. He could not wait," murmured Peter.

Monck's frown deepened. He turned to Stella. "Go and have tea, dear, and then rest! Don't wait for me! I must go round to the Club and get on the telephone at once."

The grimness of his face startled her. "To Kurrumpore?" she asked quickly. "Is there something wrong?"

"Not yet," he said curtly. "Don't you worry! I shall be back as soon as possible."

"Let me come too!" she said.

He shook his head. "No. Go and rest!"

He was gone with the words, striding swiftly down the path. As he passed out on to the road, he broke into a run. She stood and listened to his receding footsteps with foreboding in her heart.

"Tea is ready, my *mem-sahib*" said Peter softly behind her.

She thanked him with a smile and went in.

He followed her and waited upon her with all a woman's solicitude.

For a while she suffered him in silence, then suddenly, "Peter," she said, "what was the messenger like?"

Peter hesitated momentarily. Then, "He was old, *mem-sahib*," he said, "old and ragged, not worthy of your august consideration."

She turned in her chair. "Was he—was he anything like—that—that holy man—Peter, you know who I mean?" Her face was deathly as she uttered the question.

"Let my *mem-sahib* be comforted!" said Peter soothingly. "It was not the holy man—the bearer of evil tidings."

"Ah!" The words sank down through her heart like a stone dropped into a well. "But I think the tidings were evil all the same. Did he say what it was? But—" as a sudden memory shot across her, "I ought not to ask. I wish—I wish the captain—*sahib* would come back."

"Let my *mem-sahib* have patience!" said Peter gently. "He will soon come now."

The blue jay laughed at the gate gleefully, uproariously, derisively. Stella shivered.

"He is coming!" said Peter.

She started up. Monck was returning. He came up the compound like a man who has been beaten in a race. His face was grey, his eyes terrible.

Stella went swiftly to the verandah-steps to meet him. "Everard! What is it? Oh, what is it?" she said.

He took her arm, turning her back. "Have you had tea?" he said.

His voice was low, but absolutely steady. Its deadly quietness made her tremble.

"I haven't finished," she said. "I have been waiting for you."

"You needn't have done that," he said. "I won't have any, Peter," he turned on the waiting servant, "get me some brandy!"

He sat down, setting her free. But she remained beside him, and after a moment laid her hand lightly upon his shoulder, without words.

He reached up instantly, caught and held it in a grip that almost made her wince. "Stella," he said, "it's been a very short honeymoon, but I'm afraid it's over. I've got to get back at once."

"I am coming with you," she said quickly.

He looked up at her with eyes that burned with a strange intensity but he did not speak in answer.

An awful dread clutched her. She knelt swiftly down beside him. "Everard, listen! I don't care what has happened or what is likely to happen. My place is by your side—and nowhere else. I am coming with you. Nothing on earth shall prevent me."

Her words were quick and vehement, her whole being pulsated. She challenged his look with eyes of shining resolution.

His arms were round her in a moment; he held her fast. "My Stella! My wife!" he said.

She clung closely to him. "By your side, I will face anything. You know it, darling. I am not afraid."

"I know, I know," he said. "I won't leave you behind. I couldn't now. But a time will come when we shall have to separate. We've got to face that."

"Wait till it comes!" she whispered. "It isn't—yet."

He kissed her on the lips. "No, not yet, thank heaven. You want to know what has happened. I will tell you. Ermsted—you know Ermsted—was shot in the jungle near Khanmulla this afternoon, about half an hour ago."

"Oh, Everard!" She started back in horror and was struck afresh by the awful intentness of his eyes.

"Yes," he said. "And if I had been here to receive that message, I could have prevented it."

"Oh, Everard!" she said again.

He went on doggedly. "I ought to have been here. My agent knew I was in the place. I ought to have stayed within reach. These warnings might arrive at any time. I was a damned lunatic, and Ermsted has paid the price." He stopped, and his look changed. "Poor girl! It's been a shock to you," he said, "a beastly awakening for us both."

Stella was very pale. "I feel," she said slowly, "as if I were pursued by a remorseless fate."

"You?" he questioned. "This had nothing to do with you."

She leaned against him. "Wherever I go, trouble follows. Haven't you noticed it? It seems as if—as if—whichever way I turn—a flaming sword is stretched out, barring the way." Her voice suddenly quivered. "I know why,—oh, yes, I know why. It is because once—like the man without a wedding-garment, I found my way into a forbidden paradise. They hurled me out, Everard. I was flung into a desert of ashes. And now—now that I have dared to approach by another way—the sentence has gone forth that wherever I pass, something shall die. That dreadful man—told me on the day that Ralph was taken away from me—that the Holy Ones were angry. And—my dear—he was right. I shall never be pardoned until I have—somehow—expiated my sin."

"Stella! Stella!" He broke in upon her sharply. "You are talking wildly. Your sin, as you call it, was at the most no more than a bad mistake. Can't you put it from you?—get above it? Have you no faith? I thought all women had that."

She looked at him strangely. "I wasn't brought up to believe in God," she said. "At least not personally, not intimately. Were you?"

"Yes," he said.

"Ah!" Her eyes widened a little. "And you still believe in Him—still believe He really cares—even when things go hopelessly wrong?"

"Yes," he said again. "I can't talk about Him. But I know He's there."

She still regarded him with wonder. "Oh, my dear," she said finally, "are you behind me, or a very, very long way in front?"

He smiled faintly, grimly. "Probably a thousand miles behind," he said. "But I have been given long sight, that's all."

She rose to her feet with a sigh. "And I," she said very sadly, "am blind."

Down by the gate the blue jay laughed again, laughed and flew away.

CHAPTER III

THE BEAST OF PREY

In a darkened room Netta Ermsted lay, trembling and unnerved. As usual in cases of adversity, Mrs. Ralston had taken charge of her; but there was very little that she could do. It was more a matter for her husband's skill than for hers, and he could only prescribe absolute quiet. For Netta was utterly broken. Since the fatal moment when she had returned from a call in her 'rickshaw to find Major Burton awaiting her with the news that Ermsted had been shot on the jungle-road while riding home from Khanmulla, she had been as one distraught. They had restrained her almost forcibly from rushing forth to fling herself upon his dead body, and now that it was all over, now that the man who had loved her and whom she had never loved was in his grave, she lay prostrate, refusing all comfort.

Tessa, wide-eyed and speculative, was in the care of Mrs. Burton, alternately quarrelling vigorously with little Cedric Burton whose intellectual leanings provoked her most ardent contempt, and teasing the luckless Scooter out of sheer boredom till all the animal's ideas in life centred in a desperate desire to escape.

It was Tessa to whom Stella's pitying attention was first drawn on the day after her return to The Green Bungalow. Tommy, finding her raging in the road like a little tiger-cat over some small *contretemps* with Mrs. Burton, had lifted her on to his shoulders and brought her back with him.

"Be good to the poor imp!" he muttered to his sister. "Nobody wants her."

Certainly Mrs, Burton did not. She passed her on to Stella with her two-edged smile, and Tessa and Scooter forthwith cheerfully took up their abode at The Green Bungalow with whole-hearted satisfaction.

Stella experienced little difficulty in dealing with the child. She found herself the object of the most passionate admiration which went far towards simplifying the problem of managing her. Tessa adored her and followed her like her shadow whenever she was not similarly engrossed with her beloved Tommy. Of Monck she stood in considerable awe. He did not take much notice of her. It seemed to Stella that he had retired very deeply into his shell of reserve during those days. Even with herself he was reticent, monosyllabic, obviously absorbed in matters of which she had no knowledge.

But for her small worshipper she would have been both lonely and anxious. For he was often absent, sometimes for hours at a stretch wholly without warning, giving no explanation upon his return. She asked no questions. She schooled herself to patience. She tried to be content with the close holding of his arms when they were together and the certainty that all the desire of his heart was for her alone. But she could not wholly, drive away the conviction that at the very gates of her paradise the sword she dreaded had been turned against her. They were back in the desert again, and the way to the tree of life was barred.

Perhaps it was natural that she should turn to Tessa for consolation and distraction. The child was original in all her ways. Her ideas of death were wholly devoid of tragedy, and she was too accustomed to her father's absence to feel any actual sense of loss.

"Do you think Daddy likes Heaven?" she said to Stella one day. "I hope Mother will be quick and go there too. It would be better for her than staying behind with the Rajah. I always call him 'the slithy tove.' He is so narrow and wriggly. He wanted me to kiss him once, but I wouldn't. He looked so—so mischievous." Tessa tossed her golden-brown head. "Besides, I only kiss white men."

"Hear, hear!" said Tommy, who was cleaning his pipe on the verandah. "You stick to that, my child!"

"Mother said I was very silly," said Tessa. "She was quite cross. But the Rajah only laughed in that nasty, slippy way he has and took her cigarette away and smoked it himself. I hated him for that," ended Tessa with a little gleam of the tiger-cat in her blue eyes. "It—it was a liberty."

Tommy's guffaw sounded from the verandah. It went into a greeting of Monck who came up unexpectedly at the moment and sat down on a wicker-chair to examine a handful of papers. Stella, working within the room, looked up swiftly at his coming, but if he had so much as glanced in her direction he was fully engrossed with the matter in hand ere she had time to observe it. He had been out since early morning and she had not seen him for several hours.

Tessa, who possessed at times an almost uncanny shrewdness, left her and went to stand on one leg in the doorway. "Most people," she observed, "say 'Hullo!' to their wives when they come in."

"Very intelligent of 'em," said Tommy. "Do you think the Rajah does?"

"I don't know," said Tessa seriously. "I went to the palace at Bhulwana once to see them. But the Rajah wasn't there. They were very kind," she added dispassionately, "but rather silly. I don't wonder the Rajah likes white men's wives best."

"Oh, quite natural," agreed Tommy.

"He gave Mother a beautiful ring with a diamond in it," went on Tessa, delighted to have secured his attention and watching furtively for some sign of interest from Monck also. "It was worth hundreds and hundreds of pounds. That was the last thing Daddy was cross about. He was cross."

"Why?" asked Tommy.

"'Cos he was jealous, I expect," said Tessa wisely. "I thought he was going to give her a whipping. And I hid in his dressing-room to see. Mother was awful frightened. She went down on her knees to him. And he was just going to do it. I know he was. And then he came into the dressing-room and found me. And so he whipped me instead." Tessa ended on a note of resentment.

"Served you jolly well right," said Tommy.

"No, it didn't," said Tessa. "He only did it 'cos Mother had made him angry. It wasn't a child's whipping at all. It was a grown-up's whipping. And he used a switch. And it hurt—worse than anything ever hurt before. That's why I didn't mind when he went to Heaven the other day. I hope I shan't go there for a long time yet. It isn't nice to be whipped like that. And I wasn't going to say I was sorry either. I knew that would make him crosser than anything."

"Poor chap!" said Tommy suddenly.

Tessa came a step nearer to him. "*Ayah* says the man who did it will be hanged if they catch him," she said. "If it is the Rajah, will you manage so as I can go and see? I should like to."

"Tessa!" exclaimed Stella.

Tessa turned flushed cheeks and shining eyes upon her. "I would!" she declared stoutly. "I would! There's nothing wrong in that. He's a horrid man. It isn't wrong, is it, Captain Monck? But if he shot my Daddy?" She went swiftly to Monck with the words and leaned ingratiatingly against him. "You'd kill a man yourself that did a thing like that, wouldn't you?"

"Very likely," said Monck.

She gazed at him admiringly. "I expect you've killed lots and lots of men, haven't you?" she said.

He smiled with a touch of grimness. "Do you think I'm going to tell a scaramouch like you?" he said.

"Everard!" Stella rose and came to the window. "Do—please—make her understand that people don't murder each other just whenever they feel like it—even in India!"

He raised his eyes to hers, and an odd sense of shock went through her. It was as if in some fashion he had deliberately made her aware of that secret chamber which she might not enter. "I think you would probably be more convincing on that point than I should," he said.

She gave a little shudder; she could not restrain it. That look in his eyes reminded her of something, something dreadful. What was it? Ah yes, she remembered now. He had had that look on that night of terror when he had first called her his wife, when he had barred the window behind her and sworn to slay any man who should come between them.

She turned aside and went in without another word. India again! India the savage, the implacable, the ruthless! She felt as a prisoner who battered fruitlessly against an iron door.

Tessa's inquisitive eyes followed her. "She's going to cry," she said to Monck.

Tommy turned sharply upon his friend with accusation in his glance, but the next instant he summoned Tessa as if she had been a terrier and walked off into the compound with the child capering at his side.

Monck sat for a moment or two looking straight before him; then he packed together the papers in his hand and stepped through the open window into the room behind. It was empty.

He went through it without a pause, and turned along the passage to the door of his wife's room. It stood half-open. He pushed it wider and entered.

She was standing by her dressing-table, but she turned at his coming, turned and faced him.

He came straight to her and took her by the shoulders. "What is the matter?" he said.

She met his direct look, but there was shrinking in her eyes. "Everard," she said, "there are times when you make me afraid."

"Why?" he said.

She could not put it into words. She made a piteous gesture with her clasped hands.

His expression changed, subtly softening. "I can't always wear kid gloves, my Stella," he said. "When there is rough work to be done, we have to strip to the waist sometimes to get to it. It's the only way to get a sane grip on things."

Her lips were quivering. "But you—you like it!" she said.

He smiled a little. "I plead guilty to a sporting instinct," he said.

"You hunt down murderers—and call it—sport!" she said slowly.

"No, I call it justice." He still spoke gently though his face had hardened again. "That child has a sense of justice, quite elementary, but a true one. If I could get hold of the man who killed Ermsted, I would cheerfully kill him with my own hand—unless I could be sure that he would get his deserts from the Government who are apt to be somewhat slack in such matters."

Stella shivered again. "Do you know, Everard, I can't bear to hear you talk like that? It is the untamed, savage part of you."

He drew her to him. "Yes, the soldier part. I know. I know quite well. But my dear, do me the justice at least to believe that I am on the side of right! I can't do other than talk generalities to you. You simply wouldn't understand. But there are some criminals who can only be beaten with their own weapons, remember that. Nicholson knew that—and applied it. I follow—or try to follow—in Nicholson's steps."

She clung to him suddenly and closely. "Oh, don't—don't! This is another age. We have advanced since then."

"Have we?" he said sombrely. "And do you think the India of to-day can be governed by weakness any more successfully than the India of Nicholson's time? You have no idea what you say when you talk like that. Ermsted is not the first Englishman to be killed in this State. The Rajah of Markestan is too wily a beast to go for the large game at the outset, though—probably—the large game is the only stuff he cares about. He knows too well that there are eyes that watch perpetually, and he won't expose himself—if he can help it. The trouble is he doesn't always know where to look for the eyes that watch."

A certain exultation sounded in his voice, but the next instant he bent and kissed her.

"Why do you dwell on these things? They only trouble you. But I think you might remember that since they exist, someone has to deal with them."

"You don't trust Ahmed Khan?" she said. "You think he is treacherous?"

He hesitated; then: "Ahmed Khan is either a tiger or—merely a jackal," he said. "I don't know which at present. I am taking his measure."

She still held him closely. "Everard," her voice came low and breathless, "you think he was responsible for Captain Ermsted's death. May he not have been also for—for—"

He checked her sharply before Ralph Dacre's name could leave her lips. "No. Put that out of your mind for good! You have no reason to suspect foul play where he was concerned."

He spoke with such decision that she looked at him in surprise. "I often have suspected it," she said.

"I know. But you have no reason for doing so. I should try to forget it if I were you. Let the past be past!"

It was evident that he would not discuss the matter, and, wondering somewhat, she let it pass. The bare mention of Dacre seemed to be unendurable to him. But the suspicion which his words had started remained in her mind, for it was beyond her power to dismiss it. The conviction that he had met his death by foul means was steadily gaining ground within her, winding serpent-like ever more closely about her shrinking heart.

Monck went his way, whether deeply disappointed or not she knew not. But she realized that he would not reopen the subject. He had made his explanation, but—and for this she honoured him—he would not seek to convince her against her will. It was even possible that he preferred her to keep her own judgment in the matter.

They dined at the Mansfields' bungalow that night, a festivity for which she felt small relish, more especially as she knew that Mrs. Ralston would not be present. To be received with icy ceremony by Lady Harriet and sent in to dinner with Major Burton was a state of affairs that must have dashed the highest spirits. She tried to make the best of it, but it was impossible to be entirely unaffected by the depressing chill of the atmosphere. Conversation turned upon Mrs. Ermsted, regarding whom the report had gone forth that she was very seriously ill. Lady Harriet sought to probe Stella upon the subject and was plainly offended when she pleaded ignorance. She also tried to extract Monck's opinion of poor Captain Ermsted's murder. Had it been committed by a mere *budmash* for the sake of robbery, or did he consider that any political significance was attached to it? Monck drily expressed the opinion that something might be said for either theory. But when Lady Harriet threw discretion to the winds and desired to know if it were generally believed in official circles that the Rajah was implicated, he raised his brows in stern surprise and replied that so far as his information went the Rajah was a loyal servant of the Crown.

Lady Harriet was snubbed, and she felt the effects of it for the rest of the evening. Walking home with her husband through the starlight later, Stella laughed a little over the episode; but Monck was not responsive. He seemed engrossed in thought.

He went with her to her room, and there bade her good-night, observing that he had work to do and might be late.

"It is already late," she said. "Don't be long! I shall only lie awake till you come."

He frowned at her. "I shall be very angry if you do."

"I can't help that," she said. "I can't sleep properly till you come."

He looked her in the eyes. "You're not nervous? You've got Peter."

"Oh, I am not in the least nervous on my own account," she told him.

"You needn't be on mine," he said.

She laughed, but her lips were piteous. "Well, don't be long anyway!" she pleaded. "Don't forget I am waiting for you!"

"Forget!" he said. For an instant his hold upon her was passionate. He kissed her fiercely, blindly, even violently; then with a muttered word of inarticulate apology he let her go.

She heard him stride away down the passage, and in a few moments Peter came and very softly closed the door. She knew that he was there on guard until his master should return.

She sat down with a beating heart and leaned back with closed eyes. A heavy sense of foreboding oppressed her. She was very tired, but yet she knew that sleep was far away. Just as once she had felt a dread that was physical on behalf of Ralph Dacre, so now she felt weighed down by suspense and loneliness. Only now it was a thousand times magnified, for this man was her world. She tried to picture to herself what it would have meant to her had that shot in the jungle slain him instead of Captain Ermsted. But the bare thought was beyond endurance. Once she could have borne it, but not now—not now! Once she could have denied her love and fared forth alone into the desert. But he had captured her, and now she was irrevocably his. Her spirit pined almost unconsciously whenever he was absent from her. Her body knew no rest without him. From the moment of his leaving her, she was ever secretly on fire for his return.

Had they been in England she knew that it would have been otherwise. In a calm and temperate atmosphere she could have attained a serene, unruffled happiness. But India, fevered and pitiless, held her in scorching grip. She dwelt as it were on the edge of a roaring furnace that consumed some victims every day. Her life was strung up to a pitch that frightened her. The very intensity of the love that Everard Monck had practically forced into being within her was almost more than she could bear. It hurt her like the searing of a flame, and yet in the hurt there was rapture. For the icy blast of the desert could never reach her now. Unless—unless—ah, was there not a flaming sword still threatening her wherever she pitched her camp? Surround herself as she would with the magic essences of love, did not the vengeance await her—even now—even now? Could she ever count herself safe so long as she remained in this land of treachery and terrible vengeance? Could there ever be any peace so near to the burning fiery furnace?

Slowly the night wore on. The air blew in cool and pure with a soft whispering of spring and the brief splendour of the rose-time. The howl of a prowling jackal came now and then to her ears, making her shiver with the memory of Monck's words. Away in the jungle the owls were calling upon notes that sounded like weird cries for help.

Once or twice she heard a shuffling movement outside the door and knew that Peter was still on guard. She wondered if he ever slept. She wondered if Tommy had returned. He often dropped into the Club on his way back, and sometimes stayed late. Then, realizing how late it was, she came to the conclusion that she must have dozed in her chair.

She got up with a sense of being weighted in every limb, and began to undress. Everard would be vexed if he returned and found her still up. Not that she expected him to return for a long time. His absence lasted sometimes till the night was nearly over.

She never questioned him regarding it, and he never told her anything. Dacre's revelation on that night so long ago had never left her memory. He was engaged upon secret affairs. Possibly he was down in the native quarter, disguised as a native, carrying his life in his hand. He had a friend in the bazaar, she knew; a man she had never seen, but whose shop he had once pointed out to her though he would not suffer her—and indeed she had no desire—to enter. This man—Rustam Karin—was a dealer in native charms and trinkets. The business was mainly conducted by a youth of obsequious and insincere demeanour called Hafiz. The latter she knew and instinctively disliked, but her feeling for the unknown master was one of more active aversion. In the depths of that dark native stall she pictured him, a watcher, furtive and avaricious, a man who lent himself and his shrewd and covetous brain to a Government he probably despised as alien.

Tommy had once described the man to her and her conception of him was a perfectly clear one. He was black-bearded and an opium-smoker, and she hated to think of Everard as in any sense allied with him. Dark, treacherous, and terrible, he loomed in her imagination. He represented India and all her subtleties. He was a serpent underfoot, a knife in the dark, an evil dream.

She could not have said why the personality of a man she did not know so affected her, save that she believed that all Monck's secret expeditions were conceived in the gloom of that stall she had never entered in the heart of the native bazaar. The man was in Monck's confidence. Perhaps, being a woman, that hurt her also. For though she recognized—as in the case of that native lair down in the bazaar—that it were better never to set foot in that secret chamber, yet she resented the thought that any other should have free access to it. She was beginning to regard that part of Monck's life with a dread that verged upon horror—a feeling which her very love for the man but served to intensify. She was as one clinging desperately to a treasure which might at any moment be wrested from her.

Stiffly and wearily she undressed. Tommy must surely have returned ages ago, though probably late, or he would have come to bid her good-night. Why did not Everard return?

At the last she extinguished her light and went to the window to gaze wistfully out across the verandah. That secret whispering—the stirring of a thousand unseen things—was abroad in the night. The air was soft and scented with a fragrance intangible but wholly sweet. India, stretched out beneath the glittering stars, stirred with half-opened eyes, and smiled. Stella thought she heard the flutter of her robe.

Then again the mystery of the night was rent by the cry of some beast of prey, and in a second the magic was gone. The shadows were full of evil. She drew back with swift, involuntary shrinking; and as she did so, she heard the dreadful answering cry of the prey that had been seized.

India again! India the ruthless! India the bloodthirsty! India the vampire!

For a few palpitating moments she leaned against the wall feeling physically sick. And as she leaned, there passed before her inner vision the memory of that figure which she had seen upon the verandah on that terrible night when Everard had been stricken with fever. The look in her husband's eyes that day had brought it back to her, and now like a flashlight it leapt from point to point of her brain, revealing, illuminating.

That figure on the verandah and the unknown man of the bazaar were one. It was Rustam Karin whom she had seen that night—Rustam Karin, Everard's trusted friend and ally—the Rajah's tool also though Everard would never have it so—and (she was certain of it now with that certainty which is somehow all the greater because without proof) this was the man who had followed Ralph Dacre to Kashmir and lured him to his death. This was the beast of prey who when the time was ripe would destroy Everard Monck also.

CHAPTER IV

THE FLAMING SWORD

The conviction which came upon Stella on that night of chequered starlight was one which no amount of sane reasoning could shake. She made no attempt to reopen the subject with Everard, recognizing fully the futility of such a course; for she had no shadow of proof to support it. But it hung upon her like a heavy chain. She took it with her wherever she went.

More than once she contemplated taking Tommy into her confidence. But again that lack of proof deterred her. She was certain that Tommy would give no credence to her theory. And his faith in Monck—his wariness, his discretion—was unbounded.

She did question Peter with regard to Rustam Karin, but she elicited scant satisfaction from him. Peter went but little to the native bazaar, and like herself had never seen the man. He appeared so seldom and then only by night. There was a rumour that he was leprous. This was all that Peter knew.

And so it seemed useless to pursue the matter. She could only wait and watch. Some day the man might emerge from his lair, and she would be able to identify him beyond all dispute. Peter could help her then. But till then there was nothing that she could do. She was quite helpless.

So, with that shrinking still strongly upon her that made all mention of Ralph Dacre's death so difficult, she buried the matter deep in her own heart, determined only that she also would watch with a vigilance that never slackened until the proof for which she waited should be hers.

The weeks had begun to slip by with incredible swiftness. The tragedy of Ermsted's death had ceased to be the talk of the station. Tessa had gone back to her mother who still remained a semi-invalid in the Ralstons' hospitable care. Netta's plans seemed to be of the vaguest; but Home leave was due to Major Ralston the following year, and it seemed likely that she would drift on till then and return in their company.

Stella did not see very much of her friend in those days. Netta, exacting and peevish, monopolized much of the latter's time and kept her effectually at a distance. The days were growing hotter moreover, and her energies flagged, though all her strength was concentrated upon concealing the fact from Everard. For already the annual exodus to Bhulwana was being discussed, and only the possibility that the battalion might be moved to a healthier spot for the summer had deferred it for so long.

Stella clung to this possibility with a hope that was passionate in its intensity. She had a morbid dread of separation, albeit the danger she feared seemed to have sunk into obscurity during the weeks that had intervened. If there yet remained unrest in the State, it was below the surface. The Rajah came and went in his usual romantic way, played polo with his British friends, danced and gracefully flattered their wives as of yore.

On one occasion only did he ask Stella for a dance, but she excused herself with a decision there was no mistaking. Something within her revolted at the bare idea. He went away smiling, but he never asked her again.

Definite orders for the move to Udalkhand arrived at length, and Stella's heart rejoiced. The place was situated on the edge of a river, a brown and turgid torrent in the rainy weather, but no more than a torpid, muddy stream before the monsoon. A native town and temple stood upon its banks, but a sandy road wound up to higher ground on which a few bungalows stood, overlooking the grim, parched desert below.

The jungle of Khanmulla was not more than five miles distant, and Kurrumpore itself barely ten. But yet Stella felt as if a load had been lifted from her. Surely the danger here would be more remote! And she would not need to leave her husband now. That thought set her very heart a-singing.

Monck said but little upon the subject. He was more non-committal than ever in those days. Everyone said that Udalkhand was healthier and cooler than Kurrumpore and he did not contradict the statement. But yet Stella came to perceive after a time something in his silence which she found unsatisfactory. She believed he watched her narrowly though he certainly had no appearance of doing so, and the suspicion made her nervous.

There were a few—Lady Harriet among the number—who condemned Udalkhand from the outset as impossible, and departed for Bhulwana without attempting to spend even the beginning of the hot season there. Netta Ermsted also decided against it though Mrs. Ralston declared her intention of going thither, and she and Tessa departed for that universal haven The Grand Stand before any one else.

This freed Mrs. Ralston, but Stella had grown a little apart from her friend during that period at Kurrumpore, and a measure of reserve hung between them though outwardly they were unchanged. A great languor had come upon Stella which seemed to press all the more heavily upon her because she only suffered herself to indulge it in Everard's absence. When he was present she was almost feverishly active, but it needed all her strength of will to achieve this, and she had no energy over for her friends.

Even after the move to Udalkhand had been accomplished, she scarcely felt the relief which she so urgently needed. Though the place was undoubtedly more airy than Kurrumpore, the air came from the desert, and sand-storms were not infrequent.

She made a brave show nevertheless, and with Peter's help turned their new abode into as dainty a dwelling-place as any could desire. Tommy also assisted with much readiness though the increasing heat was anathema to him also. He was more considerate for his sister just then than he had ever been before. Often in Monck's absence he would spend much of his time with her, till she grew to depend upon him to an extent she scarcely realized. He had taken up wood-carving in his leisure hours and very soon she was fully occupied with executing elaborate designs for his workmanship. They worked very happily together. Tommy declared it kept him out of mischief, for violent exercise never suited him in hot weather.

And it was hot. Every day seemed to bring the scorching reality of summer a little nearer. In spite of herself Stella flagged more and more. Tommy always kept a brave front. He was full of devices for ameliorating their discomfort. He kept the punkah-coolie perpetually at his task. He made the water-coolie spray the verandah a dozen times a day. He set traps for the flies and caught them in their swarms.

But he could not take the sun out of the sky which day by day shone from horizon to horizon as a brazen shield burnished to an intolerable brightness, while the earth—- parched and cracked and barren—fainted beneath it. The nights had begun to be oppressive also. The wind from the desert was as the burning breath from a far-off forest-fire which hourly drew a little nearer. Stella sometimes felt as if a monster-hand were slowly closing upon her, crushing out her life.

But still with all her might she strove to hide from Monck the ravages of the cruel heat, even stooping to the bitter subterfuge of faintly colouring the deathly whiteness of her cheeks. For the wild-rose bloom had departed long since, as Netta Ermsted had predicted, though her beauty remained—the beauty of the pure white rose which is fairer than any other flower that grows.

There came a burning day at last, however, when she realized that the evening drive was almost beyond her powers. Tommy was on duty at the barracks. Everard had, she believed, gone down to Khanmulla to see Barnes of the Police. She decided in the absence of both to indulge in a rest, and sent Peter to countermand the carriage.

Then a great heaviness came upon her, and she yielded herself to it, lying inert upon the couch in the drawing-room dully listening to the creak of the punkah that stirred without cooling the late afternoon air.

Some time must have passed thus and she must have drifted into a species of vague dreaming that was not wholly sleep when suddenly there came a sound at the darkened window; the blind was lifted and Monck stood in the opening.

She sprang up with a startled sense of being caught off her guard, but the next moment a great dizziness came upon her and she reeled back, groping for support.

He dropped the blind and caught her. "Why, Stella!" he said.

She clung to him desperately. "I am all right—I am all right! Hold me a minute! I—I tripped against the matting." Gaspingly she uttered the words, hanging upon him, for she knew she could not stand alone.

He put her gently down upon the sofa. "Take it quietly, dear!" he said.

She leaned back upon the cushions with closed eyes, for her brain was swimming. "I am all right," she reiterated. "You startled me a little. I—didn't expect you back so soon."

"I met Barnes just after I started," he made answer. "He is coming to dine presently."

Her heart sank. "Is he?" she said faintly.

"No." Monck's tone suddenly held an odd note that was half-grim and half-protective. "On second thoughts, he can go to the Mess with Tommy. I don't think I want him any more than you do."

She opened her eyes and looked up at him. "Everard, of course he must dine here if you have asked him! Tell Peter!"

Her vision was still slightly blurred, but she saw that the set of his jaw was stubborn. He stooped after a moment and kissed her forehead. "You lie still!" he said. "And mind—you are not to dress for dinner."

He turned with that and left her.

She was not sorry to be alone, for her head was throbbing almost unbearably, but she would have given much to know what was in his mind.

She lay there passively till presently she heard Tommy dash in to dress for mess, and shortly after there came the sound of men's voices in the compound, and she knew that Monck and Barnes were walking to and fro together.

She got up then, summoning her energies, and stole to her own room. Monck had commanded her not to change her dress, but the haggardness of her face shocked her into taking refuge in the remedy which she secretly despised. She did it furtively, hoping that in the darkened drawing-room he had not noted the ghastly pallor which she thus sought to conceal.

Before she left her room she heard Tommy and Barnes departing, and when she entered the dining-room Monck came in alone at the window and joined her.

She met him somewhat nervously, for she thought his face was stern. But when he spoke, his voice held nought but kindness, and she was reassured. He did not look at her with any very close criticism, nor did he revert to what had passed an hour before.

They were served by Peter, swiftly and silently, Stella making a valiant effort to simulate an appetite which she was far from possessing. The windows were wide to the night, and from the river bank below there came the thrumming of some stringed instrument, which had a weird and strangely poignant throbbing, as if it voiced some hidden distress. There were a thousand sounds besides, some near, some distant, but it penetrated them all with the persistence of some small imprisoned creature working perpetually for freedom.

It began to wear upon Stella's nerves at last. It was so futile, yet so pathetic—the same soft minor tinkle, only a few stray notes played over and over, over and over, till her brain rang with the maddening little refrain. She was glad when the meal was over, and she could make the excuse to move to the drawing-room. There was a piano here, a rickety instrument long since hammered into tunelessness. But she sat down before it. Anything was better than to sit and listen to that single, plaintive little voice of India crying in the night.

She thought and hoped that Monck would smoke his cigarette and suffer himself to be lulled into somnolence by such melody as she was able to extract from the crazy old instrument; but he disappointed her.

He smoked indeed, lounging out in the verandah, while she sought with every allurement to draw him in and charm him to blissful, sleepy contentment. But it presently came to her that there was something dogged in his

75

refusal to be so drawn, and when she realized that she brought her soft *nocturne* to a summary close and turned round to him with just a hint of resentment.

He was leaning in the doorway, the cigarette gone from his lips. His face was turned to the night. His attitude seemed to express that patience which attends upon iron resolution. He looked at her over his shoulder as she paused.

"Why don't you sing?" he said.

A little tremor of indignation went through her. He spoke with the gentle indulgence of one who humours a child. Only once had she ever sung to him, and then he had sat in such utter immobility and silence that she had questioned with herself afterwards if he had cared for it.

She rose with a wholly unconscious touch of majesty. "I have no voice to-night," she said.

"Then come here!" he said.

His voice was still absolutely gentle but it held an indefinable something that made her raise her brows.

She went to him nevertheless, and he put his hand through her arm and drew her close to his side. The night was heavy with a brooding heat-haze that blotted out the stars. The little twanging instrument down by the river was silent.

For a space Monck did not speak, and gradually the tension went out of Stella. She relaxed at length and laid her cheek against his shoulder.

His arm went round her in a moment; he held her against his heart. "Stella," he said, "do you ever think to yourself nowadays that I am a very formidable person to live with?"

"Never," she said.

His arm tightened about her. "You are not afraid of me any longer?"

She smiled a little. "What is this leading up to?"

He bent suddenly, his lips against her forehead. "Dear heart, if I am wrong—forgive me! But—why are you trying to deceive me?"

She had never heard such tenderness in his voice before; it thrilled her through and through, checking her first involuntary dismay. She hid her face upon his breast, clasping him close, trembling from head to foot.

He turned, still holding her, and led her to the sofa. They sat down together.

"Poor girl!" he said softly. "It hasn't been easy, has it?"

Then she realized that he knew all that she had so strenuously sought to hide. The struggle was over and she was beaten. A great wave of emotion went through her. Before she could check herself, she was shaken with sobs.

"No, no!" he said, and laid his hand upon her head. "You mustn't cry. It's all right, my darling. It's all right. What is there to cry about?"

She clung faster to him, and her hold was passionate. "Everard," she whispered, "Everard,—I—can't leave you!"

"Ah!" he said "We are up against it now."

"I can't!" she said again. "I can't."

His hand was softly stroking her hair. Such tenderness as she had never dreamed of was in his touch. "Leave off crying!" he said. "God knows I want to make things easier for you—not harder."

"I can bear anything," she told him brokenly, "anything in the world—if only I am with you. I can't leave you. You won't—you can't—force me to that."

"Stella! Stella!" he said.

His voice checked her. She knew that she had hurt him. She lifted her face quickly to his.

"Oh, darling, forgive me!" she said. "I know you would not."

He kissed the quivering lips she raised without words, and thereafter there fell a silence between them while the mystery of the night seemed to press closer upon them, and the veiled goddess turned in her sleep and subtly smiled.

Stella uttered a long, long sigh at last. "You are good to bear with me like this," she said rather piteously.

"Better now?" he questioned gently.

She closed her eyes from the grave scrutiny of his. "I am—quite all right, dear," she said. "And I am taking great care of myself. Please—please don't worry about me!"

His hand sought and found hers. "I have been worrying about you for a long time," he said.

She gave a start of surprise. "I never thought you noticed anything."

"Yes." With a characteristic touch of grimness he answered her. "I noticed when you first began to colour your cheeks for my benefit. I knew it was only for mine, or of course I should have been furious."

"Oh, Everard!" She hid her face against him again with a little shamed laugh.

He went on without mercy. "I am not an easy person to deceive, you know. You really might have saved yourself the trouble. I hoped you would give in sooner. That too would have saved trouble."

"But I haven't given in," she said.

His hand closed upon hers. "You would kill yourself first if I would let you," he said. "But—do you think I am going to do that?"

"It would kill me to leave you," she said.

"And what if it kills you to stay?" He spoke with sudden force. "No, listen a minute! I have something to tell you. I have been worried about you—as I said—for some time. To-day I was working in the orderly-room, and Ralston chanced to come in. He asked me how you were. I said, 'I am afraid the climate is against her. What do you think of her?' He replied, 'I'll tell you what I think of you, if you like. I think you're a damned fool.' That opened my eyes." Monck ended on the old grim note. "I thanked him for the information, and told him to come over here and see you on the earliest opportunity. He has promised to come round in the morning."

"Oh, but Everard!" Stella started up in swift protest. "I don't want him! I won't see him!"

He kept her hand in his. "I am sorry," he said. "But I am going to insist on that."

"You—insist!" She looked at him curiously, a quivering smile about her lips.

His eyes met hers uncompromisingly. "If necessary," he said.

She made a movement to free herself, but he frustrated her, gently but with indisputable mastery.

"Stella," he said, "things may be difficult. I know they are. But, my dear, don't make them impossible! Let us pull together in this as in everything else!"

She met his look steadily. "You know what will happen, don't you?" she said. "He will order me to Bhulwana."

Monck's hand tightened upon hers. "Better that," he said, under his breath, "than to lose you altogether!"

"And if it kills me to leave you?" she said. "What then?"

He made a gesture that was almost violent, but instantly restrained himself. "I think you are braver than that," he said.

Her lips quivered again piteously. "I am not brave at all," she said. "I left all my courage—all my faith—in the mountains one terrible morning—when God cursed me for marrying a man I did not love—and took—the man—- away."

"My darling!" Monck said. He drew her to him again, holding her passionately close, kissing the trembling lips till they clung to his in answer. "Can't you forget all that," he said, "put it right away from you, think only of what lies before."

Her arms were round his neck. She poured out her very soul to him in that close embrace. But she said no word in answer, and her silence was the silence of despair. It seemed to her that the flaming sword she dreaded had flashed again across her path, closing the way to happiness.

CHAPTER V

TESSA

The blue jay was still laughing on the pine-clad slopes of Bhulwana when Stella returned thither. It was glorious summer weather. There was life in the air—such life as never reached the Plains.

The bungalow up the hill, called "The Nest," which once Ralph Dacre had taken for his bride, was to be Stella's home for the period of her sojourn at Bhulwana. It was a pretty little place twined in roses, standing in a shady compound that Tessa called "the jungle." Tessa became at once her most constant visitor. She and Scooter were running wild as usual, but Netta was living in strict retirement. People said she looked very ill, but she seemed to resent all sympathy. There was an air of defiance about her which kept most people at a distance.

Stories were rife concerning her continued intimacy with the Rajah who was now in residence at his summer palace on the hill. They went for gallops together in the early morning, and in the evenings they sometimes flashed along the road in his car. But he was seldom observed to enter the bungalow she occupied, and even Tessa had no private information to add to the general gossip. Netta seldom went to race course or polo-ground, where the Rajah was most frequently to be found.

Stella, who had never liked Netta Ermsted, took but slight interest in her affairs. She always welcomed Tessa, however, and presently, since her leisure was ample and her health considerably improved, she began to give the child a few lessons which soon became the joy of Tessa's heart. She found her quick and full of enthusiasm. Her devotion to Stella made her tractable, and they became fast friends.

It was in June just before the rains, that Monck came up on a week's leave. He found Tessa practically established as Stella's companion. Her mother took no interest in her doings. The *ayah* was responsible for her safety, and even if Tessa elected to spend the night with her friend, Netta raised no objection. It had always been her way to leave the child to any who cared to look after her, since she frankly acknowledged that she was quite incapable of managing her herself. If Mrs. Monck liked to be bothered with her, it was obviously her affair, not Netta's.

And so Stella kept the little girl more and more in her own care, since Mrs. Ralston was still at Udalkhand, and no one else cared in the smallest degree for her welfare. She would not keep her for good, though, so far as her mother was concerned, she might easily have done so. But she did occasionally—as a great treat—have her to sleep with her, generally when Tessa's looks proclaimed her to be in urgent need of a long night. For she was almost always late to bed when at home, refusing to retire before her mother, though there was little of companionship between them at any time.

Stella investigated this resolution on one occasion, and finally extracted from Tessa the admission that she was afraid to go to bed early lest her mother should go out unexpectedly, in which event the *ayah* would certainly retire to the servants' quarters, and she would be alone in the bungalow. No amount of reasoning on Stella's part could shake this dread. Tessa's nerves were strung to a high pitch, and it was evident that she felt very strongly on the subject. So, out of sheer pity, Stella sometimes kept her at "The Nest," and Tessa's gratitude knew no bounds. She was growing fast, and ought to have been in England for the past year at least; but Netta's plans were still vague. She supposed she would have to go when the Ralstons did, but she saw no reason for hurry. Lady Harriet remonstrated with her on the subject, but obtained no satisfaction. Netta was her own mistress now, and meant to please herself.

Monck arrived late one evening on the day before that on which he was expected, and found Tessa and Peter playing with a ball in the compound. The two were fast friends and Stella often left Tessa in his charge while she rested.

She was resting now, lying in her own room with a book, when suddenly the sound of Tessa's voice raised in excited welcome reached her. She heard Monck's quiet voice make reply, and started up with every pulse quivering. She had not seen him for nearly six weeks.

She met him in the verandah with Tessa hanging on his arm. Since her great love for Stella had developed, she had adopted Stella's husband also as her own especial property, though it could scarcely be said that Monck gave her much encouragement. On this occasion she simply ceased to exist for him the moment he caught sight of Stella's face. And even Stella herself forgot the child in the first rapture of greeting.

But later Tessa asserted herself again with a determination that would not be ignored. She begged hard to be allowed to remain for the night; but this Stella refused to permit, though her heart smote her somewhat when she saw her finally take her departure with many wistful backward glances.

Monck was hard-hearted enough to smile. "Let the imp go! She has had more than her share already," he said. "I'm not going to divide you with any one under the sun."

Stella was lying on the sofa. She reached out and held his hand, leaning her cheek against his sleeve. "Except—" she murmured.

He bent to her, his lips upon her shining hair. "Ah, I have begun to do that already," he said, with a touch of sadness. "I wonder if you are as lonely up here as I am at Udalkhand."

She kissed his sleeve. "I miss you—unspeakably," she said.

His fingers closed upon hers. "Stella, can you keep a secret?"

She looked up swiftly. "Of course—of course. What is it? Have they made you Governor-General of the province?"

He smiled grimly. "Not yet. But Sir Reginald Bassett—you know old Sir Reggie?—came and inspected us the other day, and we had a talk. He is one of the keenest empire-builders that I ever met." An odd thrill sounded in

Monck's voice. "He asked me if presently—when the vacancy occurred—I would be his secretary, his political adviser, as he put it. Stella, it would be a mighty big step up. It would lead—it might lead—to great things."

"Oh, my darling!" She was quivering all over. "Would it—would it mean that we should be together? No," she caught herself up sharply, "that is sheer selfishness. I shouldn't have asked that first."

His lips pressed hers. "Don't you know it is the one thing that comes first of all with me too?" he said. "Yes, it would mean far less of separation. It would probably mean Simla in the hot weather, and only short absences for me. It would mean an end of this beastly regimental life that you hate so badly. What? Did you think I didn't know that? But it would also mean leaving poor Tommy at the grindstone, which is hard."

"Dear Tommy! But he has lots of friends. You don't think he would get up to mischief?"

"No, I don't think so. He is more of a man than he was. And I could keep an eye on him—even from a distance. Still, it won't come yet,—not probably till the end of the year. You are fairly comfortable here—you and Peter?"

She smiled and sighed. "Oh yes, he keeps away the bogies, and Tessa chases off the blues. So I am well taken care of!"

"I hope you don't let that child wear you out," Monck said. "She is rather a handful. Why don't you leave her to her mother?"

"Because she is utterly unfit to have the care of her." Stella spoke with very unusual severity. "Since Captain Ermsted's death she seems to have drifted into a state of hopeless apathy. I can't bear to think of a susceptible child like Tessa brought up in such an atmosphere."

"Apathetic, is she? Do you often see her?" Monck spoke casually, as he rolled a cigarette.

"Very seldom. She goes out very little, and then only with the Rajah. They say she looks ill, but that is not surprising. She doesn't lead a wholesome life!"

"She keeps up her intimacy with His Excellency then?" Monck still spoke as if his thoughts were elsewhere.

Stella dismissed the subject with a touch of impatience. She had no desire to waste any precious moments over idle gossip. "I imagine so, but I really know very little. I don't encourage Tessa to talk. As you know, I never could bear the man."

Monck smiled a little. "I know you are discretion itself," he said. "But you are not to adopt Tessa, mind, whatever the state of her mother's morals!"

"Ah, but I must do what I can for the poor waif," Stella protested. "There isn't much that I can do when I am away from you,—not much, I mean, that is worth while."

"All right," Monck said with finality, "so long as you don't adopt her."

Stella saw that he did not mean to allow Tessa a very large share of her attention during his leave. She did not dispute the point, knowing that he could be as adamant when he had formed a resolution.

But she did not feel happy about the child. There was to her something tragic about Tessa, as if the evil fate that had overtaken the father brooded like a dark cloud over her also. Her mind was not at rest concerning her.

In the morning, however, Tessa arrived upon the scene, impudent and cheerful, and she felt reassured. Her next anxiety became to keep her from annoying Monck upon whom naturally Tessa's main attention was centered. Tessa, however, was in an unusually tiresome mood. She refused to be contented with the society of the ever-patient Peter, repudiated the bare idea of lesson books, and set herself with fiendish ingenuity to torment the new-comer into exasperation.

Stella could have wept over her intractability. She had never before found her difficult to manage. But Netta's perversity and Netta's devilry were uppermost in her that day, and when at last Monck curtly ordered her not to worry herself but to leave the child alone, she gave up her efforts in despair. Tessa was riding for a fall.

It came eventually, after two hours' provocation on her part and stern patience on Monck's. Stella, at work in the drawing-room, heard a sudden sharp exclamation from the verandah where Monck was seated before a table littered with Hindu literature, and looked up to see Tessa, with a monkey-like grin of mischief, smoking the cigarette which she had just snatched from between Monck's lips. She was dancing on one leg just out of reach, ready to take instant flight should the occasion require.

Stella was on the point of starting up to intervene, but Monck stopped her with a word. He was quieter than she had ever seen him, and that fact of itself warned her that he was angry at last.

"Come here!" he said to Tessa.

Tessa removed the cigarette to poke her tongue out at him, and continued her war-dance just out of reach. It was Netta to the life.

Monck glanced at the watch on his wrist. "I give you one minute," he said, and returned to his work."

"Why don't you chase me?" gibed Tessa.

He said nothing further, but to Stella his silence was ominous. She watched him with anxious eyes.

Tessa continued to smoke and dance, posturing like a *nautch-girl* in front of the wholly unresponsive and unappreciative Monck.

The minute passed, Stella counting the seconds with a throbbing heart. Monck did not raise his eyes or stir, but there was to her something dreadful in his utter stillness. She marvelled at Tessa's temerity.

Tessa continued to dance and jeer till suddenly, finding that she was making no headway, a demon of temper entered into her. She turned in a fury, sprang from the verandah to the compound, snatched up a handful of small stones and flung them full at the impassive Monck.

They fell around him in a shower. He looked up at last.

What ensued was almost too swift for Stella's vision to follow. She saw him leap the verandah-balustrade, and heard Tessa's shrill scream of fright. Then he had the offender in his grasp, and Stella saw the deadly determination of his face as he turned.

In spite of herself she sprang up, but again his voice checked her. "All right. This is my job. Bring me the strap off the bag in my room!"

"Everard!" she cried aghast.

Tessa was struggling madly for freedom. He mastered her as he would have mastered a refractory puppy, carrying her up the steps ignominiously under his arm.

"Do as I say!" he commanded.

And against her will Stella turned and obeyed. She fetched the strap, but she held it back when he stretched a hand for it.

"Everard, she is only a child. You won't—you won't——"

"Flay her with it?" he suggested, and she saw his brief, ironic smile. "Not at present. Hand it over!"

She gave it reluctantly. Tessa squealed a wild remonstrance. The merciless grip that held her had sent terror to her heart.

Monck, still deadly quiet, set her on her feet against one of the wooden posts that supported the roof of the verandah, passed the strap round her waist and buckled it firmly behind the post.

Then he stood up and looked again at the watch on his wrist. "Two hours!" he said briefly, and went back to his work at the other end of the verandah.

Stella went back to the drawing-room, half-relieved and half-dismayed. It was useless to interfere, she saw; but the punishment, though richly deserved, was a heavy one, and she wondered how Tessa, the ever-restless, wrought up to a high pitch of nervous excitement as she was, would stand it.

The thickness of the post to which she was fastened made it impossible for her to free herself. The strap was a very stout one, and the buckle such as only a man's fingers could loosen. It was an undignified position, and Tessa valued her dignity as a rule.

She cast it to the winds on this occasion, however, for she fought like a wild cat for freedom, and when at length her absolute helplessness was made quite clear even to her, she went into a paroxysm of fury, hurling every kind of invective that occurred to her at Monck who with the grimness of an executioner sat at his table in unbroken silence.

Having exhausted her vocabulary, both English and Hindustani, Tessa broke at last into tears and wept stormily for many minutes. Monck sat through the storm without raising his eyes.

From the drawing-room Stella watched him. She was no longer afraid of any unconsidered violence. He was completely master of himself, but she thought there was a hint of cruelty about him notwithstanding. There was ruthlessness in his utter immobility.

The hour for *tiffin* drew near. Peter came out on to the verandah to lay the cloth. Monck gathered up books and papers and rose.

The great Sikh looked at the child shaken with passionate sobbing in the corner of the verandah and from her to Monck with a touch of ferocity in his dark eyes. Monck met the look with a frown and turned away without a word. He passed down the verandah to his own room, and Peter with hands that shook slightly proceeded with his task.

Tessa's sobbing died down, and there fell a strained silence. Stella still sat in the drawing-room, but she was out of sight of the two on the verandah. She could only hear Peter's soft movements.

Suddenly she heard a tense whisper. "Peter! Peter! Quick!"

Like a shadow Peter crossed her line of vision. She heard a murmured, "Missy *baba!*" and rising, she bent forward and saw him in the act of severing Tessa's bond with the bread-knife. It was done in a few hard-breathing seconds. The child was free. Peter turned in triumph,—and found Monck standing at the other end of the verandah, looking at him.

Stella stepped out at the same moment and saw him also. She felt the blood rush to her heart. Only once had she seen Monck look as he looked now, and that on an occasion of which even yet she never willingly suffered herself to think.

Peter's triumph wilted. "Run, Missy *baba!*" he said, in a hurried whisper, and moved himself to meet the wrath of the gods.

Tessa did not run. Neither did she spring to Stella for protection. She stood for a second or two in indecision; then with an odd little strangled cry she darted in front of Peter, and went straight to Monck.

"It—it wasn't Peter's fault!" she declared breathlessly. "I told him to!"

Monck's eyes went over her head to the native beyond her. He spoke—a few, brief words in the man's own language—and Peter winced as though he had been struck with a whip, and bent himself in an attitude of the most profound humility.

Monck spoke again curtly, and as if at the sudden jerk of a string the man straightened himself and went away.

Then Tessa, weeping, threw herself upon Monck. "Do please not be angry with him! It was all my fault. You—you—you can whip me if you like! Only you mustn't be cross with Peter! It isn't—it isn't—fair!"

He stood stiffly for a few seconds, as if he would resist her; and Stella leaned against the window-frame, feeling physically sick as she watched him. Then abruptly his eyes came to hers, and she saw his face change. He put his hand on Tessa's shoulder.

"If you want forgiveness for yourself—and Peter," he said grimly, "go back to your corner and stay there!"

Tessa lifted her tear-stained face, looked at him closely for a moment, then turned submissively and went back.

Monck came down the verandah to his wife. He put his arm around her, and drew her within.

"Why are you trembling?" he said.

She leaned her head against him. "Everard, what did you say to Peter?"

"Never mind!" said Monck.

She braced herself. "You are not to be angry with him. He—is my servant. I will reprimand him—if necessary."

"It isn't," said Monck, with a brief smile. "You can tell him to finish laying the cloth."

He kissed her and let her go, leaving her with a strong impression that she had behaved foolishly. If it had not been for that which she had seen in his eyes for those few awful seconds, she would have despised herself for her utter imbecility. But the memory was one which she could not shake from her. She did not wonder that even Peter, proud Sikh as he was, had quailed before that look. Would Monck have accepted even Tessa's appeal if he had not found her watching? She wondered. She wondered.

She did not look forward to the meal on the verandah, but Monck realized this and had it laid in the dining-room instead. At his command Peter carried a plate out to Tessa, but it came back untouched, Peter explaining in a very low voice that 'Missy *baba* was not hungry.' The man's attitude was abject. He watched Monck furtively from behind Stella's chair, obeying his every behest with a promptitude that expressed the most complete submission.

Monck bestowed no attention upon him. He smiled a little when Stella expressed concern over Tessa's failure to eat anything. It was evident that he felt no anxiety on that score himself. "Leave the imp alone!" he said. "You are not to worry yourself about her any more. You have done more than enough in that line already."

There was insistence in his tone—an insistence which he maintained later when he made her lie down for her afternoon rest, steadily refusing to let her go near the delinquent until she had had it.

Greatly against her will she yielded the point, protesting that she could not sleep nevertheless. But when he had gone she realized that the happenings of the morning had wearied her more than she knew. She was very tired, and she fell into a deep sleep which lasted for nearly two hours.

Awakening from this, she got up with some compunction at having left the child so long, and went to her window to look for her. She found the corner of Tessa's punishment empty. A little further along the verandah Monck lounged in a deep cane chair, and, curled in his arms asleep with her head against his neck was Tessa.

Monck's eyes were fixed straight before him. He was evidently deep in thought. But the grim lines about his mouth were softened, and even as Stella looked he stirred a little very cautiously to ease the child's position. Something in the action sent the tears to her eyes. She went back into her room, asking herself how she had ever doubted for a moment the goodness of his heart.

Somewhere down the hill the blue jay was laughing hilariously, scoffingly, as one who marked, with cynical amusement the passing show of life; and a few seconds later the Rajah's car flashed past, carrying the Rajah and a woman wearing a cloudy veil that streamed far out behind her.

CHAPTER VI

THE ARRIVAL

Two months later, on a dripping evening in August, Monck stood alone on the verandah of his bungalow at Udalkhand with a letter from Stella in his hand. He had hurried back from duty on purpose to secure it, knowing that it would be awaiting him. She had become accustomed to the separation now, though she spoke yearningly of his next leave. Mrs. Ralston had joined her, and she wrote quite cheerfully. She was very well, and looking forward—oh, so much—to the winter. There was certainly no sadness to be detected between the lines, and Monck folded up the letter and looked across the dripping compound with a smile in his eyes.

When the winter came, he would probably have taken up his new appointment. Sir Reginald Bassett—a man of immense influence and energy—was actually in Udalkhand at that moment. He was ostensibly paying a friendly visit at the Colonel's bungalow, but Monck knew well what it was that had brought him to that steaming corner of Markestan in the very worst of the rainy season. He had come to make some definite arrangement with him. Probably before that very night was over, he would have begun to gather the fruit of his ambition. He had started already to climb the ladder, and he would raise Stella with him, Stella and that other being upon whom he sometimes suffered his thoughts to dwell with a semi-humorous contemplation as—his son. A fantastic fascination hung about the thought. He could not yet visualize himself as a father. It was easier far to picture Stella as a mother. But yet, like a magnet drawing him, the vision seemed to beckon. He walked the desert with a lighter step, and Tommy swore that he was growing younger.

There was an enclosure in Stella's letter from Tessa, who called him her darling Uncle Everard and begged him to come soon and see how good she was getting. He smiled a little over this also, but with a touch of wonder. The child's worship seemed extraordinary to him. His conquest of Tessa had been quite complete, but it was odd that in consequence of it she should love him as she loved no one else on earth. Yet that she did so was an indubitable fact. Her devotion exceeded even that of Tommy, which was saying much. She seemed to regard him as a sacred being, and her greatest pleasure in life was to do him service.

He put her letter away also, reflecting that he must manage somehow to make time to answer it. As he did so, he heard Tommy's voice hail him from the compound, and in a moment the boy raced into sight, taking the verandah steps at a hop, skip, and jump.

"Hullo, old chap! Admiring the view eh? What? Got some letters? Have you heard from your brother yet?"

"Not a word for weeks." Monck turned to meet him. "I can't think what has happened to him."

"Can't you though? I can!" Tommy seized him impetuously by the shoulders; he was rocking with laughter. "Oh, Everard, old boy, this beats everything! That brother of yours is coming along the road now. And he's travelled all the way from Khanmulla in a—in a bullock-cart!"

"What?" Monck stared in amazement. "Are you mad?" he inquired.

"No—no. It's true! Go and see for yourself, man! They're just getting here, slow and sure. He must be well stocked with patience. Come on! They're stopping at the gate now."

He dragged his brother-in-law to the steps. Monck went, half-suspicious of a hoax. But he had barely reached the path below when through the rain there came the sound of wheels and heavy jingling.

"Come on!" yelled Tommy. "It's too good to miss!"

But ere they arrived at the gate it was blocked by a massive figure in a streaming black mackintosh, carrying a huge umbrella. "I say," said a soft voice, "what a damn' jolly part of the world to live in!"

"Bernard!" Monck's voice sounded incredulous, yet he passed Tommy at a bound.

"Hullo, my boy, hullo!" Cheerily the newcomer made answer. "How do you open this beastly gate? Oh, I see! Swelled a bit from the rain. I must see to that for you presently. Hullo, Everard! I chanced to find myself in this direction so thought I would look up you and your wife. How are you, my boy?"

An immense hand came forth and grasped Monck's. A merry red face beamed at him from under the great umbrella. Twinkling eyes with red lashes shone with the utmost good-will.

Monck gripped the hand as if he would never let it go. But "My good man, you're mad to come here!" were the only words of welcome he found to utter.

"Think so?" A humorous chuckle accompanied the words. "Well, take me indoors and give me a drink! There are a few traps in the cart outside. Had we better collect 'em first?"

"I'll see to them," volunteered Tommy, whose sense of humour was still somewhat out of control. "Take him in out of the rain, Everard! Send the *khit* along!"

He was gone with the words, and Everard, with his brother's hand pulled through his arm, piloted him up to the bungalow.

In the shelter of the verandah they faced each other, the one brother square and powerful, so broad as to make his height appear insignificant; the other, brown, lean, muscular, a soldier in every line, his dark, resolute face a strange contrast to the ruddy open countenance of the man who was the only near relation he possessed in the world.

"Well,—boy! I believe you've grown." The elder brother, surveyed the younger with his shrewd, twinkling eyes. "By Jove, I'm sure you have! I used not to have to look up to you like this. Is it this devilish climate that does it? And what on earth do you live on? You look a positive skeleton."

"Oh, that's India, yes." Everard brushed aside all personal comment as superfluous. "Come along in and refresh! What particular star have you fallen from? And why in thunder didn't you say you were coming?"

The elder man laughed, slapping him on the shoulder with hearty force. His clean-shaven face was as free from care as a boy's. He looked as if life had dealt kindly with him.

"Ah, I know you," he said. "Wouldn't you have written off post-haste—if you hadn't cabled—and said, 'Wait till the rains are over?' But I had raised my anchor and I didn't mean to wait. So I dispensed with your brotherly counsel, and here I am! You won't find me in the way at all. I'm dashed good at effacing myself."

"My dear good chap," Everard said, "you're about the only man in the world who need never think of doing that."

Bernard's laugh was good to hear. "Who taught you to turn such a pretty compliment? Where is your wife? I want to see her."

"You don't suppose I keep her in this filthy place, do you?" Everard was pouring out a drink as he spoke. "No, no! She has been at Bhulwana in the Hills for the past three months. Now, St. Bernard, is this as you like it?"

The big man took the glass, looking at him with a smile of kindly criticism. "Well, you won't bore each other at that rate, anyhow," he remarked. "Here's to you both! I drink to the greatest thing in life!" He drank deeply and set down the glass. "Look here! You're just off to mess. Don't let me keep you! All I want is a cold bath. And then—if you've got a spare shakedown of any sort—going to bed is mere ritual with me. I can sleep on my head—anywhere."

"You'll sleep in a decent bed," declared Everard. "But you're coming along to mess with me first. Oh yes, you are. Of course you are! There's an hour before us yet though. Hullo, Tommy! Let me introduce you formally to my brother! St. Bernard,—my brother-in-law Tommy Denvers."

Tommy came in through the window and shook hands with much heartiness.

"The *khit* is seeing to everything. Pleased to meet you, sir! Beastly wet for you, I'm afraid, but there's worse things than rain in India. Hope you had a decent voyage."

Bernard laughed in his easy, good-humoured fashion. "Like the niggers, I can make myself comfortable most anywheres. We had rather a foul time after leaving Aden. Ratting in the hold was our main excitement when we weren't sweating at the pumps. Oh no, I didn't come over in one of your majestic liners. I have a sailor's soul."

A flicker of admiration shot through the merriment in Tommy's eyes. "Wish I had," he observed. "But the very thought of the sea turns mine upside down. If you're keen on ratting, there's plenty of sport of that kind to be had here. The brutes hold gymkhanas on the verandah every, night. I sit up with a gun sometimes when Everard is out of the way."

"Yes, he's a peaceful person to live with," remarked Everard. "Have something to eat, St. Bernard!"

"No, no, thanks! My appetite will keep. A cold bath is my most pressing need. Can I have that?"

"Sure!" said Tommy. "You're coming to mess with us of course? Old Reggie Bassett is honouring us with his presence to-night. It will be a historic occasion, eh, Everard?"

He smiled upon the elder brother with obvious pleasure at the prospect. Bernard Monck always met with a welcome wherever he went, and Tommy was prepared to like any one belonging to Everard. It was good too to see Everard with that eager light in his eyes. During the whole of their acquaintance he had never seen him look so young.

Bernard held a somewhat different opinion, however, and as he found himself alone again with his brother he took him by the shoulders, and held him for a closer survey.

"What has India been doing to you, dear fellow?" he said. "You look about as ancient as the Sphinx. Been working like a dray-horse all this time?"

"Perhaps." Everard's smile held something of restraint. "We can't all of us stand still, St. Bernard. Perpetual youth is given only to the favoured few."

"Ah!" The older man's eyes narrowed a little. For a moment there existed a curious, wholly indefinite, resemblance between them. "And you are happy?" he asked abruptly.

Everard's eyes held a certain hardness as he replied, "Provisionally, yes. I haven't got all I want yet—if that's what you mean. But I am on the way to getting it."

Bernard Monck looked at him a moment longer, and let him go. "Are you sure you're wanting the right thing?" he said.

It was not a question that demanded an answer, and Everard made none. He turned aside with a scarcely perceptible lift of the shoulders.

"You haven't told me yet how you come to be here," he said. "Have you given up the Charthurst chaplaincy?"

"It gave me up." Bernard spoke quietly, but there was deep regret in his voice. "A new governor came—a man of curiously rigid ideas. Anyway, I was not parson enough for him. We couldn't assimilate. I tried my hardest, but we couldn't get into touch anywhere. I preached the law of Divine liberty to the captives. And he—good man! preferred to keep them safely locked in the dungeon. I was forced to quit the position. I had no choice."

"What a fool!" observed Everard tersely.

Bernard's ready smile re-appeared. "Thanks, old chap!" he said. "That's just the point of view I wanted you to take. Now I have other schemes on hand. I'll tell you later what they are. I think I'd better have that cold bath next if you're really going to take me along to mess with you. By Jove, how it does rain! Does it ever leave off in these parts?"

"Not very often this time of the year. I'm not going to let you stay here for long." Everard spoke with his customary curt decision. "It's no place for fellows like you. You must go to Bhulwana and join my wife."

"Many thanks!" Bernard made a grotesque gesture of submission. "What sort of woman is your wife, my son? Do you think she will like me?"

Everard turned and smote him on the shoulder. "Of course she will! She will adore you. All women do."

"Oh, not quite!" protested Bernard modestly. "I'm not tall enough to please everyone of the feminine gender. But you think your wife will overlook that?"

"I know," said Everard, with conviction.

His brother laughed with cheery self-satisfaction. "In that case, of course I shall adore her," he said.

CHAPTER VII

FALSE PRETENCES

They were a merry party at mess that night. General Sir Reginald Bassett was a man of the bluff soldierly order who knew how to command respect from his inferiors while at the same time he set them at their ease. There was no pomp and circumstance about him, yet in the whole of the Indian Empire there was not an officer more highly honoured and few who possessed such wide influence as "old Sir Reggie," as irreverent subalterns fondly called him.

The new arrival, Bernard Monck, diffused a genial atmosphere quite unconsciously wherever he went, and he and the old Indian soldier gravitated towards each other almost instinctively. Colonel Mansfield declared later that they made it impossible for him to maintain order, so spontaneous and so infectious was the gaiety that ran round the board. Even Major Ralston's leaden sense of humour was stirred. As Tommy had declared, it promised to be a historic occasion.

When the time for toasts arrived and, after the usual routine, the Colonel proposed the health of their honoured guest of the evening, Sir Reginald interposed with a courteous request that that of their other guest might be coupled with his, and the dual toast was drunk with acclamations.

"I hope I shall have the pleasure of seeing more of you during your stay in India," the General remarked to his fellow-guest when he had returned thanks and quiet was restored. "You have come for the winter, I presume."

Bernard laughed. "Well, no, sir, though I shall hope to see it through. I am not globe-trotting, and times and seasons don't affect me much. My only reason for coming out at all was to see my brother here. You see, we haven't met for a good many years."

The statement was quite casually made, but Major Burton, who was seated next to him, made a sharp movement as if startled. He was a man who prided himself upon his astuteness in discovering discrepancies in even the most truthful stories.

"Didn't you meet last year when he went Home?" he said.

"Last year! No. He wasn't Home last year." Bernard looked full at his questioner, understanding neither his tone nor look.

A sudden silence had fallen near them; it spread like a widening ring upon disturbed waters.

Major Burton spoke, in his voice, a queer, scoffing inflection. "He was absent on Home leave anyway. We all understood—were given to understand—that you had sent him an urgent summons."

"I?" For an instant Bernard Monck stared in genuine bewilderment. Then abruptly he turned to his brother who was listening inscrutably on the other side of the table. "Some mistake here, Everard," he said. "You haven't been Home for seven years or more have you?"

There was dead silence in the room as he put the question—a silence, so full of expectancy as to be almost painful. Across the table the eyes of the two brothers met and held.

Then, "I have not," said Everard Monck with quiet finality.

There was no note of challenge in his voice, neither was there any dismay. But the effect of his words upon every man present was as if he had flung a bomb into their midst. The silence endured tensely for a couple of seconds, then there came a hard breath and a general movement as if by common consent the company desired to put an end to a situation, that had become unendurable.

Bertie Oakes dug Tommy in the ribs, but Tommy was as white as death and did not even feel it. Something had happened, something that made him feel giddy and very sick. That significant silence was to him nothing short of tragedy. He had seen his hero topple at a touch from the high pinnacle on which he had placed him, and he felt as if the very ground under his feet had become a quicksand.

As in a maze of shifting impressions he heard Sir Reginald valiantly covering the sudden breach, talking inconsequently in a language which Tommy could not even recognize as his own. And the Colonel was seconding his efforts, while Major Burton sat frowning at the end of his cigar as if he were trying to focus his sight upon something infinitesimal and elusive. No one looked at Monck, in fact everyone seemed studiously to avoid doing so. Even his brother seemed lost in meditation with his eyes fixed immovably upon a lamp that hung from the ceiling and swayed ponderously in the draught.

Then at last there came a definite move, and Bertie Oakes poked him again. "Are you moonstruck?" he said.

Tommy got up with the rest, still feeling sick and oddly unsure of himself. He pushed his brother-subaltern aside as if he had been an inanimate object, and somehow, groping, found his way to the door and out to the entrance for a breath of air.

It was raining heavily and the odour of a thousand intangible things hung in the atmosphere. For a space he leaned in the doorway undisturbed; then, heralded by the smell of a rank cigar, Ralston lounged up and joined him.

"Are you looking for a safe corner to catch fever in?" he inquired phlegmatically, after a pause.

Tommy made a restless movement, but spoke no word.

Ralston smoked for a space in silence. From behind them there came the rattle of billiard-balls and careless clatter of voices. Before them was a pall-like darkness and the endless patter of rain.

Suddenly Ralston spoke. "Make no mistake!" he said. "There's a reason for everything."

The words sounded irrelevant; they even had a sententious ring. Yet Tommy turned towards him with an impulsive gesture of gratitude.

"Of course!" he said.

Ralston relapsed into a ruminating silence. A full minute elapsed before he spoke again. Then: "You don't like taking advice I know," he said, in his stolid, somewhat gruff fashion. "But if you're wise, you'll swallow a stiff dose of quinine before you turn in. Good-night!"

He swung round on his heel and walked away. Tommy knew that he had gone for his nightly game of chess with Major Burton and would not exchange so much as another half-dozen words with any one during the rest of the evening.

He himself remained for a while where he was, recovering his balance; then at length donned his mackintosh, and tramped forth into the night. Ralston was right. Doubtless there was a reason. He would stake his life on Everard's honour whatever the odds.

In a quiet corner of the ante-room sat Everard Monck, deeply immersed in a paper. Near him a group of bridge-players played an almost silent game. Sir Reginald and his brother had followed the youngsters to the billiard-room, the Colonel had accompanied them, but after a decent interval he left the guests to themselves and returned to the ante-room.

He passed the bridge-players by and came to Monck. The latter glanced up at his approach.

"Are you looking for me, sir?"

"If you can spare me a moment, I shall be glad," the Colonel said formally.

Monck rose instantly. His dark face had a granite-like look as he followed his superior officer from the room. The bridge-players watched him with furtive attention, and resumed their game in silence.

The Colonel led the way back to the mess-room, now deserted. "I shall not keep you long," he said, as Monck shut the door and moved forward. "But I must ask of you an explanation of the fact which came to light this evening." He paused a moment, but Monck spoke no word, and he continued with growing coldness. "Rather more than a year ago you refused a Government mission, for which your services were urgently required, on the plea of pressing business at Home. You had Home leave—at a time when we were under-officered—to carry this business through. Now, Captain Monck, will you be good enough to tell me how and where you spent that leave? Whatever you say I shall treat as confidential."

He still spoke formally, but the usual rather pompous kindliness of his face had given place to a look of acute anxiety.

Monck stood at the table, gazing straight before him. "You have a perfect right to ask, sir," he said, after a moment. "But I am not in a position to answer."

"In other words, you refuse to answer?" The Colonel's voice had a rasp in it, but that also held more of anxiety than anger.

Monck turned and directly faced him. "I am compelled to refuse," he said.

There was a brief silence. Colonel Mansfield was looking at him as if he would read him through and through. But no stone mask could have been more impenetrable than Monck's face as he stood stiffly waiting.

When the Colonel spoke again it was wholly without emotion. His tones fell cold and measured. "You obtained that leave upon false pretences? You had no urgent business?"

Monck answered him with machine-like accuracy. "Yes, sir, I deceived you. But my business was urgent nevertheless. That is my only excuse."

"Was it in connection with some Secret Service requirement?" The Colonel's tone was strictly judicial now; he had banished all feeling from face and manner.

And again, like a machine, Monck made his curt reply. "No, sir."

"There was nothing official about it?"

"Nothing."

"I am to conclude then—" again the rasp was in the Colonel's voice, but it sounded harsher now—"that the business upon which you absented yourself was strictly private and personal?"

"It was, sir."

The commanding officer's brows contracted heavily. "Am I also to conclude that it was something of a dishonourable nature?" he asked.

Monck made a scarcely perceptible movement. It was as if the point had somehow pierced his armour. But he covered it instantly. "Your deductions are of your own making, sir," he said.

"I see." The Colonel's tone was openly harsh. "You are ashamed to tell me the truth. Well, Captain Monck, I cannot compel you to do so. But it would have been better for your own sake if you had taken up a less reticent attitude. Of course I realize that there are certain shameful occasions regarding which any man must keep silence, but I had not thought you capable of having a secret of that description to guard. I think it very doubtful if General Bassett will now require your services upon his staff."

He paused. Monck's hands were clenched and rigid, but he spoke no word, and gave no other sign of emotion.

"You have nothing to say to me?" the Colonel asked, and for a moment the official air was gone. He spoke as one man to another and almost with entreaty.

But, "Nothing, sir," said Monck firmly, and the moment passed.

The Colonel turned aside. "Very well," he said briefly.

Monck swung round and opened the door for him, standing as stiffly as a soldier on parade.

He went out without a backward glance.

CHAPTER VIII

THE WRATH OF THE GODS

It was nearly an hour later that Everard Monck and his brother left the mess together and walked back through the dripping darkness to the bungalow on the hill overlooking the river. The rush of the swollen stream became audible as they drew near. The sound of it was inexpressibly wild and desolate.

"It's an interesting country," remarked Bernard, breaking a silence. "I don't wonder she has got hold of you, my son. What does your wife think of it? Is she too caught in the toils?"

Not by word or look had he made the smallest reference to the episode at the mess-table. It was as if he alone of those present had wholly missed its significance.

Everard answered him quietly, without much emphasis. "I believe my wife hates it from beginning to end. Perhaps it is not surprising. She has been through a good deal since she came out. And I am afraid there is a good deal before her still."

Bernard's big hand closed upon his arm. "Poor old chap!" lie said. "You Indian fellows don't have any such time of it, or your women folk either. How long is she a fixture at Bhulwana?"

"The baby is expected in two months' time." Everard spoke without emotion, his voice sounded almost cold. "After that, I don't know what will happen. Nothing is settled. Tell me your plans now! No, wait! Let's get in out of this damned rain first!"

They entered the bungalow and sat down for another smoke in the drawing-room.

Down by the river a native instrument thrummed monotonously, like the whirring of a giant mosquito in the darkness. Everard turned with a slight gesture of impatience and closed the window.

He established his brother in a long chair with a drink at his elbow, and sat down himself without any pretence at taking his ease.

"You don't look particularly comfortable," Bernard observed.

"Don't mind me!" he made curt response. "I've got a touch of fever to-night. It's nothing. I shall be all right in the morning."

"Sure?" Bernard's eyes suddenly ceased to be quizzical; they looked at him straight and hard.

Everard met the look, faintly smiling. "I don't lie about—unimportant things," he remarked cynically. "Light up, man, and fire away!"

He struck a match for his brother's pipe and kindled his own cigarette thereat.

There fell a brief silence. Bernard did not look wholly satisfied. But after a few seconds he seemed to dismiss the matter and began to talk of himself.

"You want to know my plans, old chap. Well, as far as I know 'em myself, you are quite welcome. With your permission, I propose, for the present, to stay where I am."

"I shouldn't if I were you." Everard spoke with brief decision. "You'd be far better off at Bhulwana till the end of the rains."

Bernard puffed forth a great cloud of smoke and stared at the ceiling. "That is as may be, dear fellow," he said, after a moment. "But I think—if you'll put up with me—I'll stay here for the present all the same."

He spoke in that peculiarly gentle voice of his that yet held considerable resolution. Everard made no attempt to combat the decision. Perhaps he realized the uselessness of such a proceeding.

"Stay by all means!" he said, "but what's the idea?"

Bernard took his pipe from his mouth. "I have a big fight before me, Everard boy," he said, "a fight against the sort of prejudice that kicked me out of the Charthurst job. It's got to be fought with the pen—since I am no street corner ranter. I have the solid outlines of the campaign in my head, and I have come out here to get right away from things and work it out."

"Going to reform creation?" suggested Everard, with his grim smile.

Bernard shook his head, smiling in answer as though the cynicism had not reached him. "No, that's not my job. I am only a man under authority—like yourself. I don't see the result at all. I only see the work, and with God's help, that will be exactly what He intended it should be when He gave it to me to do."

"Lucky man!" said Everard briefly.

"Ah! I didn't think myself lucky when I had to give up the Charthurst chaplaincy." Bernard spoke through a haze of smoke. "I'm afraid I kicked a bit at first—which was a short-sighted thing to do, I admit. But I had got to look on it as my life-work, and I loved it. It held such opportunities." He broke off with a sharp sigh. "I shall be at it again if I go on. Can't you give me something pleasanter to think about? Haven't you got a photograph of your wife to show me?"

Everard got up. "Yes, I have. But it doesn't do her justice." He took a letter-case from his pocket and opened it. A moment he stood bent over the portrait he withdrew from it, then turned and handed it to his brother.

Bernard studied it in silence. It was an unmounted amateur photograph of Stella standing on the creeper-grown verandah of the Green Bungalow. She was smiling, but her eyes were faintly sad, as though shadowed by the memory of some past pain.

For many seconds Bernard gazed upon the pictured face. Finally he spoke.

"Your wife must be a very beautiful woman."

"Yes," said Everard quietly.

He spoke gravely. His brother's eyes travelled upwards swiftly. "That was not what you married her for, eh?"

Everard stooped and took the portrait from him. "Well, no—not entirely," he said.

Bernard smiled a little. "You haven't told me much about her, you know. How long have you been acquainted?"

"Nearly two years. I think I mentioned in my letter that she was the widow of a comrade?"

"Yes, I remember. But you were rather vague about it. What happened to him? Didn't he meet with a violent death?"

There was a pause. Everard was still standing with his eyes fixed upon the photograph. His face was stern.

"What was it?" questioned Bernard. "Didn't he fall over a precipice?"

"Yes," abruptly the younger man made answer. "It happened in Kashmir when they were on their honeymoon."

"Ah! Poor girl! She must have suffered. What was his name? Was he a pal of yours?"

"More or less." Everard's voice rang hard. "His name was Dacre."

"Oh, to be sure. The man I wrote to you about just before poor Madelina Belleville died in prison. Her husband's name was Dacre. He was in the Army too, and she thought he was in India. But it's not a very uncommon name." Bernard spoke thoughtfully. "You said he was no relation."

"I said to the best of my belief he was not." Everard turned suddenly and sat down. "People are not keen, you know, on owning to shady relations. He was no exception to the rule. But if the woman died, it's of no great consequence now to any one. When did she die?"

Bernard took a long pull at his pipe. His brows were slightly drawn. "She died suddenly, poor soul. Did I never tell you? It must have been immediately after I wrote that letter to you. It was. I remember now. It was the very day after.... She died on the twenty-first of March—the first day of spring. Poor girl! She had so longed for the spring. Her time would have been up in May."

Something in the silence that followed his words made him turn his head to look at his brother. Everard was sitting perfectly rigid in his chair staring at the ground between his feet as if he saw a serpent writhing there. But before another word could be spoken, he got up abruptly, with a gesture as of shaking off the loathsome thing, and went to the window. He flung it wide, and stood in the opening, breathing hard as a man half-suffocated.

"Anything wrong, old chap?" questioned Bernard.

He answered him without turning. "No; it's only my infernal head. I think I'll turn in directly. It's a fiendish night."

The rain was falling in torrents, and a long roll of thunder sounded from afar. The clatter of the great drops on the roof of the verandah filled the room, making all further conversation impossible. It was like a tattoo of devils.

"A damn' pleasant country this!" murmured the man in the chair.

The man at the window said no word. He was gasping a little, his face to the howling night.

For a space Bernard lay and watched him. Then at last, somewhat ponderously he arose.

Everard could not have heard his approach, but he was aware of it before he reached him. He turned swiftly round, pulling the window closed behind him.

They stood facing each other, and there was something tense in the atmosphere, something that was oddly suggestive of mental conflict. The devils' tattoo on the roof had sunk to a mere undersong, a fitting accompaniment as it were to the electricity in the room.

Bernard spoke at length, slowly, deliberately, but not unkindly. "Why should you take the trouble to—fence with me?" he said. "Is it worth it, do you think?"

Everard's face was set and grey like a stone mask. He did not speak for a moment; then curtly, noncommittally, "What do you mean?" he said.

"I mean," very steadily Bernard made reply, "that the scoundrel Dacre, who married Madelina Belleville and then deserted her, left her to go to the dogs, and your brother-officer who was killed in the mountains on his honeymoon, were one and the same man. And you knew it."

"Well?" The words seemed to come from closed lips. There was something terrible in the utter quietness of its utterance.

Bernard searched his face as a man might search the walls of an apparently impregnable fortress for some vulnerable spot. "Ah, I see," he said, after a moment. "You must have believed Madelina to be still alive when Dacre married. What was the date of his marriage?"

"The twenty-fifth of March." Again the grim lips spoke without seeming to move.

A gleam of relief crossed his brother's face. "In that case no one is any the worse. I'm sorry you've carried that bugbear about with you for so long. What an infernal hound the fellow was!"

"Yes," assented Everard.

He moved to the table and poured himself out a drink.

His brother still watched him. "One might almost say his death was providential," he observed. "Of course—your wife—never knew of this?"

"No." Everard lifted the glass to his lips with a perfectly steady hand and drank. "She never will know," he said, as he set it down.

"Certainly not. You can trust me never to tell her." Bernard moved to his side, and laid a kindly hand on his shoulder. "You know you can trust me, old fellow?"

Everard did not look at him. "Yes, I know," he said.

His brother's hand pressed upon him a little. "Since they are both gone," he said, "there is nothing more to be said on the subject. But, oh, man, stick to the truth, whatever else you let go of! You never lied to me before."

His tone was very earnest. It held urgent entreaty. Everard turned and met his eyes. His dark face was wholly emotionless. "I am sorry, St. Bernard," he said.

Bernard's kindly smile wrinkled his eyes. He grasped and held the younger man's hand. "All right, boy. I'm going to forget it," he said. "Now what about turning in?"

They parted for the night immediately after, the one to sleep as serenely as a child almost as soon as he lay down, the other to pace to and fro, to and fro, for hours, grappling—and grappling in vain—with the sternest adversary he had ever had to encounter.

For upon Everard Monck that night the wrath of the gods had descended, and against it, even his grim fortitude was powerless to make a stand. He was beaten before he could begin to defend himself, beaten and flung aside as contemptible. Only one thing remained to be fought for, and that one thing he swore to guard with the last ounce of his strength, even at the cost of life itself.

All through that night of bitter turmoil he came back again and again to that, the only solid foothold left him in the shifting desert-sand. So long as his heart should beat he would defend that one precious possession that yet remained,—the honour of the woman who loved him and whom he loved as only the few know how to love.

PART IV

CHAPTER I

DEVILS' DICE

"It's a pity," said Sir Reginald.

"It's a damnable pity, sir," Colonel Mansfield spoke with blunt emphasis. "I have trusted the fellow almost as I would have trusted myself. And he has let me down."

The two were old friends. The tie of India bound them both. Though their ways lay apart and they met but seldom, the same spirit was in them and they were as comrades. They sat together in the Colonel's office that looked over the streaming parade-ground. A gleam of morning sunshine had pierced the clouds, and the smoke of the Plains went up like a furnace.

"I shouldn't be too sure of that," said Sir Reginald, after a thoughtful moment. "Things are not always what they seem. One is apt to repent of a hasty judgment."

"I know." The Colonel spoke with his eyes upon the rising cloud of steam outside. "But this fellow has always had my confidence, and I can't get over what he himself admits to have been a piece of double-dealing. I suppose it was a sudden temptation, but he had always been so straight with me; at least I had always imagined him so. He has rendered some invaluable services too."

"That is partly why I say, don't be too hasty," said Sir Reginald. "We can't afford—India can't afford—to scrap a single really useful man."

"Neither can she afford to make use of rotters," rejoined the Colonel.

Sir Reginald smiled a little. "I am not so sure of that, Mansfield. Even the rotters have their uses. But I am quite convinced in my own mind that this man is very far from being one. I feel inclined to go slow for a time and give him a chance to retrieve himself. Perhaps it may sound soft to you, but I have never floored a man at his first slip. And this man has a clean record behind him. Let it stand him in good stead now!"

"It will take me some time to forget it," the Colonel said. "I can forgive almost anything except deception. And that I loathe."

"It isn't pleasant to be cheated, certainly," Sir Reginald agreed. "When did this happen? Was he married at the time?"

"No." The Colonel meditated for a few seconds "He only married last spring. This was considerably more than a year ago. It must have been the spring of the preceding year. Yes, by Jove, it was! It was just at the time of poor Dacre's marriage. Dacre, you know, married young Denvers' sister—the girl who is now Monck's wife. Dacre was killed on his honeymoon only a fortnight after the wedding. You remember that, Burton?" He turned abruptly to the Major who had entered while he was speaking.

Burton came to a stand at the table. His eyes were set very close together, and they glittered meanly as he made reply. "I remember it very well indeed. His death coincided with this mysterious leave of Monck's, and also with the unexpected absence of our man Rustam Karin just at a moment when Barnes particularly needed him."

"Who is Rustam Karin?" asked Sir Reginald.

"A police agent. A clever man. I may say, an invaluable man." Colonel Mansfield was looking hard at the Major's ferret-like face as he made reply. "No one likes the fellow. He is suspected of being a leper. But he is clever. He is undoubtedly clever. I remember his absence. It was at the time of that mission to Khanmulla, the mission I wanted Monck to take in hand."

"Exactly." Major Burton rapped out the word with a sound like the cracking of a nut. "We—or rather Barnes—tried to pump Hafiz about it, but he was a mass of ignorance and lies. I believe the old brute turned up again before Monck's return, but he wasn't visible till afterwards. He and Monck have always been thick as thieves—thick as thieves." He paused, looking at Sir Reginald. "A very fishy transaction, sir," he observed.

Sir Reginald's eyes met his. "Are you," he said calmly, "trying to establish any connection between the death of Dacre and the absence from Kurrumpore of this man Rustam Karin?"

"Not only Rustam Karin, sir," responded the Major sharply.

"Ah! Quite so. How did Dacre die?" Sir Reginald still spoke quietly, judicially. There was nothing encouraging in his aspect.

Burton hesitated momentarily, as if some inner warning prompted him to go warily.

"That was what no one knew for certain, sir. He disappeared one night. The story went that he fell over a precipice. Some old native beggar told the tale. No one knows who the man was."

"But you have your eye upon Rustam Karin?" suggested Sir Reginald.

Burton hesitated again. "One doesn't trust these fellows, sir," he said.

"True!" Sir Reginald's voice sounded very dry. "Perhaps it is a mistake to trust any one too far. This is all the evidence you can muster?"

"Yes, sir." Burton looked suddenly embarrassed. "Of course it is not evidence, strictly speaking," he said. "But when mysteries coincide, one is apt to link them together. And the death of Captain Dacre always seemed to me highly mysterious."

"The death of Captain Ermsted was no less so," put in the Colonel abruptly. "Have you any theories on that subject also?"

Burton smiled, showing his teeth. "I always have theories," he said.

Sir Reginald made a slight movement of impatience. "I think this is beside the point," he said. "Captain Ermsted's murderer will probably be traced one day."

"Probably, sir," agreed Major Burton, "since I hear unofficially that Captain Monck has the matter in hand. Ah!"

He broke off short as, with a brief knock at the door, Monck himself made an abrupt appearance.

He came forward as if he saw no one in the room but the Colonel. His face wore a curiously stony look, but his eyes burned with a fierce intensity. He spoke without apology or preliminary of any sort.

"I have just had a message, sir, from Bhulwana," he said. "I wish to apply for immediate leave."

The Colonel looked at him in surprise. "A message, Captain Monck?"

"From my wife," Monck said, and drew a hard breath between his teeth. His hands were clenched hard at his sides. "I've got to go!" he said. "I've got to go!"

There was a moment's silence. Then: "May I see the message?" said the Colonel.

Monck's eyelids flickered sharply, as if he had been struck across the face. He thrust out his right hand and flung a crumpled paper upon the table. "There, sir!" he said harshly.

There was violence in the action, but it did not hold insolence. Sir Reginald leaning forward, was watching him intently. As the Colonel, with a word of excuse to himself, took up and opened the paper, he rose quietly and went up to Monck. Thin, wiry, grizzled, he stopped beside him.

Major Burton retired behind the Colonel, realizing himself as unnecessary but too curious to withdraw altogether.

In the pause that followed, a tense silence reigned. Monck was swaying as he stood. His eyes had the strained and awful look of a man with his soul in torment. After that one hard breath, he had not breathed at all.

The Colonel looked up. "Go, certainly!" he said, and there was a touch of the old kindliness in his voice that he tried to restrain. "And as soon as possible! I hope you will find a more reassuring state of affairs when you get there."

He held out the telegram. Monck made a movement to take it, but as he did so the tension in which he gripped himself suddenly gave way. He blundered forward, his hands upon the table.

"She will die," he said, and there was utter despair in his tone. "She is probably dead already."

Sir Reginald took him by the arm. His face held nought but kindliness, which he made no attempt to hide. "Sit down a minute!" he said. "Here's a chair! Just a minute. Sit down and get your wind! What is this message? May I read it?"

He murmured something to Major Burton who turned sharply and went out. Monck sank heavily into the chair and leaned upon the table, his head in his hands. He was shaking all over, as if seized with an ague.

Sir Reginald read the message, standing beside him, a hand upon his shoulder. "Stella desperately ill. Come. Ralston," were the words it contained.

He laid the paper upon the table, and looked across at the Colonel. The latter nodded slightly, almost imperceptibly.

Monck spoke without moving. "She is dead," he said. "My God! She is dead!" And then, under his breath, "After all,—counting me out—it's best—it's best. I couldn't ask for anything better at this devils' game. Someone's got to die."

He checked himself abruptly, and again a terrible shivering seized him.

Sir Reginald bent over him. "Pull yourself together, man! You'll need all your strength. Please God, she'll be better when you get there!"

Monck raised himself with a slow, blind movement. "Did you ever dice with the devil?" he said. "Stake your honour—stake all you'd got—to save a woman from hell? And then lose—my God—lose all—even even—the woman?" Again he checked himself. "I'm talking like a damned fool. Stop me, someone! I've come through hell-fire and it's scorched away my senses. I never thought I should blab like this."

"It's all right," Sir Reginald said, and in his voice was steady reassurance. "You're with friends. Get a hold on yourself! Don't say any more!"

"Ah!" Monck drew a deep breath and seemed to come to himself. He lifted a face of appalling whiteness and looked at Sir Reginald. "You're very good, sir," he said. "I was knocked out for the moment. I'm all right now."

He made as if he would rise, but Sir Reginald checked him. "Wait a moment longer! Major Burton will be back directly."

"Major Burton?" questioned Monck.

"I sent him for some brandy to steady your nerves," Sir Reginald said.

"You're very good," Monck said again. He leaned his head on his hand and sat silent.

Major Burton returned with Tommy hovering anxiously behind him. The boy hesitated a little upon entering, but the Colonel called him in.

"You had better see the message too," he said. "Your sister is ill. Captain Monck is going to her."

Tommy read the message with one eye upon Monck, who drank the brandy Burton brought and in a moment stood up.

"I am sorry to have made such a fool of myself, sir," he said to Sir Reginald, with a faint, grim smile. "I shall not forget your kindness, though I hope you will forget my idiocy."

Sir Reginald looked at him closely for a second. His grizzled face was stern. Yet he held out his hand.

"Good-bye, Captain Monck!" was all he said.

Monck stiffened. The smile passed from his face, leaving it inscrutable, granite-like in its composure. It was as the donning of a mask.

"Good-bye, sir!" he said briefly, as he shook hands.

Tommy moved to his side impulsively. He did not utter a word, but as they went out his hand was pushed through Monck's arm in the old confidential fashion, the old eager affection was shining in his eyes.

"He has one staunch friend, anyhow," Sir Reginald muttered to the Colonel.

"Yes," the Colonel answered gravely. "He has done a good deal for young Denvers. It's the boy's turn to make good now. There isn't much left him besides."

"Poor devil!" said Sir Reginald.

CHAPTER II

OUT OF THE DARKNESS

"You said Everard was coming. Why doesn't he come? It's very dark—it's very dark! Can he have missed the way?"

Feebly, haltingly, the words seemed to wander through the room, breaking a great silence as it were with immense effort. Mrs. Ralston bent over the bed and whispered hushingly that it was all right, all right, Everard would be there soon.

"But why does he take so long?" murmured Stella. "It's getting darker every minute. And it's so steep. I keep slipping—slipping. I know he would hold me up." And then after a moment, "Oh, Mary, am I dying? I believe I am. But—he—wouldn't let me die."

Mrs. Ralston's hand closed comfortingly upon hers. "You're quite safe, dearest," she said. "Don't be afraid!"

"But it's so dreadfully dark," Stella said restlessly. "I shouldn't mind if I could see the way. But I can't—I can't."

"Be patient, darling!" said Mrs. Ralston very tenderly. "It will be lighter presently."

It was growing very late. She herself was listening for every sound, hoping against hope to hear the firm quiet step of the man who alone could still her charge's growing distress.

"It would be so dreadful to miss him," moaned Stella. "I have waited so long. Mary, why don't they light a lamp?"

A shaded lamp was burning on the table by the bed. Mrs. Ralston turned and lifted the shade. But Stella shook her head with a weary discontent.

"That doesn't help. It's in the desert that I mean—so that he shan't miss me when he comes."

"He cannot miss you, darling," Mrs. Ralston assured her; but in her own heart she doubted. For the doctor had told her that he did not think she would live through the night.

Again she strained her ears to listen. She had certainly heard a sound outside the door; but it might be only Peter who, she knew, crouched there, alert for any service.

It was Peter; but it was not Peter only, for even as she listened, the handle of the door turned softly and someone entered. She looked up eagerly and saw the doctor.

He was a thin, grey man for whom she entertained privately a certain feeling of contempt. She was so sure her own husband would have somehow managed the case better. He came to the bedside, and looked at Stella, looked closely; then turned to her friend watching beside her.

"I wonder if it would disturb her to see her husband for a moment," he said.

Mrs. Ralston suppressed a start with difficulty. "Is he here?" she whispered.

"Just arrived," he murmured back, and turned again to look at Stella who lay motionless with closed eyes, scarcely seeming to breathe.

Mrs. Ralston's whisper smote the silence, and it was the doctor's turn to start. "Send him in at once!" she said.

So insistent was her command that he stood up as if he had been prodded into action. Mrs. Ralston was on her feet. She waved an urgent hand.

"Go and get him!" she ordered almost fiercely. "It's the only chance left. Go and fetch him!"

He looked at her doubtfully for a second, then, impelled by an authority that overrode every scruple, he turned in silence and tiptoed from the room.

Mrs. Ralston's eyes followed him with scorn. How was it some doctors managed—notwithstanding all their experience—to be such hopeless idiots?

The soft opening of the door again a few seconds later banished her irritation. She turned with shining welcome in her look, and met Monck with outstretched hands.

"You're in time," she said.

He gripped her hands hard, but he scarcely looked at her. In a moment he was bending over the bed.

"Stella girl! Stella!" he said.

"Everard!" The weak voice thrilled like a loosened harp-string, and the man's dark face flashed into sudden passionate tenderness.

He went down upon his knees beside the bed and gathered her to his breast. She clung to him feebly, her lips turned to his.

"My darling—oh, my darling—have you come at last?" she whispered. "Hold me—hold me!—Don't let me die!"

He held her closer and closer to his heart, so that its fierce throbbing beat against her own. "You shan't die," he said, "you can't die—with me here."

She laughed a little, sobbingly. "You saved Tommy—twice over. I knew you would save me—if you came in time. Oh, darling, how I have wanted you! It's been—so dark and terrible."

"But you held on!" Monck's voice was very low; it came with a manifest effort. He was holding her to his breast as if he could never let her go.

"Yes, I held on. I knew—I knew—how—how it would hurt you—to find me gone." Her trembling hands moved fondly about his head and finally clasped his neck. "It's all right now," she said, with a sigh of deep content.

Monck's lips pressed hers again and again, and Mrs. Ralston went away to the window to hide her tears. "Please, God, don't separate them now!" she whispered.

It was many minutes later that Stella spoke again, softly, into Monck's ear. "Everard—darling husband—the baby—our baby—don't you—wouldn't you like to see it?"

"The baby!" He spoke as if startled. Somehow he had concluded from the first that the baby would be dead, and the rapture of finding her still living had driven the thought of everything else from his mind.

"Don't move!" whispered Stella, clasping him closer. "Ask them to bring it!"

He spoke over his shoulder to Mrs. Ralston, his voice oddly cold, almost reluctant. "Would you be good enough to bring the baby in?"

She turned at once, smiling upon him shakily. But his dark face remained wholly inscrutable, wholly unresponsive. There was something about him that smote her with a curious chill, but she told herself that he was worn out with hard travel and anxiety as she went from the room to comply with his curt request.

Lying against his shoulder, Stella whispered a few halting sentences. "It—happened so suddenly. The Rajah drives so fiercely—like a man possessed. And the car skidded on the hill. Netta Ermsted was in it, and she screamed, and I—I was terrified because Tessa—Tessa—brave mite—sprang in front of me. I don't know what she thought she could do. I think partly she was angry, and lost her head. And she meant—to help—to protect me—somehow. After that, I fainted—and when I came round, they had brought me back here. That was ever so long ago." She shuddered convulsively. "I've been through a lot since then."

Monck's teeth closed upon his lip. He had not suspected an accident.

Tremulously Stella went on. "It—was so much too soon. I was—dreadfully—afraid for the poor wee baby. But the doctor said—the doctor said—it was all right—only small. And oh, Everard—" her voice thrilled again with a quivering joy—"it is a boy. I so wanted—a son—for you."

"God bless you!" he said almost inarticulately, and kissed her white face again burningly, even with violence. She smiled at his intensity, though it made her gasp. "I know—I know—you will be great," she said. "And—your son—must carry on your greatness. He shall learn to love—the Empire—as you do. We will teach him together—you and I."

"Ah!" Monck said, and drew the hard breath of a man struggling in deep waters.

Mrs. Ralston returned softly with a white bundle in her arms, and Stella's hold relaxed. Her heavy lids brightened eagerly.

"My dear," Mrs. Ralston said, "the doctor has commanded me to turn your husband out immediately. He must just peep at the darling baby and go."

"Tell him to go himself—to blazes!" said Monck forcibly, and then reached up, still curiously grim to Mrs. Ralston's observing eyes, and, without rising from his knees, took his child into his arms.

He laid it against the mother's breast, and tenderly uncovered the tiny, sleeping face.

"Oh, Everard!" she said.

And Mrs. Ralston turned away with a little sob. She did not believe any longer that Stella would die. The sweet, thrilling happiness of her voice seemed somehow to drive out the very thought of death. She had never in her life seen any one so supremely happy. But yet—though she was reassured—there was something else in the atmosphere that disturbed her. She could not have said wherefore, but she was sorry for Monck—deeply, poignantly sorry. She was certain, with that inner conviction that needs no outer evidence, that it was more than weariness and the strain of anxiety that had drawn those deep lines about his eyes and mouth. He looked to her like a man who had been smitten down in the pride of his strength, and who knew his case to be hopeless.

As for Monck, he went through his ordeal unflinching, suffering as few men are called upon to suffer and hiding it away without a quiver. All through the hours of his journeying, he had been prepared to face—he had actually expected—- the worst. All through those hours he had battled to reach her indeed, straining every faculty, resisting with almost superhuman strength every obstacle that arose to bar his progress. But he had not thought to find her, and throughout the long-drawn-out effort he had carried in his locked heart the knowledge that if when he came at last to her bedside he found her—this woman whom he loved with all the force of his silent soul—white and cold in death, it would be the best fate that he could wish her, the best thing that could possibly happen, so far as mortal sight could judge, for either.

But so it had not been. At the very Gate of Death she had waited for his coming, and now he knew in his heart that she would return. The love between them was drawing her, and the man's heart in him battled fiercely to rejoice even while wrung with the anguish of that secret knowledge.

He hardly knew how he went through those moments which to her were such pure ecstasy. The blood was beating wildly in his brain, and he thought of that devils' tattoo on the roof at Udalkhand when first that dreadful knowledge had sprung upon him like an evil thing out of the night. But he held himself in an iron grip; he forced his mind to clearness. Even to himself he would not seem to be aware of the agony that tore him.

They whispered together for a while over the baby's head, but he never remembered afterwards what passed or how long he knelt there. Only at last there came a silence that drifted on and on and he knew that Stella was asleep.

Later Mrs. Ralston stooped over him and took the baby away, and he laid his head down upon the pillow by Stella's and wished with all his soul that the Gate before which her feet had halted would open to them both.

Someone came up behind them, and stood for a few seconds looking down upon them. He was aware of a presence, but he knelt on without stirring—as one kneeling entranced in a sacred place. Then two hands he knew grasped him firmly by the shoulders, raising him; he looked up half-dazed into his brother's face.

"Come along, old chap!" Bernard whispered. "You mustn't faint in here."

The words roused him. The old sardonic smile showed for a moment about his lips. He faint! But he had not slept for two nights. That would account for that curious top-heavy feeling that possessed him. He suffered Bernard to help him up,—good old Bernard who had watched over him like a mother refusing flatly to remain behind, waiting upon him hand and foot at every turn.

"You come into the next room!" he whispered. "You shall be called immediately if she wakes and wants you. But you'll crumple up if you don't rest."

There was truth in the words. Everard realized it as he went from the room, leaning blindly upon the stout, supporting arm. His weariness hung upon him like an overwhelming weight.

He submitted himself almost mechanically to his brother's ordering, feeling as if he moved in a dream. As in a dream also he saw Peter at the door move, noiseless as a shadow, to assist him on the other side. And he tried to laugh off his weakness, but the laugh stuck in his throat.

Then he found himself in a chair drinking a stiff mixture of brandy and water, again at Bernard's behest, while Bernard stood over him, watching with the utmost kindness in his blue eyes.

The spirit steadied him. He came to himself, sat up slowly, and motioned Peter from the room. He was his own master again. He turned to his brother with a smile.

"You're a friend in need, St. Bernard. That dose has done me good. Open the window, old fellow, will you? Let's have some air!"

Bernard flung the window wide, and the warm wet air blew in laden with the fragrance of the teeming earth. Everard turned his face to it, drawing in great breaths. The dawn was breaking.

"She is better?" Bernard questioned, after a few moments.

"Yes. I believe she has turned the corner." Everard spoke without turning. His eyes were fixed.

"Thank God!" said Bernard gently.

Everard's right hand made a curious movement. It was as if it closed upon a weapon. "You can do that part," he said, and he spoke with constraint. "But you'd do it in any case. It's a way you've got. See the light breaking over there? It's like a sword—turning all ways." He rose with an obvious effort and passed his hand across his eyes. "What of you, man?" he said. "Have they been looking after you?"

"Oh, never mind me!" Bernard rejoined. "Have something to eat and turn in! Yes, of course I'll join you with pleasure." He clapped an affectionate hand upon his brother's shoulder. "It's a boy, I'm told. Old fellow, I congratulate you—may he be a blessing to you all your lives! I'll drink his health if it isn't too early."

Everard broke into a brief, discordant laugh. "You'd better go to church, St. Bernard," he said, "and pray for us!"

He swung away abruptly with the words and crossed the room. The crystal-clear rays of the new day smote full upon him as he moved, and Bernard saw for the first time that his hair was streaked with grey.

CHAPTER III

PRINCESS BLUEBELL

To Bernard, sprawling at his ease with a pipe on the verandah some hours later, the appearance of a small girl with bare brown legs and a very abbreviated white muslin frock, hugging an unwilling mongoose to her breast, came as a surprise; for she entered as one who belonged to the establishment.

"Who are you, please?" she demanded imperiously, halting before him while she disentangled the unfortunate Scooter's rebellious legs from her hair.

Bernard sat up and removed his pipe. Meeting eyes of the darkest, intensest blue that he had ever seen, he gave her appropriate greeting,

"Good morning, Princess Bluebell! I am a humble, homeless beggar, at present living upon the charity of my brother, Captain Monck."

She came a step nearer. "Why do you call me that? You are not Captain Monck's brother really, are you?"

He spread out his hands with a deprecating gesture. "I never contradict royal ladies, Princess, but I have always been taught to believe so."

"Why do you call me Princess?" she asked, halting between suspicion and gratification.

"Because it is quite evident that you are one. There is a—bossiness about you that proclaims the fact aloud." Bernard smiled upon her—the smile of open goodfellowship. "Beggars always know princesses when they see them," he said.

She scrutinized him severely for a moment or two, then suddenly melted into a gleaming, responsive smile that illuminated her little pale face like a shaft of sunlight. She came close to him, and very graciously proffered Scooter for a caress. "You needn't be afraid of him. He doesn't bite," she said.

"I suppose he is a bewitched prince, is he?" asked Bernard, as he stroked the furry little animal.

The great blue eyes were still fixed upon him. "No," said Tessa, after a thoughtful moment or two. "He's only a mongoose. But I think you are a bewitched prince. You're so big. And they always pretend to be beggars too," she added.

"And the princesses always fall in love with them before they find out," said Bernard, looking quizzical.

Tessa frowned a little. "I don't think falling in love is a very nice game," she said. "I've seen a lot of it."

"Have you indeed?" Bernard's eyes screwed up for a moment, but were hastily restored to an expression of becoming gravity. "I don't know much about it myself," he said. "You see, I'm an old bachelor."

"Haven't you—ever—been in love?" asked Tessa incredulously.

He held out his hand to her. "Yes, I'm in love at the present moment—quite the worst sort too—love at first sight."

"You are rather old, aren't you?" said Tessa dispassionately, but she laid her hand in his notwithstanding.

"Quite old enough to be kissed," he assured her, drawing her gently to him. "Shall I tell you a secret? I'm rather fond of kissing little girls."

Tessa went into the circle of his arm with complete confidence. "I don't mind kissing white men," she said, and held up her red lips. "But I wouldn't kiss an Indian—not even Peter, and he's a darling."

"A very wise rule, Princess," said Bernard. "And I feel duly honoured."

"How is my darling Aunt Stella this morning?" demanded Tessa suddenly. "You made me forget. *Ayah* said she would be all right, but *Ayah* says just anything. Is she all right?"

"She is better," Bernard said. "But wait a minute!" He caught her arm as she made an impetuous movement to leave him. "I believe she's asleep just now. You don't want to wake her?"

Tessa turned upon him swiftly—wide horror in her eyes. "Is that your way of telling me she is dead?" she said in a whisper.

"No, no, child!" Bernard's reply came with instant reassurance. "But she has been—she still is—ill. She was upset, you know. Someone in a car startled her."

"I know I was there." Tessa came close to him again, speaking in a tense undertone; her eyes gleamed almost black. "It was the Rajah that frightened her so—the Rajah—and my mother. I'm never going to ask God to bless her again. I—hate her! And him too!"

There was such concentrated vindictiveness in her words that even Bernard, who had looked upon many bitter things, was momentarily startled.

"I think God would be rather sorry to hear you say that," he remarked, after a moment. "He likes little girls to pray for their mothers."

"I don't see why," said Tessa rebelliously, "not if He hasn't given them good ones. Mine isn't good. She's very, very bad."

"Then there's all the more reason to pray for her," said Bernard. "It's the least you can do. But I don't think you ought to say that of your mother, you know, even if you think it. It isn't loyal."

"What's loyal?" said Tessa.

"Loyalty is being true to any one—not telling tales about them. It's about the only thing I learnt at school worth knowing." Bernard smiled at her in his large way. "Never tell tales of anyone, Princess!" he said. "It isn't cricket. Now look here! I've an awfully interesting piece of news for you. Come quite close, and I'll whisper. Do you know—last night—when Aunt Stella was lying ill, something happened. An angel came to see her."

"An angel!" Tessa's eyes grew round with wonder, and bluer than the bluest bluebell. "What was he like?" she whispered breathlessly. "Did you see him?"

"No, I didn't. I think it was a she," Bernard whispered back. "And what do you think she brought? But you'll never guess."

"Oh, what?" gasped Tessa, trembling.

Bernard's arm slipped round her, and Scooter with a sudden violent effort freed himself, and was gone.

"Never mind! I can get him again," said Tessa. "Or Peter will. Tell me—quick!"

"She brought—" Bernard was speaking softly into her ear—"a little boy-baby. Think of that! A present straight from God!"

"Oh, how lovely!" Tessa gazed at him with shining eyes. "Is it here now? May I see it? Is the angel still here?"

"No, the angel has gone. But the baby is left. It is Stella's very own, and she is to take care of it."

"Oh, I hope she'll let me help her!" murmured Tessa in awe-struck accents. "Does Uncle Everard know yet?"

"Yes. He and I got here in the night two or three hours after the baby arrived. He was very tired, poor chap. He is resting."

"And the baby?" breathed Tessa.

"Mrs. Ralston is taking care of the baby. I expect it's asleep," said Bernard. "So we'll keep very quiet."

"But she'll let me see it, won't she?" said Tessa anxiously.

"No doubt she will, Princess. But I shouldn't disturb them yet. It's early you know."

"Mightn't I just go in and kiss Uncle Everard?" pleaded Tessa. "I love him so very much. I'm sure he wouldn't mind."

"Let him rest a bit longer!" advised Bernard. "He is worn out. Sit down here, on the arm of my chair, and tell me about yourself! Where have you come from?"

Tessa jerked her head sideways. "Down there. We live at The Grand Stand. We've been there a long time now, nearly ever since Daddy went away. He's in Heaven. A *budmash* shot him in the jungle. Mother made a great fuss about it at the time, but she doesn't care now she can go motoring with the Rajah. He is a nasty beast," said Tessa with emphasis. "I always did hate him. And he frightened my darling Aunt Stella at the gate yesterday. I—could have—killed him for it."

"What did he do?" asked Bernard.

"I don't know quite; but the car twisted round on the hill, and Aunt Stella thought it was going to upset. I tried to take care of her, but we were both nearly run over. He's a horrid man!" Tessa declared. "He caught hold of me the other day because I got between him and Mother when they were sitting smoking together. And I bit him." Vindictive satisfaction sounded in Tessa's voice. "I bit him hard. He soon let go again."

"Wasn't he angry?" asked Bernard.

"Oh, yes, very angry. So was Mother. She told him he might whip me if he liked. Fancy being whipped by a native!" High scorn thrilled in the words. "But he didn't. He laughed in his slithery way and showed his teeth like a jackal and said—and said—I was too pretty to be whipped." Tessa ground her teeth upon the memory. It was evidently even-more humiliating than the suggested punishment. "And then he kissed me—he kissed me—" she shuddered at the nauseating recollection—"and let me go."

Bernard was listening attentively. His eyes were less kindly than usual. They had a steely look. "I should keep out of his way, if I were you," he said.

"I will—I do!" declared Tessa. "But I do hate the way he goes on with Mother. He'd never have dared if Daddy had been here."

"He is evidently a bounder," said Bernard.

They sat for some time on the verandah, growing pleasantly intimate, till presently Peter came out with an early breakfast for Bernard. He invited Tessa to join him, which she consented to do with alacrity.

"We must find Scooter afterwards," she said, as she proudly poured out his coffee. "And then perhaps, if I keep good, Aunt Mary will let me see the baby."

"Wonder if you will manage to keep good till then," observed a voice behind them.

She turned with a squeak of delight and sprang to meet Everard.

He was looking haggard in the morning light, but he smiled upon her in a way she had never seen before, and he stooped and kissed her with a tenderness that amazed her.

"Stella tells me you were very brave yesterday," he said.

"Was I? When?" Tessa opened her blue eyes to their widest extent. "Oh, I was only—angry," she said then. "Darling Aunt Stella was frightened."

He patted her shoulder. "You meant to take care of her, so I'm grateful all the same," he said.

Tessa clung to his arm. "I'd like to come and take care of her always," she said, rather wistfully. "I can easily be spared, Uncle Everard. And I'm really not nearly so naughty as I used to be."

He smiled at the words, but did not respond. "Where's Scooter?" he said.

They spent some time hunting for him, but it was left to Peter finally to unearth him, for in the middle of the search Mrs. Ralston came softly out upon the verandah with the baby in her arms, and at once all Tessa's thoughts were centred upon the new arrival. She had never before seen anything so tiny, so red, or so utterly beautiful!

Bernard left his breakfast to join the circle of admirers, and when the doctor arrived a few minutes later he was in triumphant possession of the small bundle that held them all spellbound. He knew how to handle a baby, and was extremely proud of the accomplishment.

It was not till two days later, however, that he was admitted to see the mother. She had turned the corner, they said, but she was terribly weak. Yet, as soon as she heard of the presence of her brother-in-law, she insisted upon seeing him.

Everard brought him in to her, but for the first time in her life she dismissed him when the introduction was effected.

"We shall get on better alone," she said, with a smile. "You come back—afterwards."

So Everard withdrew, and Bernard sat down by her side, his big hand holding hers.

"That is nice," she said, her pale face turned to him. "I have been wanting to know you ever since Everard first told me of you."

He bent with a little smile and kissed the slender fingers he held. "Then the desire has been mutual," he said.

"Thank you." Stella's eyes were fixed upon his face. "I was afraid," she said, with slight hesitation, "that you might think—when you saw Everard—that marriage hadn't altogether agreed with him."

Bernard's kindly blue eyes met hers with absolute directness. "No, I shouldn't have thought that," he said. "But I see a change in him of course. He is growing old much too fast. What is it? Overwork?"

"I don't know." She still spoke with hesitation. "I think it is a good deal—anxiety."

"Ah!" Bernard's hand closed very strongly upon hers. "He is not the only person that suffers from that complaint, I think."

She smiled rather wanly. "I ought not to worry. It's wrong, isn't it?"

"It's unnecessary," he said. "And it's a handicap to progress. But it's difficult not to when things go wrong, I admit. We need to keep a very tight hold on faith. And even then—"

"Yes, even then—" Stella said, her lips quivering a little—"when the one beloved is in danger, who can be untroubled?"

"We are all in the same keeping," said Bernard gently. "I think that's worth remembering. If we can trust ourselves to God, we ought to be able to trust even the one beloved to His care."

Stella's eyes were full of tears. "I am afraid I don't know Him well enough to trust Him like that," she said.

Bernard leant towards her. "My dear," he said, "it is only by faith that you can ever come to knowledge. You have to trust without definitely knowing. Knowledge—that inner certainty—comes afterwards, always afterwards. You can't get it for yourself. You can only pray for it, and prepare the ground."

Her fingers pressed his feebly. "I wonder," she said, "if you have ever known what it was to walk in darkness."

Bernard smiled. "Yes, I have floundered pretty deep in my time," he said. "There's only one thing for it, you know; just to keep on till the light comes. You'll find, when the lamp shines across the desert at last, that you're not so far out of the track after all—if you're only keeping on. That's the main thing to remember."

"Ah!" Stella sighed. "I believe you could help me a lot."

"Delighted to try," said Bernard.

But she shook her head. "No, not now, not yet. I want you—to take care of Everard for me."

"Can't he take care of himself?" questioned Bernard. "I thought I had taught him to be fairly independent."

"Oh, it isn't that," she said. "It is—it is—India."

He leaned nearer to her, the smile gone from his eyes. "I thought so," he said. "You needn't be afraid to speak out to me. I am discretion itself, especially where he is concerned. What has India been doing to him?"

With a faint gesture she motioned him nearer still. Her face was very pale, but resolution was shining in her eyes. "Don't let us be disturbed!" she whispered. "And I—I will tell you—all I know."

CHAPTER IV

THE SERPENT IN THE DESERT

The battalion was ordered back to Kurrumpore for the winter months, ostensibly to go into a camp of exercise, though whispers of some deeper motive for the move were occasionally heard. Markestan, though outwardly calm and well-behaved, was not regarded with any great confidence by the Government, so it was said, though, officially, no one had the smallest suspicion of danger.

It was with mixed feelings that Stella returned at length to The Green Bungalow, nearly three months after her baby's birth. During that time she had seen a good deal of her brother-in-law, who, nothing daunted by the discomforts of the journey, went to and fro several times between Bhulwana and the Plains. They had become close friends, and Stella had grown to regard his presence as a safeguard and protection against the nameless evils that surrounded Everard, though she could not have said wherefore.

He it was who, with Peter's help, prepared the bungalow for her coming. It had been standing empty all through the hot weather and the rains. The compound was a mass of overgrown verdure, and the bungalow itself was in some places thick with fungus.

When Stella came to it, however, all the most noticeable traces of neglect had been removed. The place was scrubbed clean. The ragged roses had been trained along the verandah-trellis, and fresh Indian matting had been laid down everywhere.

The garden was still a wilderness, but Bernard declared that he would have it in order before many weeks had passed. It was curious how, with his very limited knowledge of natives and their ways, he managed to extract the most willing labour from them. Peter the Great smiled with gratified pride whenever he gave him an order, and all the other servants seemed to entertain a similar veneration for the big, blue-eyed *sahib* who was never heard to speak in anger or impatience, and yet whose word was one which somehow no one found it possible to disregard.

Tommy had become fond of him also. He was wont to say that Bernard was the most likable fellow he had ever met. An indefinable barrier had grown up between him and his brother-in-law, which, desperately though he had striven against it, had made the old easy intercourse impossible. Bernard was in a fashion the link between them. Strangely they were always more intimate in his presence than when alone, less conscious of unknown ground, of reserves that could not be broached.

Strive as he might, Tommy could not forget that evening at the mess—the historic occasion, as he had lightly named it—when like an evil magic at work he had witnessed the smirching of his hero's honour. He had sought to bury the matter deep, to thrust it out of all remembrance, but the evil wrought was too subtle and too potent. It reared itself against him and would not be trampled down.

Had any of his brother-officers dared to mention the affair to him, he would have been furious, would strenuously have defended that which apparently his friend did not deem it worth his while to defend. But no one ever spoke of it. It dwelt among them, a shameful thing, ignored yet ever present.

Everard came and went as before, only more reticent, more grim, more unapproachable than he had ever been in the old days. His utter indifference to the cold courtesy accorded him was beyond all scorn. He simply did not see when men avoided him. He was supremely unaware of the coldness that made Tommy writhe in impotent rebellion. He had never mixed very freely with his fellows. Upon Tommy alone had he bestowed his actual friendship, and to Tommy alone did he now display any definite change of front. His demeanour towards the boy was curiously gentle. He never treated him confidentially or spoke of intimate things. That invincible barrier which Tommy strove so hard to ignore, he seemed to take for granted. But he was invariably kind in all his dealings with him, as if he realized that Tommy had lost the one possession he prized above all others and were sorry for him.

Whatever Tommy's mood, and his moods varied considerably, he was never other than patient with him, bearing with him as he would never have borne in the byegone happier days of their good comradeship. He never rebuked him, never offered him advice, never attempted in any fashion to test the influence that yet remained to him. And his very forbearance hurt Tommy more poignantly than any open rupture or even tacit avoidance could have hurt him. There were times when he would have sacrificed all he had, even down to his own honour, to have forced an understanding with Monck, to have compelled him to yield up his secret. But whenever he braced himself to ask for an explanation, he found himself held back. There was a boundary he could not pass, a force relentless and irresistible, that checked him at the very outset. He lacked the strength to batter down the iron will that opposed him behind that unaccustomed gentleness. He could only bow miserably to the unspoken word of command that kept him at a distance.

He was too loyal ever to discuss the matter with Bernard, though he often wondered how the latter regarded his brother's attitude. At least there was no strain in their relationship though he was fairly convinced that Everard had not taken Bernard into his confidence. This fact held a subtle solace for him, for it meant that Bernard, who was as open as the day, was content to be in the dark, and satisfied that it held nothing of an evil nature. This unquestioning faith on Bernard's part was Tommy's one ray of light. He knew instinctively that Bernard was not a man to compromise with evil. He carried his banner that all might see. He was not ashamed to confess his Master before all men, and Tommy mutely admired him for it.

He marked with pleasure the intimacy that existed between this man and his sister. Like Stella, though in a different sense, he had grown imperceptibly to look upon him as a safeguard. He was a sure antidote to nervous forebodings. The advent of the baby also gave him keen delight. Tommy was a lover of all things youthful. He declared he had never felt so much at home in India before.

Peter also was almost as much in the baby's company as was its *ayah*. The administration of the bottle was Peter's proudest privilege, and he would walk soft-footed to and fro for any length of time carrying the infant in his arms. Stella was always content when the baby was in his charge. Her confidence in Peter's devotion was unbounded. The child was not very strong and needed great care. The care Peter lavished upon it was as tender as her own. There was something of a feud between him and the *ayah*, but no trace of this was ever apparent in her presence. As for the baby, he seemed to love Peter better than any one else, and was generally at his best when in his arms.

The Green Bungalow became a favourite meeting-place with the ladies of the station, somewhat, to Stella's dismay. Lady Harriet swept in at all hours to hold inspections of the infant's progress and give advice, and everyone who had ever had a baby seemed to have some fresh warning or word of instruction to bestow.

They were all very kind to her. She received many invitations to tea, and smiled over her sudden popularity. But—it dawned upon her when, she had been about three weeks in the station—no one but the Ralstons seemed to think of asking her and her husband to dine. She thought but little of the omission at first. Evening entertainments held but slight attraction for her, but as time went on and Christmas festivities drew near, she could not avoid noticing that practically every invitation she received was worded in so strictly personal a fashion that there could be no doubt that Everard was not included in it. Bernard was often asked separately, but he generally refused on the score of the evening being his best working time.

Also, after a while, she could not fail to notice that Tommy was no longer at his ease in Everard's presence. The old careless *camaraderie* between them was gone, and she missed it at first vaguely, later with an uneasiness that she could not stifle. There was something in Tommy's attitude towards his friend that hurt her. She knew by instinct that the boy was not happy. She wondered at first if there could be some quarrel between them, but decided in face of Everard's unvarying kindness to Tommy that this could not be.

Another thing struck her as time went on. Everard always checked all talk of his prospects. He was so repressive on the subject that she could not possibly pursue it, and she came at last to conclude that his hope of preferment had vanished like a mirage in the desert.

He was very good to her, but his absences continued in the old unaccountable way, and her dread of Rustam Karin, which Bernard's presence had in a measure allayed, revived again till at times it was almost more than she could bear.

She did not talk of it any further to Bernard. She had told him all her fears, and she knew he was on guard, knew instinctively that she could count upon him though he never reverted to the matter. Somehow she could not bring herself to speak to him of the strange avoidance of her husband that was being practised by the rest of the station either. She endured it dumbly, holding herself more and more aloof in consequence of it as the days went by. Ever since the days of her own ostracism she had placed a very light price upon social popularity. The love of such women as Mary Ralston—and the love of little Tessa—were of infinitely greater value in her eyes.

Tessa and her mother were once more guests in the Ralstons' bungalow. Netta had desired to stay at the new hotel which—as also at Udalkland—native enterprise had erected near the Club; but Mrs. Ralston had vetoed this plan with much firmness, and after a little petulant argument Netta had given in. She did not greatly care for staying with the Ralstons. Mary was a dear good soul of course, but inclined to be interfering, and now that the zest of life was returning to Netta, her desire for her own way was beginning to reassert itself. However, the Ralstons' bungalow also was in close proximity to the Club, and in consideration of this she consented to take up her abode there. Her days of seclusion were over. She had emerged from them with a fevered craving for excitement of any description mingled with that odd defiance that had characterized her almost ever since her husband's death. She had never kept any very great control upon her tongue, but now it was positively venomous. She seemed to bear a grudge against all the world.

Tessa, with her beloved Scooter, went her own way as of yore, and spent most of her time at The Green Bungalow where there was always someone to welcome her. She arrived there one day in a state of great indignation, Scooter as usual clinging to her hair and trying his utmost to escape.

Like a whirlwind she burst upon Stella, who was sitting with her baby in the French window of her room.

"Aunt Stella," she cried breathlessly, "Mother says she's sure you and Uncle Everard won't go to the officers' picnic at Khanmulla this year. It isn't true, is it, Aunt Stella? You will go, and you'll take me with you, won't you?"

The officers' picnic at Khanmulla! The words called up a flood of memory in Stella's heart. She looked at Tessa, the smile of welcome still upon her face; but she did not see her. She was standing once more in the moonlight, listening to the tread of a man's feet on the path below her, waiting—waiting with a throbbing heart—for the sound of a man's quiet voice.

Tessa came nearer to her, looking at her with an odd species of speculation. "Aunt Stella," she said, "that wasn't—all—Mother said. She made me very, very angry. Shall I tell you—would you like to know—why?"

Stella's eyes ceased to gaze into distance. She looked at the child. Some vague misgiving stirred within her. It was the instinct of self-defence that moved her to say, "I don't want to listen to any silly gossip, Tessa darling."

"It isn't silly!" declared Tessa. "It's much worse than that. And I'm going to tell you, cos I think I'd better. She said that everybody says that Uncle Everard won't go to the picnic on Christmas Eve cos he's ashamed to look people in the face. I said it wasn't true." Very stoutly Tessa brought out the assertion; then, a moment later, with a queer sidelong glance into Stella's face, "It isn't true, dear, is it?"

Ashamed! Everard ashamed! Stella's hands clasped each other unconsciously about the sleeping baby on her lap. Strangely her own voice came to her while she was not even aware of uttering the words. "Why should he be ashamed?"

Tessa's eyes were dark with mystery. She pressed against Stella with a small protective gesture. "Darling, she said horrid things, but they aren't true any of them. If Uncle Everard had been there, she wouldn't have dared. I told her so."

With an effort Stella unclasped her hands. She put her arm around the little girl. "Tell me what they are saying, Tessa," she said. "I think with you that I had better know."

Tessa suffered Scooter to escape in order to hug Stella close. "They are saying things about when he went on leave just after you married Captain Dacre, how he said he wanted to go to England and didn't go, and how—how—" Tessa checked herself abruptly. "It came out at mess one night," she ended.

A faint smile of relief shone in Stella's eyes. "But I knew that, Tessa," she said. "He told me himself. Is that all?"

"You knew?" Tessa's eyes shone with sudden triumph. "Oh, then do tell them what he was doing and stop their horrid talking! It was Mrs. Burton began it. I always did hate her."

"I can't tell them what he was doing," Stella said, feeling her heart sink again.

"You can't? Oh!" Keen disappointment sounded in Tessa's voice. "But p'raps he would," she added reflectively, "if he knew what beasts they all are. Shall I ask him to, Aunt Stella?"

"Tell me first what they are saying!" Stella said, bracing herself to face the inevitable.

Tessa looked at her dubiously for a moment. Somehow she would have found it easier to tell this thing to Monck himself than to Stella. And yet she had a feeling that it must be told, that Stella ought to know. She clung a little closer to her.

"I always did hate Major Burton," she said sweepingly. "I know he started it in the first place. He said—and now she says—that—that it's very funny that the leave Uncle Everard had when he pretended to go to England should have come just at the time that Captain Dacre was killed in the mountains, and that a horrid old man Uncle Everard knows called Rustam Karin who lives in the bazaar was away at the same time. And they just wonder if p'raps he—the old man—had anything to do with Captain Dacre dying like he did, and if Uncle Everard knows—something—about it. That's how they put it, Aunt Stella. Mother only told me to tease me, but that's what they say."

She stopped, pressing Stella's hand very tightly to her little quivering bosom, and there followed a pause, a deep silence that seemed to have in it something of an almost suffocating quality.

Tessa moved at last because it became unbearable, moved and looked down into Stella's face as if half afraid. She could not have said what she expected to see there, but she was undoubtedly relieved when the beautiful face, white as death though it was, smiled back at her without a tremor.

Stella kissed her tenderly and let her go. "Thank you for telling me, darling," she said gently. "It is just as well that I should know what people say, even though it is nothing but idle gossip—idle gossip." She repeated the words with emphasis. "Run and find Scooter, sweetheart!" she said. "And put all this silly nonsense out of your dear little head for good! I must take baby to *ayah* now. By and by we will read a fairy-tale together and enjoy ourselves."

Tessa ran away comforted, yet also vaguely uneasy. Her tenderness notwithstanding, there was something not quite normal about Stella's dismissal of her. This kind friend of hers had never sent her away quite so summarily before. It was almost as if she were half afraid that Tessa might see—or guess—too much.

As for Stella, she carried her baby to the *ayah*, and then shut herself into her own room where she remained for a long time face to face with these new doubts.

He had loved her before her marriage; he had called their union Kismet. He wielded a strange, almost an uncanny power among natives. And there was Rustam Karin whom long ago she had secretly credited with Ralph Dacre's death—the serpent in the garden—the serpent in the desert also—whose evil coils, it seemed to her, were daily tightening round her heart.

CHAPTER V

THE WOMAN'S WAY

It was three days later that Tommy came striding in from the polo-ground in great excitement with the news that Captain Ermsted's murderer had been arrested.

"All honour to Everard!" he said, flinging himself into a chair by Stella's side. "The fellow was caught at Khanmulla. Barnes arrested him, but he gives the credit of the catch to Everard. The fellow will swing, of course. It will be a sensational trial, for rumour has it that the Rajah was pushing behind. He, of course, is smooth as oil. I saw him at the Club just now, hovering round Mrs. Ermsted as usual, and she encouraging him. That girl is positively infatuated. Shouldn't wonder if there's a rude awakening before her. I beg your pardon, sir. You spoke?" He turned abruptly to Bernard who was seated near.

"I was only wondering what Everard's share had been in tracking this charming person down," observed the elder Monck, who was smiling a little at Tommy's evident excitement.

"Oh, everyone knows that Everard is a regular sleuth-hound," said Tommy. "He is more native than the natives when there is anything of this kind in the wind. He is a born detective, and he and that old chap in the bazaar are such a strong combination that they are practically infallible and invincible."

"Do you mean Rustam Karin?" Stella spoke very quietly, not lifting her eyes from her work.

Tommy turned to her. "That's the chap. The old beggar fellow. At least they say he is. He never shows. Hafiz does all the show part. The old boy is the brain that works the wires. Everard has immense faith in him."

"I know," Stella said.

Her voice sounded strangled, and Bernard looked across at her; but she continued to work without looking up.

Tommy lingered for a while, expatiating upon Everard's astuteness, and finally went away to dress for mess still in a state of considerable excitement.

Stella and Bernard sat in silence after his departure. There seemed to be nothing to say. But when, after a time, he got up to go, she very suddenly raised her eyes.

"Bernard!"

"My dear!" he said very kindly.

She put out a hand to him, almost as if feeling her way in a dark place. "I want to ask you," she said, speaking hurriedly, "whether you know—whether you have ever heard—the things that are being said about—about Everard and this man—Rustam Karin."

She spoke with immense effort. It was evident that she was greatly agitated.

Bernard stopped beside her, holding her hand firmly in his. "Tell me what they are!" he said gently.

She made a hopeless gesture. "Then you do know! Everyone knows. Naturally I am the last. You knew I connected that dreadful man long ago with—with Ralph's death. I had good reason for doing so after—after I had actually seen him on the verandah here that awful night. But—but now it seems—because he and Everard have always been in partnership—because they were both absent at the time of Ralph's death, no one knew where—people are talking and saying—and saying—" She broke off with a sharp, agonized sound. "I can't tell you what they are saying!" she whispered.

"It is false!" said Bernard stoutly. "It's a foul lie of the devil's own concocting! How long have you known of this? Who was vile enough to tell you?"

"You knew?" she whispered.

"I never heard the thing put into words but I had my own suspicions of what was going about," he admitted. "But I never believed it. Nothing on this earth would induce me to believe it. You don't believe it, either, child. You know him better than that."

She hid her face from him with a smothered sob. "I thought I did—once."

"You did," he asserted staunchly. "You do! Don't tell me otherwise, for I shan't believe you if you do! What kind friend told you? I want to know."

"Oh, it was only little Tessa. You mustn't blame her. She was full of indignation, poor child. Her mother taunted her with it. You know—or perhaps you don't know—what Netta Ermsted is."

Bernard's face was very grim as he made reply. "I think I can guess. But you are not going to be poisoned by her venom. Why don't you tell Everard, have it out with him? Say you don't believe it, but it hurts you to hear a damnable slander like this and not be able to refute it! You are not afraid of him, Stella? Surely you are not afraid of him!"

But Stella only hid her face a little lower, and spoke no word.

He laid his hand upon her as she sat. "What does that mean?" he said. "Isn't your love equal to the strain?"

She shook her head dumbly. She could not meet his look.

"What?" he said. "Is my love greater than yours then? I would trust his honour even to the gallows, if need be. Can't you say as much?"

She answered him with her head bowed, her words barely audible. "It isn't a question of love. I—should always love him—whatever he did."

"Ah!" The flicker of a smile crossed Bernard's face. "That is the woman's way. There's a good deal to be said for it, I daresay."

"Yes—yes." Quiveringly she made answer. "But—if this thing were true—my love would have to be sacrificed, even—even though it would mean tearing out my very heart. I couldn't go on—with him. I couldn't—possibly."

Her words trembled into silence, and the light died out of Bernard's eyes. "I see," he said slowly. "But, my dear, I can't understand how you—loving him as you do—can allow for a moment, even in your most secret heart, that such a thing as this could be true. That is where you begin to go wrong. That is what does the harm."

She looked up at last, and the despair in her eyes went straight to his heart. "I have always felt there was—something," she said. "I can't tell you exactly how. But it has always been there. I tried hard not to love him—not to marry him. But it was no use. He mastered me with his love. But I always knew—I always knew—that there was something hidden which I might not see. I have caught sight of it a dozen times, but I have never really seen it." She suppressed a quick shudder. "I have been afraid of it, and—I have always looked the other way."

"A mistake," Bernard said. "You should always face your bogies. They have a trick of swelling out of all proportion to their actual size if you don't."

"Yes, I know. I know." Stella pressed his hand and withdrew her own. "You are very good," she said. "I couldn't have said this to any one but you. I can't speak to Everard. It isn't entirely my own weakness. He holds me off. He makes me feel that it would be a mistake to speak."

"Will you let me?" Bernard suggested, taking out his pipe and frowning over it.

She shook her head instantly. "No!—no! I am sure he wouldn't answer you, and—and it would hurt him to know that I had turned to any one else, even to you. It would only make things more difficult to bear." She stopped short with a nervous gesture. "He is coming now," she said.

There was a sound of horse's hoofs at the gate, and in a moment Everard Monck came into view, riding his tall Waler which was smothered with dust and foam.

He waved to his wife as he rode up the broad path. His dark face was alight with a grim triumph. A *saice* ran forward to take his animal, and he slid to the ground and stamped his feet as if stiff.

Then without haste he mounted the steps and came to them.

"I am not fit to come near you," he said, as he drew near. "I have been right across the desert to Udalkhand, and had to do some hard riding to get back in time." He pulled off his glove and just touched Stella's cheek in passing. "Hullo, Bernard! About time for a drink, isn't it?"

He looked momentarily surprised when Stella swiftly turned her head and kissed the hand that had so lightly caressed her. He stopped beside her and laid it on her shoulder.

"I am afraid you won't approve of me when I tell you what I have been doing," he said.

She looked up at him. "I know. Tommy came in and told us. You—seem to have done something rather great. I suppose we ought to congratulate you."

He smiled a little. "It is always satisfactory when a murderer gets his deserts," he said, "though I am afraid the man who does the job is not in all cases the prime malefactor."

"Ah!" Stella said. She folded up her work with hands that were not quite steady; her face was very pale.

Everard stood looking down at the burnished coils of her hair. "Are you going to the dance at the Club to-night?" he asked, after a moment.

She shook her head instantly. "No."

"Why not?" he questioned.

She leaned back in her chair, and looked up at him. "As you know, I never was particularly fond of the station society."

He frowned a little. "It's better than nothing. You are too given to shutting yourself up. Bernard thinks so too."

Stella glanced towards her brother-in-law with a slight lift of the eyebrows. "I don't think he does. But in any case, we are engaged to-night. It is Tessa's birthday, and she and Scooter are coming to dine."

"Coming to dine! What on earth for?" Everard looked his astonishment.

"My doing," said Bernard. "It's a surprise-party. Stella very kindly fell in with the plan, but it originated with me. You see, Princess Bluebell is ten years old to-day, and quite grown up. Mrs. Ralston had a children's party for her this afternoon which I was privileged to attend. I must say Tessa made a charming hostess, but she confided to me at parting that the desire of her life was to play Cinderella and go out to dinner in a 'rickshaw all by herself. So I undertook then and there that a 'rickshaw should be waiting for her at the gate at eight o'clock, and she should have a stodgy grown-up entertainment to follow. She was delighted with the idea, poor little soul. The Ralstons are going to the Club dance, and of course Mrs. Ermsted also, but Tommy is giving up the first half to come and amuse Cinderella. Mrs. Ralston thinks the child will be ill with so much excitement, but a tenth birthday is something of an occasion, as I pointed out. And she certainly behaved wonderfully well this afternoon, though she was about the only child who did. I nearly throttled the Burton youngster for kicking the *ayah*, little brute. He seemed to think it was a very ordinary thing to do." Bernard stopped himself with a laugh. "You'll be bored with all this, and I must go and make ready. There are to be Chinese lanterns to light the way and a strip of red cloth on the steps. Peter is helping as usual, Peter the invaluable. We shan't keep it up very late. Will you join us? Or are you also bound for the Club?"

"I will join you with pleasure," Everard said. "I haven't seen the imp for some days. There has been too much on hand. How is the boy, Stella? Shall we go and say good-night to him?"

Stella had risen. She put her hand through his arm. "Bernard and Tommy are to do all the entertaining, and you and I can amuse each other for once. We don't often have such a chance."

She smiled as she spoke, but her lips were quivering. Bernard sauntered away, and as he went, Everard stooped and kissed her upturned face.

He did not speak, and she clung to him for a moment passionately close. Wherefore she could not have said, but there was in her embrace something to restrain her tears. She forced them back with her utmost resolution as they went together to see their child.

CHAPTER VI

THE SURPRISE PARTY

Punctually at eight o'clock Tessa arrived, slightly awed but supremely happy, seated in a 'rickshaw, escorted by Bernard, and hugging the beloved Scooter to her eager little breast.

Her eyes were shining with mysterious expectation. As her cavalier handed her from her chariot up the red-carpeted steps she moved as one who treads enchanted ground. The little creature in her arms wore an air of deep suspicion. His pointed head turned to and fro with ferret-like movements. His sharp red eyes darted hither and thither almost apprehensively. He was like a toy on wires.

"He is going—p'raps—to turn into a fairy prince soon," explained Tessa. "I'm not sure that he quite likes the idea though. He would rather kill a dragon. P'raps he'll do both."

"P'raps," agreed Bernard.

He led the little girl along the vernadah under the bobbing lanterns. Tessa looked about her critically. "There aren't any other children, are there?" she said.

"Not one," said Bernard, "unless you count me. We are going to dine together, you and I, quite alone—if you can put up with me. And after that we will hold a reception for grown-ups only."

"I shall like that," said Tessa graciously. "Ah, here is Peter! Peter, will you please bring a box for Scooter while I have my dinner? He wants to go snake-hunting," she added to Bernard. "And if he does that, I shan't have him again for the rest of the evening."

"You don't get snakes this time of year, do you?" asked Bernard.

"Oh yes, sometimes. I saw one the other day when I was out with Major Ralston. He tried to kill it with his stick, but it got away. And Scooter wasn't there. They like to hide under bits of carpet like this," said Tessa in an instructive tone, pointing to the strip that had been laid in her honour. "Are you afraid of snakes, Uncle St. Bernard?"

"Yes," said Bernard with simplicity. "Aren't you?"

Tessa looked slightly surprised at the admission. "I don't know. I expect I am. Peter isn't. Peter's very brave."

"He has been more or less brought up with them," said Bernard. "Scorpions too. He smiled the other day when I fled from a scorpion in the garden. And I believe he has a positively fatherly feeling for rats."

Tessa shivered a little. "Scooter killed a rat the other day, and it squealed dreadfully. I don't think he ought to do things like that, but of course he doesn't know any better."

"He looks as if he knows a lot," said Bernard.

"Yes, I wish he would learn to talk. He's awful clever. Do you think we could ever teach him?" asked Tessa.

Bernard shook his head. "No. It would take a magician to do that. We are not clever enough, either of us. Peter now—"

"Oh, is Peter a magician?" said Tessa, with shining eyes. "Peter, dear Peter," turning to him ecstatically as he appeared with a box in which to imprison her darling, "do you think you could possibly teach my little Scooter to talk?"

Peter smiled all over his bronze countenance. "Missy *sahib*, only the Holy Ones can do that," he said.

Tessa's face fell. "That's as bad as telling you to pray for anything, isn't it?" she said to Bernard. "And my prayers never come true. Do yours?"

"They always get answered," said Bernard, "some time or other."

"Oh, do they?" Tessa regarded him with interest. "Does God come and talk to you then?" she said.

He smiled a little. "He speaks to all who wait to hear, my princess," he said.

"Only to grown-ups," said Tessa, looking incredulous.

Bernard put his arm round her. "No," he said. "It's the children who come first with Him. He may not give them just what they ask for, but it's generally something better."

Tessa stared at him, her eyes round and dark. "S'pose," she said suddenly, "a big snake was to come out of that corner, and I was to say, 'Don't let it bite me, Lord!' Do you think it would?"

"No," said Bernard very decidedly.

"Oh!" said Tessa. "Well, I wish one would then, for I'd love to see if it would or not."

Bernard pulled her to him and kissed her. "We won't talk any more about snakes or you'll be dreaming of them," he said. "Come along and dine with me! Rather sport having it all to ourselves, eh?"

"Where's Aunt Stella and Uncle Everard?" asked Tessa.

"Oh, they're preparing for the reception. Let me take your Highness's cloak! This is the banqueting-room."

He threw the cloak over a chair in the verandah, and led her into the drawing-room, where a small table lighted by candles with crimson shades awaited them.

"How pretty!" cried Tessa, clapping her hands.

Peter in snowy attire, benign and magnificent, attended to their wants, and the feast proceeded, vastly enjoyed by both. Tessa had never been so *fêted* in all her small life before.

When, at the end of the repast, to an accompaniment of nuts and sweetmeats, Bernard poured her a tiny ruby-coloured liqueur glass of wine, her delight knew no bounds.

"I've never enjoyed myself so much before," she declared. "What a ducky little glass! Now I'm going to drink your health!"

"No. I drink yours first." Bernard arose, holding his glass high. "I drink to the Princess Bluebell. May she grow fairer every day! And may her cup of blessing be always full!"

"Thank you," said Tessa. "And now, Uncle St. Bernard, I'm going to drink to you. May you always have lots to laugh at! And may your prayers always come true! That rhymes, doesn't it?" she added complacently. "Do I drink all my wine now, or only a sip?"

"Depends," said Bernard.

"How does it depend?"

"It depends on how much you love me," he explained. "If there's any one else you love better, you save a little for him."

She looked straight at him with a hint of embarrassment in her eyes. "I'm afraid I love Uncle Everard best," she said.

Bernard smiled upon her with reassuring kindliness. "Quite right, my child. So you ought. There's Tommy too and Aunt Stella. I am sure you want to drink to them."

Tessa slipped round the table to his side, clasping her glass tightly. As she came within the circle of his arm she whispered, "Yes, I love them ever such a lot. But I love you best of all, except Uncle Everard, and he doesn't want me when he's got Aunt Stella. I s'pose you never wanted a little girl for your very own did you?"

He looked down at her, his blue eyes full of tenderness. "I've often wanted you, Tessa," he said.

"Have you?" she beamed upon him, rubbing her flushed cheek against his shoulder. "I'm sure you can have me if you like," she said.

He pressed her to him. "I don't think your mother would agree to that, you know."

Tessa's red lips pouted disgust. "Oh, she wouldn't care! She never cares what I do. She likes it much best when I'm not there."

Bernard's brows were slightly drawn. His arm held the little slim body very closely to him.

"You and I would be so happy," insinuated Tessa, as he did not speak. "I'd do as you told me always. And I'd never, never be rude to you."

He bent and kissed her. "I know that, my darling."

"And when you got old, dear Uncle St. Bernard,—really old, I mean—I'd take such care of you," she proceeded. "I'd be—more—than a daughter to you."

"Ah!" he said. "I should like that, my princess of the bluebell eyes."

"You would?" she looked at him eagerly. "Then don't you think you might tell Mother you'll have me? I know she wouldn't mind."

He smiled at her impetuosity. "We must be patient, my princess," he said. "These things can't be done offhand, if at all."

She slid her arm round his neck and hugged him. "But there is the weeniest, teeniest chance, isn't there? 'Cos you do think you'd like to have me if I was good, and I'd—love—to belong to you. Is there just the wee-est little chance, Uncle St. Bernard? Would it be any good praying for it?"

He took her little hand into his warm kind grasp, for she was quivering all over with excitement.

"Yes, pray, little one!" he said. "You may not get exactly what you want. But there will be an answer if you keep on. Be sure of that!"

Tessa nodded comprehension. "All right. I will. And you will too, won't you? It'll be fun both praying for the same thing, won't it? Oh, my wine! I nearly spilt it."

"Better drink it and make it safe!" he said with a twinkle. "I'm going to drink mine, and then we'll go on to the verandah and wait for something to happen."

"Is something going to happen?" asked Tessa, with a shiver of delighted anticipation.

He laughed. "Perhaps,—if we live long enough."

Tessa drank her wine almost casually. "Come on!" she said. "Let's go!"

But ere they reached the French window that led on to the verandah, a sudden loud report followed by a succession of minor ones coming from the compound told them that the happenings had already begun. Tessa gave one great jump, and then literally danced with delight.

"Fireworks!" she cried. "Fireworks! That's Tommy! I know it is. Do let's go and look!" They went, and hung over the verandah-rail to watch a masked figure attired in an old pyjama suit of vivid green and white whirling a magnificent wheel of fire that scattered glowing sparks in all directions.

Tessa was wild with excitement. "How lovely!" she cried. "Oh, how lovely! Dear Uncle St. Bernard, mayn't I go down and help him?"

But Bernard decreed that she should remain upon the verandah, and, strangely, Tessa submitted without protest. She held his hand tightly, as if to prevent herself making any inadvertent dash for freedom, but she leapt to and fro like a dog on the leash, squeaking her ecstasy at every fresh display achieved by the bizarre masked figure below them.

Bernard watched her with compassionate sympathy in his kindly eyes. Little Tessa had won a very warm place in his heart. He marvelled at her mother's attitude of callous indifference.

Certainly Tessa had never enjoyed herself more thoroughly than on that evening of her tenth birthday. Time flew by on the wings of delight. Tommy's exhibition was appreciated with almost delirious enthusiasm on the verandah, and a little crowd of natives at the gate pushed and nudged each other with an admiration quite as heartfelt though carefully suppressed.

The display had been going on for some time when Stella came out alone and joined the two on the verandah. To Tessa's eager inquiry for Uncle Everard she made answer that he had been called out on business, and to Bernard she added that Hafiz had sent him a message by one of the servants, and she supposed he had gone to Rustam Karin's stall in the bazaar. She looked pale and dispirited, but she joined in Tessa's delighted appreciation of the entertainment which now was drawing to a close.

It was getting late, and as with a shower of coloured stars the magician in the compound accomplished a grand *finale*, Bernard put his arm around the narrow shoulders and said, with a kindly squeeze, "I am going to see my princess home again now. She mustn't lose all her beauty-sleep."

She lifted her face to kiss him. "It has been—lovely," she said. "I do wish I needn't go back to-night. Do you think Aunt Mary would mind if I stayed with you?"

He smiled at her whimsically. "Perhaps not, princess; but I am going to take you back to her all the same. Say good-night to Aunt Stella! She looks as if a good dose of bed would do her good."

Tommy, with his mask in his hand, came running up the verandah-steps, and Tessa sprang to meet him.

"Oh, Tommy—darling, I have enjoyed myself so!"

He kissed her lightly. "That's all right, scaramouch. So have I. I must get out of this toggery now double-quick. I suppose you are off in your 'rickshaw? I'll walk with you. It'll be on the way to the Club."

"Oh, how lovely! You on one side and Uncle St. Bernard on the other!" cried Tessa.

"The princess will travel in state," observed Bernard. "Ah! Here comes Peter with Scooter! Have your cloak on before you take him out!"

The cloak had fallen from the chair. Peter set down Scooter in his prison, and picked it up. By the light of the bobbing, coloured lanterns he placed it about her shoulders.

Tessa suddenly turned and sat down. "My shoe is undone," she said, extending her foot with a royal air. "Where is the prince?"

The words were hardly out of her mouth before another sound escaped her which she hastily caught back as though instinct had stifled it in her throat. "Look!" she gasped.

Peter was nearest to her. He had bent to release Scooter, but like a streak of light he straightened himself. He saw—before any one else had time to realize—- the hideous thing that writhed in momentary entanglement in the folds of Tessa's cloak, and then suddenly reared itself upon her lap as she sat frozen stiff with horror.

He stooped over the child, his hands outspread, waiting for the moment to swoop. "Missy *sahib*, not move—not move!" he said softly above her. "My missy *sahib* not going to be hurt. Peter taking care of Missy *sahib*."

And, with glassy eyes fixed and white lips rigid, Tessa's strained whisper came in answer. "O Lord, don't let it bite me!"

Tommy would have flung himself forward then, but Bernard caught and held him. He had seen the look in the Indian's eyes, and he knew beyond all doubting that Tessa was safe, if any human power could make her so.

Stella knew it also. In that moment Peter loomed gigantic to her. His gleaming eyes and strangely smiling face held her spellbound with a fascination greater even than that wicked, vibrating thing that coiled, black and evil, on the white of Tessa's frock could command. She knew that if none intervened, Peter would accomplish Tessa's deliverance.

But there was one factor which they had all forgotten. In those tense seconds Scooter the mongoose by some means invisible became aware of the presence of the enemy. The lid of his box had already been loosened by Peter. With a frantic effort he forced it up and leapt free.

In that moment Peter, realizing that another instant's delay might be fatal, pounced forward with a single swift swoop and seized the serpent-in his naked hands.

Tessa uttered the shriek which a few seconds before sheer horror had arrested, and fell back senseless in her chair.

Peter, grim and awful in the uncertain light, fought the thing he had gripped, while a small, red-eyed monster clawed its way up him, fiercely clambering to reach the horrible, writhing creature in the man's hold.

It was all over in a few hard-breathing seconds, over before either of the men in front of Peter or a shadowy figure behind him that had come up at Tessa's cry could give any help.

With a low laugh that was more terrible than any uttered curse, Peter flung the coiling horror over the verandah-rail into the bushes of the compound. Something else went with it, closely locked. They heard the thud of the fall, and there followed an awful, voiceless struggling in the darkness.

"Peter!" a voice said.

Peter was leaning against a post of the verandah. "Missy *sahib* is quite safe," he said, but his voice sounded odd, curiously lifeless.

The shadow that had approached behind him swept forward into the light. The lanterns shone upon a strange figure, bent, black-bearded, clothed in a long, dingy garment that seemed to envelop it from head to foot.

Peter gave a violent start and spoke a few rapid words in his own language.

The other made answer even more swiftly, and in a second there was the flash of a knife in the fitful glare. Bernard and Tommy both started forward, but Peter only thrust out one arm with a grunt. It was a gesture of submission, and it told its own tale.

"The poor devil's bitten!" gasped Tommy.

Bernard turned to Tessa and lifted the little limp body in his arms.

He thought that Stella would follow him as he bore the child into the room behind, but she did not.

The place was in semi-darkness, for they had turned down the lamps to see the fireworks. He laid her upon a sofa and turned them up again.

The light upon her face showed it pinched and deathly. Her breathing seemed to be suspended. He left her and went swiftly to the dining-room in search of brandy.

Returning with it, he knelt beside her, forcing a little between the rigid white lips. His own mouth was grimly compressed. The sight of his little playfellow lying like that cut him to the soul. She was uninjured, he knew, but he asked himself if the awful fright had killed her. He had never seen so death-like a swoon before.

He had no further thought for what was passing on the verandah outside. Tommy had said that Peter was bitten, but there were three people to look after him, whereas Tessa—poor brave mite—had only himself. He chafed her icy cheeks and hands with a desperate sense of impotence.

He was rewarded after what seemed to him an endless period of suspense. A tinge of colour came into the white lips, and the closed eyelids quivered and slowly opened. The bluebell eyes gazed questioningly into his.

"Where—where is Scooter?" whispered Tessa.

"Not far away, dear," he made answer soothingly. "We will go and find him presently. Drink another little drain of this first!"

She obeyed him almost mechanically. The shadow of a great horror still lingered in her eyes. He gathered her closely to him.

"Try and get a little sleep, darling! I'm here. I'll take care of you."

She snuggled against him. "Am I going to stay all night!" she asked.

"Perhaps, little one, perhaps!" He pressed her closer still. "Quite comfy?"

"Oh, very comfy; ever—so—comfy," murmured Tessa, closing her eyes again. "Dear—dear Uncle St. Bernard!"

She sank down in his hold, too spent to trouble herself any further, and in a very few seconds her quiet breathing told him that she was fast asleep.

He sat very still, holding her. The awful peril through which she had come had made her tenfold more precious in his eyes. He could not have loved her more tenderly if she had been indeed his own. He fell to dreaming with his cheek against her hair.

CHAPTER VII

RUSTAM KARIN

How long a time passed he never knew. It could not in actual fact have been more than a few minutes when a sudden sound from the verandah put an end to his reverie.

He laid the child back upon the sofa and got up. She was sleeping off the shock; it would be a pity to wake her. He moved noiselessly to the window.

As he did so, a voice he scarcely recognized—a woman's voice—spoke, tensely, hoarsely, close to him.

"Tommy, stop that man! Don't let him go! He is a murderer,—do you hear? He is the man who murdered my husband!"

Bernard stepped over the sill and closed the window after him. The lanterns were still swaying in the night-breeze. By their light he took in the group upon the verandah. Peter was sitting bent forward in the chair from which he had lifted Tessa. His snowy garments were deeply stained with blood. Beside him in a crouched and apelike attitude, apparently on the point of departure, was the shadowy native who had saved his life. Tommy, still fantastic and clown-like in his green and white pyjama-suit, was holding a glass for Peter to drink. And upright before them all, with accusing arm outstretched, her eyes shining like stars out of the shadows, stood Stella.

She turned to Bernard as he came forward. "Don't let him escape!" she said, her voice deep with an insistence he had never heard in it before. "He escaped last time. And there may not be another chance."

Tommy looked round sharply. "Leave the man alone!" he said. "You don't know what you're talking about, Stella. This affair has upset you. It's only old Rustam Karin."

"I know. I know. I have known for a long time that it was Rustam Karin who killed Ralph." Stella's voice vibrated on a strange note. "He may be Everard's chosen friend," she said. "But a day will come when he will turn upon him too. Bernard," she spoke with sudden appeal, "you know everything. I have told you of this man. Surely you will help me! I have made no mistake. Peter will corroborate what I say. Ask Peter!"

At sound of his name Peter lifted a ghastly face and tried to rise, but Tommy swiftly prevented him.

"Sit still, Peter, will you? You're much too shaky to walk. Finish this stuff first anyhow!"

Peter sank back, but there was entreaty in his gleaming eyes. They had bandaged his injured arm across his breast, but with his free hand he made a humble gesture of submission to his mistress.

"*Mem-sahib*," he said, his voice low and urgent, "he is a good man—a holy man. Suffer him to go his way!"

The man in question had withdrawn into the shadows. He was in fact beating an unobtrusive retreat towards the corner of the bungalow, and would probably have effected his escape but for Bernard, who, moved by the anguished entreaty in Stella's eyes, suddenly strode forward and gripped him by his tattered garment.

"No harm in making inquiries anyway!" he said. "Don't you be in such a hurry, my friend. It won't do you any harm to come back and give an account of yourself—that is, if you are harmless."

He pulled the retreating native unceremoniously back into the light. The man made some resistance, but there was a mastery about Bernard that would not be denied. Hobbling, misshapen, muttering in his beard, he returned.

"*Mem-sahib!*" Again Peter's voice spoke, and there was a break in it as though he pleaded with Fate itself and knew it to be in vain. "He is a good man, but he is leprous. *Mem-sahib,* do not look upon him! Suffer him to go!"

Possibly the words might have had effect, for Stella's rigidity had turned to a violent shivering and it was evident that her strength was beginning to fail. But in that moment Bernard broke into an exclamation of most unwonted anger, and ruthlessly seized the ragged wisp of black beard that hung down over his victim's hollow chest.

"This is too bad!" he burst forth hotly. "By heaven it's too bad! Man, stop this tomfool mummery, and explain yourself!"

The beard came away in his indignant hand. The owner thereof straightened himself up with a contemptuous gesture till he reached the height of a tall man. The enveloping *chuddah* slipped back from his head.

"I am not the fool," he said briefly.

Stella's cry rang through the verandah, and it was Peter who, utterly forgetful of his own adversity, leapt up like a faithful hound to protect her in her hour of need.

The glass in Tommy's hand fell with a crash. Tommy himself staggered back as if he had been struck a blow between the eyes.

And across the few feet that divided them as if it had been a yawning gulf, Everard Monck faced the woman who had denounced him.

He did not utter a word. His eyes met hers unflinching. They were wholly without anger, emotionless, inscrutable. But there was something terrible behind his patience. It was as if he had bared his breast for her to strike.

And Stella—Stella looked upon him with a frozen, incredulous horror, just as Tessa had looked upon the snake upon her lap only a little while before.

In the dreadful silence that hung like a poisonous vapour upon them, there came a small rustling close to them, and a wicked little head with red, peering eyes showed through the balustrade of the verandah.

In a moment Scooter with an inexpressibly evil air of satisfaction slipped through and scuttled in a zigzag course over the matting in search of fresh prey.

It was then that Stella spoke, her voice no more than a throbbing whisper. "Rustam Karin!" she said.

Very grimly across the gulf, Everard made answer. "Rustam Karin was removed to a leper settlement before you set foot in India."

"By—Jupiter!" ejaculated Tommy.

No one else spoke till slowly, with the gesture of an old and stricken woman, Stella turned away. "I must think," she said, in the same curious vibrating whisper, as though she held converse with herself. "I must—think."

No one attempted to detain her. It was as though an invisible barrier cut her off from all but Peter. He followed her closely, forgetful of his wound, forgetful of everything but her pressing need. With dumb devotion he went after her, and they vanished beyond the flicker of the bobbing lanterns.

Of the three men left, none moved or spoke for several difficult seconds. Finally Bernard, with an abrupt gesture that seemed to express exasperation, turned sharply on his heel and without a word re-entered the room in which he had left Tessa asleep, and fastened the window behind him. He left the tangle of beard on the matting, and Scooter stopped and nosed it sensitively till Everard stooped and picked it up.

"That show being over," he remarked drily, "perhaps I may be allowed to attend to business without further interference."

Tommy gave a great start and crunched some splinters of the shattered glass under his heel. He looked at Everard with an odd, challenging light in his eyes.

"If you ask me," he said bluntly, "I should say your business here is more urgent than your business in the bazaar."

Everard raised his brows interrogatively, and as if he had asked a question Tommy made sternly resolute response.

"I've got to have a talk with you. Shall I come into your room?"

Just for a second the elder man paused; then: "Are you sure that is the wisest thing you can do?" he said.

"It's what I'm going to do," said Tommy firmly.

"All right." Everard stooped again, picked up the inquiring Scooter, and dropped him into the box in which he had spent the evening.

Then without more words, he turned along the verandah and led the way to his own room.

Tommy came close behind. He was trembling a little but his agitation only seemed to make him more determined.

He paused a moment as he entered the room behind Everard to shut the window; then valiantly tackled the hardest task that had ever come his way.

"Look here!" he said. "You must see that this thing can't be left where it is."

Everard threw off the garment that encumbered him and gravely faced his young brother-in-law.

"Yes, I do see that," he said. "I seem to have exhausted my credit all round. It's decent of you, Tommy, to have been as forbearing as you have. Now what is it you want to know?"

Tommy confronted him uncompromisingly. "I want to know the truth, that's all," he said. "Can't you stop this dust-throwing business and be straight with me?"

His tone was stubborn, his attitude almost hostile. Yet beneath it all there ran a vein of something that was very like entreaty. And Everard, steadily watching him, smiled—the faint grim smile of the fighter who sees a gap in his enemy's defences.

"I'm afraid not," he said. "I don't want to be brutal, but—you see, Tommy—it's not your business."

Tommy flinched a little, but he stood his ground. "I think you're forgetting," he said, "that Stella is my sister. It's up to me to protect her."

"From me?" Everard's words came swift and sharp as a sword-thrust.

Tommy turned suddenly white, but he straightened himself with a gesture that was not without dignity. "If necessary—yes," he said.

An abrupt silence followed his words. They stood facing each other, and the stillness between them was such that they could hear Scooter beyond the closed window scratching against his prison-walls for freedom.

It seemed endless to Tommy. He came through it unfaltering, but he felt physically sick, as if he had been struck in the back.

When Everard spoke at last, his hands clenched involuntarily. He half expected violence. But there was no hint of anger about the elder man. He had himself under iron control. His face was flint-like in its composure, his mouth implacably grim.

"Thanks for the warning!" he said briefly. "It's just as well to know how we stand. Is that all you wanted to say?"

The dismissal was as definite as if he had actually seized and thrown him out of the room. And yet there was not even suppressed wrath in his speech. It was indifferent, remote as a voice from the desert-distance. His eyes looked upon Tommy without interest or any sort of warmth, as though he had been a total stranger.

In that moment Tommy saw that sacred thing, their friendship, shattered and lying in the dust. It was not he who had flung it there, yet his soul cried out in bitter self-reproach. This was the man who had been closer to him than a brother, the man who had saved him from disaster physically and morally, watching over him with a grim tenderness that nothing had ever changed.

And now it was all done with. There was nothing left but to turn and go.

But could he? He stood irresolute, biting his lips, held there by a force that seemed outside himself. And it was Everard who made the first move, turning from him as if he had ceased to count and pulling out a note-book that he always carried to make some entry.

Tommy stood yet a moment longer as if, had it been possible, he would have broken through the barrier between them even then. But Everard did not so much as glance in his direction, and the moment passed.

In utter silence he turned and went out as he had entered. There was nothing more to be said.

CHAPTER VIII

PETER

Tessa went back to the Ralstons' bungalow that night borne in Bernard's arms. She knew very little about it, for she scarcely awoke, only dimly realizing that her friend was at hand. Tommy went with them, carrying Scooter. He said he must show himself at the Club, though Bernard suspected this to be merely an excuse for escaping for a time from The Green Bungalow. For it was evident that Tommy had had a shock.

He himself was merely angry at what appeared to him a wanton trick, too angry to trust himself in his brother's company just then. He regarded it as no part of his business to attempt to intervene between Everard and his wife, but his sympathies were all with the latter. That she in some fashion misconstrued the whole affair he could not doubt, but he was by no means sure that Everard had not deliberately schemed for some species of misunderstanding. He had, to serve his own ends, personated a man who was apparently known to be disreputable, and if he now received the credit for that man's misdeeds he had himself alone to thank. Obviously a mistake had been made, but it seemed to him that Everard had intended it to be made, had even worked to bring it about. What his object had been Bernard could not bring to conjecture. But his instinctive, inborn hatred of all underhand dealings made him resent his brother's behaviour with all the force at his command. He was too angry to attempt to unravel the mystery, and he did not broach the subject to Tommy who evidently desired to avoid it.

The whole business was beyond his comprehension and, he was convinced, beyond Stella's also. He did not think Everard would find it a very easy task to restore her confidence. Perhaps he would not attempt to do so. Perhaps he was too engrossed with the service of his goddess to care that he and his wife should drift asunder. And yet—the memory of the morning on which he had first seen those streaks of grey in his brother's hair came upon him, and an unwilling sensation of pity softened his severity. Perhaps he had been drawn in in spite of himself. Perhaps the poor beggar was a victim rather than a worshipper. Most certainly—whatever his faults—he cared deeply.

Would he be able to make Stella realize that? Bernard wondered, and shook his head in doubt.

The thought of Stella turning away with that look of frozen horror on her face pursued him through the night. Poor girl! She had looked as though the end of all things had come for her. Could he have helped her? Ought he to have left her so? He quickened his pace almost insensibly. No, he would not interfere of his own free will. But if she needed his support, if she counted upon him, he would not be found wanting. It might even be given to him eventually to help them both.

He had not seen her again. She had gone to her room with Peter in attendance, Peter who owed his life to the knife in Everard's girdle. He had had a strong feeling that Peter was the only friend she needed just then, and certainly Tessa had been his first responsibility. But the feeling that possibly she might need him was growing upon him. He wished he had satisfied himself before starting that this was not the case. But he comforted himself with the thought of Peter. He was sure that Peter would take care of her.

Yes, Peter would care for his beloved *mem-sahib*, whatever his physical disabilities. He would never fail in the execution of that his sacred duty while the power to do so was his. If all others failed her, yet would Peter remain faithful. Even then with his dog-like devotion was he crouched upon her threshold, his dark face wrapped in his garment, yet alert for every sound and mournfully aware that his mistress was not resting. Of his own wound he thought not at all. He had been very near the gate of death, and the only man in the world for whom he entertained the smallest feeling of fear had snatched him back. To his promptitude alone did Peter owe his life. He had cut out that deadly bite with a swiftness and a precision that had removed all danger of snake-poison, and in so doing he had exposed the secret which he had guarded so long and so carefully. The first moment of contact had betrayed him to Peter, but Peter was very loyal. Had he been the only one to recognize him, the secret would have been safe. He had done his best to guard it, but Fate had been against them. And the *mem-sahib*—the *mem-sahib* had turned and gone away as one heart-broken.

Peter yearned to comfort her, but the whole situation was beyond him. He could only mount guard in silence. Perhaps—presently—the great *sahib* himself would come, and make all things right again. The night was advancing. Surely he would come soon.

Barely had he begun to hope for this when the door he guarded was opened slightly from within. His *mem-sahib*, strangely white and still, looked forth.

"Peter!" she said gently.

He was up in a moment, bending before her, his black eyes glowing in the dim light.

She laid her slender hand upon his shoulder. She had ever treated him with the graciousness of a queen. "How is your wound?" she asked him in her soft, low voice. "Has it been properly bathed and dressed?"

He straightened himself, looking into her beautiful pale face with the loving reverence that he always accorded her. "All is well, my *mem-sahib*," he said. "Will you not be graciously pleased to rest?"

She shook her head, smiling faintly—a smile that somehow tore his heart. She opened her door and motioned him to enter. "I think I had better see for myself," she said. "Poor Peter! How you must have suffered, and how splendidly brave you are! Come in and let me see what I can do!"

He hung back protesting; but she would take no refusal, gently but firmly overruling all his scruples.

"Why was the doctor not sent for?" she said. "I ought to have thought of it myself."

She insisted upon washing and bandaging his wound anew. It was a deep one. Necessity had been stern, and Everard had not spared. It had bled freely, and there was no sign of any poisonous swelling. With tender hands Stella treated it, Peter standing dumbly submissive the while.

When she had finished, she arranged the injured arm in a sling, and looked him in the eyes.

"Peter, where is the captain *sahib*?"

"He went to his room, my *mem-sahib*," said Peter. "Bernard *sahib* carried the little missy *sahib* back, and Denvers *sahib* went with him. I did not see the captain *sahib* again."

He spoke wistfully, as one who longed to help but recognized his limitations.

Stella received his news in silence, her face still and white as the face of a marble statue. She felt no resentment against Peter. He had acted almost under compulsion. But she could not discuss the matter with him.

At length: "You may go, Peter," she said. "Please let no one come to my door to-night! I wish to be undisturbed."

Peter salaamed low and withdrew. The order was a very definite one, and she knew she could rely upon him to carry it out. As the door closed softly upon him, she turned towards her window. It opened upon the verandah. She moved across the room to shut it; but ere she reached it, Everard Monck came noiselessly through on slippered feet and bolted it behind him.

CHAPTER IX

THE CONSUMING FIRE

As he turned towards her, there came upon Stella, swift as a stab through the heart, the memory of that terrible night more than a year before when he had drawn her into his room and fastened the window behind her—against whom? His wild words rushed upon her. She had deemed them to be directed against the unknown intruder on the verandah. She knew now that the madness that had loosed his tongue had moved him to utter his fierce threat against a man who was dead—against the man whom he had—She stopped the thought as she would have checked the word half-spoken. She turned shivering away. The man on the verandah, that vision of the night-watches, she saw it all now—she saw it all. And he had loved her before her marriage. And he had known—and he had known—that, given opportunity, he could win her for his own.

Like a throbbing undersong—the fiendish accompaniment to the devils' chorus—the gossip of the station as detailed by Tessa ran with glib mockery through her brain. Ah, they only suspected. But she knew—she knew! The door of that secret chamber had opened wide to her at last, and perforce she had entered in.

He had moved forward, but he had not spoken. At least she fancied not, but all her senses were in an uproar. And above it all she seemed to hear that dreadful little thrumming instrument down by the river at Udalkhand—the tinkling, mystic call of the vampire goddess,—India the insatiable who had made him what he was.

He came to her, and every fibre of her being was aware of him and thrilled at his coming. Never had she loved him as she loved him then, but her love was a fiery torment that burned and consumed her soul. She seemed to feel it blistering, shrivelling, in the cruel heat.

Almost before she knew it, she had broken her silence, speaking as it were in spite of herself, scarcely knowing in her anguish what she said.

"Yes, I know. I know what you are going to say. You are going to tell me that I belong to you. And of course it is true,—I do. But if I stay with you, I shall be—a murderess. Nothing will alter that."

"Stella!" he said.

His voice was stern, so stern that she flinched. He laid his hand upon her, and she shrank as she would have shrunk from a hot iron searing her flesh. She had a wild thought that she would bear the brand of it for ever.

"Stella," he said again, and in both tone and action there was compulsion. "I have come to tell you that you are making a mistake. I am innocent of this thing you suspect me of."

She stood unresisting in his hold, but she was shaking all over. The floor seemed to be rising and falling under her feet. She knew that her lips moved several times before she could make them speak.

"But I don't suspect," she said. "The others suspect. I—know."

He received her words in silence. She saw his face as through a shifting vapour, very pale, very determined, with eyes of terrible intensity dominating her own.

Half mechanically she repeated herself. It was as if that devilish thrumming in her brain compelled her. "The others suspect. I—know."

"I see," he said at last. "And nothing I can say will make any difference?"

"Oh, no!" she made answer, and scarcely knew that she spoke, so cold and numb had she become. "How could it—now?"

He looked at her, and suddenly he saw that to which his own suffering had momentarily blinded him. He saw her utter weakness. With a swif passionate movement he caught her to him. For a second or two he held her so, strained against his heart, then almost fiercely he turned her face up to his own and kissed the stiff white lips.

"Be it so then!" he said, and in his voice was a deep note as though he challenged all the powers of evil. "You are mine—and mine you will remain."

She did not resist him though the touch of his lips was terrible to her. Only as they left her own, she turned her face aside. Very strangely that savage lapse of his had given her strength.

"Physically—perhaps—but only for a little while," she said gaspingly. "And in spirit, never—never again!"

"What do you mean?" he said, his arms tightening about her.

She kept her face averted. "I mean—that some forms of torture are worse than death. If it comes to that—if you compel me—I shall choose death."

"Stella!" He let her go so suddenly that she nearly fell. The utterance of her name was as a cry wrung from him by sheer agony. He turned from her with his hands over his face. "My God!" he said, and again almost inarticulately, "My—God!"

The low utterance pierced her, yet she stood motionless, her hands gripped hard together. He had forced the words from her, and they were past recall. Nor would she have recalled them, had she been able, for it seemed to her that her love had become an evil thing, and her whole being shrank from it in a species of horrified abhorrence, even though she could not cast it out.

He had turned towards the window, and she watched him, her heart beating in slow, hard strokes with a sound like a distant drum. Would he go? Would he remain? She almost prayed aloud that he would go.

But he did not. Very suddenly he turned and strode back to her. There was purpose in every line of him, but there was no longer any violence.

He halted before her. "Stella," he said, and his voice was perfectly steady and controlled, "do you think you are being altogether fair to me?"

She wrung her clasped hands. She could not answer him.

He took them into his own very quietly. "Just look me in the face for a minute!" he said.

She yearned to disobey, but she could not. Dumbly she raised her eyes to his.

He waited a moment, very still and composed. Then he spoke. "Stella, I swear to you—and I call God to witness—that I did not kill Ralph Dacre."

A dreadful shiver went through her at the bald brief words. She felt, as Tommy had felt a little earlier, physically sick. The beating of her heart was getting slower and slower. She wondered if presently it would stop.

"Do you believe me?" he said, still holding her eyes with his, still clasping her icy hands firmly between his own.

She forced herself to speak before that horrible sense of nausea overcame her. "Perhaps—David—said the same thing—about Uriah the Hittite."

His face changed a little, but it was a change she could not have defined. His eyes remained inscrutably fixed upon hers. They seemed to enchain her quivering soul.

"No," he said quietly. "Nor did I employ any one else to do it."

"But you were there!" The words seemed suddenly to burst from her without her own volition.

He drew back sharply, as if he had been struck. But he kept his eyes upon hers. "I can't explain anything," he said. "I am not here to explain. I only came to see if your love was great enough to make you believe in me—in spite of all there seems to be against me. Is it, Stella? Is it?"

His words seemed to go through her, tearing a way to her heart; the agony was more than she could bear. She uttered an anguished cry, and wrenched herself from him. "It isn't a question of love!" she said. "You know it isn't a question of love! I never wanted to love you. I never wholly trusted you. But you forced my love—though you couldn't compel my trust. And now that I know—now that I know—" her voice broke as if the torture were too great for her; she flung out her hands with a gesture of driving him from her—"oh, it is hell on earth—hell on earth!"

He drew back for a second before her, his face deathly white. And then suddenly an awful light leapt in his eyes. He gripped her outflung hands. The fire had kindled to a flame and the torture was too much for him also.

"Then you shall love me—even in hell!" he said, through his clenched teeth, and locked her in the iron circle of his arms.

She did not resist him. She was very near the end of her strength. Only, as he held her, her eyes met his, mutely imploring him....

It reached him even in his madness, that unspoken appeal. It checked him in the mid-furnace of his passion. His hold relaxed as if at a word of command. He put her into a chair and turned himself from her.

The next moment he was fumbling desperately at the window fastening. The night met him on the threshold. He heard her weeping, piteously, hopelessly, as he went away.

CHAPTER X

THE DESERT PLACE

A single light shone across the verandah when Bernard Monck returned late in the night. It drew his steps though it did not come from any of the sitting-rooms. With the light tread often characteristic of heavy men, he approached it, realizing only at the last moment that it came from the window of his brother's room.

Then for a second he hesitated. He was angry with Everard, more angry than he could remember that he had ever been before. He questioned with himself as to the wisdom of seeing him again that night. He doubted if he could be ordinarily civil to him at present, and a quarrel would help no one.

Still why was the fellow burning a light at that hour? An unacknowledged uneasiness took possession of him and drove him forward. People seemed to do all manner of extravagant things in this fantastic country that they would never have dreamed of doing in homely old England. There must be something electric in the atmosphere that penetrated the veins. Even he had been aware of it now and then, a strange and potent influence that drove a man to passionate deeds.

He reached the window without sound just as Stella had reached it on that night of rain long ago. With no consciousness of spying, driven by an urgent impulse he could not stop to question, he looked in.

The window was ajar, as if it had been pushed to negligently by someone entering, and in a flash Bernard had it wide. He went in as though he had been propelled.

A man—Everard—was standing half-dressed in the middle of the room. He was facing the window, and the light shone with ghastly distinctness upon his face. But he did not look up. He was gazing fixedly into a glass of water he held in his hand, apparently watching some minute substance melting there.

It was not the thing he held, but the look upon his face, that sent Bernard forward with a spring. "Man!" he burst forth. "What are you doing?"

Everard gave utterance to a fierce oath that was more like the cry of a savage animal than the articulate speech of a man. He stepped back sharply, and put the glass to his lips. But no drop that it contained did he swallow, for in the same instant Bernard flung it violently aside. The glass spun across the room, and they grappled

115

together for the mastery. For a few seconds the battle was hot; then very suddenly the elder man threw up his hands.

"All right," he said, between short gasps for breath. "You can hammer me—if you want someone to hammer. Perhaps—it'll do you good."

He was free on the instant. Everard flung round and turned his back. He did not speak, but crossed the room and picked up the glass which lay unbroken on the floor.

Bernard followed him, still gasping for breath, "Give that to me!" he said.

His soft voice was oddly stern. Everard looked at him. His hand, shaking a little, was extended. After a very definite pause, he placed the glass within it. There was a little white sediment left with a drain of water at the bottom. With his blue eyes full upon his brother's face, Bernard lifted it to his own lips.

But the next instant it was dashed away, and the glass shivered to atoms against the wall. "You—fool!" Everard said.

A faint, faint smile that very strangely proclaimed a resemblance between them which was very seldom perceptible crossed Bernard's face. "I—thought so," he said. "Now look here, boy! Let's stop being melodramatic for a bit! Take a dose of quinine instead! It seems to be the panacea for all evils in this curious country."

His voice was perfectly kind, even persusaive, but it carried a hint of authority as well, and Everard gave him a keen look as if aware of it.

He was very pale but absolutely steady as he made reply. "I don't think quinine will meet the case on this occasion."

"You prefer another kind of medicine," Bernard suggested. And then with sudden feeling he held out his hand. "Everard, old chap, never do that while you've a single friend left in the world! Do you want to break my heart? I only ask to stand by you. I'll stand by you to the very gates of hell. Don't you know that?"

His voice trembled slightly. Everard turned and gripped the proffered hand hard in his own.

"I suppose I—might have known," he said. "But it's a bit rash of you all the same."

His own voice quivered though he forced a smile. He would have turned away, but Bernard restrained him.

"I don't care a tinker's damn what you've done," he said forcibly. "Remember that! We're brothers, and I'll stick to you. If there's anything in life that I can do to help, I'll do it. If there isn't, well, I won't worry you, but you know you can count on me just the same. You'll never stand alone while I live."

It was generously spoken. The words came straight from his soul. He put his hand on his brother's shoulder as he uttered them. His eyes were as tender as the eyes of a woman.

And suddenly, without warning, Everard's strength failed him. It was like the snapping of a stretched wire. "Oh, man!" he said, and covered his face.

Bernard's arm was round him in a moment, a staunch, upholding arm. "Everard—dear old chap—can't you tell me what it is?" he said. "God knows I'll die sooner than let you down."

Everard did not answer. His breathing was hard, spasmodic, intensely painful to hear. He had the look of a man stricken in his pride.

For a space Bernard stood dumbly supporting him. Then at length very quietly he moved and guided him to a chair.

"Take your time!" he said gently. "Sit down!"

Mutely Everard submitted. The agony of that night had stripped his manhood of its reserve. He sat crouched, his head bowed upon his clenched hands.

"Wait while I fetch you a drink!" Bernard said.

He was gone barely two minutes. Returning, he fastened the window and drew the curtain across. Then he bent again over the huddled figure in the chair.

"Take a mouthful of this, old fellow! It'll pull you together."

Everard groped outwards with a quivering hand. "Give me strength—to shoot myself," he muttered.

The words were only just audible, but Bernard caught them. "No,—give you strength to play the game," he said, and held the glass he had brought to his brother's lips.

Everard drank with closed eyes and sat forward again motionless. His face was bloodless. "I'm sorry, St. Bernard," he said, after a moment. "Forgive me for manhandling you—and all the rest, if you can!" He drew a long, hard breath. "Thanks for everything! Good-night!"

"But I'm not leaving you," said Bernard, gently. "Not like this."

"Like what?" Everard opened his eyes with an abrupt effort. "Oh, I'm all right. Don't you bother about me!" he said.

Their eyes met. For a second longer Bernard stood over him. Then he went down upon his knees by his side. "I swear I won't leave you," he said, "until you've told me this trouble of yours."

Everard shook his head instantly, but his hand went out and closed upon the arm that had upheld him. He was beginning to recover his habitual self-command. "It's no good, old chap. I can't," he said. And added almost involuntarily, "That's—the hell of it!"

"But you can," Bernard said. He still looked him straight in the eyes. "You can and you will. Call it a confession—I've heard a good many in my time—and tell me everything!"

"Confess to you!" A hint of surprise showed in Everard's heavy eyes. "You'd better not tempt me to do that," he said. "You might be sorry afterwards."

"I will risk it," Bernard said.

"Risk being made an accessory to—what you may regard as a crime?" Everard said. "Forgive me—you're a parson, I know,—but are you sure you can play the part?"

Bernard smiled a little at the question. "Yes, I can," he said. "A confession is sacred—whatever it is. And I swear to you—by God in Heaven—to treat it as such."

Everard was looking at him fixedly, but something of the strain went out of his look at the words. A gleam of relief crossed his face.

"All right. I will—confess to you," he said. "But I warn you beforehand, you'll be horribly shocked. And—you won't feel like absolving me afterwards."

"That's not my job, dear fellow," Bernard answered gently. "Go ahead! You're sure of my sympathy anyway."

"Am I? You're a good chap, St. Bernard. Look here, don't kneel there! It's not suitable for a father confessor," Everard's faint smile showed for a moment.

Bernard's hand closed upon his. "Go ahead!" he said again, "I'm all right."

Everard made an abrupt gesture that had in it something of surrender. "It's soon told," he said, "though I don't know why I should burden you with it. That fellow Ralph Dacre—I didn't murder him. I wish to Heaven I had. So far as I know—he is alive."

"Ah!" Bernard said

Jerkily, with obvious effort, Everard continued. "I'm a murderous brute no doubt. But if I had the chance to kill him now, I'd take it. You see what it means, don't you? It means that Stella—that Stella—" He broke off with a convulsive movement, and dropped back into a tortured silence.

"Yes. I see what it means," Bernard said.

After an interval Everard forced out a few more words. "About a fortnight after their marriage I got your letter telling me he had a wife living. I went straight after them in native disguise, and made him clear out. That's the whole story."

"I see," Bernard said again.

Again there fell a silence between them. Everard sat bowed, his head on his hand. The awful pallor was passing, but the stricken look remained.

Bernard spoke at last. "You have no idea what became of him?"

"Not the faintest. He went. That was all that concerned me." Grimly, without lifting his head, he made answer. "You know the rest—or you can guess. Then you came, and told me that the woman—Dacre's wife—died before his marriage to Stella. I've been in hell ever since."

"I wish to Heaven I'd stopped away!" Bernard exclaimed with sudden vehemence.

Everard shifted his position slightly to glance at him. "Don't wish that!" he said. "After all, it would probably have come out somehow."

"And—Stella?" Bernard spoke with hesitation, as if uncertain of his ground. "What does she think? How much does she know?"

"She thinks like the rest. She thinks I murdered the hound. And I'd rather she thought that," there was dogged suffering in Everard's voice, "than suspected the truth."

"You think—" Bernard still spoke with slight hesitation—"that will hurt her less?"

"Yes." There was stubborn conviction in the reply. Everard slowly straightened himself and faced his brother squarely. "There is—the child," he said.

Bernard shook his head slightly. "You're wrong, old fellow. You're making a mistake. You are choosing the hardest course for her as well as yourself."

Everard's jaw hardened. "I shall find a way out for myself," he said. "She shall be left in peace."

"What do you mean?" Bernard said. Then as he made no reply, he took him firmly by the shoulders. "No—no! You won't. You won't," he said. "That's not you, my boy—not when you've sanely thought it out."

Everard suffered his hold; but his face remained set in grim lines. "There is no other way," he said. "Honestly, I see no other way."

"There is another way." Very steadily, with the utmost confidence, Bernard made the assertion. "There always is. God sees to that. You'll find it presently."

Everard smiled very wearily at the words. "I've given up expecting any light from that quarter," he said. "It seems to me that He hasn't much use for the wanderers once they get off the beaten track."

"Oh, my dear chap!" Bernard's hands pressed upon him suddenly. "Do you really believe He has no care for that which is lost? Have you blundered along all this time and never yet seen the lamp in the desert? You will see it—like every other wanderer—sooner or later, if you only have the pluck to keep on."

"You seem mighty sure of that." Everard looked at him with a species of dull curiosity. "Are you sure?"

"Of course I am sure." Bernard spoke vigorously. "And so are you in your heart. You know very well that if you only push on you won't be left to die in the wilderness. Have you never thought to yourself after a particularly dark spell that there has always been a speck of light somewhere—never total darkness for any length of time? That's the lamp in the desert, old chap. And—whether you realize it or not—God put it there."

He ceased to speak, and rose quietly to his feet; then, as Everard stretched a hand to him, gave him a steady pull upwards. They stood face to face.

"And that," Bernard added, after a few moments, "is all I've got to say. You turn in now and get a rest! If you want me, well, you know where to find me—just any time."

"Thanks!" Everard said. His hand held his brother's hard. "But—before you go—there's one thing I want to say—no, two." A shadowy smile touched his grim lips and vanished. His eyes were still and wholly remote, sheltering his soul.

"Go ahead!" said Bernard gently.

Everard paused for a second. "You have asked no promise of me," he said then; "but—I'll make you one. And I want one from you in return."

Again he paused, as if he had some difficulty in finding words.

"You can rely on me," Bernard said.

"Yes, old fellow." For an instant his eyes smiled also. "I know it. It's by that fact alone that you've gained your point. And so I'll hang on somehow for the present—find another way—anyhow hang on, just because you are what you are—and because—" his voice sank a little—"you care."

"Don't you know I love you before any one else in the world?" Bernard said, giving him a mighty grip.

"Yes," Everard looked him straight in the face, "I do. And it means more to me than perhaps you think. In fact—it's everything to me just now. That's why I want you to promise me—whatever happens—whatever I decide to do—that you will stay within reach of—that you will take care of—my—my—of Stella." He ended abruptly, with a quick gesture that held entreaty.

And Bernard's reply came instantly, almost before he had ceased to speak. "Before God, old chap, I will."

"Thanks," Everard said again. He stood for a few moments as if debating something further, but in the end he freed himself and turned away. "She will be all right, with you," he said. "You're—safe anyhow."

"Quite safe," said Bernard steadily.

PART V

CHAPTER I

GREATER THAN DEATH

"If you ask me," said Bertie Oakes, propping himself up in an elegant attitude against a pillar of the Club verandah, "it's my belief that there's going to be—a bust-up."

"Nobody did ask you," observed Tommy rudely.

He generally was rude nowadays, and had been haled before a subalterns' court-martial only the previous evening for that very reason. The sentence passed had been of a somewhat drastic nature, and certainly had not improved his temper or his manners. To be stripped, bound scientifically, and "dipped" in the Club swimming-bath till, as Oakes put it, all the venom had been drenched out of him, was an experience for which only one utterly reckless would qualify twice.

Tommy had come through it with a dumb endurance which had somewhat spoilt the occasion for his tormentors, had gone back to The Green Bungalow as soon as his punishment was over, and for the first time had drunk heavily in the privacy of his room.

He sat now in a huddled position on the Club verandah, "looking like a sick chimpanzee" as Oakes assured him, "ready to bite—if he dared—at a moment's notice."

Mrs. Ralston was seated near. She had a motherly eye upon Tommy.

"Now what exactly do you mean by a 'bust-up,' Mr. Oakes?" she asked with her gentle smile.

Oakes blew a cloud of smoke upwards. He liked airing his opinions, especially when there were several ladies within earshot.

"What do I mean?" he said, with a pomposity carefully moulded upon the Colonel's mode of delivery on a guest-night. "I mean, my dear Mrs. Ralston, that which would have to be suppressed—a rising among the native element of the State."

"Ape!" growled Tommy under his breath.

Oakes caught the growl, and made a downward motion with his thumb which only Tommy understood.

Mrs. Burton's soft, false laugh filled the pause that followed his pronouncement. "Surely no one could openly object to the conviction of a native murderer!" she said. "I hear that the evidence is quite conclusive. Captain Monck has spared no pains in that direction."

"Captain Monck," observed Lady Harriet, elevating her long nose, "seems to be exceptionally well qualified for that kind of service."

"Set a thief to catch a thief, what?" suggested Oakes lightly. "Yes, he seems to be quite good at it. Just as well in a way, perhaps. Someone has got to do the dirty work, though it would be preferable for all of us if he were a policeman by profession."

It was too carelessly spoken to sound actively malevolent. But Tommy, with his arms gripped round his knees, raised eyes of bloodshot fury to the speaker's face.

"If any one could take a first class certificate for dirty work, it would be you," he said, speaking very distinctly between clenched teeth.

A sudden silence fell upon the assembly. Oakes looked down at Tommy, and Tommy glared up at Oakes.

Then abruptly Major Ralston, who had been standing in the background with a tall drink in his hand, slouched forward and let himself down ponderously on the edge of the verandah by Tommy's side.

"Go away, Bertie!" he said. "We've listened to your wind instrument long enough. Tommy, you shut up, or I'll give you the beastliest physic I know! What were we talking about? Mary, give us a lead!"

He appealed to his wife, who glanced towards Lady Harriet with a hint of embarrassment.

Major Ralston at once addressed himself to her. He was never embarrassed by any one, and never went out of his way to be pleasant without good reason.

"This murder trial is going to be sensational," he said, "I've just got back from giving evidence as to the cause of death and I have it on good authority that a certain august personage in Markestan is shaking in his shoes as to the result of the business."

"I have heard that too," said Lady Harriet.

It was a curious fact that though she was always ready, and would even go out of her way, to snub the surgeon's wife, she had never once been other than gracious to the surgeon.

"I don't suppose he will be actively implicated. He's too wily for that," went on Major Ralston. "But there's not much doubt according to Barnes, that he was in the know—very much so, I should imagine." He glanced about him. "Mrs. Ermsted isn't here, is she?"

"No dear. I left her resting," his wife said. "This affair is very trying for her—naturally." He assented somewhat grimly. "I wonder she stayed for it. Now Tessa on the other hand yearns for the murderer's head in a charger. That child is getting too Eastern in her ideas. It will be a good thing to get her Home."

Mrs. Burton intervened with a simper. "Yes, she really is a naughty little thing, and I cannot say I shall be sorry when she is gone. My small son is at such a very receptive age."

"Yes, he's old enough to go to school and be licked into shape," said Major Ralston brutally. "He flings stones at my car every time I pass. I shall stop and give him a licking myself some day when I have time."

"Really, Major Ralston, I hope you will not do anything so cruel," protested Mrs. Burton. "We never correct him in that way ourselves."

"Pity you don't," said Major Ralston. "An unlicked cub is an insult to creation. Give him to me for a little while! I'll undertake to improve him both morally and physically to such an extent that you won't know him."

Here Tommy uttered a brief, wholly involuntary guffaw.

"What's the matter with you?" said Ralston.

"Nothing." His gloom dropped upon him again like a mantle. "Have you been at Khanmulla all day?"

"Yes; a confounded waste of time it's been too." Ralston took a deep drink and set down his glass.

"You always think it's a waste of time if you can't be doctoring somebody," muttered Tommy.

"Don't be offensive!" said Ralston. "I know what's the matter with you, my son, but I should keep it to myself if I were you. As a matter of fact I did give medical advice to somebody this afternoon—which of course he won't take."

Tommy's face was suddenly scarlet. It was solely the maternal protective instinct that induced Mrs. Ralston to bend forward and speak.

"Do you mean Captain Monck, Gerald?" she asked.

Major Ralston cast a comprehensive glance around the little group assembled near him, finishing his survey upon Tommy's burning countenance. "Yes—Monck," he said. "He's staying with Barnes at Khanmulla to see this affair through. If I were Mrs. Monck I should be pretty anxious about him. He says it's insomnia."

"Is he ill?" It was Tommy who spoke, his voice quick and low, all the sullen embarrassment gone from his demeanour.

The doctor's eyes dwelt upon him for a moment longer before he answered. "I never saw such a change in any man in such a short time. He'll have a bad break-down if he doesn't watch out."

"He works too hard," said Mrs. Ralston sympathetically.

Her husband nodded. "If it weren't for that sickly baby of hers, I should advise his wife to go straight to him and look after him. But perhaps when this trial is over he will be able to take a rest. I shall order the whole family to Bhulwana if I get the chance." He got up with the words, and faced the company with a certain dogged aggressiveness that compelled attention. "It's hard," he said, "to see a fine chap like that knocked out. He's about the best man we've got, and we can't afford to lose him."

He waited for someone to take up the challenge, but no one showed any inclination to do so. Only after a moment Tommy also sprang up as if there was something in the situation that chafed him beyond endurance.

Ralston looked at him again, critically, not over-favourably. "Where are you off to in such a hurry?" he said.

Tommy hunched his shoulders, all defiance in a second. "Going for a ride," he growled. "Any objection?"

Ralston turned away. "None whatever, my young porcupine. Have mercy on your nag, that's all—and don't break your own neck!"

Tommy strode wrathfully away to the sound of Mrs. Burton's tittering laugh. With the exception of Mrs. Ralston, who really did not count, he hated every one of the party that he left behind on the Club verandah, and he did not attempt to disguise the fact.

But when an hour later he rolled off his horse in the compound of the policeman's bungalow at Khanmulla, his mood had undergone a complete change. There was nothing defiant or even assertive about him as he applied for admittance. He looked beaten, tried beyond his strength.

It was growing rapidly dark as he followed Barnes's *khansama* into the long bare room which he used as his private office. The man brought him a lamp and told him that the *sahibs* would be back soon. They had gone down to the Court House again, but they might return at any time.

He also brought him whisky and soda which Tommy did not touch, spending the interval of waiting that ensued in fevered tramping to and fro.

He had not seen Monck alone since the evening of Tessa's birthday-party nearly three weeks before. On the score of business connected with the approaching trial, Monck had come to Khanmulla immediately afterwards, and no one at Kurrumpore had had more than an occasional glimpse of him since. But he meant to see him alone now, and he had given very explicit instructions to that effect to the servant, accompanied by a substantial species of persuasion that could not fail to achieve its object.

When the sound of voices told him at last of the return of the two men, he drew back out of sight of the window while the obsequious *khansama* went forth upon his errand. Then a moment or two later he heard them separate, and one alone came in his direction. Everard entered with the gait of a tired man.

The lamp dazzled him for a second, and Tommy saw him first. He smothered an involuntary exclamation and stepped forward.

"Tommy!" said Monck, as if incredulous.

Tommy stood in front of him, his hands at his sides. "Yes, it's me. I had to come over—just to have a look at you. Ralston said—said—oh, damn it, it doesn't matter what he said. Only I had to—just come and see for myself. You see, I—I—" he faltered badly, but recovered himself under the straight gaze of Everard's eyes—"I can't get the thought of you out of my mind. I've been a damn' cur. You won't want to speak to me of course, but when Ralston started jawing about you this afternoon, I found—I found—" he choked suddenly—"I couldn't stand it any longer," he said in a strangled whisper.

Monck was looking full at him by the merciless glare of the lamp on the table, which revealed himself very fully also. All the grim lines in his face seemed to be accentuated. He looked years older. The hair above his temples gleamed silver where it caught the light.

He did not speak at once. Only as Tommy made a blind movement as if to go, he put forth a hand and took him by the arm.

"Tommy," he said, "what have you been doing?"

Out of deep hollows his eyes looked forth, indomitable, relentless as they had ever been, searching the boy's downcast face.

Tommy quivered a little under their piercing scrutiny, but he made no attempt to avoid it.

"Look at me!" Monck commanded.

He raised his eyes for a moment, and in spite of himself Monck was softened by the utter misery they held.

"You always were an ass," he commented. "But I thought you had more strength of mind than this."

Tommy made an impotent gesture. "I'm a beast—I'm a skunk!" he declared, with tremulous vehemence. "I'm not fit to speak to you!"

The shadow of a smile crossed Monck's face. "And you've come all this way to tell me so?" he said. "You've no business here either. You ought to be at the Mess."

"Damn the Mess!" said Tommy fiercely. "They'll tell me I ratted to-morrow. I don't care. Let 'em say what they like! It's you that matters. Man, how infernally ill you look!"

Monck checked the personal allusion. "I'm not ill. But what have you been up to? Are you in a row?"

Tommy essayed a laugh. "No, nothing serious. The blithering idiots ducked me yesterday for being disrespectful, that's all. I don't care. It's you I care about, Everard, old chap!"

His voice held sudden pleading, but his face was turned away. He had meant to say more, but could not. He stood biting his lips desperately in a mute struggle for self-control.

Everard waited a few seconds, giving him time; then abruptly he moved, slapped a hand on Tommy's shoulder and gave him a shake.

"Tommy, don't be so beastly cheap! I'm ashamed of you. What's the matter?"

Tommy yielded impulsively to the bracing grip, but he kept his face averted. "That's just it," he blurted out. "I feel cheap. Fact is, I came—I came to ask you to—forgive me. But now I'm here,—I'm damned if I have the cheek."

"What do you want my forgiveness for? I thought I was the transgressor." Everard's voice was a curious blend of humour and sadness.

Tommy turned to him with a sudden boyish gesture so spontaneous as to override all barriers. "Oh, I know all that. But it doesn't count. See? I don't know how I ever had the infernal presumption to think it did, or to ask you—you, of all men—to explain your actions. I don't want any explanation. I believe in you without, simply because I can't help it. I know—without any proof,—that you're sound. And—and—I beg your pardon for being such a cur as to doubt you. There! That's what I came to say. Now it's your turn."

The tears were in his eyes, but he made no further attempt to hide them. All that was great in his nature had come to the surface, and there was no room left for self-consciousness.

Monck realized it, and it affected him deeply, depriving him of the power to respond. He had not expected this from Tommy, had not believed him capable of it. But there was no doubting the boy's sincerity. Through those tears which Tommy had forgotten to hide, he saw the old loving trust shine out at him, the old wholehearted admiration and honour offered again without reservation and without stint.

He opened his lips to speak, but something rose in his throat, preventing him. He held out his hand in silence, and in that wordless grip the love which is greater than death made itself felt between them—a bond imperishable which no earthly circumstance could ever again violate—the Power Omnipotent which conquers all things.

CHAPTER II

THE LAMP

The orange light of the morning was breaking over the jungle when two horsemen rode out upon the Kurrumpore road and halted between the rice fields.

"I say, come on a bit further!" Tommy urged. "There's plenty of time."

But the other shook his head. "No, I can't. I promised Barnes to be back early. Good-bye, Tommy my lad! Keep your end up!"

"I will," Tommy promised, and thrust out a hand. "And you'll hang on, won't you? Promise!"

"All right; for the present. My love to Bernard." Everard spoke with his usual brevity, but his handclasp was remembered by Tommy for a very long time after.

"And to Stella?" he said, pushing his horse a little nearer till it muzzled against its fellow.

Everard's eyes, grave and dark, looked out to the low horizon. "I think not," he said. "She has—no further use for it."

"She will have," said Tommy quickly.

But Everard passed the matter by in silence. "You must be getting on," he said, and relaxed his grip. "Good-bye, old chap! You've done me good, if that is any consolation to you."

"Oh, man!" said Tommy, and coloured like a girl. "Not—not really!"

Everard uttered his curt laugh, and switched Tommy's mount across the withers. "Be off with you, you—cuckoo!" he said.

And Tommy grinned and went.

Half-an-hour later he was sounding an impatient tatto upon his sister's door.

She came herself to admit him, but the look upon her face checked the greeting on his lips.

"What on earth's the matter?" he said instead.

She was shivering as if with cold, though the risen sun had filled the world with spring-like warmth. It occurred to him as he entered, that she was looking pinched and ill, and he put a comforting arm around her.

"What is it, Stella girl? Tell me!"

She relaxed against him with a sob. "I've been—horribly anxious about you," she said.

"Oh, is that all?" said Tommy. "What a waste of time! I was only over at Khanmulla. I spent the night at Barnes's bungalow because they wouldn't trust me in the jungle after dark."

"They?" she questioned.

"Barnes and Everard," Tommy said, and faced her squarely. "I went to see Everard."

"Ah!" She caught her breath. "Major Ralston has been here. He told me—he told me—" her voice failed; she laid her head down upon Tommy's shoulder.

He tightened his arm about her. "It's a shame of Ralston to frighten you. He isn't ill." Then a sudden thought striking him, "What was he doing here so early? Isn't the kid up to the mark?"

She shivered against him again. "He had a strange attack in the night, and Major Ralston said—said—oh, Tommy," she suddenly clung to him, "I am going to lose him. He—isn't—like other children."

"Ralston said that?" demanded Tommy.

"He didn't tell me. He told Bernard. I practically forced Bernard to tell me, but I think he thought I ought to know. He said—he said—it isn't to be desired that my baby should live."

"What?" said Tommy in dismay. "Oh, my darling girl, I am sorry! What's wrong with the poor little chap?"

With her face hidden against him she made whispered answer. "You know he—came too soon. They thought at first he was all right, but now—symptoms have begun to show themselves. We thought he was just delicate, but it isn't only that. Last night—in the night—" she shuddered suddenly and violently and paused to control herself—"I can't talk about it. It was terrible. Major Ralston says he doesn't suffer, but it looks like suffering. And, oh, Tommy,—he is all I have left."

Tommy held her comfortingly close. "I say, wouldn't you like Everard to come to you?" he said.

"Oh no! Oh no!" Her refusal was instant. "I can't see him. Tommy, why suggest such a thing? You know I can't."

"I know he's a good man," Tommy said steadily. "Just listen a minute, old girl! I know things look black enough against him, so black that it's probable he'll have to send in his papers. But I tell you he's all right. I didn't think so at first. I thought the same as you do. But somehow that suspicion has got worn out. It was pretty beastly while it lasted, but I came to my senses at last. And I've been to tell him so. He was jolly decent about it, though he didn't tell me a thing. I didn't want him to. Besides, he always is decent. How could he be otherwise? And now we're just as we were—friends."

There was no mistaking the satisfaction in Tommy's voice. He even spoke with pride, and hearing it, Stella withdrew herself slowly and wearily from his arms.

"It's rather different for you, Tommy," she said. "A man's standards are different, I know. There may be what you call extenuating circumstances—though I can't quite imagine it. I'm too tired to argue about it, Tommy dear, and you mustn't be vexed with me. I can't go into it with you, but I feel as if it is I—I myself—who have committed an awful sin. And it has got to be expiated, perhaps that is why my baby is to be taken from me. Bernard says it is not so. But then—Bernard is a man too." There was a sound of heartbreak in her voice as she ended. She put up her hands with a gesture as of trying to put away some monstrous thing that threatened to crush her—a gesture that went straight to Tommy's warm heart.

"Oh, poor old girl!" he said impulsively, and took the hands into his own. "I say, ought I to be in here? Aren't you supposed to be resting?"

She smiled at him wanly. "I believe I am. Major Ralston left a soothing draught, but I wouldn't take it, in case—" she broke off. "Peter is on guard as well as *Ayah*, and he has promised to call me if—if—" Again she stopped. "I don't think *Ayah* is much good," she resumed. "She was nearly frightened out of her senses last night. She seems to think there is something—supernatural about it. But Peter—Peter is a tower of strength. I trust him implicitly."

"Yes, he's a good chap," said Tommy. "I'm glad you've got him anyway. I wish I could be more of a help to you."

She leaned forward and kissed him. "You are very dear to me, Tommy. I don't know what I should do without you and Bernard."

"Where is the worthy padre?" asked Tommy.

"He may be working in his room. He is certainly not far away. He never is nowadays."

"I'll go and find him," said Tommy. "But look here, dear! Have that draught of Ralston's and lie down! Just to please me!"

She began to refuse, but Tommy could be very persuasive when he chose, and he chose on this occasion. Finally, with reluctance she yielded, since, as he pointed out, she needed all the strength she could muster.

He tucked her up with motherly care, feeling that he had accomplished something worth doing, and then, seeing that exhaustion would do the rest, he left her and went softly forth in search of Bernard.

The latter, however, was not in the bungalow, and since it was growing late Tommy had a hurried bath and dressed for parade. He was bolting a hasty *tiffin* in the dining-room when a quiet step on the verandah warned him of Bernard's approach, and in a moment or two the big man entered, a pipe in his mouth and a book under his arm.

"Hullo, Tommy!" he said with his genial smile. "So you haven't been murdered this time. I congratulate you."

"Thanks!" said Tommy.

"I congratulate myself also," said Bernard, patting his shoulder by way of greeting. "If it weren't against my principles, I should have been very worried about you, my lad. For I couldn't get away to look for you."

"Of course not," said Tommy. "And I was safe enough. I've been over to Khanmulla. Everard made me spend the night, and we rode back this morning."

"Everard! He isn't here?" Bernard looked round sharply.

"No," said Tommy bluntly. "But he ought to be. He went back again. He is wanted for that trial business. I say, things are pretty rotten here, aren't they? Is the little kid past hope?"

"I am afraid so." Bernard spoke very gravely. His kindly face was more sombre than Tommy had ever seen it.

"But can nothing be done?" the boy urged. "It'll break Stella's heart to lose him."

Bernard shook his head. "Nothing whatever I am afraid. Major Ralston has suspected trouble for some time, it seems. We might of course get a specialist's opinion at Calcutta, but the baby is utterly unfit for a journey of any kind, and it is doubtful if any doctor would come all this way—especially with things as they are."

"What do you mean?" said Tommy.

Bernard looked at him. "The place is a hotbed of discontent—if not anarchy. Surely you know that!"

Tommy shrugged his shoulders. "That's nothing new. It's what we're here for."

"Yes. And matters are getting worse. I hear that the result of this trial will probably mean the Rajah's enforced abdication. And if that happens there is practically bound to be a rising."

Tommy laughed. "That's been the situation as long as I've been out. We're giving him enough rope, and I hope he'll hang, though I'm afraid he won't. The rising will probably be a sort of Chinese cracker affair—a fizz, a few bangs, and a splutter-out. No honour and glory for any one!"

"I hope you are right," said Bernard.

"And I hope I'm wrong," said Tommy lightly. "I like a run for my money."

"You forget the women," said Bernard abruptly.

Tommy opened his eyes. "No, I don't. They'll be all right. They'll have to clear out to Bhulwana a little earlier than usual. They'll be safe enough there. You can go and look after 'em, sir. They'll like that."

"Thank you, Tommy." Bernard smiled in spite of himself. "It's kind of you to put it so tactfully. Now tell me what you think of Everard. Is he really ill?"

"No; worried to death, that's all. He's talking of sending in his papers. Did you know?"

"I suspected he would," Bernard spoke thoughtfully.

"He mustn't do it!" said Tommy with vehemence. "He's worth all the rest of the Mess put together. You mustn't let him."

Bernard lifted his brows. "I let him!" he said. "Do you think he is going to do what I tell him?"

"I know you have influence—considerable influence—with him," Tommy said. "You ought to use it, sir. You really ought. It's up to you and no one else."

He spoke insistently. Bernard looked at him attentively.

"You've changed your tune somewhat, haven't you, Tommy?" he said.

"Yes," said Tommy bluntly. "I have. I've been a damn' fool if you want to know—the biggest, damnedest fool on the face of creation. And I've been and told him so."

"For no particular reason?" Bernard's blue eyes grew keener in their regard. He looked at Tommy with more interest than he had ever before bestowed upon him.

Tommy's face was red, but he replied without embarrassment. "Certainly. I've come to my senses, that's all. I've come to realize—what I really knew all along—that he's a white man, white all through, however black he chooses to be painted. And I'm ashamed that I ever doubted him."

"He hasn't told you anything?" questioned Bernard, still closely surveying the flushed countenance.

"No!" said Tommy, and his voice rang on a note of indignant pride. "Why the devil should he tell me anything? I'm his friend. Thank the gods, I can trust him without."

Bernard held out his hand suddenly. The interest had turned to something warmer. He looked at the boy with genuine admiration. "I take off my hat to you, Tommy," he said. "Everard is a deuced lucky man."

"What?" said Tommy, and turned deep crimson. "Oh, rot, sir! That's rot!" He gripped the extended hand with warmth notwithstanding. "It's all the other way round. I can't tell you what he's been to me. Why, I—I'd die for him, if I had the chance."

"Yes," Bernard said with simplicity. "I'm sure you would, boy. And it's just that I like about you. You're just the sort of friend he needs—the sort of friend God sends along to hold up the lamp when the night is dark. There! You want to be off. I won't keep you. But you're a white man yourself, Tommy, and I shan't forget it."

"Oh, rats—rats—rats!" said Tommy rudely, and escaped through the window at headlong speed.

CHAPTER III

TESSA'S MOTHER

"It really isn't my fault," said Netta fretfully. "I don't see why you should lecture me about it, Mary. I can't help being attractive."

"My dear," said Mrs. Ralston patiently, "that was not my point. I am only urging you to show a little discretion. You do not want to be an object of scandal, I am sure. The finger of suspicion has been pointed at the Rajah a good many times lately, and I do think that for Tessa's sake, if not for your own, you ought to put a check upon your intimacy with him."

"Bother Tessa!" said Netta. "I don't see that I owe her anything."

Mrs. Ralston sighed a little, but she persevered. "The child is at an age when she needs the most careful training. Surely you want her to respect you!"

Netta laughed. "I really don't care a straw what she does. Tessa doesn't interest me. I wanted a boy, you know. I never had any use for girls. Besides, she gets on my nerves at every turn. We shall never be kindred spirits."

"Poor little Tessa!" said Mrs. Ralston gently. "She has such a loving heart."

"She doesn't love me," said Tessa's mother without regret. "I suppose you'll say that's my fault too. Everything always is, isn't it?"

"I think—in fact I am sure—that love begets love," said Mrs. Ralston. "Perhaps when you and she get to England together, you will become more to each other."

"Out of sheer *ennui*?" suggested Netta. "Oh, don't let's talk of England—I hate the thought of it. I'm sure I was created for the East. Hence the sympathy that exists between the Rajah and myself. You know, Mary, you really are absurdly prejudiced against him. Richard was the same. He never had any cause to be jealous. They simply didn't come into the same category."

Mrs. Ralston looked at her with wonder in her eyes. "You seem to forget," she said, "that Richard's murderer is being tried, and that this man is very strongly suspected of being an abettor if not the actual instigator of the crime."

Netta flicked the ash from her cigarette with a gesture of impatience. "I only wish you would let me forget these unpleasant things," she said. "Why don't you go and preach a sermon to the beautiful Stella Monck on the same text? Ralph Dacre's death was quite as much of a mystery. And the kindly gossips are every bit as busy with Captain Monck's reputation as with His Excellency's. But I suppose her devotion to that wretched little imbecile baby of hers renders her immune!"

She spoke with intentional malice, but she scarcely expected to strike home. Mary was not, in her estimation, over-endowed with brains, and she never seemed to mind a barbed thrust or two. But on this occasion Mrs. Ralston upset her calculations.

She arose in genuine wrath. "Netta!" she said. "I think you are the most heartless, callous woman I have ever met!"

And with that she went straight from the room, shutting the door firmly behind her.

"Good gracious!" commented Netta. "Mary in a tantrum! What an exciting spectacle!"

She stretched her slim body like a cat as she lay with the warm sunshine pouring over her, and presently she laughed.

"How funny! How very funny! Netta, my dear, they'll be calling you wicked next."

She pursed her lips over the adjective as if she rather enjoyed it, then stretched herself again luxuriously, with sensuous enjoyment. She had ridden with the Rajah in the early morning, and was pleasantly tired.

The sudden approach of Tessa, scampering along the verandah in the wake of Scooter, sent a quick frown to her face, which deepened swiftly as Scooter, dodging nimbly, ran into the room and went to earth behind a bamboo screen.

Tessa sprang in after him, but pulled up sharply at sight of her mother. The frown upon Netta's face was instantly reflected upon her own. She stood expectant of rebuke.

"What a noisy child you are!" said Netta. "Are you never quiet, I wonder? And why did you let that horrid little beast come in here? You know I detest him."

"He isn't horrid!" said Tessa, instantly on the defensive. "And I couldn't help him coming in. I didn't know you were here, but it isn't your bungalow anyway, and Aunt Mary doesn't mind him."

"Oh, go away!" said Netta with irritation. "You get more insufferable every day. Take the little brute with you and shut him up—or drown him!"

Tessa came forward with an insolent shrug. There was more than a spice of defiance in her bearing.

"I don't suppose I can catch him," she said. "But I'll try."

The chase of the elusive Scooter that followed would have been an affair of pure pleasure to the child, had it not been for the presence of her mother and the growing exasperation with which she regarded it. It was all sheer fun to Scooter who wormed in and out of the furniture with mirth in his gleaming eyes, and darted past the window a dozen times without availing himself of that means of escape.

Netta's small stock of patience was very speedily exhausted. She sat up on the sofa and sternly commanded Tessa to desist.

"Go and tell the *khit* to catch him!" she said.

Tessa, however, by this time had also warmed to the game. She paid no more attention to her mother's order than she would have paid to the buzzing of a mosquito. And when Scooter dived under the sofa on which Netta had been reclining, she burrowed after him with a squeal of merriment.

It was too much for Netta whose feelings had been decidedly ruffled before Tessa's entrance. As Scooter shot out on the other side of her, running his queer zigzag course, she snatched the first thing that came to hand, which chanced to be a heavy bronze weight from the writing-table at her elbow, and hurled it at him with all her strength.

Scooter collapsed on the floor like a broken mechanical toy. Tessa uttered a wild scream and flung herself upon him.

Netta gasped hysterically, horrified but still angry. "It serves him right—serves you both right! Now go away!" she said.

Tessa turned on her knees on the floor. Scooter was feebly kicking in her arms. The missile had struck him on the head and one eye was terribly injured. She gathered him up to her little narrow chest, and he ceased to kick and became quite still.

Over his lifeless body she looked at her mother with eyes of burning furious hatred. "You've killed him!" she said, her voice sunk very low. "And I hope—oh, I do hope—some day—someone—will kill you!"

There was that about her at the moment that actually frightened Netta, and it was with undoubted relief that she saw the door open and Major Ralston's loose-knit lounging figure block the entrance.

"What's all this noise about?" he began, and stopped short.

Behind him stood another figure, broad, powerful, not overtall. At sight of it, Tessa uttered a hard sob and scrambled to her feet. She still clasped poor Scooter's dead body to her breast, and his blood was on her face and on the white frock she wore.

"Uncle St. Bernard! Look! Look!" she said. "She's killed my Scooter!"

Netta also arose at this juncture. "Oh, do take that horrible thing away!" she said. "If it's dead, so much the better. It was no more than a weasel after all. I hate such pets."

Major Ralston found himself abruptly though not roughly pushed aside. Bernard Monck swooped down with the action of a practised footballer and took the furry thing out of Tessa's hold. His eyes were very bright and intensely alert, but he did not seem aware of Tessa's mother.

"Come with me, darling!" he said to the child. "P'raps I can help."

He trod upon the carved bronze that had slain Scooter as he turned, and he left the mark of his heel upon it— the deep impress of an angry giant.

The door closed with decision upon himself and the child, and Major Ralston was left alone with Netta.

She looked at him with a flushed face ready to defy remonstrance, but he stooped without speaking and picked up the thing that Bernard had tried to grind to powder, surveyed it with a lifted brow and set it back in its place.

Netta promptly collapsed upon the sofa. "Oh, it is too bad!" she sobbed. "It really is too bad! Now I suppose you too—are going to be brutal."

Major Ralston cleared his throat. There was certainly no sympathy in his aspect, but his manner was wholly lacking in brutality. He was never brutal to women, and Netta Ermsted was his guest as well as his patient.

After a moment he sat down beside her, and there was nothing in the action to mark it as heroic, or to betray the fact that he yearned to stamp out of the room after Bernard and leave her severely to her hysterics.

"No good in being upset now," he remarked. "The thing's done, and crying won't undo it."

"I don't want to undo it!" declared Netta. "I always did detest the horrible ferrety thing. Tessa couldn't have taken it Home with her either, so it's just as well it's gone." She dried her eyes with a vindictive gesture, and reached for the cigarettes. Hysterics were impossible in this man's presence. He was like a shower of cold water.

"I shouldn't if I were you," remarked Major Ralston with the air of a man performing a laborious duty. "You smoke too many of 'em."

Netta ignored the admonition. "They soothe my nerves," she said. "May I have a light?"

He searched his pockets, and apparently drew a blank.

Netta frowned in swift irritation. "How stupid! I thought all men carried matches."

Major Ralston accepted the reproof in silence. He was like a large dog, gravely presenting his shoulder to the nips of a toy terrier.

"Well?" said Netta aggressively.

He looked at her with composure. "Talking about going Home," he said, "at the risk of appearing inhospitable, I think it is my duty to advise you very strongly to go as soon as possible."

"Indeed!" She looked back with instant hostility. "And why?"

He did not immediately reply. Whether with reason or not, he had the reputation for being slow-witted, in spite of the fact that he was a brilliant chess-player.

She laughed—a short, unpleasant laugh. She was never quite at her ease with him, notwithstanding his slowness. "Why the devil should I, Major Ralston?"

He shrugged his shoulders with massive deliberation. "Because," he said slowly, "there's going to be the devil's own row if this man is hanged for your husband's murder. We have been warned to that effect."

She shrugged her shoulders also with infinite daintiness, "Oh, a native rumpus! That doesn't impress me in the least. I shan't go for that."

Major Ralston's eyes wandered round the room as if in search of inspiration. "Mary is going," he observed.

Netta laughed again, lightly, flippantly. "Good old Mary! Where is she going to?"

His eyes came down upon her suddenly like the flash of a knife. "She has consented to go to Bhulwana with the rest," he said. "But I beg you will not accompany her there. As Captain Ermsted's widow and—" he spoke as one hewing his way—"the chosen friend of the Rajah, your position in the State is one of considerable difficulty—possibly even of danger. And I do not propose to allow my wife to take unnecessary risks. For that reason I must ask you to go before matters come to a head. You have stayed too long already."

"Good gracious!" said Netta, opening her eyes wide. "But if Mary's sacred person is to be safely stowed at Bhulwana, what is to prevent my remaining here if I so choose?"

"Because I don't choose to let you, Mrs. Ermsted," said Major Ralston steadily.

She gazed at him. "You—don't—choose! You!"

His eyes did battle with hers. Since that slighting allusion to his wife, he had no consideration left for Netta. "That is so," he said, in his heavy fashion. "I have already pointed out that you would be well-advised on your own account to go—not to mention the child's safety."

"Oh, the child!" There was keenness about the exclamation which almost amounted to actual dislike. "I'm tired to death of having Tessa's welfare and Tessa's morals rammed down my throat. Why should I make a fetish of the child? What is good enough for me is surely good enough for her."

"I am afraid I don't agree with you," said Major Ralston.

"You wouldn't," she rejoined. "You and Mary are quite antediluvian in your idea. But that doesn't influence me. I am glad to say I am more up to date. If I can't stay here, I shall go to Udalkhand. There's a hotel there as well as here."

"Of sorts," said Major Ralston. "Also Udalkhand is nearer to the seat of disturbance."

"Well, I don't care." Netta spoke recklessly. "I'm not going to be dictated to. What a mighty scare you're all in! What can you think will happen even if a few natives do get out of hand?"

"Plenty of things might happen," he rejoined, getting up. "But that by the way. If you won't listen to reason I am wasting my time. But—" he spoke with abrupt emphasis—"you will not take Tessa to Udalkhand."

Netta's eyes gleamed. "I shall take her to Kamtchatka if I choose," she said.

For the first time a smile crossed Major Ralston's face. He turned to the door. "And if she chooses," he said, with malicious satisfaction.

The door closed upon him, and Netta was left alone.

She remained motionless for a few moments showing her teeth a little in an answering smile; then with a swift, lissom movement, that would have made Tommy compare her to a lizard, she rose.

With a white, determined face she bent over the writing-table and scribbled a hasty note. Her hand shook, but she controlled it resolutely.

Words flicked rapidly into being under her pen: "I shall be behind the tamarisks to-night."

CHAPTER IV

THE BROAD ROAD

Bernard Monck never forgot the day of Scooter's death. It was as indelibly fixed in his memory as in that of Tessa.

The child's wild agony of grief was of so utterly abandoned a nature as to be almost Oriental in its violence. The passionate force of her resentment against her mother also was not easy to cope with though he quelled it eventually. But when that was over, when she had wept herself exhausted in his arms at last, there followed a period of numbness that made him seriously uneasy.

Mrs. Ralston had gone out before the tragedy had occurred, but Major Ralston presently came to his relief. He stooped over Tessa with a few kindly words, but when he saw the child's face his own changed somewhat.

"This won't do," he said to Bernard, holding the slender wrist. "We must get her to bed. Where's her *ayah*?"

Tessa's little hand hung limply in his hold. She seemed to be half-asleep. Yet when Bernard moved to lift her, she roused herself to cling around his neck.

"Please keep me with you, dear Uncle St. Bernard! Oh, please don't go away!"

"I won't, sweetheart," he promised her.

The *ayah* was nowhere to be found, but it was doubtful if her presence would have made much difference, since Tessa would not stir from her friend's sheltering arms, and wept again weakly even at the doctor's touch.

So it was Bernard who carried her to her room, and eventually put her to bed under Major Ralston's directions. The latter's face was very grave over the whole proceeding and he presently fetched something in a medicine-glass and gave it to Bernard to administer.

Tessa tried to refuse it, but her opposition broke down before Bernard's very gentle insistence. She would do anything, she told him piteously, if only—if only—he would stay with her.

So Bernard stayed, sending a message to The Green Bungalow to explain his absence, which found Mrs. Ralston as well as Stella and brought the former back in haste.

Tessa was in a deep sleep by the time she arrived, but, hearing that Stella did not need him, Bernard still maintained his watch, only permitting Mrs. Ralston to relieve him while he partook of luncheon with her husband.

Netta did not appear for the meal to the unspoken satisfaction of them both. They ate almost in silence, Major Ralston being sunk in a species of moody abstraction which Bernard did not disturb until the meal was over.

Then at length, ere he rose to go, he deliberately broke into his host's gloomy reflections. "Will you tell me," he said courteously, "exactly what it is that you fear with regard to the child?"

Major Ralston continued to be abstracted for fully thirty seconds after the quiet question; then, as Bernard did not repeat it but merely waited, he replied to it.

"There are plenty of things to be feared for a child like that. It's a criminal shame to have kept her out here so long. What I actually believe to be the matter at the present moment, is heart trouble."

"Ah! I thought so." Bernard looked across at him with grave comprehension. "She had a bad shock the other day."

"Yes; a shock to the whole system. She lives on wires in any case. I am going to examine her presently, but I am pretty sure I am right. What she really wants—" Major Ralston stopped himself abruptly, so abruptly that a twinkle of humour shone momentarily in Bernard's eyes.

"Don't jam on the brakes on my account!" he protested gently. "I am with you all the way. What does she really want?"

Major Ralston uttered a gruff laugh. It was practically impossible not to confide in Bernard Monck. "She wants to get right away from that vicious little termagant of a mother of hers. There's no love between them and never will be, so what's the use of pretending? She wants to get into a wholesome bracing, outdoor atmosphere with someone who knows how to love her. She'll probably go straight to the bad if she doesn't—that is, if she lives long enough."

The humour had died in Bernard's eyes. They shone with a very different light as he said, "I have thought the same thing myself." He paused a moment, then slowly, "Do you think her mother would be persuaded to hand her over to me?" he said.

Ralston's brows went up. "To you! For good and all do you mean?"

"Yes." In his steady unhurried fashion Bernard made answer. "I have been thinking of it for some time. As a matter of fact, it was to consult you about it that I came here to-day. I want it more than ever now."

Ralston was staring openly. "You'd have your hands full," he remarked.

Bernard smiled. "I daresay. But, you see, we're chums. To use your own expression I know how to love her. I could make her happy—possibly good as well."

Ralston never paid compliments, but after a considerable pause he said, "It would be the best thing that ever happened to the imp. So far as her mother's permission goes, I should say she is cheap enough to be had almost without asking. You won't need to use much persuasion in that direction."

"An infernal shame!" said Bernard, the hot light again in his eyes.

Ralston agreed with him. "All the same, Tessa can be a positive little demon when she likes. I've seen it, so I know. She has got a good deal of her mother's temperament only with a generous allowance of heart thrown in."

"Yes," Bernard said. "And it's the heart that counts. You can do practically anything with a child like that."

Ralston got up. "Well, I'm going to have another look at her, and then I'm due at The Green Bungalow. I can't say what is going to happen there. You ought to clear out, all of you; but a journey would probably be fatal to Mrs. Monck's infant just now. I can't advise it."

"Wherever Stella goes, I go," said Bernard firmly.

"Yes, that's understood." Ralston gave him a keen look. "You're in charge, aren't you? But those who can go, must go, that's certain. That scoundrel will be convicted in a day or two. And then—look out for squalls!"

Bernard's smile was scarcely the smile of the man of peace. "Oh yes, I shall look out," he said mildly. "And—incidentally—Tommy is teaching me how to shoot."

They returned to Tessa who was still sleeping, and Mrs. Ralston gave up her place beside her to Bernard, who settled down with a paper to spend the afternoon. Major Ralston departed for The Green Bungalow, and the silence of midday fell upon the place.

It was still early in the year, but the warmth was as that of a soft summer day in England. The lazy drone of bees hung on the air, and somewhere among the tamarisks a small, persistent bird, called and called perpetually, receiving no reply.

"A fine example of perseverance," Bernard murmured to himself.

He had plenty of things to think about—to worry about also, had it been his disposition to worry; but the utter peace that surrounded him made him drowsy. He nodded uncomfortably for a space, then finally—since he seldom did things by halves—laid aside his paper, leaned back in his chair, and serenely slept.

Twice during the afternoon Mrs. Ralston tiptoed along the verandah, peeped in upon them, and retired again smiling. On the second occasion she met her husband on the same errand and he drew her aside, his hand through her arm.

"Look here, Mary! I've talked to that little spitfire without much result. She talks in a random fashion of going to Udalkhand. What her actual intentions are I don't know. Possibly she doesn't know herself. But one thing is certain. She is not going to be attached to your train any longer, and I have told her so."

"Oh, Gerald!" She looked at him in dismay. "How—inhospitable of you!"

"Yes, isn't it?" His hand was holding her arm firmly. "You see, I chance to value your safety more than my reputation for kindness to outsiders. You are going to Bhulwana at the end of this week. Come! You promised."

"Yes, I know I did." She looked at him with distress in her eyes. "I've wished I hadn't ever since. There is my poor Stella in bad trouble for one thing. She says she will have to change her *ayah*. And there is—"

"She has got Peter—and her brother-in-law. She doesn't want you too," said her husband.

"And now there is little Tessa," proceeded Mrs. Ralston, growing more and more worried as she proceeded.

"Yes, there is Tessa," he agreed. "You can offer to take her to Bhulwana with you if you like. But not her mother as well. That is understood. It won't break her heart to part with her, I fancy. As for you, my dear," he gave her a whimsical look, "the sooner you are gone the better I shall be pleased. Lady Harriet and the Burton contingent left to-day."

"I hate going!" declared Mrs. Ralston almost tearfully. "I shouldn't have promised if I could have foreseen all that was going to happen."

He squeezed her arm. "All the same—you promised. So don't be silly!"

She turned suddenly and clung to him.

"Gerald! I want to stay with you. Let me stay! I can't bear the thought of you alone and in danger."

He stared for a moment in astonishment. Demonstrations of affection were almost unknown between them. Then, with a shamefaced gesture, he bent and kissed her.

"What a silly old woman!" he said.

That ended the discussion and she knew that her plea had been refused. But the fashion of its refusal brought the warm colour to her faded face, and she was even near to laughing in the midst of her woe. How dear of Gerald to put it like that! She did not feel that she had ever fully realized his love for her until that moment.

Seeing that her presence in her own bungalow was not needed just then, she betook herself once more to Stella, and again the afternoon silence fell like a spell of enchantment. That there could be any element of unrest anywhere within that charmed region seemed a thing impossible. The peace of Eden brooded everywhere.

The evening was drawing on ere Bernard slowly emerged from his serene slumber and looked at the child beside him. Some invisible influence—or perhaps some bond of sympathy between them—had awakened her at the same moment, for her eyes were fixed upon him. They shone intensely, mysteriously blue in the subdued light, wistful, searching eyes, wholly unlike the eyes of a child.

Her hand came out to his. "Have you been here all the time, dear?" she said.

She seemed to be still half-wrapped in the veil of sleep. He leaned to her, holding the little hand up against his cheek.

"Almost, my princess," he said.

She nestled to him snuggling her fair head into his shoulder. "I've been dreaming," she whispered.

"Have you, my darling?" He gathered her close with a compassionate tenderness for the frailty of the little throbbing body he held.

Tessa's arms crept round his neck. "I dreamt," she said, "that you and I, Uncle St. Bernard, were walking in a great big city, and there was a church with a golden spire. There were a lot of steps up to it—and Scooter—" a sob rose in her throat and was swiftly suppressed—"was sunning himself on the top. And I tried to run up the steps and catch him, but there were always more and more and more steps, and I couldn't get any nearer. And I cried at last, I was so tired and disappointed. And then—" the bony arms tightened—"you came up behind me, and took my hand and said, 'Why don't you kneel down and pray? It's much the quickest way.' And so I did," said Tessa simply. "And all of a sudden the steps were gone, and you and I went in together. I tried to pick up Scooter, but he ran away, and I didn't mind 'cos I knew he was safe. I was so happy, so very happy. I didn't want to wake again." A doleful note crept into Tessa's voice; she swallowed another sob.

Bernard lifted her bodily from the bed to his arms. "Don't fret, little sweetheart! I'm here," he said.

She lifted her face to his, very wet and piteous. "Uncle St. Bernard, I've been praying and praying—ever such a lot since my birthday-party. You said I might, didn't you? But God hasn't taken any notice."

He held her close. "What have you been praying for, my darling?" he said.

"I do—so—want to be your little girl," answered Tessa with a break in her voice. "I never really prayed for anything before—only the things Aunt Mary made me say—and they weren't what I wanted. But I do want this. And I believe I'd get quite good if I was your little girl. I told God so, but I don't think He cared."

"Yes. He did care, darling." Very softly Bernard reassured her. "Don't you think that ever! He is going to answer that prayer of yours—pretty soon now."

"Oh, is He?" said Tessa, brightening. "How do you know? Is He going to say Yes?"

"I think so." Bernard's voice and touch were alike motherly. "But you must be patient a little longer, my princess of the bluebell. It isn't good for us to have things straight off when we want them."

"You do want me?" insinuated Tessa, squeezing his neck very hard.

"Yes. I want you very much," he said.

"I love you," said Tessa with passionate warmth, "better—yes, better now than even Uncle Everard. And I didn't think I ever could do that."

"God bless you, little one!" he said.

Later, when Major Ralston had seen her again, they had another conference. The doctor's suspicions were fully justified. Tessa would need the utmost care.

"She shall have it," Bernard said. "But—I can't leave Stella now. I shall see my way clearer presently."

"Quite so," Ralston agreed. "My wife shall look after the child at Bhulwana. It will keep her quiet." He gave Bernard a shrewd look. "Perhaps you—and Mrs. Monck also—will be on your way Home before the hot weather," he said. "In that case she could go with you."

Bernard was silent. It was impossible to look forward. One thing was certain. He could not desert Stella.

Ralston passed on. Being reticent himself he respected a man who could keep his own counsel. "What about Mrs. Ermsted?" he said. "When will you see her?"

"To-night," said Bernard, setting his jaw.

Ralston smiled briefly. That look recalled his brother. "No time like the present," he said.

But the time for consultation with Netta Ermsted upon the future of her child was already past. When Bernard, very firm and purposeful, walked down again after dinner that night, Ralston met him with a wry expression and put a crumpled note into his hand.

"Mrs. Ermsted has apparently divined your benevolent intentions," he said.

Bernard read in silence, with meeting brows.

DEAR MARY:

This is to wish you and all kind friends good-bye. So that there may be no misunderstanding on the part of our charitable gossips, pray tell them at once that I have finally chosen the broad road as it really suits me best. As for Tessa—I bequeath her and her little morals to the first busybody who cares to apply for them. Perhaps the worthy Father Monck would like to acquire virtue in this fashion. I find the task only breeds vice in me. Many thanks for your laborious and, I fear, wholly futile attempts to keep me in the much too narrow way.

Yours,

NETTA.

Bernard looked up from the note with such fiery eyes that Ralston who was on the verge of a scathing remark himself had to stop out of sheer curiosity to see what he would say.

"A damnably cruel and heartless woman!" said Bernard with deliberation.

Ralston's smile expressed what for him was warm approval. "She's nothing but an animal," he said.

Bernard took him up short. "You wrong the animals," he said. "The very least of them love their young."

Ralston shrugged his shoulders. "All the better for Tessa anyhow."

Bernard's eyes softened very suddenly. He crumpled the note into a ball and tossed it from him. "Yes," he said quietly. "God helping me, it shall be all the better for her."

CHAPTER V

THE DARK NIGHT

An owl hooted across the compound, and a paraquet disturbed by the outcry uttered a shrill, indignant protest. An immense moon hung suspended as it were in mid-heaven, making all things intense with its radiance. It was the hour before the dawn.

Stella stood at her window, gazing forth and numbly marvelling at the splendour. As of old, it struck her like a weird fantasy—this Indian enchantment—poignant, passionate, holding more of anguish than of ecstasy, yet deeply magnetic, deeply alluring, as a magic potion which, once tasted, must enchain the senses for ever.

The extravagance of that world of dreadful black and dazzling silver, the stillness that was yet indescribably electric, the unreality that was allegorically real, she felt it all as a vague accompaniment to the heartache that never left her—the scornful mockery of the goddess she had refused to worship.

There were even times when the very atmosphere seemed to her charged with hostility—a terrible overwhelming antagonism that closed about her in a narrowing ring which serpent-wise constricted her ever more and more, from which she could never hope to escape. For—still the old idea haunted her—she was a trespasser upon forbidden ground. Once she had been cast forth. But she had dared to return, braving the flaming sword. And now—and now—it barred her in, cutting off her escape.

For she was as much a prisoner as if iron walls surrounded her. Sentence had gone forth against her. She would not be cast forth again until she had paid the uttermost farthing, endured the ultimate torture. Then only—childless and desolate and broken—would she be turned adrift in the desert, to return no more for ever.

The ghastly glamour of the night attracted and repelled her like the swing of a mighty pendulum. She was trying to pray—that much had Bernard taught her—but her prayer only ran blind and futile through her brain. The hour should have been sacred, but it was marred and desecrated by the stark glare of that nightmare moon. She was worn out with long and anxious watching, and she had almost ceased to look for comfort, so heavy were the clouds that menaced her.

The thought of Everard was ever with her, strive as she might to drive it out. At such moments as these she yearned for him with a sick and desperate longing—his strength, his tenderness, his understanding. He, and he alone, would have known how to comfort her now with her baby dying before her eyes. He would have held her up through her darkest hours. His arm would have borne her forward however terrible the path.

She had Bernard and she had Tommy, each keen and ready in her service. She sometimes thought that but for Bernard she would have been overwhelmed long since. But he could not fill the void within her. He could not even touch the aching longing that gnawed so perpetually at her heart. That was a pain she would have to endure in silence all the rest of her life. She did not think she would ever see Everard again. Though only a few miles lay between them at present he might have been already a world away. She was sure he would not come back to her unless she summoned him. The manner of his going, though he had taken no leave of her, had been somehow final. And she could not call him back even if she would. He had deceived her cruelly, of set intention, and she could never trust him again. The memory of Ralph Dacre tainted all her thoughts of him. He had sworn he had not killed him. Perhaps not—perhaps not! Yet was the conviction ever with her that he had sent him to his death, had intended him to die.

She had given up reasoning the matter. It was beyond her. She was too hopelessly plunged in darkness. Tommy with all his staunchness could not lift that overwhelming cloud. And Bernard? She did not know what Bernard thought save that he had once reminded her that a man should be regarded as innocent unless he could be proved guilty.

It was common talk now that Everard's Indian career was ended. It was only the trial at Khanmulla that had delayed the sending in of his papers. He was as much a broken man, however hotly Tommy contested the point, as if he had been condemned by a court-martial. Surely, had he been truly innocent he would have demanded a court-martial and vindicated himself. But he had suffered his honour to go down in silence. What more damning evidence could be supplied than this?

The dumb sympathy of Peter's eyes kept the torturing thought constantly before her. She felt sure that Peter believed him guilty of Dacre's murder though it was more than possible that in his heart he condoned the offence. Perhaps he even admired him for it, she reflected shudderingly. But his devotion to her, as always, was uppermost. His dog-like fidelity surrounded her with unfailing service. The *ayah* had gone, and he had slipped into her place as naturally as if he had always occupied it. Even now, while Stella stood at her window gazing forth into the garish moonlight, was he softly padding to and fro in the room adjoining hers, hushing the poor little wailing infant to sleep. She could trust him implicitly, she knew, even in moments of crisis. He would gladly work himself to death in her service. But with Mrs. Ralston gone to Bhulwana, she knew she must have further help. The strain was incessant, and Major Ralston insisted that she must have a woman with her.

All the ladies of the station, save herself, had gone. She knew vaguely that some sort of disturbance was expected at Khanmulla, and that it might spread to Kurrumpore. But her baby was too ill for travel; she had practically forced this truth from Major Ralston, and so she had no choice but to remain. She knew very well at the heart of her that it would not be for long.

No thought of personal danger troubled her. Sinister though the night might seem to her stretched nerves, yet no sense of individual peril penetrated the weary bewilderment of her brain. She was tired out in mind and body, and had yielded to Peter's persuasion to take a rest. But the weird cry of the night-bird had drawn her to the window and the glittering splendour of the night had held her there. She turned from it at last with a long, long sigh, and lay down just as she was. She always held herself ready for a call at any time. Those strange seizures came so suddenly and were becoming increasingly violent. It was many days since she had permitted herself to sleep soundly.

She lay for awhile wide-eyed, almost painfully conscious, listening to Peter's muffled movements in the other room. The baby had ceased to cry, but he was still prowling to and fro, tireless and patient, with an endurance that was almost superhuman.

She had done the same thing a little earlier till her limbs had given way beneath her. In the daytime Bernard helped her, but she and Peter shared the nights.

Her senses became at last a little blurred. The night seemed to have spread over half a lifetime—a practically endless vista of suffering. The soft footfall in the other room made her think of the Sentry at the Gate, that Sentry with the flaming sword who never slept. It beat with a pitiless thudding upon her brain....

Later, it grew intermittent, fitful, as if at each turn the Sentry paused. It always went on again, or so she thought. And she was sure she was not deeply sleeping, or that haunting cry of an owl had not penetrated her consciousness so frequently.

Once, oddly, there came to her—perhaps it was a dream—a sound as of voices whispering together. She turned in her sleep and tried to listen, but her senses were fogged, benumbed. She could not at the moment drag herself free from the stupor of weariness that held her. But she was sure of Peter, quite sure that he would call her if any emergency arose. And there was no one with whom he could be whispering. So she was sure it must be a dream. Imperceptibly she sank still deeper into slumber and forgot....

It was several hours later that Tommy, returned from early parade, flung himself impetuously down at the table opposite Bernard with a brief, "Now for it!"

Bernard was reading a letter, and Tommy's eyes fastened upon it as his were lifted.

"What's that? A letter from Everard?" he asked unceremoniously.

"Yes. He has written to tell me definitely that he has sent in his resignation—and it has been accepted." Bernard's reply was wholly courteous, the boy's bluntness notwithstanding. He had a respect for Tommy.

"Oh, damn!" said Tommy with fervor. "What is he going to do now?"

"He doesn't tell me that." Bernard folded the letter and put it in his pocket. "What's your news?" he inquired.

Tommy marked the action with somewhat jealous eyes. He had been aware of Everard's intention for some time. It had been more or less inevitable. But he wished he had written to him also. There were several things he would have liked to know.

He looked at Bernard rather blankly, ignoring his question. "What the devil is he going to do?" he said. "Dropout?"

Bernard's candid eyes met his. "Honestly I don't know," he said. "Perhaps he is just waiting for orders."

"Will he come back here?" questioned Tommy.

Bernard shook his head. "No. I'm pretty sure he won't. Now tell me your news!"

"Oh, it's nothing!" said Tommy impatiently. "Nothing, I mean, compared to his clearing out. The trial is over and the man is condemned. He is to be executed next week. It'll mean a shine of some sort—nothing very great, I am afraid."

"That all?" said Bernard, with a smile.

"No, not quite all. There was some secret information given which it is supposed was rather damaging to the Rajah, for he has taken to his heels. No one knows where he is, or at least no one admits he does. You know these Oriental chaps. They can cover the scent of a rotten herring. He'll probably never turn up again. The place is too hot to hold him. He can finish his rotting in another corner of the Empire; and I wish Netta Ermsted joy of her bargain!" ended Tommy with vindictive triumph.

"My good fellow!" protested Bernard.

Tommy uttered a reckless laugh. "You know it as well as I do. She was done for from the moment he taught her the opium habit. There's no escape from that, and the devil knew it. I say, what a mercy it will be when you can get Tessa away to England."

"And Stella too," said Bernard, turning to the subject with relief.

"You won't do that," said Tommy quickly.

"How do you know that?" Bernard's look had something of a piercing quality.

But Tommy eluded all search. "I do know. I can't tell you how. But I'm certain—dead certain—that Stella won't go back to England with you this spring."

"You're something of a prophet, Tommy," remarked Bernard, after an attentive pause.

"It's not my only accomplishment," rejoined Tommy modestly. "I'm several things besides that. I've got some brains too—just a few. Funny, isn't it? Ah, here is Stella! Come and break your fast, old girl! What's the latest?"

He went to meet her and drew her to the table. She smiled in her wan, rather abstracted way at Bernard whom she had seen before.

"Oh, don't get up!" she said. "I only came for a glimpse of you both. I had *tiffin* in my room. Peter saw to that. Baby is very weak this morning, and I thought perhaps, Tommy dear, when, you go back you would see Major Ralston for me and ask him to come up soon." She sat down with an involuntary gesture of weariness.

"Have you slept at all?" Bernard asked her gently.

"Oh yes, thank you. I had three hours of undisturbed rest. Peter was splendid."

"You must have another *ayah*," Bernard said. "It isn't fit for you to go on in this way."

"No." She spoke with the docility of exhaustion. "Peter is seeing to it. He always sees to everything. He knows a woman in the bazaar who would do—an elderly woman—I think he said she is the grandmother of Hafiz who sells trinkets. You know Hafiz, I expect? I don't like him, but he is supposed to be respectable, and Peter is prepared to vouch for the woman's respectability. Only she has been terribly disfigured by an accident, burnt I think he said, and she wears a veil. I told him that didn't matter. Baby is too ill to notice, and he evidently wants me to have her. He says she has been used to English children, and is a good nurse. That is what matters chiefly, so I have told him to engage her."

"I am very glad to hear it," Bernard said.

"Yes, I think it will be a relief. Those screaming fits are so terrible." Stella checked a sharp shudder. "Peter would not recommend her if he did not personally know her to be trustworthy," she added quietly.

"No. Peter's safe enough," said Tommy. He was bolting his meal with great expedition. "Is the kiddie worse, Stella?"

She looked at him with that in her tired eyes that went straight to his heart. "He is a little worse every day," she said.

Tommy swore into his cup and asked no further.

A few moments later he got up, gave her a brief kiss, and departed.

Stella sat on with her chin in her hand, every line of her expressing the weariness of the hopeless watcher. She looked crushed, as if a burden she could hardly support had been laid upon her.

Bernard looked at her once or twice without speaking. Finally he too rose, went round to her, knelt beside her, put his arm about her.

Her face quivered a little. "I've got—to keep strong," she said, in the tone of one who had often said the same thing in solitude.

"I know," he said. "And so you will. There's special strength given for such times as these. It won't fail you now."

She put her hand into his. "Thank you," she said. And then, with an effort, "Do you know, Bernard, I tried—I really tried—to pray in the night before I lay down. But—there was something so wicked about it—I simply couldn't."

"One can't always," he said.

"Oh, have you found that too?" she asked.

He smiled at the question. "Of course I have. So has everybody. We're only children, Stella. God knows that. He doesn't expect of us more than we can manage. Prayer is only one of the means we have of reaching Him. It can't be used always. There are some people who haven't time for prayer even, and yet they may be very near to God. In times of stress like yours one is often much nearer than one realizes. You will find that out quite suddenly one of these days, find that through all your desert journeying, He has been guiding you, protecting you, surrounding you with the most loving care. And—because the night was dark—you never knew it."

"The night is certainly very dark," Stella said with a tremulous smile. "If it weren't for you I don't think I could ever get through."

"Oh, don't say that!" he said. "If it weren't me it would be someone else—or possibly a closer vision of Himself. There is always something—something to which later you will look back and say, 'That was His lamp in the desert, showing the way.' Don't fret if you can't pray! I can pray for you. You just keep on being brave and patient! He understands."

Stella's fingers pressed upon his. "You are good to me, Bernard," she said. "I shall think of what you say—the next time I am alone in the night."

His arm held her sustainingly. "And if you're very desolate, child, come and call me!" he said. "I'm always at hand, always glad to serve you."

She smiled—a difficult smile. "I shall need you more—afterwards," she said under her breath. And then, as if words had suddenly become impossible to her, she leaned against him and kissed him.

He gathered her up close, as if she had been a weary child. "God bless you, my dear!" he said.

CHAPTER VI

THE FIRST GLIMMER

It was from the Colonel himself that Stella heard of Everard's retirement.

He walked back from the Mess that night with Tommy and asked to see her for a few minutes alone. He was always kinder to her in his wife's absence.

She was busy installing the new *ayah* whom Peter with the air of a magician who has but to wave his wand had presented to her half an hour before. The woman was old and bent and closely veiled—so closely that Stella strongly suspected her disfigurement to be of a very ghastly nature, but her low voice and capable manner inspired her with instinctive confidence. She realized with relief from the very outset that her faithful Peter had not made a mistake. She was sure that the new-comer had nursed sickly English children before. She went to the Colonel, leaving the strange woman in charge of her baby and Peter hovering reassuringly in the background.

His first greeting of her had a touch of diffidence, but when he saw the weary suffering of her eyes this was swallowed up in pity. He took her hands and held them.

"My poor girl!" he said.

She smiled at him. Pity from an outsider did not penetrate to the depths of her. "Thank you for coming," she said.

He coughed and cleared his throat. "I hope it isn't an intrusion," he said.

"But of course not!" she made answer. "How could it be? Won't you sit down?"

He led her to a chair; but he did not sit down himself. He stood before her with something of the air of a man making a confession.

"Mrs. Monck," he said, "I think I ought to tell you that it was by my advice that your husband resigned his commission."

Her brows drew together a little as if at a momentary dart of pain. "Has he resigned it?" she said.

"Yes. Didn't he tell you?" He frowned. "Haven't you seen him? Don't you know where he is?"

She shook her head. "I can only think of my baby just now," she said.

He swung round abruptly upon his heel and paced the room. "Oh yes, of course. I know that. Ralston told me. I am very sorry for you, Mrs. Monck,—very, very sorry."

"Thank you," she said.

He continued to tramp to and fro. "You haven't much to thank me for. I had to think of the Regiment; but I considered the step very carefully before I took it. He had rendered invaluable service—especially over this Khanmulla trial. He would have been decorated for it if—" he pulled up with a jerk—"if things had been different. I know Sir Reginald Bassett thought very highly of him, was prepared to give him an appointment on his personal staff. And no doubt eventually he would have climbed to the top of the tree. But—this affair has destroyed him." He paused a moment, but he did not look at her. "He has had every chance," he said then. "I kept an open mind. I wouldn't condemn him unheard until—well until he refused flatly to speak on his own behalf. I went over to Khanmulla and talked to him—talked half the night. I couldn't move him. And if a man won't take the trouble to defend his own honour, it isn't worth—that!" He snapped his fingers with a bitter gesture; then abruptly wheeled and came back to her. "I didn't come here to distress you," he said, looking down at her again. "I know your cup is full already. And it's a thankless task to persuade any woman that her husband is unworthy of her, besides being an impertinence. But what I must say to you is this. There is nothing left to wait for, and it would be sheer madness to stay on any longer. The Rajah has been deeply incriminated and is in hiding. The Government will of course take over the direction of affairs, but there is certain—absolutely certain—to be a disturbance when Ermsted's murderer is executed. I hope an adequate force will soon be at our disposal to cope with it, but it has not yet been provided. Therefore I cannot possibly permit you to stay here any longer. As Monck's wife, it is more than likely that you might be made an object of vengeance. I can't risk it. You and the child must go. I will send an escort in the morning."

He stopped at last, partly for lack of breath, partly because from her unmoved expression he fancied that she was not taking in his warning words. She sat looking straight before her as one rapt in reverie. It was almost as though she had forgotten him, suffered some more absorbing matter to crowd him out of her thoughts.

"You do follow me?" he questioned at length as she did not speak.

She lifted her eyes to him again though he felt it was with a great effort. "Oh, yes," she said. "I quite understand you, Colonel Mansfield. And—I am quite grateful to you. But I am not staying here for my husband's sake at all. I—do not suppose we shall ever see each other any more. All that is over."

He started. "What! You have given him up?" he said, uttering the words almost involuntarily, so quiet was she in her despair.

She bent her head. "Yes, I have given him up. I do not know where he is—or anything about him. I am staying here now—I must stay here now—for my baby's sake. He is too ill to bear a journey."

She lifted her face again with the words, and in its pale resolution he saw that he would spend himself upon further argument in vain. Moreover, he was for the moment too staggered by the low-spoken information to concentrate his attention upon persuasion. Her utter quietness silenced him.

He stood for a moment or two looking down at her, then abruptly bent and took her hand. "You're a very brave woman," he said, a quick touch of feeling in his voice. "You've had a fiendish time of it out here from start to finish. It'll be a good thing for you when you can get out of it and go Home. You're young; you'll start again."

It was clumsy consolation, but his hand-grip was fatherly. She smiled again at him, and got up.

"Thank you very much, Colonel. You have always been kind. Please don't bother about me any more. I am really not a bit afraid. I have too much to think about. And really I don't think I am important enough to be in any real danger. You will excuse me now, won't you? I have just got a new *ayah*, and they always need superintending. Perhaps you will join my brother-in-law. I know he will be delighted."

She extricated herself with a gentle aloofness more difficult to combat than any open opposition, and he went away to express himself more strongly to Bernard Monck from whom he was sure at least of receiving sympathy if not support.

Stella returned to her baby with a stunned feeling of having been struck, and yet without consciousness of pain. Perhaps she had suffered so much that her faculties were getting numbed. She knew that the Colonel was surprised that his news concerning Everard had affected her so little. She was in a fashion surprised herself. Was she then so absorbed that she had no room for him in her thoughts? And yet only the previous night how she had yearned for him!

It was the end of everything for him—the end of his ambition, of his career, of all his cherished hopes. He was a broken man and he would drop out as other men had dropped out. His love for her had been his ruin. And yet her brain seemed incapable of grasping the meaning of the catastrophe. The bearing of her burden occupied the whole of her strength.

The rest of the Colonel's news scarcely touched her at all, save that the thought flashed upon her once that if the danger were indeed so great Everard would certainly come to her. That sent a strange glow through her that died as swiftly as it was born. She did not really believe in the danger, and Everard was probably far away already.

She went back to her baby and the *ayah*, Hanani, over whom Peter was mounting guard with a queer mixture of patronage and respect. For though he had procured the woman and obviously thought highly of her, he seemed to think that none but himself could be regarded as fully qualified to have the care of his *mem-sahib's* fondly cherished *baba*.

Stella heard him giving some low-toned directions as she entered, and she wondered if the new *ayah* would resent his lordly attitude. But the veiled head bent over the child expressed nothing but complete docility. She answered Peter in few words, but with the utmost meekness.

Her quietness was a great relief to Stella. There was a self-reliance about it that gave her confidence. And presently, tenderly urged by Peter, she went to the adjoining room to rest, on the understanding that she should be called immediately if occasion arose. And that was the first night of many that she passed in undisturbed repose.

In the early morning, entering, she found Peter in sole possession and very triumphant. They had divided the night, he said, and Hanani had gone to rest in her turn. All had gone well. He had slept on the threshold and knew. And now his *mem-sahib* would sleep through every night and have no fear.

She smiled at his solicitude though it touched her almost to tears, and gathered in silence to her breast the little frail body that every day now seemed to feel lighter and smaller. It would not be for very long—their planning and contriving. Very soon now she would be free—quite free—to sleep as long as she would. But her tired heart warmed to Peter and to that silent *ayah* whom he had enlisted in her service. Through the dark night of her grief the love of her friends shone with a radiance that penetrated even the deepest shadows. Was this the lamp in the desert of which Bernard had spoken so confidently—the Lamp that God had lighted to guide her halting feet? Was it by this that she would come at last into the Presence of God Himself, and realize that the wanderers in the wilderness are ever His especial care?

Certainly, as Peter had intimated, she knew her baby to be safe in their joint charge. As the days slipped by, it seemed to her that Peter had imbued the *ayah* with something of his own devotion, for, though it was proffered almost silently, she was aware of it at every turn. At any other time her sympathy for the woman would have fired her interest and led her to attempt to draw her confidence. But the slender thread of life they guarded, though it bound them with a tie that was almost friendship, seemed so to fill their minds that they never spoke of anything else. Stella knew that Hanani loved her and considered her in every way, but she gave Peter most of the credit for it, Peter and the little dying baby she rocked so constantly against her heart. She knew that many an *ayah* would lay down her life for her charge. Peter had chosen well.

Later—when this time of waiting and watching was over, when she was left childless and alone—she would try to find out something of the woman's history, help her if she could, reward her certainly. It was evident that she was growing old. She had the stoop and the deliberation of age. Probably, she would not have obtained an *ayah's* post under any other circumstances. But, notwithstanding these drawbacks, she had a wonderful endurance, and she was never startled or at a loss. Stella often told herself that she would not have exchanged her for another woman—even a white woman—out of the whole of India had the chance offered. Hanani, grave, silent, capable, met every need.

CHAPTER VII

THE FIRST VICTIM

An ominous calm prevailed at Khanmulla during the week that followed the conviction of Ermsted's murderer and the disappearance of the Rajah. All Markestan seemed to be waiting with bated breath. But, save for the departure of the women from Kurrumpore, no sign was given by the Government of any expectation of a disturbance. The law was to take its course, and no official note had been made of the absence of the Rajah. He had always been sudden in his movements.

Everything went as usual at Kurrumpore, and no one's nerves seemed to feel any strain. Even Tommy betrayed no hint of irritation. A new manliness had come upon Tommy of late. He was keeping himself in hand with a steadiness which even Bertie Oakes could not ruffle and which Major Ralston openly approved. He had always known that Tommy had the stuff for great things in him.

A species of bickering friendship had sprung up between them, founded upon their tacit belief in the honour of a man who had failed. They seldom mentioned his name, but the bond of sympathy remained, oddly tenacious and unassailable. Tommy strongly suspected, moreover, that Ralston knew Everard's whereabouts, and of this even Bernard was ignorant at that time. Ralston never boasted his knowledge, but the conviction had somehow taken hold of Tommy, and for this reason also he sought the surgeon's company as he had certainly never sought it before.

Ralston on his part was kind to the boy partly because he liked him and admired his staunchness, and partly because his wife's unwilling departure had left him lonely. He and Major Burton for some reason were not so friendly as of yore, and they no longer spent their evenings in strict seclusion with the chess-board. He took to walking back from the Mess with Tommy, and encouraged the latter to drop in at his bungalow for a smoke whenever he felt inclined. It was but a short distance from The Green Bungalow, and, as he was wont to remark, it was one degree more cheerful for which consideration Tommy was profoundly grateful. Notwithstanding Bernard's kind and wholesome presence, there were times when the atmosphere of The Green Bungalow was almost more than he could bear. He was powerless to help, and the long drawn-out misery weighed upon him unendurably. He infinitely preferred smoking a silent pipe in Ralston's company or messing about with him in his little surgery as he was sometimes permitted to do.

On the evening before the day fixed for the execution at Khanmulla, they were engaged in this fashion when the *khitmutgar* entered with the news that a *sahib* desired to speak to him.

"Oh, bother!" said Ralston crossly. "Who is it? Don't you know?"

The man hesitated, and it occurred to Tommy instantly that there was a hint of mystery in his manner. The *sahib* had ridden through the jungle from Khanmulla, he said. He gave no name.

"Confounded fool!" said Ralston. "No one but a born lunatic would do a thing like that. Go and see what he wants like a good chap, Tommy! I'm busy."

Tommy rose with alacrity. His curiosity was aroused. "Perhaps it's Monck," he said.

"More likely Barnes," said Ralston. "Only I shouldn't have thought he'd be such a fool. Keep your eyes skinned!" he added, as Tommy went to the door. "Don't get shot or stuck by anybody! If I'm really wanted, I'll come."

Tommy grinned at the caution and departed. He had ceased to anticipate any serious trouble in the State, and nothing really exciting ever came his way.

He went through the bungalow to the dining-room still half expecting to find his brother-in-law awaiting him. But the moment he entered, he had a shock. A man in a rough tweed coat was sitting at the table in an odd, hunched attitude, almost as if he had fallen into the chair that supported him.

He turned his head a little at Tommy's entrance, but not so that the light revealed his face. "Hullo!" he said. "That you, Ralston? I've got a bullet in my left shoulder. Do you mind getting it out?"

Tommy stopped dead. He felt as if his heart stopped also. He knew—surely he knew—that voice! But it was not that of Everard or Barnes, or of any one he had ever expected to meet again on earth.

"What—what—" he gasped feebly, and went backwards against the door-post. "Am I drunk?" he questioned with himself.

The man in the chair turned more fully. "Why, it's Tommy!" he said.

The light smote full upon him now throwing up every detail of a countenance which, though handsome, had begun to show unmistakable signs of coarse and intemperate habits. He laughed as he met the boy's shocked eyes, but the laugh caught in his throat and turned to a strangled oath. Then he began to cough.

"Oh—my God!" said Tommy.

He turned then, horror urging him, and tore back to Ralston, as one pursued by devils. He burst in upon him headlong.

"For heaven's sake, come! That fellow—it's—it's——"

"Who?" said Ralston sharply.

"I don't know!" panted back Tommy. "I'm mad, I think. But come—for goodness' sake—before he bleeds to death!"

Ralston came with a velocity which exceeded even Tommy's wild rush. Tommy marvelled at it later. He had not thought the phlegmatic and slow-moving Ralston had it in him. He himself was left well behind, and when he re-entered the dining-room Ralston was already bending over the huddled figure that sprawled across the table.

"Come and lend a hand!" he ordered. "We must get him on the floor. Poor devil! He's got it pretty straight."

He had not seen the stricken man's face. He was too concerned with the wound to worry about any minor details for the moment.

Tommy helped him to the best of his ability, but he was trembling so much that in a second Ralston swooped scathingly upon his weakness.

"Steady man! Pull yourself together! What on earth's the matter? Never seen a little blood before? If you faint, I'll—I'll kick you! There!"

Tommy pulled himself together forthwith. He had never before submitted to being bullied by Ralston; but he submitted then, for speech was beyond him. They lowered the big frame between them, and at Ralston's command he supported it while the doctor made a swift examination of the injury.

Then, while this was in progress, the wounded man recovered his senses and forced a few husky words. "Hullo,—Ralston! Have they done me in?"

Ralston's eyes went to his face for the first time, shot a momentary glance at Tommy, and returned to the matter in hand.

"Don't talk!" he said.

A few seconds later he got to his feet. "Keep him just as he is! I must go and fetch something. Don't let him speak!"

He was gone with the words, and Tommy, still feeling bewildered and rather sick, knelt in silence and waited for his return.

But almost immediately the husky voice spoke again. "Tommy—that you?"

Tommy felt himself begin to tremble again and put forth all his strength to keep himself in hand. "Don't talk!" he said gruffly.

"I've—got to talk." The words came, forced by angry obstinacy. "It's no—damnation—good. I'm done for—beaten on the straight. And that hell hound Monck—"

"Damn you! Be quiet!" said Tommy in a furious undertone.

"I won't be quiet. I'll have—my turn—such as it is. Where's Stella? Fetch Stella! I've a right to that anyway. She is—my lawful wife!"

"I can't fetch her," said Tommy.

"All right then. You can tell her—from me—that she's been duped—as I was. She's mine—not his. He came—with that cock-and-bull story about—the other woman. But she was dead—I've found out since. She was dead—and he knew it. He faked up the tale—to suit himself. He wanted her—the damn skunk—wanted her—and cheated—cheated—to get her."

He stopped, checked by a terrible gurgle in the throat. Tommy, white with passion, broke fiercely into his gasping silence.

"It's a damned lie! Monck is a white man! He never did—a thing like that!"

And then he too stopped in sheer horror at the devilish hatred that gleamed in the rolling, bloodshot eyes.

A few dreadful seconds passed. Then Ralph Dacre gathered his ebbing life in one last great effort of speech. "She is my wife. I hold the proof. If it hadn't been for this—I'd have taken her from him—to-night. He ruined me—and he robbed me. But I—I'll ruin him now. It's my turn. He is not—her husband, and she—she'll scorn him after this—if I know her. Consoled herself precious soon. Yes, women are like that. But they don't forgive so easily. And she—is not—the forgiving sort—anyway. She'll never forgive him for tricking her—the hound! She'll never forget that the child—her child—is a bastard. And—the Regiment—won't forget either. He's down—and out."

He ceased to speak. Tommy's hands were clenched. If the man had been on his feet, he would have struck him on the mouth. As it was, he could only kneel in impotence and listen to the amazing utterance that fell from the gasping lips.

He felt stunned into passivity. His anger had strangely sunk away, though he regarded the man he supported with such an intensity of loathing that he marvelled at himself for continuing to endure the contact. The astounding revelation had struck him like a blow between the eyes. He felt numb, almost incapable of thought.

He heard Ralston returning and wondered what he could have been doing in that interminable interval. Then, reluctant but horribly fascinated, his look went back to the upturned, dreadful face. The malignancy had gone out of it. The eyes rolled no longer, but gazed with a great fixity at something that seemed to be infinitely far away. As Tommy looked, a terrible rattling breath went through the heavy, inert form. It seemed to rend body and soul asunder. There followed a brief palpitating shudder, and the head on his arm sank sideways. A great stillness fell....

Ralston knelt and freed him from his burden. "Get up!" he said.

Tommy obeyed though he felt more like collapsing. He leaned upon the table and stared while Ralston laid the big frame flat and straight upon the floor.

"Is he dead?" he asked in a whisper, as Ralston stood up.

"Yes," said Ralston.

"It wasn't my fault, was it?" said Tommy uneasily. "I couldn't stop him talking."

"He'd have died anyhow," said Ralston. "It's a wonder he ever got here if he was shot in the jungle as he must have been. That means—probably—that the brutes have started their games to-night. Odd if he should be the first victim!"

Tommy shuddered uncontrollably.

Ralston gripped his arm. "Don't be a fool now! Death is nothing extraordinary, after all. It's an experience we've all got to go through some time or other. It doesn't scare me. It won't you when you're a bit older. As for this fellow, it's about the best thing that could happen for everyone concerned. Just rememer that! Providence works pretty near the surface at times, and this is one of 'em. You won't believe me, I daresay, but I never really felt that Ralph Dacre was dead—until this moment."

He led Tommy from the room with the words. It was not his custom to express himself so freely, but he wanted to get that horror-stricken look out of the boy's eyes. He talked to give him time.

"And now look here!" he said. "You've got to keep your head—for you'll want it. I'll give you something to steady you, and after that you'll be on your own. You must cut back to The Green Bungalow and find Bernard Monck and tell him just what has happened—no one else mind, until you've seen him. He's discreet enough. I'm going round to the Colonel. For if what I think has happened, those devils are ahead of us by twenty-four hours, and we're not ready for 'em. They've probably cut the wires too. When you've done that, you report down at the barracks! Your sister will probably have to be taken there for safety. And there may be some tough work before morning."

These last words of his had a magical effect upon Tommy. His eyes suddenly shone. Ralston had accomplished his purpose. Nevertheless, he took him back to the surgery and made him swallow some *sal volatile* in spite of protest.

"And now you won't be a fool, will you?" he said at parting. "I should be sorry if you got shot to no purpose. Monck would be sorry too."

"Do you know where he is?" questioned Tommy point-blank.

"Yes." Blunt and uncompromising came Ralston's reply. "But I'm not going to tell you, so don't you worry yourself! You stick to business, Tommy, and for heaven's sake don't go round and make a mush of it!"

"Stick to business yourself!" said Tommy rudely, suddenly awaking to the fact that he was being dictated to; then pulled up, faintly grinning. "Sorry: I didn't mean that. You're a brick. Consider it unsaid! Good-bye!"

He held out his hand to Ralston who took it and thumped him on the back by way of acknowledgment.

"You're growing up," he remarked with approval, as Tommy went his way.

CHAPTER VIII

THE FIERY VORTEX

"There is nothing more to be done," said Peter with mournful eyes upon the baby in the *ayah's* arms. "Will not my *mem-sahib* take her rest?"

Stella's eyes also rested upon the tiny wizen face. She knew that Peter spoke truly. There was nothing more to be done. She might send yet again for Major Ralston. But of what avail? He had told her that he could do no more. The little life was slipping swiftly, swiftly, out of her reach. Very soon only the desert emptiness would be left.

"The *mem-sahib* may trust her *baba* to Hanani," murmured the *ayah* behind the enveloping veil. "Hanani loves the *baba* too."

"Oh, I know," Stella said.

Yet she hung over the *ayah's* shoulder, for to-night of all nights she somehow felt that she could not tear herself away.

There had been a change during the day—a change so gradual as to be almost imperceptible save to her yearning eyes. She was certain that the baby was weaker. He had cried less, had, she believed, suffered less; and now he lay quite passive in the *ayah's* arms. Only by the feeble, fluttering breath that came and went so fitfully could she have told that the tiny spark yet lingered in the poor little wasted frame.

Major Ralston had told her earlier in the evening that he might go on in this state for days, but she did not think it probable. She was sure that every hour now brought an infinitesimal difference. She felt that the end was drawing near.

And so a great reluctance to go possessed her, even though she would be within call all night. She had a hungry longing to stay and watch the little unconscious face which would soon be gone from her sight. She wanted to hold each minute of the few hours left.

Very softly Peter came to her side. "My *mem-sahib* will rest?" he said wistfully.

She looked at him. His faithful eyes besought her like the eyes of a dog. Their dumb adoration somehow made her want to cry.

"If I could only stay to-night, Peter!" she said.

"*Mem-sahib*," he urged very pleadingly, "the *baba* sleeps now. It may be he will want you to-morrow. And if my *mem-sahib* has not slept she will be too weary then."

Again she knew that he spoke the truth. There had been times of late when she had been made aware of the fact that her strength was nearing its limit. She knew it would be sheer madness to neglect the warning lest, as Peter suggested, her baby's need of her outlasted her endurance. She must husband all the strength she had.

With a sigh she bent and touched the tiny forehead with her lips. Hanani's hand, long and bony, gently stroked her arm as she did so.

"Old Hanani knows, *mem-sahib*," she whispered under her breath.

The tears she had barely checked a moment before sprang to Stella's eyes. She held the dark hand in silence and was subtly comforted thereby.

Passing through the door that Peter held open for her, she gave him her hand also. He bent very low over it, just as he had bent on that first wedding-day of hers so long—so long—ago, and touched it with his forehead. The memory flashed back upon her oddly. She heard again Ralph Dacre's voice speaking in her ear. "You, Stella,—you are as ageless as the stars!" The pride and the passion of his tones stabbed through her with a curious poignancy. Strange that the thought of him should come to her with such vividness to-night! She passed on to her room, as one moving in a painful trance.

For a space she lingered there, hardly knowing what she did; then she remembered that she had not bidden Bernard good-night, and mechanically her steps turned in his direction.

He was generally smoking and working on the verandah at that hour. She made her way to the dining-room as being the nearest approach.

But half-way across the room the sound of Tommy's voice, sharp and agitated, came to her: Involuntarily she paused. He was with Bernard on the verandah.

"The devils shot him in the jungle, but he came on, got as far as Ralston's bungalow, and collapsed there. He was dead in a few minutes—before anything could be done."

The words pierced through her trance, like a naked sword flashing with incredible swiftness, cutting asunder every bond, every fibre, that held her soul confined. She sprang for the open window with a great and terrible cry.

"Who is dead? Who? Who?"

The red glare of the lamp met her, dazzled her, seemed to enter her brain and cruelly to burn her; but she did not heed it. She stood with arms flung wide in frantic supplication.

"Everard!" she cried. "Oh God! My God! Not—Everard!"

Her wild words pierced the night, and all the voices of India seemed to answer her in a mad discordant jangle of unintelligible sound. An owl hooted, a jackal yelped, and a chorus of savage, yelling laughter broke hideously across the clamour, swallowing it as a greater wave swallows a lesser, overwhelming all that has gone before.

The red glare of the lamp vanished from Stella's brain, leaving an awful blankness, a sense as of something burnt out, a taste of ashes in the mouth. But yet the darkness was full of horrors; unseen monsters leaped past her as in a surging torrent, devils' hands clawed at her, devils' mouths cried unspeakable things.

She stood as it were on the edge of the vortex, untouched, unafraid, beyond it all since that awful devouring flame had flared and gone out. She even wondered if it had killed her, so terribly aloof was she, so totally distinct from the pandemonium that raged around her. It had the vividness and the curious lack of all physical feeling of a nightmare. And yet through all her numbness she knew that she was waiting for someone—someone who was dead like herself.

She had not seen either Bernard or Tommy in that blinding moment on the verandah. Doubtless they were fighting in that raging blackness in front of her. She fancied once that she heard her brother's voice laughing as she had sometimes heard him laugh on the polo-ground when he had executed a difficult stroke. Immediately before her, a Titanic struggle was going on. She could not see it, for the light in the room behind had been extinguished also, but the dreadful sound of it made her think for a fleeting second of a great bull-stag being pulled down by a score of leaping, wide-jawed hounds.

And then very suddenly she herself was caught—caught from behind, dragged backwards off her feet. She cried out in a wild horror, but in a second she was silenced. Some thick material that had a heavy native scent about it—such a scent as she remembered vaguely to hang about Hanani the *ayah*—was thrust over her face and head muffling all outcry. Muscular arms gripped her with a fierce and ruthless mastery, and as they lifted and bore her away the nightmare was blotted from her brain as if it had never been. She sank into oblivion....

CHAPTER IX

THE DESERT OF ASHES

Was it night? Was it morning? She could not tell. She opened her eyes to a weird and incomprehensible twilight, to the gurgling sound of water, the booming croak of a frog.

At first she thought that she was dreaming, that presently these vague impressions would fade from her consciousness, and she would awake to normal things, to the sunlight beating across the verandah, to the cheery call of Everard's *saice* in the compound, and the tramp of impatient hoofs. And Everard himself would rise up from her side, and stoop and kiss her before he went.

She began to wait for his kiss, first in genuine expectation, later with a semi-conscious tricking of the imagination. Never once had he left her without that kiss.

But she waited in vain, and as she waited the current of her thoughts grew gradually clearer. She began to remember the happenings of the night. It dawned upon her slowly and terribly that Everard was dead.

When that memory came to her, her brain seemed to stand still. There was no passing on from that. Everard had been shot in the jungle—just as she had always known he would be. He had ridden on in spite of it. She pictured his grim endurance with shrinking vividness. He had ridden on to Major Ralston's bungalow and had collapsed there,—collapsed and died before they could help him. Clearly before her inner vision rose the scene,—Everard sinking down, broken and inert, all the indomitable strength of him shattered at last, the steady courage quenched.

Yet what was it he had once said to her? It rushed across her now—words he had uttered long ago on the night he had taken her to the ruined temple at Khanmulla. "My love is not the kind that burns and goes out." She remembered the exact words, the quiver in the voice that had uttered them. Then, that being so, he was loving her still. Across the desert—her bitter desert of ashes—the lamp was shining even now. Love like his was immortal. Love such as that could never die.

That comforted her for a space, but soon the sense of desolation returned. She remembered their cruel estrangement. She remembered their child. And that last thought, entering like an electric force, gave her strength. Surely it was morning, and he would be needing her! Had not Peter said he would want her in the morning?

With a sharp effort she raised herself; she must go to him.

The next moment a sharp breath of amazement escaped her. Where was she? The strange twilight stretched up above her into infinite shadow. Before her was a broken archway through which vaguely she saw the heavy foliage of trees. Behind her she yet heard the splash and gurgle of water, the croaking of frogs. And near at hand some tiny creature scratched and scuffled among loose stones.

She sat staring about her, doubting the evidence of her senses, marvelling if it could all be a dream. For she recognized the place. It was the ruined temple of Khanmulla in which she sat. There were the crumbling steps on which she had stood with Everard on the night that he had mercilessly claimed her love, had taken her in his arms and said that it was Kismet.

It was then that like a dagger-thrust the realization of his loss went through her. It was then that she first tasted the hopeless anguish of loneliness that awaited her, saw the long, long desert track stretching out before her, leading she knew not whither. She bowed her head upon her arms and sat crushed, unconscious of all beside....

It must have been some time later that there fell a soft step beside her; a veiled figure, bent and slow of movement, stooped over her.

"*Mem-sahib!*" a low voice said.

She looked up, startled and wondering. "Hanani!" she said.

"Yes, it is Hanani." The woman's husky whisper came reassuringly in answer. "Have no fear, *mem-sahib!* You are safe here."

"What—happened?" questioned Stella, still half-doubting the evidence of her senses. "Where—where is my baby?"

Hanani knelt down by her side. "*Mem-sahib*," she said very gently, "the *baba* sleeps—in the keeping of God."

It was tenderly spoken, so tenderly that—it came to her afterwards—she received the news with no sense of shock. She even felt as if she must have somehow known it before. In the utter greyness of her desert—she had walked alone.

"He is dead?" she said.

"Not dead, *mem-sahib*," corrected the *ayah* gently. She paused a moment, then in the same hushed voice that was scarcely more than a whisper: "He—passed, *mem-sahib*, in these arms, so easily, so gently, I knew not when the last breath came. You had been gone but a little space. I sent Peter to call you, but your room was empty. He returned, and I went to seek you myself. I reached you only as the storm broke."

"Ah!" A sharp shudder caught Stella. "What—happened?" she asked again.

"It was but a band of *budmashes, mem-sahib*." A note of contempt sounded in the quiet rejoinder. "I think they were looking for Monck *sahib*—for the captain *sahib*. But they found him not."

"No," Stella said. "No. They had killed him already—in the jungle. At least, they had shot him. He died—afterwards." She spoke dully; she felt as if her heart had grown old within her, too old to feel poignantly any more. "Go on!" she said, after a moment. "What happened then? Did they kill Bernard *sahib* and Denvers *sahib*, too?"

"Neither, my *mem-sahib*." Hanani's reply was prompt and confident. "Bernard *sahib* was struck on the head and senseless when we dragged him in. Denvers *sahib* was not touched. It was he who put out the lamp and saved their lives. Afterwards, I know not how, he raised a great outcry so that they thought they were surrounded and fled. Truly, Denvers *sahib* is great. After that, he went for help. And I, *mem-sahib*, fearing they might return to visit their vengeance upon you—being the wife of the captain *sahib* whom they could not find—I wrapped a *saree* about your head and carried you away." Humble pride in the achievement sounded in Hanani's voice. "I knew that here you would be safe," she ended. "All evil-doers fear this place. It is said to be the abode of unquiet spirits."

Again Stella gazed around the place. Her eyes had become accustomed to the green-hued twilight. The crumbling, damp-stained walls stretched away into darkness behind her, but the place held no terrors for her. She was too tired to be afraid. She only wondered, though without much interest, how Hanani had managed to accomplish the journey.

"Where is Peter?" she asked at last.

"Peter remained with Bernard *sahib*," Hanani answered. "He will tell them where to seek for you."

Again Stella gazed about the place. It struck her as strange that Peter should have relinquished his guardianship of her, even in favour of Hanani. But the thought did not hold her for long. Evidently he had known that he could trust the woman as he trusted himself and her strength must be almost superhuman. She was glad that he had stayed behind with Bernard.

She leaned her chin upon her hands and sat silent for a space. But gradually, as she reviewed the situation, curiosity began to struggle through her lethargy. She looked at Hanani crouched humbly beside her, looked at her again and again, and at last her wonder found vent in speech.

"Hanani," she said, "I don't quite understand everything. How did you get me here?"

Hanani's veiled head was bent. She turned it towards her slowly, almost reluctantly it seemed to Stella.

"I carried you, *mem-sahib*," she said.

"You—carried—me!" Stella repeated the word incredulously. "But it is a long way—a very long way—from Kurrumpore."

Hanani was silent for a moment or two, as though irresolute. Then: "I brought you by a way unknown to you, *mem-sahib*," she said. "Hafiz—you know Hafiz?—he helped me."

"Hafiz!" Stella frowned a little. Yes, by sight she knew him well. Hafiz the crafty, was her private name for him.

"How did he help you?" she asked.

Again Hanani seemed to hesitate as one reluctant to give away a secret. "From the shop of Hafiz—that is the shop of Rustam Karin in the bazaar," she said at length, and Stella quivered at the name, "there is a passage that leads under the ground into the jungle. To those who know, the way is easy. It was thus, *mem-sahib*, that I brought you hither."

"But how did you get me to the bazaar?" questioned Stella, still hardly believing.

"It was very dark, *mem-sahib*; and the *budmashes* were scattered. They would not touch an old woman such as Hanani. And you, my *mem-sahib*, were wrapped in a *saree*. With old Hanani you were safe."

"Ah, why should you take all that trouble to save my life?" Stella said, a little quiver of passion in her voice. "Do you think life is so precious to me—now?"

Hanani made a protesting gesture with one arm. "Lo, it is yet night, *mem-sahib*," she said. "But is it not written in the sacred Book that with the dawn comes joy?"

"There can never be any joy for me again," Stella said.

Hanani leaned slowly forward. "Then will my *mem-sahib* have missed the meaning of life," she said. "Listen then—listen to old Hanani—who knows! It is true that the *baba* cannot return to the *mem-sahib*, but would she call him back to pain? Have I not read in her eyes night after night the silent prayer that he might go in peace? Now that the God of gods has answered that prayer—now that the *baba* is in peace—would my *mem-sahib* have it otherwise? Would she call that loved one back? Would she not rather thank the God of spirits for His great mercy—and so go her way rejoicing?"

Again the utterance was too full of tenderness to give her pain. It sank deep into Stella's heart, stilling for a space the anguish. She looked at the strange, draped figure beside her that spoke those husky words of comfort with a dawning sense of reverence. She had a curious feeling as of one being guided through a holy place.

"You—comfort me, Hanani," she said after a moment. "I don't think I am really grieving for the *baba* yet. That will come after. I know that—as you say—he is at peace, and I would not call him back. But—Hanani—that is not all. It is not even the half or the beginning of my trouble. The loss of my *baba* I can bear—I could bear—bravely. But the loss of—of—" Words failed her unexpectedly. She bowed her head again upon her arms and wept the bitter tears of despair.

Hanani the *ayah* sat very still by her side, her brown, bony hands tightly gripped about her knees, her veiled head bent slightly forward as though she watched for someone in the dimness of the broken archway.

At last very, very slowly she spoke.

"*Mem-sahib*, even in the desert the sun rises. There is always comfort for those who go forward—even though they mourn."

"Not for me," sobbed Stella. "Not for those—who part—in bitterness—and never—meet again!"

"Never, *mem-sahib*?" Hanani yet gazed straight before her. Suddenly she made a movement as if to rise, but checked herself as one reminded by exertion of physical infirmity. "The *mem-sahib* weeps for her lord," she said. "How shall Hanani comfort her? Yet never is a cruel word. May it not be that he will—even now—return?"

"He is dead," whispered Stella.

"Not so, *mem-sahib*." Very gently Hanani corrected her. "The captain *sahib* lives."

"He—lives?" Stella started upright with the words. In the gloom her eyes shone with a sudden feverish light; but it very swiftly died. "Ah, don't torture me, Hanani!" she said. "You mean well, but—it doesn't help."

"Hanani speaks the truth," protested the old *ayah*, and behind the enveloping veil came an answering gleam as if she smiled. "My lord the captain *sahib* spoke with Hafiz this very night. Hafiz will tell the *mem-sahib*."

But Stella shook her head in hopeless unbelief. "I don't trust Hafiz," she said wearily.

"Yet Hafiz would not lie to old Hanani," insisted the *ayah* in that soft, insinuating whisper of hers.

Stella reached out a trembling hand and laid it upon her shoulder. "Listen, Hanani!" she said. "I have never seen your face, yet I know you for a friend."

"Ask not to see it, *mem-sahib*," swiftly interposed the *ayah*, "lest you turn with loathing from one who loves you!"

Stella smiled, a quivering, piteous smile. "I should never do that, Hanani," she said. "But I do not need to see it. I know you love me. But do not—out of your love for me—tell me a lie! It is false comfort. It cannot help me."

"But I have not lied, *mem-sahib*." There was earnest assurance in Hanani's voice—such assurance as could not be disregarded. "I have told you the truth. The captain *sahib* is not dead. It was a false report."

"Hanani! Are you—sure?" Stella's hand gripped the *ayah*'s shoulder with convulsive, strength. "Then who—who—was the *sahib* they shot in the jungle—the *sahib* who died at the bungalow of Ralston *sahib*? Did—Hafiz—tell you that?"

"That—" said Hanani, and paused as if considering how best to present the information,—"that was another *sahib*."

"Another *sahib*?" Stella was trembling violently. Her hold upon Hanani was the clutch of desperation, "Who—what was his name?"

She felt in the momentary pause that followed that the eyes behind the veil were looking at her strangely, speculatively. Then very softly Hanani answered her.

"His name, *mem-sahib*, was Dacre."

"Dacre!" Stella repeated the name blankly. It seemed to hold too great a meaning for her to grasp.

"So Hafiz told Hanani," said the *ayah*.

"But—Dacre!" Stella hung upon the name as if it held her by a fascination from which she could not shake free. "Is that—all you know?" she said at last.

"Not all, my *mem-sahib*," answered Hanani, in the soothing tone of one who instructs a child. "Hafiz knew the *sahib* in the days before Hanani came to Kurrumpore. Hafiz told a strange story of the *sahib*. He had married and had taken his wife to the mountains beyond Srinagar. And there an evil fate had overtaken him, and she—the *mem-sahib*—had returned alone."

Hanani paused dramatically.

"Go on!" gasped Stella almost inarticulately.

Hanani took up her tale again in a mysterious whisper that crept in eerie echoes about the ruined place in which they sat. "*Mem-sahib*, Hafiz said that there was doubtless a reason for which he feigned death. He said that Dacre *sahib* was a bad man, and my lord the captain *sahib* knew it. Wherefore he followed him to the mountains and commanded him to be gone, and thus—he went."

"But who—told—Hafiz?" questioned Stella, still struggling against unbelief.

"How should Hanani know?" murmured the *ayah* deprecatingly "Hafiz lives in the bazaar. He hears many things—some true—some false. But that Dacre *sahib* returned last night and that he now is dead is true, *mem-sahib*. And that my lord the captain *sahib* lives is also true. Hanani swears it by her grey hairs."

"Then where—where is the captain *sahib*?" whispered Stella.

The *ayah* shook her head. "It is not given to Hanani to know all things," she protested. "But—she can find out. Does the *mem-sahib* desire her to find out?"

"Yes," Stella breathed.

The fantastic tale was running like a mad tarantella through her brain. Her thoughts were in a whirl. But she clung to the thought of Everard as a shipwrecked mariner clings to a rock. He yet lived; he had not passed out of her reach. It might be he was even then at Khanmulla a few short miles away. All her doubt of him, all evil suspicions, vanished in a great and overwhelming longing for his presence. It suddenly came to her that she had wronged him, and before that unquestionable conviction the story of Ralph Dacre's return was dwarfed to utter insignificance. What was Ralph Dacre to her? She had travelled far—oh, very far—through the desert since the days of that strange dream in the Himalayas. Living or dead, surely he had no claim upon her now!

Impulsively she stooped towards Hanani. "Take me to him!" she said. "Take me to him! I am sure you know where he is."

Hanani drew back slightly. "*Mem-sahib*, it will take time to find him," she remonstrated. "Hanani is not a young woman. Moreover—" she stopped suddenly, and turned her head.

"What is it?" said Stella.

"I heard a sound, *mem-sahib*." Hanani rose slowly to her feet. It seemed to Stella that she was more bent, more deliberate of movement, than usual. Doubtless the wild adventure of the night had told upon her. She watched her with a tinge of compunction as she made her somewhat difficult way towards the archway at the top of the broken marble steps. A flying-fox flapped eerily past her as she went, dipping over the bent, veiled head with as little fear as if she were a recognized inhabitant of that wild place.

A sharp sense of unreality stabbed Stella. She felt as one coming out of an all-absorbing dream. Obeying an instinctive impulse, she rose up quickly to follow. But even as she did so, two things happened.

Hanani passed like a shadow from her sight, and a voice she knew—Tommy's voice, somewhat high-pitched and anxious—called her name.

Swiftly she moved to meet him. "I am here, Tommy! I am here!"

And then she tottered, feeling her strength begin to fail.

"Oh, Tommy!" she gasped. "Help me!"

He sprang up the steps and caught her in his arms. "You hang on to me!" he said. "I've got you."

She leaned upon him quivering, with closed eyes. "I am afraid I must," she said weakly. "Forgive me for being so stupid!"

"All right, darling. All right," he said. "You're not hurt?"

"No, oh no! Only giddy—stupid!" She fought desperately for self-command. "I shall be all right in a minute."

She heard the voices of men below her, but she could not open her eyes to look. Tommy supported her strongly, and in a few seconds she was aware of someone on her other side, of a steady capable hand grasping her wrist.

"Drink this!" said Ralston's voice. "It'll help you."

He was holding something to her lips, and she drank mechanically.

"That's better," he said. "You've had a rough time, I'm afraid, but it's over now. Think you can walk, or shall we carry you?"

The matter-of-fact tones seemed to calm the chaos of her brain. She looked up at him with a faint, brave smile.

"I will walk,—of course. There is nothing the matter with me. What has happened at Kurrumpore? Is all well?"

He met her eyes. "Yes," he said quietly.

Her look flinched momentarily from his, but the next instant she met it squarely. "I know about—my baby," she said.

He bent his head. "You could not wish it otherwise," he said, gently.

She answered him with firmness, "No."

The few words helped to restore her self-possession. With her hand upon Tommy's arm she descended the steps into the green gloom of the jungle. The morning sun was smiting through the leaves. It gleamed in her eyes like the flashing of a sword. But—though the simile held her mind for a space—she felt no shrinking. She had a curious conviction that the path lay open before her at last. The Angel with the Flaming Sword no longer barred the way.

A party of Indian soldiers awaited her. She did not see how many. Perhaps she was too tired to take any very vivid interest in her surroundings. A native litter stood a few yards from the foot of the steps. Tommy guided her to it, Major Ralston walking on her other side.

She turned to the latter as they reached it. "Where is Hanani?" she said.

He raised his brows for a moment. "She has probably gone back to her people," he answered.

"She was here with me, only a minute ago," Stella said.

He glanced round. "She knows her way no doubt. We had better not wait now. If you want her, I will find her for you later."

"Thank you," Stella said. But she still paused, looking from Ralston to Tommy and back again, as one uncertain.

"What is it, darling?" said Tommy gently.

She put her hand to her head with a weary gesture of bewilderment. "I am very stupid," she said. "I can't think properly. You are sure everything is all right?"

"Quite sure, dear," he said. "Don't try to think now. You are done up. You must rest."

Her face quivered suddenly like the face of a tired child. "I want—Everard," she said piteously. "Won't you—can't you—bring him to me? There is something—I want—to say to him."

There was an instant's pause. She felt Tommy's arm tighten protectingly around her, but he did not speak.

It was Major Ralston who answered her. "Certainly he shall come to you. I will see that he does."

The confidence of his reply comforted her. She trusted Major Ralston instinctively. She entered the litter and sank down among the cushions with a sigh.

As they bore her away along the narrow, winding path which once she had trodden with Everard Monck so long, long ago, on the night of her surrender to the mastery of his love, utter exhaustion overcame her and the sleep, which for so long she had denied herself, came upon her like an overwhelming flood, sweeping her once more into the deeps of oblivion. She went without a backward thought.

CHAPTER X

THE ANGEL

It was many hours before she awoke and in all those hours she never dreamed. She only slept and slept and slept in total unconsciousness, wrapt about in the silence of her desert.

She awoke at length quite fully, quite suddenly, to a sense of appalling loneliness, to a desolation unutterable. She opened her eyes wide upon a darkness that could be felt, and almost cried aloud with the terror of it. For a few palpitating moments it seemed to her that the most dreadful thing that could possibly happen to her had come upon her unawares.

And then, even as she started up in a wild horror, a voice spoke to her, a hand touched her, and her fear was stayed.

"Stella!" the voice said, and steady fingers came up out of the darkness and closed upon her arm.

Her heart gave one great leap within her, and was still. She did not speak in answer, for she could not. She could only sit in the darkness and wait. If it were a dream, it would pass—ah, so swiftly! If it were reality, surely, surely he would speak again!

He spoke—softly through the silence. "I don't want to startle you. Are you startled? I've put out the lamp. You are not afraid?"

Her voice came back to her; her heart jerked on, beating strangely, spasmodically, like a maimed thing. "Am I awake?" she said. "Is it—really—you?"

"Yes," he said. "Can you listen to me a moment? You won't be afraid?"

She quivered at the repeated question. "Everard—no!"

He was silent then, as if he did not know how to continue. And she, finding her strength, leaned to him in the darkness, feeling for him, still hardly believing that it was not a dream.

He took her wandering hand and held it imprisoned. The firmness of his grasp reassured her, but it came to her that his hands were cold; and she wondered.

"I have something to say to you," he said.

She sat quite still in his hold, but it frightened her. "Where are you?" she whispered.

"I am just—kneeling by your side," he said. "Don't tremble—or be afraid! There is nothing to frighten you. Stella," his voice came almost in a whisper. "Hanani—the *ayah*—told you something in the ruined temple at Khanmulla. Can you remember what it was?"

"Ah!" she said. "Do you mean about—Ralph Dacre?"

"I do mean that," he said. "I don't know if you actually believed it. It may have sounded—fantastic. But—it was true."

"Ah!" she said again. And then she knew why he had turned out the lamp. It was that he might not see her face when he told her—or she his.

He went on; his hold upon her had tightened, but she knew that he was unconscious of it. It was as if he clung to her in anguish—though she heard no sign of suffering in his low voice. "I have done the utmost to keep the truth from you—but Fate has been against me all through. I sent him away from you in the first place because I heard—too late—that he had a wife in England. I married you because—" he paused momentarily—"ah well, that doesn't come into the story," he said. "I married you, believing you free. Then came Bernard, and told me that the wife—Dacre's wife—had died just before his marriage to you. That also came—too late."

He stopped again, and she knew that his head was bowed upon his arms though she could not free her hand to touch it.

"You know the rest," he said, and his voice came to her oddly broken and unfamiliar. "I kept it from you. I couldn't bear the thought of your facing—that,—especially after—after the birth of—the child. Even when you found out I had tricked you in that native rig-out, I couldn't endure the thought of your knowing. I nearly killed myself that night. It seemed the only way. But Bernard stopped me. I told him the truth. He said I was wrong not to tell you. But—somehow—I couldn't."

"Oh, I wish—I wish you had," she breathed.

"Do you? Well,—I couldn't. It's hard enough to tell you now. You were so wonderful, so beautiful, and they had flung mud at you from the beginning. I thought I had made you safe, dear, instead of—dragging you down."

"Everard!" Her voice was quick and passionate. She made a sudden effort and freed one hand; but he caught it again sharply.

"No, you mustn't, Stella! I haven't finished. Wait!"

His voice compelled her; she submitted hardly knowing that she did so.

"It is over now," he said. "The fellow is dead. But, Stella,—he had found out—what I had found out. And he was on his way to you. He meant to—claim you."

She shuddered—a hard, convulsive shudder—as if some loathsome thing had touched her. "But—I would never have gone back," she said.

"No," he answered grimly, "you wouldn't. I was here, and I should have shot him. They saved me that trouble."

"You were—here!" she said.

"Yes,—much nearer to you than you imagined." Almost curtly he answered. "Did you think I would leave you at the mercy of those devils? You!" He stopped himself sharply. "No I was here to protect you—and I would have done it—though I should have shot myself afterwards. Even Bernard would have seen the force of that. But it didn't come to pass that way. It wasn't intended that it should. Well, it is over. There are not many who know—only Bernard, Tommy, and Ralston. They are going—if possible—to keep it dark, to suppress his name. I told them they must." His voice rang suddenly harsh, but softened again immediately. "That's all, dear—or nearly all. I hope it hasn't shocked you unutterably. I think the secret is safe anyhow, so you won't have—that—to face. I'm going now. I'll send—Peter—to light the lamp and bring you something to eat. And you'll undress, won't you, and go to bed? It's late."

He made as if he would rise, but her hands turned swiftly in his, turned and held him fast.

"Everard—Everard, why should you go?" she whispered tensely into the darkness that hid his face.

He yielded in a measure to her hold, but he would not suffer himself to be drawn nearer.

"Why?" she said again insistently.

He hesitated. "I think," he said slowly "that you will find an answer to that question—possibly more than one—when you have had time to think it over."

"What do you mean?" she breathed.

"Must I put it into words?" he said.

She heard the pain in his voice, but for the first time she passed it by unheeded. "Yes, tell me!" she said. "I must know."

He was silent for a little, as if mustering his forces. Then, his hands tight upon hers, he spoke. "In the first place, you are Dacre's widow, and not—my wife."

She quivered in his hold. "And then?" she whispered.

"And then," he said, "our baby is dead, so you are free from all—obligations."

Her hands clenched hard upon his. "Is that all?"

"No." With sudden passion he answered her. "There are two more reasons why I should go. One is—that I have made your life a hell on earth. You have said it, and I know it to be true. Ah, you had better let me go—and go quickly. For your own sake—you had better!"

But she ignored the warning, holding him almost fiercely. "And the last reason?" she said.

He was silent for a few seconds, and in his silence there was something of an electric quality, something that pierced and scorched yet strangely drew her. "Someone else can tell you that," he said at length. "It isn't that I am a broken man. I know that wouldn't affect you one way or another. It is that I have done a thing that you would hate—yet that I would do again to-morrow if the need arose. You can ask Ralston what it is! Say I told you to! He knows."

"But I ask you," she said, and still her hands gripped his. "Everard, why don't you tell me? Are you—afraid to tell me?"

"No," he said.

"Then answer me!" she said, her breathing sharp and uneven. "Tell me the truth! Make me understand you—once and for all!"

"You have always understood me," he said.

"No—no!" she protested.

"Well, nearly always," he amended. "As long as you have known my love—you have known me. My love for you is myself—the immortal part. The rest—doesn't count."

"Ah!" she said, and suddenly the very soul of her rose up and spoke. "Then you needn't tell me any more, dear love—dear love. I don't need to hear it. It doesn't matter. It can't make any difference. Nothing ever can again, for, as you say, nothing else counts. Go if you must,—but if you do—I shall follow you—I shall follow you—to the world's end."

"Stella!" he said.

"I mean it," she told him, and her voice throbbed with a fiery force that was deeper than passion, stronger than aught human. "You are mine and I am yours. God knows, dear,—God knows that is all that matters now. I didn't understand before. I do now, I think—suffering has taught me—many things. Perhaps it is—His Angel."

"The Angel with the Flaming Sword," he said, under his breath.

"But the Sword is turned away," she said. "The way is open."

He got to his feet abruptly. "Wait!" he said. "Before you say that—wait!"

He freed himself from her hold gently but very decidedly. She knew that for a second he stood close above her with arms outflung before he turned away. Then there came the rasp of a match, a sudden flare in the darkness. She looked to see his face—and uttered a cry.

It was Hanani, the veiled *ayah*, who stooped to kindle the lamp....

CHAPTER XI

THE DAWN

"This country is like an infernal machine," said Bernard. "You never know when it's going to explode. There's only one reliable thing in it, and that's Peter."

He turned his bandaged head in the latter's direction, and received a tender, indulgent smile in answer. Peter loved the big blue-eyed *sahib* with the same love which he had for the children of the *sahib-log*.

"Whatever happens," Bernard continued, "there's always Peter. He keeps the whole show going, and is never absent when wanted. In fact, I begin to think that India wouldn't be India without him."

"A very handsome compliment," said Sir Reginald.

"It is, isn't it?" smiled Bernard. "I have a vast respect for him—a quite unbounded respect. He is the greatest greaser of wheels I have ever met. Help yourself, sir, won't you? I am sorry I can't join you, but Major Ralston insists that I must walk circumspectly, being on his sick list. I really don't know why my skull was not cracked. He declares it ought to have been and even seems inclined to be rather disgusted with me because it wasn't."

"You had a very lucky escape," said Sir Reginald. "Allow me to congratulate you!"

"And a very enjoyable scrap," said Bernard, with kindling eyes. "Thanks! I wouldn't have missed it for the world,—the damn' dirty blackguards!"

"Was Mrs. Monck much upset?" asked Sir Reginald. "I have never yet had the pleasure of meeting her."

"She was more upset on my brother's account than her own," Bernard said, giving his visitor a shrewd look. "She thought he had come to harm."

"Ah!" said Sir Reginald, and held his glass up to the light. "And that was not so?"

"No," said Bernard, and closed his lips.

There was a distinct pause before Sir Reginald's eyes left his glass and came down to him. They held a faint whimsical smile.

"We owe your brother a good deal," he said.

"Do we?" said Bernard.

Sir Reginald's smile became more pronounced. "I have been told that it is entirely owing to him—his forethought, secrecy, and intimate knowledge obtained at considerable personal risk—that this business was not of a far more serious nature. I was of course in constant communication with Colonel Mansfield. We knew exactly where the danger lay, and we were prepared for all emergencies."

"Except the one which actually rose," suggested Bernard.

"That?" said Sir Reginald. "That was a mere flash in the pan. But we were prepared even for that. My men were all in Markestan by daybreak, thanks to the promptitude of young Denvers."

"If all our throats had been slit the previous night, that wouldn't have helped us much," Bernard pointed out.

Sir Reginald broke into a laugh. "Well, dash it, man! We did our best. And anyway they weren't, so you haven't much cause for complaint."

"You see, I was one of the casualties," explained Bernard. "That accounts for my being a bit critical. So you expected something worse than this?"

"I did." Sir Reginald spoke soberly again. "If we hadn't been prepared, the whole of Markestan would have been ablaze by now from end to end."

"Instead of which, you have only permitted us a fizz, a few bangs, and a splutter-out, as Tommy describes it," remarked Bernard. "And you haven't even caught the Rajah."

"I wasn't out to catch him," said Sir Reginald. "But I will tell you who I am out to catch, though I am afraid I am applying in the wrong quarter."

Bernard's eyes gleamed with a hint of malicious amusement. "I thought my health was not primarily responsible for the honour of your visit, sir," he said.

"No," said Sir Reginald, with simplicity. "I really came because I want to take you into my confidence, and to ask for your confidence in return."

"I thought so," said Bernard, and slowly shook his head. "I'm afraid it's no go. I am sealed."

"Ah! And that even though I give you my word it would be to your brother's interest to break the seal?" questioned Sir Reginald.

Bernard's eyes suddenly drooped under their red brows. "And betray my trust?" he said lazily.

"I beg your pardon," said Sir Reginald.

He finished his drink with a speed that suggested embarrassment, but the next moment he smiled. "You had me there, padre. I withdraw the suggestion. I should not have made it if I could see the man himself. But he has disappeared, and even Barnes, who knows everything, can't tell us where to look for him."

"Neither can I," said Bernard. "I am not in his confidence to that extent."

"Why don't you ask his wife?" a low voice said.

Both men started. Sir Reginald sprang to his feet. "Mrs. Monck!"

"Yes," Stella said. She stood a moment framed in the French window, looking at him. Then she stepped forward with outstretched hand. The morning sunshine caught her as she moved. She was very pale and her eyes were deeply shadowed, but she was exceedingly beautiful.

"I heard your voices," she said, looking at Sir Reginald, while her hand lay in his. "I didn't mean to listen at first. But I was tempted, because you were talking of—my husband, and—" she smiled at him faintly, "I fell."

"I think you were justified," Sir Reginald said.

"Thank you," she answered gently. She turned from him to Bernard, and bending kissed him. "Are you better? Peter told me it wasn't serious. I would have come to you sooner, but I was asleep for a very long time, and afterwards—Everard wanted me."

"Everard!" he said sharply. "Is he here?"

"Sit down!" murmured Sir Reginald, drawing forward his chair.

But Stella remained standing, her hand upon Bernard's shoulder. "Thank you. But I haven't come to stay. Only to tell you—just to tell you—all the things that Bernard couldn't, without betraying his trust."

"My dear, dear child!" Bernard broke in quickly, but Sir Reginald intervened in the same moment.

"No, no! Pardon me! Let her speak! She wishes to do so, and I—wish to listen."

Stella's hand pressed a little upon Bernard's shoulder, as though she supported herself thereby.

"It is right that you should know, Sir Reginald," she said. "It is only for my sake that it has been kept from you. But I—have travelled the desert too long to mind an extra stone or two by the way. First, with regard to the suspicion which drove him out of the Army. You thought—everyone thought—that he had killed Ralph Dacre up in the mountains. Even I thought so." Her voice trembled a little. "And I had less excuse than any one else, for he swore to me that he was innocent—though he would not—could not—tell me the truth of the matter. The truth was simply this. Ralph Dacre was not dead."

"Ah!" Sir Reginald said softly.

Bernard reached up and strongly grasped the hand that rested upon him. But he spoke no word.

Stella went on with greater steadiness, her eyes resolutely meeting the shrewd old eyes that watched her. "He—Everard—came between us because only a fortnight after our marriage he received the news that Ralph had a wife living in England. Perhaps I ought to tell you—though this in no way influenced him—that my marriage to Ralph was a mistake. I married him because I was unhappy, not because I loved him. I sinned, and I have been punished."

"Poor girl!" said Sir Reginald very gently.

Her eyelids quivered, but she would not suffer them to fall. "Everard sent him away from me, made him vanish completely, and then came himself to me—he was in native disguise—and told me he was dead. I suppose it was wrong of him. If so, he too has been punished. But he wanted to save my pride. I had plenty of pride in those days. It is all gone now. At least, all I have left is for him—that his honour may be vindicated. I am afraid I am telling the story very badly. Forgive me for taking so long!"

"There is no hurry," Sir Reginald answered in the same gentle voice. "And you are telling it very well."

She smiled again—her faint, sad smile. "You are very kind. It makes it much easier. You know how clever he is in native disguise. I never recognized him. I came back, as I thought, a widow. And then—it was nearly a year after—I married Everard, because I loved him. It was just before Captain Ermsted's murder. We had to come back here in a hurry because of it. Then when the summer came we had to separate. I went to Bhulwana for the birth of my baby. And while I was there, he heard that Ralph Dacre's wife had died in England only a few days before his marriage to me. That meant of course that I was not Everard's legal wife, that the baby was illegitimate. But—I was very ill at the time—he kept it from me."

"Of course he did," said Sir Reginald.

"Of course he did," said Bernard.

"Yes," she assented. "He couldn't help himself then. But he ought to have told me afterwards—when—when I began to have that horrible suspicion that everyone else had, that he had murdered Ralph Dacre."

"A difficult point," said Sir Reginald.

"I told him he was making a mistake," said Bernard.

Stella glanced down at him. "It was a mistake," she said. "But he made it out of love for me, because he thought—he thought—that my pride was dearer to me than my love. I don't wonder he thought so. I gave him every reason. For I wouldn't listen to him, wouldn't believe him. I sent him away." Her breath caught suddenly, and she put a quick hand to her throat. "That is what hurts me most," she said after a moment,—"just to remember that,—to remember what I made him suffer—how I failed him—when Tommy, even Tommy, believed in him—went after him to tell him so."

"But we all make mistakes," said Sir Reginald gently, "or we shouldn't be human."

She controlled herself with an effort. "Yes. He said that, and told me to forget it. I don't know if I can, but I shall try. I shall try to make up to him for it for as long as I live. And I thank God—for giving me the chance."

Her deep voice quivered, and Bernard's hand tightened upon hers. "Yes," he said, looking at Sir Reginald. "Ralph Dacre is dead. He was the unknown man who was shot in the jungle two nights ago."

"Indeed!" said Sir Reginald sharply.

"Yes," Stella said. "He too had found out—about the death of his first wife. And he was on his way to me. But—" she suddenly covered her eyes—"I couldn't have borne it. I would have killed myself first."

Bernard reached up and thrust his arm about her, without speaking.

She leaned against him for a few seconds as if the story had taxed her strength too far. Then Sir Reginald came to her and with a fatherly gesture drew her hand away from her face.

"My dear," he said very kindly, "thank you a thousand times for telling me this. I know it's been infernally hard. I admire you for it more than I can say. It hasn't been too much for you I hope?"

She smiled at him through tears. "No—no! You are both—so kind."

He stooped with a very courtly gesture and carried her hand to his lips. "Everard Monck is a very lucky man," he said, "but I think he is almost worthy of his luck. And now—I want you to tell me one thing more. Where can I find him?"

Her hand trembled a little in his. "I—am not sure he would wish me to tell you that."

Sir Reginald's grey moustache twitched whimsically. "If his desire for privacy is so great, it shall be respected. Will you take him a message from me?"

"Of course," she said.

Sir Reginald patted her hand and released it. "Then please tell him," he said, "that the Indian Empire cannot afford to lose the services of so valuable a servant as he has proved himself to be, and if he will accept a secretaryship with me I think there is small doubt that it will eventually lead to much greater things."

Stella gave a great start. "Oh, do you mean that?" she said.

Sir Reginald smiled openly. "I really do, Mrs. Monck, and I shall think myself very fortunate to secure him. You will use your influence, I hope, to induce him to accept?"

"But of course," she said.

"Poor Stella!" said Bernard. "And she hates India!"

She turned upon him almost in anger. "How dare you pity me? I love anywhere that I can be with him."

"So like a woman!" commented Bernard. "Or is it something in the air? I'll never bring Tessa out here when she's grown up, or she'll marry and be stuck here for the rest of her life."

"You can do as you like with Tessa," said Stella, and turned again to Sir Reginald. "Is that all you want of me now?"

"One thing more," he answered gently. "I hope I may say it without giving offence."

With a gesture all-unconsciously regal she gave him both her hands. "You may say—anything," she said impulsively.

He bent again courteously. "Mrs. Monck, will you invite me to witness the ratification of the bond already existing between my friend Everard Monck, and the lady who is honouring him by becoming his lawful wife?"

She flushed deeply but not painfully. "I will," she said. "Bernard, you will see to that, I know."

"Yes; leave it to me, dear!" said Bernard.

"Thank you," she said; and to Sir Reginald: "Good-bye! I am going to my husband now."

"Good-bye, Mrs. Monck!" he said. "And many thanks for your graciousness to a stranger."

"Oh no!" she answered quickly. "You are a friend—of us both."

"I am proud to be called so," he said.

As she passed back into the bungalow her heart fluttered within her like the wings of a bird mounting upwards in the dawning. The sun had risen upon the desert.

CHAPTER XII

THE BLUE JAY

"Tommy says his name is Sprinter; but Uncle St. Bernard calls him Whisky. I wonder which is the prettiest," said Tessa.

"I should call him Whisky out of compliment to Uncle St. Bernard," said Mrs. Ralston.

"He certainly does whisk," said Tessa. "But then—Tommy gave him to me." She spoke with tender eyes upon a young mongoose that gambolled at her feet. "Isn't he a love?" she said. "But he isn't nearly so pretty as darling Scooter," she added loyally. "Is he, Aunt Mary?"

"Not yet, dear," said Mrs. Ralston with a smile.

"I wish Uncle St. Bernard and Tommy would come," said Tessa restlessly.

"I hope you are going to be very good," said Mrs. Ralston.

"Oh yes," said Tessa rather wearily. "But I wish I hadn't begun quite so soon. Do you think Uncle St. Bernard will spoil me, Aunt Mary?"

"I hope not, dear," said Mrs. Ralston.

Tessa sighed a little. "I wonder if I shall be sick on the voyage Home. I don't want to be sick, Aunt Mary."

"I shouldn't think about it if I were you, dear," said Mrs. Ralston sensibly.

"But I want to think about it," said Tessa earnestly. "I want to think about every minute of it. I shall enjoy it so. Dear Uncle St. Bernard said in his letter the other day that we should be like the little pigs setting out to seek their fortunes. He says he is going to send me to school—only a day school though. Aunt Mary, shall I like going to school?"

"Of course you will, dear. What sensible little girl doesn't?"

"I'm sorry I'm going away from you," said Tessa suddenly. "But you'll have Uncle Jerry, won't you? Just the same as Aunt Stella will have darling Uncle Everard. I think I'm sorriest of all for poor Tommy."

"I daresay he will get over it," said Mrs. Ralston. "We will hope so anyway."

"He has promised to write to me," said Tessa rather wistfully. "Do you think he will forget to, Aunt Mary?"

"I'll see he doesn't," said Mrs. Ralston.

"Oh, thank you." Tessa embraced her tenderly. "And I'll write to you very, very often. P'raps I'll write in French some day. Would you like that?"

"Oh, very much," said Mrs. Ralston.

"Then I will," promised Tessa. "And oh, here they are at last! Take care of Whisky for me while I go and meet them!"

She was gone with the words—a little, flying figure with arms outspread, rushing to meet her friends.

"That child gets wilder and more harum-scarum every day," observed Lady Harriet, who was passing The Grand Stand in her carriage at the moment. "She will certainly go the same way as her mother if that very easy-going parson has the managing of her."

The easy-going parson, however, had no such misgivings. He caught the child up in his arms with a whoop of welcome.

"Well run, my Princess Bluebell! Hullo, Tommy! Who are you saluting so deferentially?"

"Only that vicious old white cat, Lady Harriet," said Tommy. "Hullo, Tessa! Your legs get six inches longer every time I look at 'em. Put her down, St. Bernard! She's going to race me to The Grand Stand."

"But I want to go and see Uncle Everard and Aunt Stella at The Nest," protested Tessa, hanging back from the contest. "Besides Aunt Mary says I'm not to get hot."

"You can't go there anyway," said Tommy inexorably. "The Nest is closed to the public for to-night. They are going to have a very sacred and particular evening all to themselves. That's why they wouldn't come in here with us."

"Are they love-making?" asked Tessa, with serious eyes. "Do you know, I heard a blue jay laughing up there this morning. Was that what he meant?"

"Something of that silly nature," said Tommy. "And he's going to be a public character is Uncle Everard, so he is wise to make the most of his privacy now. Ah, Bhulwana," he stretched his arms to the pine-trees, "how I have yearned for thee!"

"And me too," said Tessa jealously.

He looked at her. "You, you scaramouch? Of course not! Whoever yearned for a thing like you? A long-legged, snub-nosed creature without any front teeth worth mentioning!"

"I have! You're horrid!" cried Tessa, stamping an indignant foot. "Isn't he horrid, Uncle St. Bernard? If it weren't for that darling mongoose, I should hate him!"

"Oh, but it's wrong to hate people, you know." Bernard passed a pacifying arm about her quivering form. "You just treat him to the contempt he deserves, and give all your attention to your doting old uncle who has honestly been longing for you from the moment you left him!"

"Oh, darling!" She turned to him swiftly. "I'll never go away from you again. I can say that now, can't I?"

Her red lips were lifted. He stooped and kissed them. "It's the one thing I love to hear you say, my princess," he said.

The sun set in a glory of red and purple that night, spreading the royal colours far across the calm sky.

It faded very quickly. The night swooped down, swift and soundless, and in the verandah of the bungalow known as The Nest a red lamp glowed with a steady beam across the darkness.

Two figures stood for a space under the acacia by the gate, lingering in the evening quiet. Now and then there was the flutter of wings above them, and the white flowers fell and scattered like bridal blossoms all around.

"We must go in," said Stella. "Peter will be disappointed if we keep the dinner waiting."

"Ah! We mustn't hurt his august feelings," conceded Everard. "We owe him a mighty lot, my Stella. I wish we could make some return."

"His greatest reward is to let him serve us," she answered. "His love is the kind that needs to serve."

"Which is the highest kind of love," said Everard holding her to him. "Do you know—Hanani discovered that for me."

She pressed close to his side. "Everard darling, why did you keep that secret so long?"

"My dear!" he said, and was silent.

"Well, won't you tell me?" she urged. "I think you might."

He hesitated a moment longer; then, "Don't let it hurt you, dear!" he said. "But—actually—I wasn't sure that you cared—until I was with you in the temple and saw you—weeping for me."

"Oh, Everard!" she said.

He folded her in his arms. "My darling, I thought I had killed your love; and even though I found then that I was wrong, I wasn't sure that you would ever forgive me for playing that last trick upon you."

"Ah!" she whispered. "And if I—hadn't—forgiven—you?"

"I should have gone away," he said.

"You would have left me?" She pressed closer.

"I should have come back to you sometimes, sweetheart, in some other guise. I couldn't have kept away for ever. But I would never have intruded upon you," he said.

"Everard! Everard!" She hid her face against him. "You make me feel so ashamed—so utterly—unworthy."

"Don't darling! Don't," he whispered. "Let us be happy—to-night!"

"And I wanted you so! I missed you so!" she said brokenly.

He turned her face up to his own. "I missed myself a bit, too," he said. "I couldn't have played the Hanani game if Peter hadn't put me up to it. Darling, are those actually tears? Because I won't have them. You are going to look forward, not back."

She clung to him closely, passionately. "Yes—yes. I will look forward. But, oh, Everard, promise me—promise me—you will never deceive me again!"

"I don't believe I could, any more," he said.

"But promise!" she urged.

"Very well, my dear one. I promise. There! Is that enough?" He kissed her quivering face, holding her clasped to his heart. "I will never trick you again as long as I live. But I had to be near you, and it was the only way. Now—am I quite forgiven?"

"Of course you are," she told him tremulously. "It wasn't a matter for forgiveness. Besides—anyhow—you were justified. And,—Everard,—" her breathing quickened a little; she just caught back a sob—"I love to think—now—that your arms held our baby—when he died."

"My darling! My own girl!" he said, and stopped abruptly, for his voice was trembling too.

The next moment very tenderly he kissed her again.

"Please God he won't be the only one!" he said softly.

"Amen!" she whispered back.

In the acacia boughs above them the blue jay suddenly uttered a rippling laugh of sheer joy and flew away.

THE END

!

Printed in Poland
by Amazon Fulfillment
Poland Sp. z o.o., Wrocław